DON'T BREATHE A WORD

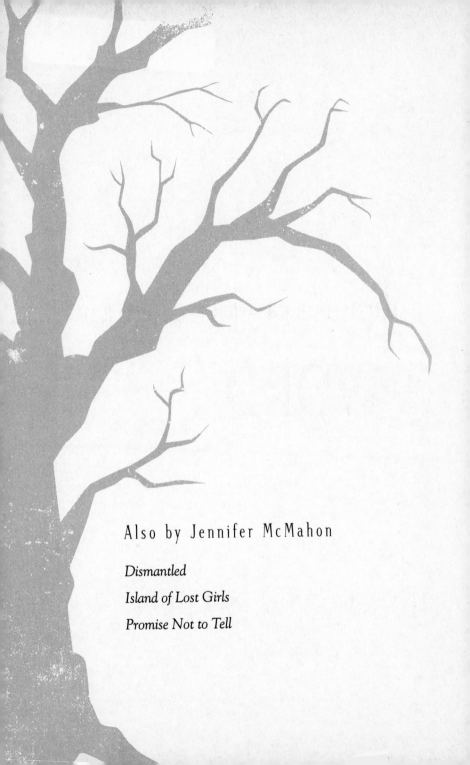

Also by Jennifer McMahon

DON'T BREATHE A WORD

A Novel

JENNIFER McMAHON

HARPER

NEW YORK • LONDON • TORONTO • SYDNEY

HARPER

This book is a work of fiction. The characters, incidents, and dialogue are drawn from the author's imagination and are not to be construed as real. Any resemblance to actual events or persons, living or dead, is entirely coincidental.

DON'T BREATHE A WORD. Copyright © 2011 by Jennifer McMahon. All rights reserved. Printed in the United States of America. No part of this book may be used or reproduced in any manner whatsoever without written permission, except in the case of brief quotations embodied in critical articles and reviews. For information address HarperCollins Publishers, 10 East 53rd Street, New York, NY 10022.

HarperCollins books may be purchased for educational, business, or sales promotional use. For information please write: Special Markets Department, HarperCollins Publishers, 10 East 53rd Street, New York, NY 10022.

FIRST EDITION

Designed by Jaime Putorti

Library of Congress Cataloging-in-Publication Data has been applied for.

ISBN 978-0-06-168937-6

11 12 13 14 15   OV/RRD   10 9 8 7 6 5 4 3 2 1

In memory of my grandmother,
Laura Koon Howard, M.D.,
who had a rational explanation
for everything

DON'T BREATHE A WORD

If you are holding this book in your hands, you are one of the chosen. You must understand that with this privilege comes great responsibility. The knowledge contained in these pages will change your life forever. But you must be very wary of who you share this knowledge with. The fate of our race depends on it. On you.

Phoebe

JUNE 23, FIFTEEN YEARS AGO

Hotter than hot, no air-conditioning, sweat pouring down in rivers, the Magic Fingers motel bed vibrating beneath her, Mr. Ice Cream doing his thing above. He's not bad-looking, a little paunch-bellied, but he's got a nice face. Blue eyes that remind her of a crystal stream. Of that song "Crystal Blue Persuasion"—something her ma listened to all the time. Of course, she told him that, and now sometimes he sings it to her, his idea of foreplay. She wishes he'd shave his mustache, but no chance, the wife loves it.

The wife, however, does not like to ride. But Phoebe does. He's got a Harley and he takes her out every Saturday, and sometimes in the evening after they close the shop. Wind in her hair, bugs in her teeth, the bike roaring like something unholy underneath her. He likes to park way out at the end of a fire trail, do it to her on his bike. Sometimes she's sure it's the motorcycle he's screwing, not her. She doesn't mind. It's hard to compete with all that glossy paint and chrome so shiny she can see their reflections. And it beats the crap out of the high school boys who don't last five minutes in the backseats of cars.

Phoebe doesn't mind, no. She's just turned twenty. Three months ago, she moved to Brattleboro with her friends Nan and Sasha. She wanted to go farther, California maybe even, to put as much distance as she could between her and her mother. But Sasha had a boyfriend in Brattleboro, and Vermont was better than the shit old mill town she'd grown up in down in Massachusetts. And when her ma calls the apartment, drunker than drunk, Nan and Sasha talk in silly accents, say she's reached the China Star restaurant. Her ma says, "Is Phoebe in?" and Nan says, "Peking duck? Okay. You want wonton? Special today." Then they all fall over laughing.

They've got a low-rent hovel of an apartment—greasy walls, squirrels nesting in the drop-down ceiling (one fell through when Sasha was cooking ramen noodles—a great story to tell at parties), but they're hardly ever there, so it's okay. Phoebe got a job scooping ice cream at the Crazy Cone, which pays her share of the rent and keeps her amused. Mostly kids come into the Crazy Cone for the arcade, dumping change into The Claw with its promise of stuffed pink poodles and fake designer sunglasses.

Her boss, Mr. Ice Cream, is twenty years older than she. He takes blood pressure medication and wears orthotics in his shoes. He has hair on his back. She tries not to touch it but always ends up running her fingers through it anyway. Being repulsed but unable to stop at the same time. Phoebe's like that.

She's on the lumpy motel mattress trying not to think about the hair on his back, or that his breath is particularly bad today. Rancid, like old meat. Maybe Mr. Ice Cream is really a werewolf. Phoebe imagines him covered in hair, sprouting fangs by the light of the full moon. Enough. She clears her mind, tries to relax, to let the Magic Fingers do their thing underneath her while he does his thing on top. She looks up at Mr. Ice Cream, who's got his eyes clamped shut, his face sweaty, lips swollen-looking under his caterpillar of a mustache (her friends think it's so cool that she's going out with an older guy, a rich guy), but what catches her eye is what's happening on the wall behind him.

The TV flickers and glows with the dull blue fire of the evening news. There's a story on about the girl who's disappeared in Harmony. Three nights ago, she went into the woods behind her house and never came out again. She said there was a door in those woods, somewhere in the ruins of an old town long abandoned. She'd told her little brother she'd met the King of the Fairies and he was going to take her home to be his queen.

The newscaster says all that remains of the village in the woods is chimneys and cellar holes. Some lilac bushes and apple trees in old dooryards. The little settlement was called Reliance, of all things, and was never shown on any maps. It disappeared without explanation. Perhaps everyone died off in the flu of 1918. Or maybe, went local legend, the fifty-odd residents were spirited away. The newscaster gets a little gleam in his eye here because everyone loves a good ghost story, don't they?

"Some of the townspeople I talked to claim to have heard strange noises coming from the woods over the years—a ghostly moaning, crying. Some even say if you pass by on the right night of the year, you'll hear the devil whisper your name. Others report seeing a green mist that sometimes takes the shape of a person."

The camera shows a close-up of an old woman with a craggy face. "It's no place for children out in them woods. Reliance is haunted and everybody knows it. I don't even let my dog run loose down there."

The newscaster says there's been no trace of the missing girl except for a single pink and silver sneaker found in a cellar hole. A size-six Nike.

Then the camera pans back and shows the woods, which could be the woods anywhere, in any small town.

Phoebe turns from the TV, tries to focus on the here and now. Runs her fingers through the pelt of fur (is there more now?) on Mr. Ice Cream's back.

But still, she finds herself thinking of those woods in Harmony, wondering where the door might be. In a thick tree trunk? Behind a rock?

Most people, they would say there's no such thing as doors like that. Imaginary.

But Phoebe knows the truth, doesn't she?

Don't look under the bed.

A drop of Mr. Ice Cream's sweat lands on her chest, giving her a chill.

It's stupid, really. Crazy. The fact that in every bed she's slept in since childhood, she stuffs everything she can underneath: heavy boxes of books she'll never read, Hefty bags full of sweaters and shoes.

"You're so organized," Nan and Sasha say.

But what she is is afraid. Because when she was a little girl, she saw the trapdoor under her bed that only appeared in the darkest hours of the night. Heard the scrabbling, the squeaking of hinges as it was opened. And she saw what came out.

And she knows (doesn't she?) that sometimes he's there still, not just under the bed but in the shadows at the bus stop, lurking with the alley cats behind the Dumpster at her apartment building. He's everywhere and nowhere. A blur caught out of the corner of her eye. A mocking smile she tells herself she's imagined.

Phoebe shivers.

Mr. Ice Cream finishes with a werewolf roar.

"How was it?" he asks once he's caught his breath.

"Like eating an ice cream sundae," she says, trying to banish all thoughts of doors and things that might come out of them.

"With a cherry on top?" he asks, smiling.

"Mmm," she says. "Gotta love that cherry."

He laughs, rolls off her.

"Hey," she says, "ain't we near Harmony?"

"*Aren't.*" He's always correcting her grammar, and the truth is, Phoebe's grammar is pretty good, she just talks like this sometimes to piss him off. "And yes, I think it's the next town over."

"Can we ride by there before we head back. I wanna see the woods where that girl was taken."

And there it is again, in the back corner of the room, just out of her range of vision. A shadowy figure nods his head, smiles. She feels it more than sees it. She turns and he's gone.

Coming into the town of Harmony, just beyond a dairy farm with a collapsing silo, they pass a massive boulder with the Lord's Prayer carved across the front. Phoebe memorized the words the year she went to Sunday school when her ma was dating the born-again trucker with the glowing plastic Jesus on his dashboard.

She tightens her arms around Mr. Ice Cream's waist as she

hears the words in her head: *Lead us not into temptation, but deliver us from evil.*

She gets a chill in spite of the heat and her ten-pound leather jacket with its million pockets and zippers—something she splurged on back when she was trying to get Mr. Ice Cream to notice her.

The road bends to the left, taking them into the center of town. On the right is the Harmony Methodist Church with a letter board out front promising a huge rummage sale on Saturday. Below that, in all caps, it says: PRAY FOR LISA'S SAFE RETURN. Across the street are a general store, a post office, and a pizza shop. It's a freaking media circus in the village, which makes Mr. Ice Cream edgy as hell—he doesn't want the wife to catch a glimpse of him and his new scoop girl on the evening news. "I'll wait here," he says, parking the bike at the general store. "You go look around."

It's not hard to find the girl's house. She turns off Main onto Spruce Street and spots a big old rambler with an overgrown lawn, peeling paint, and a porch that needs a new railing. News vans and cop cars out front. A crowd of people looking, just looking, drawn to disaster like metal filings to a magnet. Phoebe stands across the street, roasting in her heavy jacket as she studies the house, thinks that it must have been pretty once. Upstairs, in the top left window, a boy pulls open the curtain, peers down at them. He's got a Superman T-shirt on. His dark hair is shaggy, falling down into his eyes. He looks out at the crowd, at Phoebe, and suddenly she understands that she shouldn't be here. That coming was all wrong. But it's like touching the hair on Mr. Ice Cream's back.

"Are you here to see the fairies?" a girl asks her.

"Huh?" Phoebe says, turning to see who spoke.

The girl is ten maybe, dressed from head to toe in pink. She's got a plastic compass, small and cheap like a prize from a box of Cracker Jacks, pinned to her shirt. Her pale arms, sticking out from the ruffled short-sleeve blouse, have bright red welts on them. "I thought maybe you were like the others. That you came out to see the fairies. 'Cause I can show you something real special that belongs to the King of the Fairies himself. Five dollars, and I can show you."

Phoebe looks back at the window, sees the boy is gone. She reaches into her jeans, pulls out a crumpled five, hands it over.

"Follow me," the girl says.

They walk past the crowd and the news vans, down the street to a white house. They turn into the yard, walk around back, past a swing set and vegetable garden in bad need of watering. Then the girl enters the woods. "Stick close," she says.

And Phoebe wants to tell her to forget it, that she doesn't need to see. Shit, she's not sure how long Mr. Ice Cream is gonna wait, it's nearly five now, his wife expects him home in time for supper. The girl moves fast. "Wait!" Phoebe calls, chasing her.

She remembers the old woman on the newscast: *No place for children out in them woods.*

They jog through trees, over a brook, into where the woods grow dark. Phoebe wants to turn around, but it's too late. She'll never find her way back without help. There's no path, no landmarks. It's the same in all directions: trees and rocks, trees and rocks. They go down a hill where the woods open up. And then Phoebe sees that in the distance, off to her left, yellow crimescene tape is looped around the trees.

"This way," the girl says, leading her in the other direction.

"Was that it?" Phoebe asks. "Where Lisa was taken? Was that Reliance?"

The girl smiles. "All of this is Reliance, Miss."

Then, as she walks, the girl starts humming a song Phoebe half recognizes. As she hums, it turns into "Crystal Blue Persuasion," which Phoebe knows is impossible, no one under forty listens to that music, but that's what she hears.

"What's that you're humming?" she asks.

"Me? I'm not humming," the girl in pink says. "You stay here a minute. I'll be right back." The girl jogs on ahead, stopping to look over her shoulder to make sure Phoebe's staying put.

Phoebe checks her watch, anxious to get back to Main Street, to Mr. Ice Cream waiting at the general store. She imagines him browsing through racks of tacky postcards, stale maple sugar candy, bug spray. He'd make small talk with the owner. He seems to feel like he's in a club, he and all these small business owners: them against the world.

It's quiet. Too quiet. Phoebe doesn't hear a single bird or mosquito. She thinks of the Lord's Prayer. What a crazy thing to carve into a rock. Why not "Welcome to Harmony"? She starts to say the prayer, then stops herself. Idiot.

Where the hell are all the birds?

Twigs snap. A shadow moves through the trees. Phoebe holds her breath, then releases it as the girl in pink steps out from a group of little saplings up ahead. She's got a paper sack in her arms. Phoebe watches her jog over, smiling, the little compass jumping around where it's pinned to her shirt.

"Look," she says, thrusting the open bag toward Phoebe, who takes it from her and peers inside. It's the smell that hits her first: earthy and vaguely rotten. Then she understands the lump she's looking at isn't a lump at all. There are fingers, swollen and curled.

Phoebe yelps, drops the bag, steps away.

The girl gives Phoebe a disappointed shake of the head, then picks up the bag, opens it up, reaches in. Phoebe wants to scream, to beg her not to touch it, not to show her any more. But when she pulls it out, Phoebe sees it's only a glove. Tan leather, thick, and holding the shape of the hand it once covered.

"It's his," the girl says.

"Whose?" Phoebe says, stepping closer now, wanting to touch it but afraid. The glove is large, covered in brown stains, and all wrong somehow. There's an extra finger sewn to the side just past the pinkie, the stitching sloppy and in black thread like sutures. Frankenstein glove.

The girl smiles, gently caresses the soft leather of the extra finger. "The King of the Fairies."

PART I

First Contact

There is no such thing as an accident.
There's no luck or chance or coincidence.

Imagine an enormous and intricate
spiderweb connecting everything and
everyone.

We can teach you to see that web.

We can teach you to be the spider and not
the fly.

You'll understand how closely our worlds
are linked and that it is we fairies who
shape your destiny.

You'll soon see that you are never alone.

Phoebe

Are you sure this is right?" Phoebe asked, doing her best to sound like a chipper, adventure-loving girl.

Sam glanced down at the map and directions. "Positive," he said, sounding a little huffy. He was tired of having to tell her again and again that yes, they were going the right way. And no, they weren't lost.

It had been miles since they'd even passed a house. They'd gone by overgrown fields, cow pastures, a stagnant pond, and then into thick, conifer-filled woods. No sign of civilization for miles. Phoebe knew she should be used to it after living in Vermont for fifteen years, but she still got twitchy when she didn't know where the nearest McDonald's was.

"There's an old-growth forest out here somewhere," Sam said, glancing from the road back down to the map open on the seat between them. "Maybe we can hike out to it tomorrow."

"Oh joy," Phoebe said. Sam had taken her to an old-growth forest before—a bunch of big old trees with a plaque in front of them. Sam took pictures, jotted down notes in his little black hiking journal. Some guys took their girls out to dinner and the movies. A hot date with Sam involved topographical maps and trail mix.

"Or you could stay behind and play solitaire or something," Sam suggested.

Phoebe reached over and squeezed his arm. "If you're going hiking, then so am I. Old trees, here we come!" She gave an enthusiastic cowgirl *Yippee-i-o!* and Sam laughed.

Spending a weekend in an isolated cabin in the woods was not Phoebe's idea of a relaxing getaway. When Sam first told her about it, she briefly considered saying she had to work. But she realized she needed to go. Sam hadn't seen his cousin Evie since they were kids, since the summer Lisa disappeared. Last week, Evie called out of the blue and said she had news about Lisa—something she insisted on telling Sam only in person. And of course Sam told Evie about finding Lisa's old fairy book, and it was agreed that they needed to meet as soon as possible. Evie rented a cabin in Vermont's Northeast Kingdom for the weekend and called Sam back with directions. It was about an hour and a half north of where Sam and Phoebe lived.

"We'll come to you," Evie said. "I haven't been to Vermont in ages."

The cabin itself was tucked deep in the woods and could be reached only by an old logging road.

"I'm told the trail is in pretty rough shape," Evie said. When Phoebe heard this, she complained. "Why couldn't we just all meet at a Holiday Inn? Or a nice bed-and-breakfast?"

"Because," said Sam, "with Evie, everything has to be an adventure. She was always just like Lisa that way. You couldn't just ride your bike to the store to get some gum. It got turned into this life-and-death quest, a battle of good versus evil over Doublemint gum, which was really a secret antidote to some witch's deadly poison."

Evie had instructed Sam to park on a dirt pull-off on the edge of Route 12, half a mile past a WATCH FOR MOOSE sign. Evie and her husband, Elliot, would pick them up in their Jeep at five o'clock on Friday.

"Don't forget the fairy book," Evie had instructed, "and anything else you may have saved from that summer."

So here was the reason Phoebe had for joining Sam on his trip to the cabin: to learn what she could about Lisa (a subject Sam had rarely spoken of before this past week) and to perhaps finally get to see what was inside the famous *Book of Fairies*.

LEARN ALL I CAN ABOUT LISA because Sam sure as shit isn't going to tell me a thing was at the top of her to-do list in the little spiral memo pad she carried. Phoebe was a list maker. Nothing seemed to make sense until she'd written it out on paper, and nothing seemed accomplished unless she crossed it off. She was also a great one for making lists of pros and cons. She didn't have any fear of Sam discovering her memo pad and reading her secret thoughts because he (and everyone else) found her handwriting indecipherable. Hieroglyphics, he called it. It was a system she'd developed as a kid when she caught her mom reading her diary—abbreviations, writing some letters and words backward, throwing in random numbers and punctuation marks, and making all of it very, very small. When she wanted, like at work or when leaving Sam a note, she could make her handwriting legible—big block letters no one had trouble figuring out.

Sam, of course, had beautiful writing. Neat cursive almost identical to his mother's—she had taught both Lisa and him perfect Palmer-method penmanship.

They found the pull-off easily enough, but Evie and Elliot were late picking them up. Phoebe flipped the visor down, inspected herself in the mirror. She wasn't in bad shape for thirty-five, but she could already see the beginnings of tiny lines around her hazel eyes. And so far, she'd only found two or three coarse white hairs mixed in with her long, nearly black curls—she pulled them out without Sam ever noticing. Phoebe knew Sam would claim not to care, but *she* cared. Sam was only twenty-five. Phoebe was, all their friends teased, robbing the cradle. "A regular cougar," Sam joked, and she'd go along with it, giving him a throaty cat growl and clawing at the air in his direction.

She pulled her lipstick from her bag and carefully applied it. She'd toned down the makeup a lot since being with Sam—he called it war paint and swore she looked sexiest first thing in the morning before she'd done her hair or face. Even now he rolled his eyes while she touched up her lips.

"I don't know who you're trying to impress," he said. "Evie was always a tomboy."

Phoebe shrugged.

An hour and a half in the car—with its mingled bouquet of burning oil, ancient spilled coffee, and Sam's too-sweet organic herbal aftershave—was more than Phoebe could stand. Her stomach was churning in an unfriendly way. The lipstick had a greasy taste that was pushing her over the edge.

"I think I'll go stretch my legs," she said, mouth watering in the way it did that warned she might throw up any second.

Sam reached over and took her hand, stroking her knuckles with his index finger. "You okay, Bee? You're looking kind of pale." He felt her forehead to see if she might have a fever. It was a sweet gesture. She took his hand in hers and kissed his fingers. His hands were calloused from all his work in the woods, and he had deep stains in the creases that never seemed to come clean: pine pitch, chain-saw grease. Now his fingers smelled vaguely of gasoline and Lava soap.

"I'm fine," she said, gently guiding his hand away from her face. "I've just been in the car too long. A little fresh air and I'll be good as new."

Sam nodded, checked his watch. "Don't go too far. They should be here any minute."

She gave him a teasing sort of salute and stumbled from the car, pretending to check her own invisible watch (she couldn't stand the feel of anything tight around her wrist). "Watches syn-chronized, Captain," she said. "Back in ten minutes."

"And try not to get lost!" he called after her. "Leave a trail of bread crumbs or something."

Taking deep breaths to fight the nausea, Phoebe reached down to tie her green Doc Martens boots. They'd been a thrift store find and now were standard footwear on all of her wilder-ness adventures.

Boots double knotted, Phoebe headed down the start of the logging road while Sam stayed in the driver's seat studying the map to make sure they were in the right place. Sam was a map and compass kind of guy, which Phoebe found comforting. She had the sense of direction of a moth banging uselessly against a light fixture.

Sam and Phoebe had been together for three years, a fact that Phoebe still couldn't quite believe. They met at the veterinary clinic where Phoebe worked as a receptionist. Sam brought in an injured barred owl he found when he was out hiking.

"I don't know what happened," he said, out of breath, his arms bleeding from where the owl had fought him with its talons. "I just found her like this." The owl was wrapped in a red-checked flannel shirt, its face pale, its eyes a deep brown.

Sam had similar eyes—they were the color of chocolate with the most amazing eyelashes she'd ever seen on a man. Phoebe was instantly charmed by his sensitivity—unusual for Phoebe, who was ordinarily attracted to the insensitive bad-boy type. She was a pro at dead-end relationships with the type of guy whose big idea of commitment was actually showing up for a Friday night date at the Great Wall of China all-you-can-eat buffet. She had been okay with that—at least it was familiar, safe. But something happened to her when she saw Sam cradling that owl—as if a door opened up and she got a peek at what she'd been missing.

"Buckshot," Dr. Ostrum said once she had the owl on the examining table. All the fight was out of it now and the owl lay limp, breathing fast and jerky, a mass of mottled gray-brown bloody feathers.

"Can you save her?" Sam asked, his eyes red and wet, his voice soft and boyish.

Dr. O. shook her head. "The best thing we can do for this owl is euthanasia."

Sam's body crumpled, and he leaned forward, arms on the table. "Who would do this?" he asked, voice cracking. "Who would shoot an owl?"

And Phoebe did something so uncharacteristic, she felt as if it wasn't even her doing it. She reached out and put a hand on Sam's clawed-up arm, which twitched slightly at contact. She felt as if she were touching something wild and wounded, as Sam must have felt with that owl in his arms.

"Sometimes," she told him, "bad things happen and we're never meant to know why." They both stayed in the room while Dr. O., quickly and gently, gave the owl an injection. The rise and fall of its feathered breast slowed, then stopped. Phoebe helped Sam wash and bandage his arms.

"Her heartbeat was so fast," Sam said. "And those eyes . . . It was like they had a thousand things to say."

Phoebe nodded and ripped off another piece of medical tape, having no idea then that the kind guy with the bloody arms and killer eyelashes was *the* Sam, the brother of the girl who went off to see the fairies and was never seen again. The little boy in the Superman shirt she'd once glimpsed through a window.

He invited her to go hiking the following weekend, and she agreed, showing up in a miniskirt and flip-flops. "Not exactly a nature girl, huh?" Sam had said. At her insistence, they'd gone on the hike. She came out of the woods that afternoon sunburned, blisters between her big and second toes, and with a god-awful case of poison ivy. But it had been worth it. For the first time in her life, she truly understood the old saying *Opposites attract*. They were all wrong for each other and he wasn't her type at all (a college graduate and member of the Green Party?), but somehow this made the attraction stronger, more daring.

When Phoebe later asked what it was Sam saw in her, he smiled. "It's just because you're you, Bee. I never know what's going to come out of your mouth or what crazy adventure you'll have me on next. You're raw. Uncensored. You don't give a shit what other people think. And the sex is great," he said with a wink.

Sam grounded her, made her feel safe. And she taught him what it was like to be a little less grounded, a little less safe. Since they'd been together, she'd convinced him to try shoplifting (he stole a cheap plastic lighter with a NASCAR logo), sex in the back of a Greyhound bus, and horror movies (which he pretended not to like, though he was always quick to point out when a new movie was opening).

It seemed to Phoebe, back at the beginning and now, that they were exactly what the other needed; the missing piece that made everything else magically click into place.

And still, even when she was first falling in love with him, she didn't know about Lisa.

It would be months (and by then she was head over heels) before she realized who Sam really was. The man who made her feel safe, who'd driven her nightmares away, was carrying his own set of secrets, his own dark history that—if she were to be honest with herself—she ached for glimpses of.

After navigating washouts and ruts for five minutes or so, Phoebe stopped to pick up a small, smooth, orange kidney-shaped stone that caught her eye. When she emptied her pockets at the end of the day, Sam would often tease her, say she was named after the wrong sort of bird. "You're my magpie," he joked.

Their house was full of the little treasures Phoebe had gathered over the years: birds' nests, snakeskins, corroded coins, old railroad ties. The skull of a squirrel. Sam said her ever-growing collection made their house seem like the den of a voodoo priestess. When she met him, the only thing decorating his house were topographical maps tacked to his walls. Phoebe had them framed and put them up in the living room and office, where they went perfectly with Phoebe's trinkets. She bought some throw pillows and dragged Sam's Mexican blankets from the closet and used them to cover the secondhand furniture. She felt downright domestic and began to wonder what had happened to the old Phoebe who would never have imagined living with a guy, much less playing the Martha Stewart of Vermont. Still, she had to admit that part of her was waiting for the bottom to fall out—that this was too good to be true and wouldn't last. And deep down, she felt like maybe she didn't deserve it—that she belonged with the petty thieves and guys who drank Pabst Blue Ribbon for breakfast.

But the dream life continued. They soon added some framed snapshots of the two of them camping and canoeing, looking like a couple in an L.L.Bean catalog. Slowly, Phoebe's wardrobe changed from the sexy to the practical—hot pants and vintage camisoles were replaced by fleece and long johns. She let her hair grow out like a wild woman hippie chick. For Sam's birthday that first year, Phoebe bought him an Audubon print of a barred owl in tribute to the bird that had brought them together. The print hung above their bed, the owl's large eyes watching over them, casting a wise bird spell that bound them together each night.

Phoebe felt safe with Sam. For the first time in her life, there were no nightmares, no glimpses of figures watching her from the shadows or slithering out from under her bed. The foolish fears of her childhood and early adulthood vanished and came to feel far away, like something dreamed up by some other girl.

It was the first weekend in June and the blackflies were out in full force. They swarmed Phoebe, getting into her mouth, ears, and nose. She'd lived in Vermont on and off for fifteen years but had not yet gotten used to the blackflies. They didn't seem to bother Sam. Phoebe's theory was that they preferred flatlander blood, that a native Vermonter carried a certain degree of natural immunity.

She shoved the orange stone into the front pocket of her frayed Levi's that were held up with her trucker belt (another thrift store find) that had a huge silver buckle with two semis beneath the words KING OF THE ROAD. Sam teased her about the belt, but he loved it, thought it was sexy. She'd do a hip-swiveling dance, flashing the buckle, singing the Roger Miller song in a low, teasing voice: *I'm a man of means by no means, King of the Road* . . . She slid the green memo pad from her back pocket and thumbed through it to the last page she'd written on.

GOALS FOR WEEKEND:
Meet and befriend Evie
Learn all I can about Lisa and the fairies

She was staring down at her notebook when she felt it: the overwhelming sense that she was being watched. Had Sam decided to join her after all? She turned to look back down the path, half expecting to see him trotting toward her. She'd say, "What, you didn't trust me not to get lost?" and he'd laugh.

But there was nothing, no one.

Or was there? She could have sworn she saw a shadow dart swiftly behind a tree to her left, down the path about ten yards. Something too tall to be a fox or coyote. Phoebe's scalp prickled. Her arms broke out in goose bumps.

"Hello?" she called, her voice squeaking out around the lump in her throat. She closed her notebook and walked slowly toward the tree. Nothing. She let out a long shaky breath.

"You've just been in the car too damn long," she hissed to herself. Phoebe had been on edge since Evie had called. It seemed strange that the fairy book had shown up at the same time Sam's long-lost cousin did. Sam had shrugged it off, said life was full of coincidences—it was superstitious to assign meaning to every one of them.

Feeling refreshed from the brisk walk and fresh air, Phoebe hooked her fingers into the belt and did her best trucker swagger back to the car. Dodging blackflies, she prayed Sam had remembered to pack the Off!. She couldn't help walking a little faster than she had on her way down the path, or glancing back over her shoulder a few times. Once the car was in sight, she felt relieved and a little embarrassed.

Sam was still in the driver's seat but didn't notice her bowlegged trucker walk as she approached. He was looking down at the plastic Ziploc bag on his lap, the treasured *Book of Fairies* inside. All she'd seen so far was the cover: worn and green, the title handwritten in now-smudged calligraphy. Tonight, Sam and Evie were going to open it up, read through it carefully page by page. What Sam held on his lap might well be the biggest clue as to what happened to Lisa. The book, like Lisa, had been missing for fifteen years, and now here it was, balanced on Sam's lap as he sat in the driver's seat of their crappy old Mercury Sable.

Don't you think we should show it to the police?" Sam's mother, Phyllis, had asked after they discovered the fairy book, just last week, in an attic crawl space in her house. She gazed down at the book worriedly, wringing her hands together. "Why don't you leave it here and I'll call them, have them come out and pick it up."

Sam shook his head. "I just want a little time to look it over myself first," Sam had said. "Then I'll bring it back and we can call the police together."

But he hadn't looked it over. At far as Phoebe knew, he hadn't even been able to open the cover. He sealed it in a large Ziploc, like a cop bagging evidence, and hid it away someplace so secret, he wouldn't even tell Phoebe. She didn't press him. Phoebe knew she'd see the book soon enough. She just had to be patient.

They'd told his mom they'd found the book by chance, that Sam was looking through the attic for a box of old baseball cards that might be worth some money on eBay, but that wasn't the truth. What really happened was that Phoebe had gotten a phone call from a little girl.

"Are you sure it was a girl? Like what age?" Sam had asked when he got home from work and she told him about the call. His words came hard and fast and sounded accusatory. Like he suspected Phoebe of imagining the whole thing.

"I don't know. She sounded young. I could barely hear her."

Phoebe left out her biggest impression: she sounded scared. And nearly breathless.

"She said, 'Tell Sammy to look in the crawl space, behind the insulation.' Then she hung up."

Sam got pale.

"Does that mean something to you?"

He nodded. "It's in the attic at my mom's. A place Lisa used to play."

At ten of six, Sam's cousin and her husband arrived in a black Jeep with the top down. Sam had tried calling them, but there was no cell service this far out. The Jeep had Massachusetts plates.

"I thought they were from Philadelphia," she said.

"Huh?" Sam replied, the question lost as he jumped out of the car to meet his cousin.

"Sorry we're late," announced Evie as she bounded out of the Jeep and threw her arms around Sam. She held him tight and said, "God, I can't believe it's you. It's been way too long, Sammy!"

Sam had shown Phoebe an old snapshot of Evie at thirteen: chunky, bad haircut, wearing a pair of greasy mechanic's coveralls and huge work boots. This woman bore no resemblance to that girl. She was in excellent shape, had neatly styled dark hair with highlights, and wore red lipstick in just the right shade for her complexion.

Elliot shook their hands and helped them get their stuff into the back of the Jeep. He was a gregarious, outdoorsy type dressed in jeans, a T-shirt, and one of those vests with a hundred pockets. He had a neatly trimmed beard and wore wire-framed glasses.

"Ready?" he asked. "It's not far. About two miles in."

Phoebe and Sam climbed into the backseat. As Elliot navigated the Jeep along the washed-out once-upon-a-time road, Phoebe noticed what she thought at first glance was a ring, then realized was a tattoo: a band of Celtic knots around the ring finger of his left hand. Evie had a matching tattoo on her left ring finger. Permanent wedding bands. Evie was also, much to poor Sam's half-disguised horror, a hugger. Evie had given them each a total of three hugs—excited, squeezy, full-body hugs—before they even stepped into the cabin. She smelled vaguely of patchouli (another thing Sam hated: he said it was such a cliché, though Phoebe was never sure a scent could count as a cliché).

Phoebe and Evie found themselves alone in the kitchen putting away provisions while the men unpacked the Jeep. Phoebe felt the other woman studying her. She stopped what she was doing to turn and catch Evie staring, a strange smile on her face.

Phoebe smiled back, nervous. "What?" she asked at last, feeling like there must be something she'd missed. She felt a little defensive, too, like maybe the joke was on her and she didn't even realize it.

"What?" Phoebe repeated when Evie wouldn't stop grinning.

Evie looked straight into Phoebe's eyes and asked, "When are you due?"

Phoebe actually stumbled from the shock of the question, bumping against the worn Formica counter.

"What?" Phoebe whimpered.

"You're pregnant, aren't you?" Evie asked.

"Pregnant? No, I'm not. What made you think that?" She

glanced self-consciously down at her stomach, wondering if the India pale ale she and Sam were so fond of was giving her a beer belly.

"Your eyes," Evie explained. "You can always tell a pregnant woman by the light in her eyes."

"Well, I'm not." Most definitely not. Phoebe was sure she wasn't even capable of having children. Over the years, she'd been less than careful numerous times and still, every twenty-eight days, her period came like clockwork. Just like it would now. She'd packed tampons for the weekend, sure it was getting to be that time.

Evie laughed, reaching out to put a hand on Phoebe's belly, just above the King of the Road belt buckle. "My mistake. I'm sorry."

Phoebe jumped a little at the strangely forward gesture but then caught herself and forced a smile.

"It's fine," she said, struggling to remember how long it had been since her last period.

Was it possible she was late?

She reached into her pocket to rub the little orange stone. Worry stone.

CHAPTER 2

Lisa

When Lisa first heard the bells, it was as if the whole forest was singing.

"Shh," she said to Sam and Evie, finger over her lips. "Listen."

Off in the distance, from the bottom of the hill, came the faintest tinkling of bells. It reminded Lisa of the little bell she'd had on her first bike that she rode up and down the driveway, dinging away as she pretended she was driving an ice cream truck or an ambulance.

"What is that?" Evie asked, scrunching her face up. Evie was thirteen—a year older than Lisa—and some people, when they first met Evie, figured she was kind of slow. She was a little overweight, never combed her hair, and dressed like a boy. Evie had real breasts already—not like the little mosquito bites Lisa had—and she tried to keep them hidden by putting on a tight white T-shirt under baggy men's clothes. She wore a pair of tan steel-toed work boots that were several sizes too big. My *shitkickers*, she called them. For a finishing touch, she had a huge hunting knife in a leather sheath strapped to her belt.

The bells went on, calling to them.

Lisa rocked back on her heels, looked up at the sky through the fringed curtain of dark bangs. She was the tallest girl in her class, with a wiry frame, and when she stood beside her short, squat cousin she felt like a different species entirely. "It's like the forest is talking to us," she said. "Doesn't it almost sound like little voices?"

"You're nuts," Sammy told her. "Trees don't talk." Sammy the serious.

"Well, what do you think it is then?" Evie asked, seeming a little twitchy, nervous.

"I don't know, but trees and leaves and rocks don't have vocal cords," he said.

"There are other ways of speaking," Lisa explained, thinking that sometimes her conversations with Sammy were more like sword fights: strike, parry, strike. "Sometimes you listen with your ears; sometimes it's like your whole body becomes this antenna and you pick up on everything." What she didn't say was how it could almost hurt, could give you a terrible headache, all the voices you could hear if you tried: the cardinals, the worms, the squirrels with their mouths full of acorns all talking over one another. Even the trees had a story to tell.

"This way," Lisa told them, galloping across the backyard and into the trees, jumping over roots and rocks.

"Wait up!" Evie called, but Lisa didn't slow.

The kids in town called Evie *Stevie*. When Evie wasn't around, Lisa hung out with other kids. Like Gerald and his sister, Pinkie, who lived down the road. But she dropped them when her cousin was visiting because they were such jerks about Evie.

"Gonna come to the movies with us, Lisa?" Gerald asked, mockingly, then added, "Oh, sorry, I forgot Stevie was here. Have fun with your favorite boy cousin!"

Everyone in school said Gerald had a crush on Lisa, but Lisa hated to think about that. She'd known him her whole life, and he was just geeky Gerald, a too-skinny boy with gold eyes who was always covered in paint and glue from the models he made.

"He's just jealous," Sam told Lisa. "You'd rather hang out with Evie than him, so he's mad."

It made Lisa's stomach hurt to think about things like jealousy, crushes, breasts, and girls who seemed to want to be boys. She hated that all of a sudden, everything seemed much more complicated. This growing-up thing kind of sucked. Some days, she wished she could go back in time instead of moving forward—just keep getting younger and younger until she was a tadpole inside her mom's belly, then a speck, then nothing at all, just the idea of Lisa O'Toole Nazzaro floating around out there in the cosmos.

"Gerald can be a jerk, but he's not bad, really," Sam said.

"I just wish he and his weirdo sister weren't so mean," Lisa said. She was disappointed in Gerald and Pinkie but also in Evie. If Evie would just try, just make some small attempt to fit in, things might have been easier. But then she wouldn't be Evie, would she?

The summer before, Evie refused to comb her hair for a month until it became one big rat's nest. Aunt Hazel finally gave Evie a buzz cut, making her head looked like a big old stubbly peeled potato. It was supposed to be this terrible punishment, to teach

her a lesson, but Evie loved it. She went around begging everyone to feel her head. "Isn't it just the best?" she asked, cooing
like an animal when people stroked her dark stubble.

"When I'm with you," she said to Lisa, "I just know something magical is bound to happen any second." Evie believed in
magic, in things like ghosts and reincarnation.

"We've known each other many lifetimes," Evie told Lisa late
at night, when they were out in the yard in sleeping bags, Sammy
passed out beside them. The crickets chirped. Evie crossed her
fingers, nails chewed ragged, and said, "You and I are like this."

Lisa looked at the fingers. Two serpents entwined.

"Snake girls," Lisa mumbled, twitching inside her sleeping
bag, moving over so that she was right up against Evie. Evie
wrapped her arm around Lisa, darted her tongue into Lisa's ear.

"*Hiss, hiss.*"

They flew through the forest, wind in their ears, branches tick-
ling their faces. They knew the way by heart. The sound of the
bells was coming from down the hill. From Reliance.

It was just getting dark, but Lisa's mom and Aunt Hazel let
them stay out late, especially with Da home from the hospital.
They were supposed to be quiet. To let him rest. "The last thing
your father needs," Lisa's mom said, "is three wild beasts racing
through the house." Lisa thought maybe a little racing might do
him some good. Still, she bit her tongue and tiptoed around him
like he was a sleeping giant. And that's all he seemed to do since
he got out—sleep. Aunt Hazel brought him trays of food, cups
of tea, and all his medicine. She was a nurse, which her mom
said was a big help right now. Hazel knew how to take care of

people like Da. He stayed on the couch, buried beneath a pile of quilts, with his eyes closed most of the time. Even when they were open, it was like he was sleeping behind them. He looked right through you, like you were the ghost.

"Boo," Lisa said to him sometimes, hoping for a reaction but getting nothing.

Reliance was full of ghosts. That's what some folks in town said, anyway. People claimed they saw green lights, mist that turned into a man who walked the edge of the woods, mumbling in a language no one had ever heard before. Mrs. Mattock, who used to run Jenny's Café before her hip got too bad, said that there was some kind of magic door hidden somewhere in the ruins of the old town. "People don't just disappear without a trace like that—not a whole town anyway. You kids shouldn't play out there."

Old Carl Jensen said he'd lost two dogs in Reliance. They went into the woods and never came back out. "The weird thing is," he'd say as he told the story over and over to whoever would listen, "sometimes, when I go walking by there, I still hear those dogs. I call to them, and they howl but never come. Once you go through that door out there, you can't come back, no matter how bad you might want to."

If there was a magic door in Reliance, Lisa was sure they would have found it by now. They'd been playing in those woods their whole lives in spite of the warnings. They knew every tree, every rock, every old mossy brick in every cellar hole. Lisa's mother and Aunt Hazel told them that once there had been five houses, two barns, a blacksmith shop, and a church down in Reliance. All that was left of them were the foundations, roughly square pits, two to four feet deep with indefinite borders, choked with weeds and dead leaves, littered with crumbling masonry. Empty now, like the sockets where teeth should be. Back then, the woods had been open pasture full of cows, sheep, and horses. Sometimes, when Lisa was down there at dusk, if she squinted her eyes just right in the dying light, she was sure she could see the buildings and fields; sometimes she even caught a glimmer of movement—a face at the window, a door opening.

A *haunted place*, people in town said, and Lisa thought maybe they were right. But it was a good kind of haunted. If there had been anything evil there, Lisa would have felt it.

On the southeast edge of the old settlement, behind the cellar hole they'd guessed was the church's foundation, there was a tiny graveyard with five headstones, the slate so weatherworn that it was impossible to make out names or dates. In the early summer, Lisa would gather forget-me-nots and leave bunches of them on each grave.

They knew to steer clear of the old well on the north side of the village, which was circled with stones and deep and dark and smelled like sulfur. They were careful not to disturb what remained of the low stone walls that encircled Reliance. Over the years, they had learned that if they went out with a shovel and dug in the right places, they'd find things: rusty bolts, buttons, bottles made of opaque glass. Once, they found a long, stained bone. "Femur," Sammy said. "Probably an animal but maybe not." Evie took the bone back home, kept it on her bookcase, told everyone it was the fossilized remains of a caveman named Herb.

Lisa led Evie and Sam down the hill, toward the sound of the bells. It was a small, tinkling sound, like delicate glass being broken.

"Wait!" she said, grabbing Sammy by the neck of his T-shirt. He stopped short, choking a little. "Look," she whispered, pulling him down so that they were both hunkered on their knees, like spies. Evie, who'd been a little behind them, caught up and crouched down with them. She had asthma, and when she ran, her breath got all whistley-sounding. It scared Lisa to death sometimes, to see her big, strong-as-an-ox cousin gasping for breath like a swollen pale fish out of water.

Lisa blinked, still not quite believing what she was seeing. "What is that?" she asked. At the bottom of the hill, inside one of the old cellar holes, little lights were dancing around. Two pinpricks of bright white light blinking, flying from one side of the cellar hole to the other, going up and down, bouncing off trees, then diving back down into the pit.

"Fireflies?" Sammy said, but these were no insects. Even Mr. Sammy Science himself knew that there was no way. Lisa could tell by the sound of his voice.

"Those," Evie said, wheezing, "aren't"—another labored breath—"fireflies." Evie put a cold, sweaty hand on Lisa's arm, giving her goose bumps.

Lisa held still, listening. But there was no sound. Only Evie's wheezing. And the faint tinkling of the bells. It was like the rest of the forest was holding its breath.

"Come on," Lisa said, pulling Sammy up. "Evie," she said, listening to her cousin's breath, realizing she didn't have her inhaler. "Stay."

"Bull crap," Evie said, standing.

They galloped down the hill, but as they were running, the lights disappeared. And the sound stopped. They crossed the tiny brook, leaping like deer.

When they got to the cellar hole, there was nothing, not even the sound of a single cricket. But the air felt electric and alive, the molecules humming.

"Do you feel that?" Lisa asked.

Evie was bent over, hands on her knees, struggling to catch her breath. She looked up. Nodded. "They're," she gasped, "watching."

Even Sammy Science seemed to pick up on it. "Let's get out of here," he said.

Lisa scanned the trees. There was no movement. No sound. But still, she felt it: somewhere out there, someone, *something*, was watching them.

CHAPTER 3

Phoebe

They had pan-fried trout with baby arugula salad and roasted corn for dinner. Evie and Elliot were excellent cooks, especially compared to Phoebe, who had the unique talent of being able to burn spaghetti. Phoebe had a glass of wine and it went straight to her head. It was pink and sweet, with a caramelized raspberry flavor. But there was something bitter underneath, something that made Phoebe's tongue feel dry and shrunken in her mouth.

"Some friends of ours make it," Evie explained.

Phoebe didn't drink any more, but everyone else polished off the bottle. Then another. They were working on their third when Sam lit the fire. Phoebe was drifting in and out, straining to pay attention to the conversation, but she felt exhausted and on information overload. She wanted to go to bed. To get under the covers and snuggle up to Sam.

All evening she'd been telling herself it wasn't possible—she couldn't be pregnant. But still, the worry nagged at her, chewing away like an old dog with a bone. She was pretty sure she'd had her period on her friend Franny's birthday, which was at the end of April. Well over a month ago.

"But if we imagined it, I mean, if it wasn't real, then how do you explain the book?" Evie asked. She was leaning toward Sam, her wine-flushed face only inches away from his. Phoebe opened her eyes wider. Was Evie flirting with Sam? Or was this just how cousins behaved? She'd never been close with any of her cousins. Couldn't even remember any of their names now, just little facts, like that one of them was pregnant at thirteen, another liked to start fires. The cream of the crop, her people. So she guessed she wasn't much of an authority on cousins, or family in general. But still, something about Evie ruffled her feathers, told her to be on guard.

Elliot seemed unfazed. He sat in a deep easy chair, paring his fingernails with a small jackknife that had come from one of the many pockets of his vest. A magician needs a vest like that, Phoebe had thought: over the course of the evening he'd pulled out matches, a corkscrew, a cell phone, a digital camera, a GPS unit, breath mints, toothpicks in a little silver holder, a pack of menthol cigarettes, even a mini first-aid kit to get a Band-Aid when Evie cut herself cleaning the fish. He had more in his vest than Phoebe ever carried in her purse, which usually had a cell phone, lipstick, a spiral-bound memo book or two, and a pocket-size word puzzle book with a stubby golf pencil.

"And what about the little gifts he left her?" Evie asked. "The ones she stuck on the charm bracelet?"

"I don't know," Sam admitted, his shoulders slouching as he sunk down in the chair, looking smaller, little-boyish. Phoebe reached over and took his hand.

Elliot, who'd been nearly silent, stood up, stretched, poured himself more wine, then walked over to the window next to the front door. He opened the window, pulled out of a pack of cigarettes, and lit one, carefully blowing the smoke out the window.

"I never heard about a charm bracelet," Phoebe said sleepily, but then again, she'd never heard a lot of the story. Not from Sam anyway. All she had was what she herself remembered and what she'd gleaned by sneaking off to the library and rereading the old newspaper stories. She was sure none of them had mentioned a bracelet. But cops did that, didn't they? Kept certain details to themselves so they'd know who had real information and who was just looking for their fifteen minutes of fame.

"God, she loved that thing," Evie said. "It was silver and she had a charm with her name on it. And one of a starfish she'd gotten earlier that summer up in Cape Cod. But then, the fairies started leaving gifts and she put them on the bracelet."

"What kinds of gifts?" Phoebe asked, sitting forward and stretching out her legs. She was looking at Sam but knew the question would be answered by Evie.

"Let's see. There was an old Indian head penny polished to a shine. A Catholic medal, too. Saint Christopher, I think. Was there anything else, Sammy?"

"I don't think so," Sam said. He had shrunk down even farther into the seat, looking like he was trying to disappear altogether.

"So whatever happened to the bracelet?" Phoebe asked.

"I'm not sure," Sam said, casting his eyes down in a way that made Phoebe wonder if he was lying.

Phoebe didn't realize who Sam was until they'd been dating for three months and Sam took her home to meet his mother.

As they came into town and passed the Lord's Prayer rock, Phoebe gave an involuntary shiver. She all but gasped when he pulled up in front of the rambling house on Spruce Street that she herself once stood in front of, lost in a crowd of gawkers.

Are you here to see the fairies?

"This is your house?" Phoebe asked, forcing the words through her rapidly constricting throat.

"Yup."

"I mean, you actually grew up here? You didn't move when you were in high school or something?"

"It's our house, Bee. My great-grandfather built it. Now come on in. My mom's dying to meet you."

She followed Sam to the front door, stopping to look up at the leftmost window on the second floor, remembering the little boy with the Superman shirt. The little boy she was destined to meet one day, by random chance, when he walked into the clinic where she worked, carrying a wounded owl wrapped in a flannel shirt. The man she'd fall in love with. It was almost too much, to think that she'd glimpsed him back when he was only ten, that she had somehow been witness to his worst moments.

She decided, as she followed Sam into the house (which was now freshly painted, the porch repaired, bright pansies in flower boxes), that she wouldn't tell him about being in the crowd on the street the week Lisa disappeared. What good would it do? Even later, when she took the time to make a list, the cons of telling him far outweighed the pros.

"What a lovely home you have," she said as she shook Phyllis's hand in the bright kitchen, determined to make a good first impression. "And what a charming little town. I think I've driven through it, but never stopped."

Sam threw another log on the fire. Elliot finished his cigarette, flinging the butt out the window into the darkness, then closing the window. Phoebe drifted. She wondered how Evie kept her lipstick so perfect while she sipped wine. Was she not letting her lips touch the glass? Was she even drinking the wine or just pretending?

"Did you bring the book?" Evie finally asked, and Sam nodded. Phoebe sat up with a start, felt her heart quicken at the thought that they were finally about to open the book that had been left for Lisa in an abandoned foundation in a ghost town: a book supposedly written by the King of the Fairies, a book with instructions Lisa followed to cross over.

"We'll look at it in the morning," Evie said, leaning back to stretch, her hand landing on Elliot's shoulder, "when our heads are a little more clear. It's getting late now." She looked at her watch.

Phoebe leaned to look at Sam's watch: nearly midnight.

"But before we go to bed, I want to show you something," Evie said. She reached into the pocket of her jeans and pulled out a folded piece of paper. She passed it over to Sam, who sat up straight to receive it. He unfolded it and smoothed it flat. Notepaper. In the upper left corner, a reproduction of an old botanical print. Lily of the valley. Tiny flowers with sleepy, nodding, bell-shaped heads. Beneath it were lines of small black script. Phoebe leaned in to get a better view of the writing.

I am back from the land of the fairies. I'll be
seeing you soon.

Lisa

"How did you get this?" Sam asked.

"It was left in my mailbox last week. Just before I called you."
She waited a minute while Sam studied it, then asked, "Do you
think it's really her? I mean, could it be? After all these years?"

"It's not possible," Sam said. His face was stony, and in it
Phoebe read the same line Sam had been reciting for years: *Lisa's
gone, taken, and there's nothing we can do but get on with our lives.*

Practical Sam. This was one of the things Phoebe admired
most about him—his ability to put the past behind him and
move on.

"But it looks sort of like her writing, doesn't it?" Evie asked. "I
went to the police with it, but they think it's someone playing a
prank. They didn't take it very seriously."

Sam shook his head, not ready to believe.

"Tell me the truth, Sammy," Evie said, leaning toward him.
"You didn't just happen to find the fairy book in the attic after
all these years, did you?"

"No," Sam admitted. "We got a call. From a girl."

"A girl?"

"Yeah," Sam explained. "Phoebe talked to her. She told us
where to find the book."

"Did she say anything else?" Evie asked, looking at Phoebe.
Her face was worried, pleading.

"No," Phoebe said.

"How did she sound?" Evie asked.

"Scared," Phoebe admitted. "She sounded scared."

All four of them, it seemed, were holding their breath while Sam traced the words on the note with a trembling finger.

I am back from the land of the fairies. I'll be seeing you soon.

The silence was destroyed by a loud rap at the door.

Everyone froze and stared wild-eyed at one another, each of them, Phoebe knew, thinking the same impossible thought: *It's Lisa. She's found us.*

CHAPTER 4

Lisa

Tell me a story," Evie begged. "P-l-eee-se!" She was in her sleeping bag on the floor beside Lisa's bed, thrashing restlessly from side to side like someone trying to escape a straitjacket. The crack of light coming in from under the door gave her face a jack-o'-lantern glow. Her head looked too big, her eyes black hollows.

Tucked under Evie's pillow was her big hunting knife. Lisa could see the edge of the leather sheath. Who exactly was Evie expecting when she hid the knife under her pillow each night?

Evie told people that the knife had belonged to her father, which was a complete load of crap—Evie had never known her father or even had a clue who he might have been. She'd found the knife in an old box of fishing tackle in her basement. Hazel, Evie's mom, was a packrat and the knife could have come from anywhere—Hazel frequented flea markets and yard sales and seemed to have a strange addiction to buying things she'd never have any use for. The more Evie told the story of how the knife had belonged to her father, the more she herself seemed to believe it was true. Lisa never argued with her about it; she understood that Evie deserved some solid thing to hold on to that tied her to her dad, even if it was made up.

Next to her pillow were her sketchbook and pens. Evie was often making scribbling drawings in it—quick sketches of gangly limbed cartoon people with long faces and dark circles under their eyes. Everything she sketched looked like something a seven-year-old had done—a very creepy seven-year-old who made everyone look like a vampire.

"Pretty please," Evie moaned again.

Lisa turned in her bed so that her back was to Evie, her nose inches from the wall. Above her hung the map of Middle Earth she'd made while reading *The Lord of the Rings*. She knew it was kind of geeky, that other girls in her class had cute movie stars and singers thumbtacked to their walls while hers were covered with maps of imaginary places, unicorns, and a drawing her father had done for her of the troll under the bridge in "Three Billy Goats Gruff"—it was pen and ink and had always terrified her. What scared her wasn't the sharp teeth or ragged claws of the troll but the hungriness in his eyes.

"With a cherry on top," Evie said.

Lisa pulled the covers up over her head. "I'll tell a story if you admit what we saw in Reliance."

Since they'd been home, whenever Lisa brought up the bells and the lights, Evie changed the subject, pretended she was totally over it. She scribbled in her sketchbook, not even making any real drawings—just spirals, *x*'s, and smudges. She pressed so hard with her pen that the paper tore.

"What is it I'm supposed to admit?" Evie wheezed.

"That it was fairies. You know it was, so why don't you just say it?"

Lisa was suffocating under the covers, but she had these little tests she gave herself—to see how long she could do uncomfortable, unpleasant things: holding her breath in the bathtub, touching raw chicken livers, roasting under covers. When it felt like she was out of air, she gave in and lifted the sheet and blanket off her face.

The dark room seemed suddenly bright. She rolled back to look at Evie, who was kicking her legs spasmodically inside the sleeping bag, her breath making a whistling sound.

Across the room was Lisa's desk. Next to it was the bookcase, full of fairy tales and fantasy stories.

"People see what they want to see," Sammy had told her earlier, when she was trying to convince Evie and him that the lights in the cellar hole had been fairies.

Maybe Sammy was right—maybe Lisa thought it was fairies because that's just what she wanted it to be, what she'd been waiting her whole life for.

But what if it worked the other way around?

What if things happened to you—special, magic things— because you'd been preparing for them? What if by believing, you opened a door?

"Say you know it was fairies and I'll tell a story. A real special one. And I'll give you a gift to go along with it—a magic talisman."

"What kind of talisman?" Evie asked.

"You'll see," Lisa promised.

It felt a little mean, manipulating Evie like this. But the truth was, Evie was being mean too. She'd been acting like a total freak since they got back from the woods, pretending nothing out of the ordinary had happened. But her twitching body showed she was thinking about it, that she was all nerved up and wheezy. And Lisa could fix all those bad feelings. She could put Evie right to sleep with her own kind of magic medicine.

Evie loved Lisa's stories. When she was worried or upset, they calmed her. When she was tossing and turning, they lulled her to sleep. Even when she was having the worst asthma attack ever, if Lisa pulled her close and whispered "Once upon a time" into her ear, Evie's lungs would open, her body would go limp against Lisa's like a giant doll. Last summer, Evie even taped Lisa telling stories so she could bring them home, play them when Lisa wasn't around. Evie had this fantasy that someday, when they were grown up, they'd make a book together—Lisa would write down all her stories and Evie would illustrate them.

"Okay," Evie said, finally holding still inside the sleeping bag. "You're right."

"Right about what?" Lisa asked. She was going to make her go all the way—say the words out loud.

Evie groaned. "Okay, okay! I think there are fairies in Reliance. Now do the story and show me the gift, okay? A deal's a deal."

Lisa smiled, put her head back on the pillow, closed her eyes. Storytelling wasn't about making things up. It was more like inviting the stories to come through her, let themselves be told.

"Make it a good one," Evie said.

"Mmm," Lisa said, taking in a breath, then starting with the four magic words that began every story.

"Once upon a time," she said, pausing, waiting, "there were two sisters, one light, one dark."

"Uh huh," Evie said, the words a soft approving sigh. Already her breath had slowed and lost some of its raspiness.

"They lived in a castle that had been enchanted by an evil witch. The castle was dark and gloomy. Everyone who set foot inside the castle, everyone but the two sisters, went mad. Their mother had hanged herself. And their father walked the halls muttering to himself and didn't seem to notice his daughters. He looked right through them, like they were ghosts."

Evie made a low *mmmm* sound and turned onto her side in the sleeping bag.

"This went on for so long that they began to wonder if maybe they *were* ghosts. If maybe they'd gone mad too, and were locked up in some deep dungeon, having a delusional dream about being sane.

" 'There's only one thing we can do,' said the fair-haired sister, 'we've got to leave this place.'

" 'Where will we go?' asked the raven-haired sister.

" 'Away. We'll look for someone or something that can help us break the spell on our castle.' "

Lisa stopped, listened to Evie's breathing, which was slow and deep—she was almost asleep.

"And so it was decided," Lisa continued. "They left the castle that night, under cover of darkness on horseback. They took a sack of bread, cheese, and fruit. The dark sister carried her father's sword. The light one carried a bow and silver arrows. And they took the one possession they had of their mother's: a small silver key she had treasured—she never told them what lock the key might fit, but promised only that one day it would save them."

Lisa rose from the bed, stepped carefully over Evie, and went to the desk. She pulled open the drawer and felt around until she found it. Then she crept over to Evie and opened her hand.

"What's this?" Evie asked, half asleep.

"The gift I promised. Your own magic key." It was an old skeleton key Lisa had found way back in the drawer of the table in the front hall, mixed in with dead batteries, dried-up pens, a bent screwdriver, and other keys abandoned because no one could remember what locks they had once fit. The skeleton key was tarnished silver and had a large tooth with several notches taken out.

Evie gripped the key tightly and smiled. "Will it save me one day?"

"Definitely," Lisa said. "It'll save both of us."

Lisa was on the back of the horse from the story, her fingers gripping its silvery-white mane. She leaned down, smelled the warm musky scent of its coat. The horse moved gently, gracefully, without making a sound. She thought for sure Evie would be there behind her, but she was alone.

The horse carried her to the edge of the yard, then into the woods. They went down the hill, across the brook. Only the brook seemed deeper, wider. The horse had to swim. Lisa thought she should be frightened, but she wasn't.

"Aren't dreams lovely?" she said out loud.

"Yes, they are," the horse told her. "Shh," the horse whispered. "You sleep now."

When she woke up at first light, she was back in her own bed, but the dark, musky smell of the horse was all around her.

A shadow moved across the corner of her vision, then was gone. The door creaked shut and she was sure she heard the sound of feet padding down the hall.

"Hello?" she said.

Evie was snoring softly on the floor beside her, the knife under her pillow and the old key clenched in her hand.

A dream. Only a dream.

Aren't dreams lovely?

Yes, they are.

She turned and saw that there on the pillow beside her was a small green velvet bag tied with a ribbon of gold.

Her heart jumped up into her throat.

Her fingers trembled as they untied the ribbon and reached inside. She pulled out three plain stones. Only when she turned on the light, she saw they weren't stones. They were large teeth: molars, brown and worn.

"Oh!" she exclaimed, and Evie bolted up like a jack-in-the-box looking for a fight.

"Where is he?" Evie asked, reaching under the pillow for her knife.

"Who?" Lisa asked.

Evie looked around, rubbing sleep from her eyes. "Forget it," she said, setting the knife in her lap.

Some kind of ruminant maybe," Sammy said when they shook him awake to show him the teeth. "Like a cow," he guessed, turning one of the teeth in his hand. "Or a horse."

Lisa got a cold chill, which Evie always said meant someone was walking over your grave.

"And you just woke up and found them?" Evie asked, her brow furrowed.

"I've told you a hundred times already," Lisa said. "They were there on my pillow."

Evie scowled.

"You think it's the fairies?" Lisa asked.

"I thought the tooth fairy was supposed to take teeth, not leave them," Sammy said.

"The tooth fairy's made up," Lisa said.

Sammy laughed, dropped the teeth back into the bag, and tied it closed. "Right. And all the other fairies are just so totally real."

CHAPTER 5

Phoebe

The knocking on the cabin door got louder, more frantic.

It was Evie who finally rose and went to answer it. She stood a second, her hand on the knob, looking back at the group near the fire, her face a question: *Do I dare?* But what choice did she have? She turned the knob and opened the door.

An old woman with short gray hair smiled in at them. She wore a straw hat rimmed with gaudy plastic flowers. Her lipstick was a garish bright red and looked as though it had been applied by an orangutan in a clownish rough circle around her mouth. She had on a pair of glasses with heavy pink plastic frames. The dress she wore was a summer muumuu—orange with hot pink tropical flowers, and over it she had on a raincoat. On her feet were a pair of red Keds, nearly worn through at the toes.

"Umm . . . can I help you?" asked Evie.

The old woman laughed.

"Are you lost?" Evie asked. "Would you like to come in?"

And then, softly at first, the old woman started to sing:

Say, say my playmate
Come out and play with me
And bring your dollies three
Climb up my apple tree
Holler down my rain barrel
Slide down my cellar door
And we'll be jolly friends, forever more!

Evie turned from her and looked back to the others for help. The old woman was clearly out of her mind.

Phoebe and Elliot both stood and walked toward the open door.

"Please come in," said Elliot.

"Yeah," said Evie, "we'll make you a cup of tea."

She stretched out her arms and, for a brief moment, Phoebe was sure the stranger was about to be enveloped in a patchouli-scented hug, but the old woman turned and took off into the dark woods.

"Wait!" Evie cried. "Come back!" But the woman was gone.

"We should go after her," Phoebe said. "She's clearly lost. I mean, we're miles from anywhere. And she doesn't seem like she's in any shape to be on her own in the woods."

"Sam and I will go," Elliot said, grabbing a flashlight. "You two stay here."

"I'm going to put some tea on," said Evie.

They were gone nearly forty-five minutes, and when they came back they said they'd seen no sign of her.

"It's pitch-black out there," Sam reported, shaking his head.

"I think it's time we all hit the hay," said Elliot as he slid the bolt on the front door, locking it.

Phoebe couldn't have agreed more. She was exhausted.

"I'm not comfortable with this," Evie said. "I feel like we should be doing more. That poor woman is out there all alone."

Elliot put his hand gently on the back of her neck and massaged it a little. "We can look around more in the morning. Then drive into town and report it if it'll make you feel better."

Evie nodded.

After saying their good nights, Phoebe and Sam closed themselves up in their room and got ready for bed. Phoebe emptied her pockets, putting the small orange stone on the windowsill beside the bed. She pulled the memo pad from her back pocket along with a stubby pencil and wrote:

WEIRD THINGS THAT HAPPENED TODAY
Evie thinking I'm pregnant (can't be, can I???)
Their car had Mass plates
Seeing the note from Lisa (can't really be her, right?)
The old woman at the door

"Mapping out your plan for world peace?" Sam teased.

"More like world domination," Phoebe said with a sly smile, tucking the notebook into her purse, then watching as Sam pulled off his T-shirt. His back was strong, arms ropy with muscles from working out in the woods. She smiled at his funny T-shirt, farm-boy tan. She couldn't wait to get into bed and feel his arms around her, telling her she was home.

He turned to face her, and her eyes went to the pale white scar just below his left collarbone. Sam never said much about the scar, and when Phoebe asked, he told her that he was young and hardly remembered what had happened. His mother didn't remember either and said only, "Little boys can be so careless—I don't recall if that was from when he got tangled in the barbed-wire fence or the time he tried to jump his bike over our Volkswagen." Phoebe still found it hard to imagine that her careful, cautious Sam had once been such a reckless daredevil.

Phoebe kicked off her boots and undressed.

"Do you think she's all right?" Phoebe asked.

"Who?"

"The old woman. I hate to think of her alone out there, lost in the woods."

Sam was silent a minute. "It was the damndest thing," he said at last, his eyes glassy, cheeks flushed from all the wine he'd had. "How she could disappear like that. And that song she sang—"

"What about it?"

"Nothing," Sam said, turning off the light and getting under the covers. "Forget it. I think I've just had too much to drink. That wine had a definite kick to it, didn't it?"

"*Mmm hmm.*"

Phoebe crawled into bed next to him. *You should tell him*, a little inner voice said. *Tell him you think your period's late. Tell him what Evie said.*

But when he spooned himself around her, and she opened her mouth to say the words, she instead found herself asking the question she'd always wanted to ask.

"Did you really see fairies?"

He was silent a moment, his body tensing against hers.

"We saw something," he mumbled into her hair.

She wanted to ask him what, wanted to know the details—were they little green figures clothed in leaves? Or only shadows? But before she could ask, he was asleep. And soon she joined him, her own hand resting over her belly as she wondered if there really could be a tiny baby in there, swimming inside her.

The trapdoor was open. She'd heard the scuttling and squeaking of hinges.

She should have piled their suitcases and bags under the bed. Sam would have made fun of her, but so what? At least they'd be safe.

Something had crawled through. She felt pressure on her abdomen, opened her eyes and looked down. A hand was working its way into an envelope of torn skin, fat, and muscle.

Your eyes, a voice was saying. *You can always tell a pregnant woman by the light in her eyes.*

She reached down, but the hand was gone. And the covers were off. Sam was beside her, cocooned in the one thin blanket they'd found on the lumpy mattress in the cabin.

It wasn't a dream, Phoebe thought, realizing at once how ridiculous this was but holding her hand protectively over her belly as she sat up.

Sam didn't understand about dreams, had little patience for listening to her retelling them.

"I don't dream," he'd told her a hundred times.

"Of course you do," she'd told him. "Everybody dreams. You just don't remember."

It was barely light out, but Phoebe was able to make out a figure at the foot of their bed.

Was her childhood shadow man back?

No. It was the old woman in the flowered hat, and she was going through their things.

Phoebe blinked, sure it was some nightmare image, a freakish hallucination.

The woman turned, looked straight at them.

This was no dream.

Phoebe screamed, clawed at Sam, who sat bolt upright and stared at the old woman with a look of stunned disbelief.

The old woman winked at Sam, then ran out of the room, nearly knocking down Elliot, who was coming from the other bedroom down the hall in only his boxers to see what all the commotion was. The old woman took off through the open front door into the dawn.

"What was she doing?" Elliot asked.

"She was going through our bags," Phoebe said.

"But how did she get in?" Elliot asked. "I bolted the door last night before bed."

Sam went to the door and checked it over. "It doesn't look forced," he said. His voice sounded high and shaky, like a little boy's.

"Maybe she got in through one of the windows," said Evie, who followed behind Elliot. She was in a red silk kimono and looked smaller, younger, without her makeup on.

Sam checked the windows. They were all closed and locked.

The trapdoor under the bed, Phoebe thought. *That's how she got in.*

But she wasn't a little kid anymore. And there was no such thing as trapdoors under beds, no such thing as the bogeyman. She had to remind herself that she no longer believed in these things. This was the new Phoebe—the woman who hadn't had a nightmare for three years. Until last night.

"Did she take anything?" Evie asked. Sam went to check, then came back to report that nothing was missing.

"Well, I say we have some breakfast, then drive into town to call the police," Evie said.

"I can't believe none of our phones work," Elliot muttered, shaking his head.

"It's like this all over Vermont," Sam said. "Too many mountains, not enough cell towers."

"I'm going to put some coffee on," said Evie, giving Elliot's arm a reassuring squeeze. "Why don't you go get your pants?"

Elliot looked down at his bare legs as if just realizing he was in his underwear. Not just any underwear, but boxers with the words LOVE SLAVE emblazoned across the front. Clearly not meant for entertaining long-lost family members in. His cheeks flushed a little. As Elliot turned to walk back to the bedroom, Phoebe noticed a tattoo on his right calf—a small, tribal design: a circle with a perpendicular line that led to an upside-down number four. A Greek letter? Some sort of fraternity thing? Phoebe had barely made it through high school, never mind college, so she was clueless. She'd ask Sam about it later.

Sam stood in the front doorway and looked out into the woods, shaking his head. "Who the hell is she?" he asked, running his fingers through his close-cropped dark hair. Phoebe came up behind him, rubbed his shoulders. His muscles felt like golf balls.

"Just some poor old crazy woman," she said.

Sam shook his head. "That stupid song she sang last night . . . ," he said.

"She's clearly ill. Probably has Alzheimer's or something and wandered off from home," Phoebe reiterated.

"It was something Lisa used to sing all the time."

Phoebe worked at the knotted muscles in his shoulders. "It's just a coincidence," she whispered. "Lots of people know that song."

But in the back of her mind, she knew she didn't really believe it.

CHAPTER 6

Lisa

There are fairies in Reliance," Lisa announced at breakfast. The light from the kitchen windows made the floating dust glow and sparkle. The cherries on the wallpaper seemed unusually bright and cheery. The chrome chair and table legs glinted in the sun. The kitchen, like most of the house, hadn't changed much since her mom and aunt were little girls. The cabinets were all white metal, the countertops worn pale yellow Formica that matched the wallpaper—a bright pattern of cherries against a creamy yellow background. The floor was simple pine planks, painted a glossy white every few years.

Lisa's mom smiled into her sweet, milky Earl Grey tea but said nothing. As always, she had gotten up early, done yoga, and taken a bath. She was dressed for the day in loose-fitting linen pants with a matching shirt that had buttons shaped like pine-cones. Her hair was still damp and neatly combed. She smelled like lavender bath salts and cold cream.

If anyone was going to believe in the fairies, it would be her mom, who'd taught her to love fairy tales, to understand the magic spell cast by the words *Once upon a time*. Lisa's earliest memory was of her mother reading "Hansel and Gretel," pulling a sheet over her head like a shawl and speaking in a crackling voice when she read the witch's parts. "Let me feel your finger, girlie," she'd say, reaching out for Lisa's tiny hand. "Oh, too thin. Much too thin."

It was her mother who told her about Reliance, that the people in town were only half right: it was an enchanted place, but the magic was good, not bad. "One day you'll see," she'd told Lisa as she brushed her hair at night. "You'll see the magic for yourself. If you're lucky, that is. If you believe."

And Lisa *did* believe. She'd spent her life believing.

Now she held her breath, waiting. Her Rice Krispies went snap, crackle, and pop. Everything spoke if you knew how to listen.

Across the red Formica tabletop, Da sat in dirty pajamas staring into his coffee cup like there was a whole complicated world inside it: little cities, farms, cyclones. He dumped some sugar in, making it snow.

Lisa hadn't figured out how to listen right with Da. There had to be a way, though. He was in there somewhere. She listened with all of her might, but Da stayed silent.

"I saw fairies, Da," she said, leaning over the table, trying to look him in the eye. He kept his head down, studying the murky coffee in his mug. "We all did," she said, raising her voice a little this time. She was sure she saw the faintest tremble of movement by his left eye.

Da had never been this bad before. Sure, there were times when he wouldn't get out of bed for days, wouldn't shower or eat or do much of anything. But this was the first time he'd given up speaking. And the closest he'd ever come to dying.

"Why hasn't he said anything?" Lisa had asked her mom earlier.

"I guess he doesn't have much to say right now," she answered. "Give him time, Lisa. He's only been out of the hospital a couple of days. The doctors say the overdose didn't do any permanent physical damage. Things will be back to normal soon."

Cat got your tongue?

That's what Da used to say to Lisa and Sam when they wouldn't answer a question right away, which was usually a sign that they had something to hide.

Da didn't want to go with them to Cape Cod on Memorial Day, which should have been a warning flag—he loved the beach. He said it had *restorative powers.*

Ever since Lisa could remember, they'd gone to Cape Cod on Memorial Day weekend. Hazel and Evie always went with them. They stayed in a tiny cottage right on the beach, had bonfires, dug for clams, and swam in the ocean no matter how cold it was.

Da and Lisa would spend hours combing the beach, looking for shells and driftwood, making necklaces out of seaweed. Last summer, Da made a whole crazy wig out of seaweed. He put it on his head and danced around shaking a piece of driftwood, singing a witch doctor song. The sand on his bare chest sparkled and his long, narrow feet made funny bird tracks in a big circle on the beach. Even Hazel laughed until she cried.

Da was a potter. He had a studio set up in the garage with a kiln, spinning wheel, and shelves full of glazes. He made mugs, bowls, vases that he sold in galleries and craft shops all over the state. He said each of the pieces he made told a story. He didn't want to go to the Cape this year because he was working on something new, he explained. "Something those tourists from New York would give their left kidney for," he said with a wink. He kissed the top of Lisa's head. "Bring me back a magic rock. And some fudge. Lots of fudge."

"Things are gonna be different when we get back," Evie told Lisa one night on the beach. They'd wandered away from the others and stood throwing stones into the waves.

"What do you mean?"

"Your dad told me. Just before we left. He said everything was going to change." Evie had a faraway look, then smiled.

"Why would he say that?" Lisa asked.

Evie shrugged. "I guess we'll just have to wait and see."

When they got home last Tuesday, sunburned and bearing gifts of saltwater taffy and fudge, they called out, but he didn't answer even though his truck was in the driveway. Sammy and Lisa raced up to the bedroom, pounced on the bed, but he wouldn't wake up. Mom called 911. Aunt Hazel took his pulse, gathered up all the empty pill bottles to give to the ambulance drivers so they'd know what they were dealing with. They found his sketchbook on the bedside table—he always used it for jotting down ideas for new pottery. Lisa turned to the last page he'd filled in. He'd drawn a dark, shadowy figure—a self-portrait, maybe. His face was nothing but a spiral of scribbles, done so hard that the paper was torn in the center.

Did he know the day he said good-bye, Lisa wondered as she watched them take Da away by ambulance. Did he have it all planned? While he was asking for fudge and magic rocks was he secretly stockpiling pills, knowing he'd never eat another bite of Cape Cod fudge? Was that what he was trying to tell Evie? And the bigger question that twisted Lisa's stomach into knots: Why give Evie his cryptic good-bye message? Why not her and Sam? Lisa wished she could ask him. She tried thinking the questions really hard, hoping some psychic part of his brain would pick up on them and send her a message back. But nothing happened.

"Fairies, Da," Lisa repeated, speaking the words right into his ear, which had two little hairs growing out of the top of it she'd never noticed before and made him look kind of werewolf-y.

"It was just fireflies," Sammy said.

Lisa kicked him under the table.

"Ow!" he yelped.

Evie flashed her a smile. She'd put the skeleton key Lisa had given her on a long rawhide bootlace and tied it around her neck. The key was hidden by her shirt, but Lisa could see the leather lace around her neck. Evie had her sketchbook and was drawing a coffee cup, only she had it all wrong—the handle was too big, the top was an oval instead of a circle.

"It was not fireflies and you know it," Lisa said. Sammy gave her a scowl, then went back to shoveling cereal into his mouth, chewing like a robot. Sammy got no pleasure from food. It was sad, really.

"Tell them, Evie," Lisa said.

Evie bit her lip, looked down at her drawing. *Scratch, scratch, scratch* went her pen. She'd given the coffee cup arms with claws.

"Evie!" Lisa snarled.

"Ha!" said Sam, smiling. "So much for your reliable witness." He laughed, shaking his head, then went back to his cereal.

Lisa bit her lip. She'd show him. She'd prove the fairies were real, make Sammy Skeptic eat his words.

"You'll see," Lisa hissed. She reached into her pocket, touched the teeth, started to pull them out, offer them up as proof. Evie caught her and threw her a warning glance. She mouthed the word *No!* and gave such a menacing look that Lisa left the teeth in her pocket.

Aunt Hazel, who'd been standing with her back to them at the stove across the room, brought over a stack of pancakes, which she called flapjacks.

"Who's going to see what?" she asked. Always the opposite of her sister, she wore an inside-out robe, scuffed-up old slippers, her hair going this way and that like an unmanageable nest of snakes. "And while we're on the subject of seeing things, maybe one of you could tell me what might have happened to the strawberry jam I bought yesterday. You know how Dave loves his jam."

Aunt Hazel was a little batty, but she was good at taking care of people. She cooked a big breakfast every day (pancakes, Canadian bacon, cinnamon buns from a can) and never lost her patience with Da, even when he peed himself or refused to eat. She worked in nursing homes mostly, so she was used to dealing with old, crazy people. But she didn't seem to keep any one job too long because of her drinking. She'd call in sick too much or show up reeking of gin. That's what Evie said anyway. And this last time was no different. According to Evie, Hazel got called in to cover an early shift at Cedar Grove Health and Rehab and was still drunk from the night before. They fired her on the spot, which, it turned out, was good luck because it meant that now Hazel was in no hurry to get back home. She could stay and help with Da until he was better.

Hazel and Evie lived only an hour away, in a dilapidated old farmhouse that was cold all winter and stifling in the summer. Hazel didn't like to drive, so they didn't come on a regular basis, but when they did, they'd stay for days, sometimes whole weeks, usually when Hazel was between jobs. Sam and Lisa rarely went to visit there—Phyllis didn't approve of her sister's housekeeping and claimed that on various occasions over the years she'd encountered bedbugs, lice, and fleas. They couldn't go in the basement because there were supposedly rats the size of small cats down there, along with toe-breaking rattraps and poison bait. Lisa was pretty sure the real reason they weren't allowed to visit much was because of Hazel's drinking. When she came to their place, Phyllis could keep a tight rein on her, but in her own environment, all bets were off. She had bottles stashed everywhere—even, Lisa recalled, in the toilet tank.

"The kids say there are fairies in Reliance, Hazel," Lisa's mom told her.

Aunt Hazel shook her head, said, "Nonsense," and flashed Lisa's mother a don't-encourage-them look. "I'd say we've got a bunch of kids with overactive imaginations. Call it a blessing, call it a curse, but there it is." With this, she turned and shuffled over to the fridge for the syrup, mumbling something about the whole family needing medication, not just Da. She stood with the door open, leaning in to the fridge and banging things around while she muttered to herself.

"You should leave them something," Mom said in a low voice so that Hazel wouldn't hear. "Fairies like gifts. Especially sweets. And shiny, sparkly things. Not iron, though. They don't like anything made from iron."

Lisa smiled. She was sure her mother would understand and know just what to do.

"Tell us again, Aunt Phyllis," Evie said. "What happened to all the people who lived in Reliance?"

Da looked up from his cup slowly, as if his head was the heaviest thing. He had a little string of drool coming from the edge of his mouth, getting caught up on the stubble covering his cheek. Aunt Hazel came back across the checkered lino-leum floor, put the syrup and butter on the table with a loud thump, and gently dabbed at Da's face with a napkin, then put a stack of flapjacks in front of him. "No jam, Dave, sorry. It's a damn mystery."

"Gone," Lisa's mom said, her voice barely above a whisper. It was her best storytelling voice. The one she used before bed each night for as long as Lisa could remember. The one that had told her "Hansel and Gretel," "Cinderella," "Snow White and Rose Red." "The whole town just disappeared. One day they were there, the next they weren't. There were dinner plates left on the tables, fires stoked, cows waiting to be milked, horses in the stable. All that was left," her mother said, her voice as hushed as she could make it while still being heard, "was one child. A baby in a cradle."

"And what happened to that baby?" Lisa asked, though she knew the story by heart.

"He was adopted by a family here in town."

"And he was our great-grandpa," Evie said.

Lisa's mom nodded. "My grandfather. Eugene O'Toole. He built this house."

"And grew up to be the town doctor," Lisa added.

"Went to medical school in Boston when he was just sixteen," her mother said, a proud smile on her face. "There was nothing that man couldn't do."

Except explain why he was the only one left behind, Lisa thought.

Lisa's mom and Hazel had grown up in this same house with their grandfather Eugene and his daughter, Rose, their mother. Their own father had left them. "House wasn't big enough for two men," Hazel always said, but Lisa never got it—the house seemed plenty big to her.

Lisa never met her great-grandpa. He died just after her parents were married. He walked out into the backyard one evening during a storm and was struck by lightning. If he was so smart, Lisa always wondered, shouldn't he have known not to be holding an umbrella in a thunderstorm? From that point on, umbrellas were outlawed in their house and Lisa had never been allowed to own one.

Lisa remembered her grandma Rose as being delicate and smelling like the menthol rub she used for her arthritis. She had a stroke and couldn't move one side of her face. She lived in a nursing home and died after having another stroke when Lisa was seven.

Sometimes Lisa would walk around the house and touch things—the red kitchen table, the milk-glass candy dish, the pipe that had belonged to Eugene that sat on the mantel—and imagine that each object was haunted in some small way by her grandmother and great-grandfather, by the ghosts of her mother and Aunt Hazel's childhood selves.

Da left his pancakes untouched, dropped his head back down, gazing into his coffee. It was a white mug with a red heart on one side, Cupid on the other. Lisa had given it to him on Valentine's Day years ago. It was full of those chalky, heart-shaped candies that had messages like *Sweet Talk* and *Be True*.

"You eat up now, Dave," Hazel told him. "You need your strength." Then she leaned over and started cutting up his pancakes for him.

Sammy stared, eyes locked on his father like someone who sees an accident and can't look away. Their mother shifted uncomfortably in her seat, said, "I wish you kids could have met your great-grandfather. Sometimes," she went on, her voice low and serious again like she was telling a story, "sometimes I'm sure I see little pieces of him in each of you."

Da took the fork Hazel handed him, stabbed at his plate, missing the pancake entirely. Hazel took the fork back and fed him herself.

Lisa's mother winced, but when she caught Lisa looking, she forced a smile. Then her mom folded her napkin, pushed her chair back away from the table, and said, "Well, if you're all set here, I think I'll go out to the garden and do some weeding."

"Of course we are," Hazel said, feeding Da another bite. "Aren't we, Dave?" Some pancake fell out of his mouth.

Lisa touched the ugly yellow teeth in her pocket. Wondered what it felt like to go crazy. If maybe it was a little like walking into a thunderstorm with an umbrella. Or maybe it started small—like thinking the kitchen table and candy dish were haunted, or insisting you've just seen fairies in the woods even though your brother and cousin, who were right there with you, seemed determined to deny it.

CHAPTER 7

Phoebe

They were finishing up a breakfast of strawberry pancakes, which Evie called flapjacks. "Like my mom," Evie said, "remember?" which gave Sam a dreamy sort of smile that made Phoebe's stomach hurt. Phoebe had very few warm, fuzzy memories from childhood, and even if she had, there was no one to share them with. No long-lost cousins to be reunited with. Before her mother's death four years ago, she'd talk to her three, maybe four times a year, and then it was usually because her ma was looking for money, not to share memories of old family recipes.

Phoebe smiled at Evie. She wasn't going to let her cruddy-ass childhood cloud the fact that she was happy for Sam. While it's true that she did feel a twinge of envy when she looked at Evie and understood all she and Sam had shared, she was determined not to screw this up. Evie seemed like the golden ticket. Just what Sam needed to start opening up about his past. And as much as she admired him for being able to move on, curiosity got the better of her. She wanted to hear about Lisa. About the Fairy King and the hidden door.

Hidden doors. Trapdoors.

Like the one the old woman must have come through last night.

Stop it, she told herself.

"Do you come from a big family, Phoebe?" Evie asked, and Phoebe stammered a bit, said, "No, it was just me and my mom. She passed away just before I met Sam."

"I'm sorry," Evie said, giving her a doe-eyed look and leaning across the table like she was thinking of embracing her in yet another hug. "Were you very close?"

Hell no! Phoebe wanted to say. Instead, she shook her head, looked down at her half-eaten pancakes. She was saved from having to explain any more when there was a quick, frantic rapping at the door.

"Jesus!" Elliot said, throwing down his fork. "Don't tell me she's back again!"

"I'll go," said Evie, reaching over to squeeze his wrist. "Maybe she'll be less intimidated if it's just me. You all finish eating."

They were all silent, listening to Evie's footsteps on the wide plank floor. Then the door opened and she said, "Hello again. Can I help you?"

This was followed by a horrible, frantic scream.

Phoebe knew the old woman in the flowered hat was back and that she'd done something awful. She raced out of the kitchen and saw Evie clutching her side, her white T-shirt stained crimson with blood. And there stood the old woman, wielding the corkscrew Elliot had pulled from his vest pocket and left on the kitchen table last night.

Phoebe was used to blood. She'd seen some pretty grue-some things at the clinic: dogs and cats carried in after hit-

and-runs; a poodle maimed by a pit bull; a shepherd that had been caught for days in a leg hold trap and had gnawed his way free.

"Let me see," she said, reaching to pull up Evie's soaked shirt, but the other woman kept her hand clamped tightly over it.

"I'm okay," Evie said, looking pale. "It's not too deep. Go get her!"

"Go!" Elliot yelled. "I'm gonna get Evie into the Jeep and go for help. Catch the bitch!"

The world was reduced to a single narrow tunnel just then, and there, at the end of that tunnel, was the only fact Phoebe could be sure of: she was going to catch up with the old woman, pin her down, and get some goddamn answers. But first, she was going to throw up.

Phoebe made it through the door just in time to vomit strawberry pancakes and coffee onto the flagstone path leading up to the cabin. Through the tearful retching, she heard the old woman singing that song in a wicked, crackling witch's voice:

> *Say, say my playmate*
> *Come out and play with me.*

"Who the hell are you?" Sam was in the open door behind Phoebe. The old woman, who was standing at the edge of the woods, shifting from foot to foot like a little girl who has to pee, stopped singing and winked at him.

"Sammy, Sammy, Sammy, weak little lamb-y!" she sang. Then the old woman dropped the corkscrew and took off into the woods, Sam right behind her. Phoebe got to her feet and followed on shaky legs, stomach churning.

Running, running. Tripping on roots and stones. Branches scratching her face. She kept sight of Sam's pale blue T-shirt through the trees. The old woman was somewhere in front of him, but she was losing her clothes.

At first, Phoebe saw the robe lying on the forest floor. Then the hat. Her dress. Shoes. At last, she saw a mass of gray hair. A wig.

The bitch had been wearing a disguise.

Phoebe pushed herself harder. Faster.

What if the wound was deeper than Evie admitted? And what if the nearest hospital turned out to be an hour away. How much damage could a corkscrew do? What if it had hit a major artery? Or an organ? Phoebe tried desperately to recall anatomy charts she'd once memorized for high school biology. What was even down there? Ovaries? Spleen? She was clueless. Damn. If she'd been a vet tech instead of a receptionist, someone with some actual medical training, she might have been able to help more.

How long had they been running? How far had they gone?

Her legs pumped, her breath whistled. Aside from the weekend hikes with Sam, Phoebe was not big on exercise. The old woman ran like a coyote. She was just a shadow in front of them. Then she was gone.

The trees were thinning. Up ahead, Phoebe saw a huge, unnaturally bright green meadow that reminded her of the plastic grass in Easter baskets. The old woman was running across it, naked.

Only she wasn't an old woman. She had short red hair and the lean, taut body of a twenty-year-old. And she was screaming.

"Help! Oh God! Somebody help me!"

It is *Lisa!* Phoebe thought. And she would have said it out loud, if she'd had the spare breath required for speaking.

"Please help me!" the naked redheaded girl wailed, her arms crisscrossed defensively across her torso, covering her small breasts. Her skin was milk white and flawless. Her cheeks were flushed but not damp. She seemed, to Phoebe, too perfect to be real.

And then, across the field came three men with golf clubs. They'd followed her out into the middle of a goddamn golf course. One of the men, the tallest one, who was dressed in plaid pants, tackled Sam. Another stood over him, golf club raised like a weapon. The third man grabbed Phoebe and pinned her hands behind her back. Phoebe screamed, "Let me go, you idiot! Grab her! She's the one! She stabbed Evie!"

The naked woman was sobbing, trying desperately to cover herself with her arms. One of the men draped a yellow sweater over her.

"What happened?" asked the man who was pinning Sam to the ground.

"They . . . they . . ." the woman in the yellow sweater sobbed and choked. "I was hitchhiking out on Route 12 last night. They picked me up. Then they took me into the woods. And they . . . they did things . . ." Her voice crumpled.

Phoebe and Sam looked at each other, stunned. "She's lying!" Phoebe screamed. "She stabbed Sam's cousin with a corkscrew! We're staying at a cabin in the woods and this old woman showed up . . ."

"What old woman?" asked one of the golfers.

"Her!" Phoebe shrieked. "She was wearing a disguise!"

She only realized how absurd it sounded after she'd said it.

"They took off my clothes and tied me to a tree," said the woman in the yellow sweater. She showed the men rope burns on her wrists.

This is not happening, thought Phoebe. *This cannot be happening.*

"What are you?" Sam asked the redhead in the yellow sweater. He looked petrified.

"I'm calling the police," announced the man who'd given the girl his sweater.

"Good," Sam said. "Tell them my cousin Evie and her husband are heading into town on Route 12 and that she's been badly hurt. They're in a black Jeep with out-of-state plates."

Soon they were joined by two state troopers in uniform and the town constable, whose name was Alfred and who smelled like he'd just come from chores in the barn. The golfers had released Sam and Phoebe but stood by with their clubs in case any attempts were made at escape. One of the men had gone back to the clubhouse and found a pair of sweatpants and a T-shirt for the naked woman. The T-shirt said FERNCREST COUNTRY CLUB.

The woman, thought Phoebe, whoever she was, was a wonderful actress. She knew just when to cry, when to look like a frightened child, and when to show anger. She had all the men but Sam hanging on her every word. She touched them each, thanked them, made them feel like her saviors. Their eyes were astonished, proud. And wasn't there something else there, too, in their watery middle-aged eyes? Phoebe recognized it at once: they were spellbound. These men were clearly captivated by this beautiful damsel in distress.

"Shit," Phoebe mumbled under her breath. She and Sam were screwed.

The mysterious victim showed off her rope burns and told her story once more to the police, who took notes. Phoebe looked over at Sam with a *what the hell is going on* expression. His eyes looked dazed and glassy. Phoebe had a sense that maybe, if she concentrated hard enough, she'd wake up back in the cabin. That she was just trapped in some nonsensical nightmare.

When they'd all had a chance to tell their stories, the police decided the only thing to do was take a walk back into the woods.

"If what you're saying is true," said Alfred the constable to Sam, "then we should have no trouble finding the woman's disguise."

"All our stuff is at the cabin. Please try to find Evie and Elliot. They'll back up our story. And Evie was injured, bleeding all over the place. I want to be sure they made it to a doctor."

But the trouble was, they couldn't find any part of the woman's disguise.

Not good, thought Phoebe. *Definitely not good.*

They fanned out through the woods and came up with nothing. Phoebe recognized landmarks: trees and rocks she'd passed, tripping over them and scratching her face, so she knew they were going the right way. But the woman's wig and clothing had disappeared. Phoebe began to feel a new and creeping dread.

Eventually (Phoebe guessed it was an hour or so since first giving chase to the old woman) they got to the cabin. Elliot's Jeep was gone. In its place was a battered Toyota pickup.

Sam was pounding on the closed cabin door, calling for Evie and Elliot.

An old man in green pants and a flannel shirt answered. His eyes seemed unnaturally blue and clear, like bright marbles set inside a sunken-faced, shriveled apple-head doll.

"Hello, Danny," the constable said to the old man. Danny nodded back and Alfred continued. "Sorry to bother you so early on a Saturday. But there's been a little trouble in the woods. These folks say they've been staying here. Is that right?"

The old man focused his piercing blue eyes on Phoebe and Sam. "Never seen them before," he said.

"And you've been here all morning?" asked one of the state policeman.

"Since yesterday afternoon."

"He's lying," moaned Sam. "We spent the night here. In the back bedroom. All our stuff is inside."

"Mind if we take a look?" asked the constable.

The old man held the door open for them. "Be my guest, Al."

The place had been cleaned up. But there were ashes in the fireplace from the night before and the air still smelled of pancakes. All the breakfast dishes had been put away. There was no sign of Evie and Elliot. Their room was empty, the bed made. When they got to the room at the end of the hall where Phoebe and Sam had spent the night, it too was tidy. Their bags were gone. The bed made.

"Our things!" Phoebe shrieked. Everything they'd brought was gone: duffel bags, her purse, their camera. The only things left were the clothes they were wearing. None of it made any sense, and she began to feel like a woman in the middle of a psychotic break, unsure what was real and what wasn't.

Then she looked, and there on the windowsill was the tiny

orange stone right where she'd put it. As the others turned from the room, she scooped up the stone and dropped it into her pocket, comforted to have a shred of proof.

Whatever was happening, she was not going crazy. They had spent the night here.

The state police took information from the owner of the cabin, then they headed back into the woods, the strange shape-shifting girl in the lead.

"Is there any word on my cousin and her husband?" Sam asked. "She was hurt badly."

"Nothing's been called in," one of troopers said. "And no female with a stab wound has shown up at the emergency room."

Phoebe took Sam's hand. One of the troopers walked in front of them, the other behind them, as if they were already prisoners.

"What's going on?" Phoebe whispered.

"I don't know," said Sam, squaring his shoulders, trying to play the part of the brave boyfriend.

"She knew your name," said Phoebe. "Just before you chased her into the woods, she said your name. Maybe she saw it when she was going through our things."

"No," said Sam. "There's more to it than that. That weak little lamb-y thing she said—it was a rhyme Lisa used to tease with me with. No one else knows about it." There went Sam's shoulders, back into the slouched, little boy position.

"So, what? Are you saying you think this girl is Lisa?"

"No! Definitely not." The state trooper ahead of them turned to look back. Sam continued, lowering his voice. "But it's like she knows her. Or knows things about her."

"Maybe she's from the land of the fairies," Phoebe ventured, knowing how ludicrous it sounded.

Sam shook his head. "Jesus! There is no land of the fairies, Bee. Lisa was taken by a real person to a real place. Shit, she probably never even made it out of those woods alive."

Phoebe felt a rush of guilt. She'd been so compelled by the idea of the fairies and the book that she'd forgotten the facts: Sam had lost his sister to what was most likely a brutal, and terribly human, crime. She needed to be more gentle and supportive, beginning with backing off from the crazy fairy talk.

She took Sam's hand, broadening her own shoulders. She would be the strong one here. She'd get them out of this. She had the stone in her pocket as proof, damn it, and that counted for something.

Eventually they came to a small clearing, and there, at the base of a tree, was a length of rope. And a pile of clothing along with a small knapsack. It was all just as the redhead described.

The girl reached into the bag and came out with a wallet. She showed the police a state college ID that said her name was just what she'd told them it was: Amy Pelletier.

"No driver's license?" one of the cops asked.

"I don't drive," Amy said.

"Maybe you should learn," suggested the constable. "I'd say it's high time you gave up hitchhiking."

"No shit," said Amy as she gathered up her belongings. "Look, I was scared out of my mind, but no harm was done, right? I'd just as soon drop the whole thing."

"But these people committed a crime. They held you against your will."

"Maybe it was just a game. Maybe at first I played along, okay? They're kind of cute, I was into it. A little bondage isn't such a bad thing. Maybe I just kind of freaked. Let's just forget it, okay? I got my stuff back. I just want to walk away and pretend it never happened."

"You don't want to press charges?" one of the cops asked, dumbfounded.

"No. I just want to go home."

Alfred the constable took the girl aside and spoke quietly to her for a minute. She shook her head, said something that made him laugh.

"If you're sure . . ." said the constable. Then he turned back to the others. His ears were bright red, like strange glowing handles on the side of his juglike head. "I'm going to give Amy a ride into town. Take her to the diner for some breakfast and a chance to get cleaned up, use the phone . . ."

The constable put his arm around the girl and nodded at the cops, then led her away, his ears and neck redder than ever.

"I think you should consider yourselves very lucky," said one of the cops. "But she could still change her mind. If she decides to press charges after all, we know where to find you." Then they turned to go.

"Wait! How do we find our car?" asked Sam.

"That way," pointed one of the cops. "Route 12 is about half a mile."

————

They walked in dazed silence.

"Shit!" Sam mumbled. "My keys. I don't have any keys. They were on the dresser at the cabin."

"There's one under the car."

"There is?"

"I put it there last winter after I locked myself out and had to call AAA. Remember?"

"I told you not to," Sam said.

"But I did it anyway, and now aren't you glad?"

He didn't say anything.

"Do you have your wallet?" she asked him.

"That's about all I do have."

"What are we going to do?"

"Go home. We're going to go home."

They walked on in silence, and by the time they reached the Mercury, they were exhausted and hungry. Phoebe looked beneath the car and found the little magnetic box under the rear bumper, right where she'd left it back in January. It had rusted closed and she pounded it open with a rock. She was bringing the key to Sam, closed in her palm like a secret, when she saw him remove a small piece of paper that had been tucked under the windshield wiper.

"A ticket? You've gotta be kidding."

"It's not a ticket," Sam said. What little color left in his face drained away as he studied the paper. Phoebe noticed the faintest tremor in his hand. She came up beside him and looked down at the paper. There were no words, only a simple picture. Lines and a circle, like something a child would do.

It was the same mark she'd seen on Elliot's calf.

"Teilo," he mumbled.

"What?"

"Not what, who. Teilo. The King of the Fairies."

CHAPTER 8

Lisa

Lisa got an old, chipped china saucer and laid out three sugar cubes, a flat piece of mica she'd found in the stream, a Lorna Doone cookie, and a juice glass full of Orange Crush.

"The only thing you're going to attract with all this is yellow jackets," Sammy complained as they made their way across their backyard and into the woods. Sammy had on a black T-shirt with a map of glow-in-the-dark star constellations. His hair was too long and was sticking out all over the place. Da always cut Sammy's hair. He'd set up a chair in the kitchen, lay out the scissors and comb, and announce, "The barbershop is open!" He'd wet Sam's hair in the kitchen sink, then drape a towel around his neck and sing out, "Shave and a haircut, two bits!" Sam would laugh and Da would talk like a barber. "What'll it be today, son? Flattop? A little off the sides? Finish it off with a dab of Brylcreem?" Sam would giggle more. "A Mohawk, perhaps?" Da would tease, combing up the sides of Sam's damp hair so that it was all in the middle, then showing him the mirror. "The stegosaurus look," Da said. "It's very in these days. You'll be a hit with the girls. A real lady killer."

Lisa was thinking that maybe she should offer to give Sam a trim but figured he'd probably refuse. He'd just let his hair keep growing until Da got better, looking more and more like a boy of the wild every day. Sammy didn't give much thought to things like being presentable.

"You don't know that," Evie said. "Aunt Phyllis said fairies like sweets."

"She's just yanking your chain," Sam said.

"So if you don't believe me, why'd you come?" Lisa asked, squinting back over her shoulder at her brother.

"'Cause I want to see your face when nothing happens," he said.

Lisa was walking extra carefully, her high-wire balance walk, so that she wouldn't spill anything on the plate. The hill that led down toward Reliance was uneven and steep in places. The ground was spongy with fallen leaves rotted to mulch. There were rocks and downed branches to trip on, but if you knew where to look, there was a path the kids kept clear that led all the way down to Reliance. All around them, young poplar and birch fought for scraps of light under the canopy of full-grown maple and beech trees. The woods had a rich, loamy scent that always made Lisa take deep, hungry breaths. Even though it was only ten, it was hot already and it felt good to enter the woods and get out of the sun. The drying sweat on her arms and legs felt prickly and cool.

"What, are you guys having a picnic or something?" called a voice from up ahead of them. Great. This was not what they needed at all. Gerald and Becca were coming up from Reliance. Gerald was wearing camouflage pants and a *Star Trek* T-shirt. He had big square wire-framed glasses that were the kind that got darker when you were out in the sun. The problem was that they seemed really slow to get back to normal, and now that he was in the dark forest, he was squinting, struggling to see through them. Becca was always in pink and today was no different—matching shorts and shirt the color of cotton candy. Pink flip-flops. Her hair was even tied back with a pink ribbon. What a kook. She was in Sammy's grade and he said that she thought she was popular, but secretly everyone kind of hated her. "She tries too hard," Sammy explained. "Like WAY too hard. It's kind of painful to watch." Her schoolmates called her Pinkie, which she liked. Lisa had thought it wasn't so bad until the day she went to the pet shop and saw that the little newborn mice they sold to people who owned snakes were called pinkies. Now, whenever she saw Becca, she thought of those tiny, blind embryo-like creatures that didn't stand a chance.

"Yup," Lisa said, wanting to get rid of them quickly, whatever it took. There was no way she was going to tell them the truth about the plate of gifts or mention anything about what they'd seen the night before. And she didn't want to give Gerald a chance to start giving Evie any crap or calling her Stevie.

"Kind of a strange-looking picnic," Gerald said, peering down at the plate now that he was up close. He'd pushed his still-too-dark glasses down and was looking over the top of them. His light brown hair was a little greasy, and his forehead was dotted with pimples.

Gerald, at least, didn't have any illusions about being popular. He had his small circle of friends—boys who liked computer games, model building, and graphic novels—and that was enough. He was content hanging out in the computer lab after school, where he and his buddies were working on designing their own game, which took place in an alternate, microscopic universe and required them to invent a whole new language they called Minarian. Lisa kind of admired Gerald for knowing just who he was and not pretending to be anything more. But still, he got teased by some of the other boys—the popular, athletic boys who already had girlfriends they went to the movies with on Friday nights.

"Ant food," Sammy said. "We're giving a picnic to the ants."

Gerald laughed. "You guys are so weird." It was a favorite line of his. Something he said to Lisa all the time: *You're so weird.* But he said it with a goofy smile on his face, like it somehow pleased him. Like he knew he was weird too, and he was acknowledging Lisa as part of his tribe.

This time, though, the smile faded quickly and his eyes went right to Evie. "Like freak show weird," he said, snorting a little. Evie clenched her jaw and her breath got whistley-sounding. Her fingers rested on the knife in its sheath.

"I like ants," Pinkie said, looking at Sam, smiling.

"You do not," Gerald said, shaking his head, pushing his glasses back up. "You hate bugs!"

"An ant can lift twenty times its own body weight," Sam told Pinkie. "That's like you lifting a car."

Pinkie giggled at this, scratched a bug bite on her arm.

"Now *that* I'd like to see," Gerald said, making a silly, forced guffawing sound. Then he grabbed the shoulder of her pink T-shirt with ruffled sleeves and gave it a tug. "Come on, Hercules," he said. Pinkie followed, still picking at the bug bite on her arm, which was now bleeding. "Au revoir!" she called back, giving a queen's wave, hand cupped and wrist twisting in an unsettling Barbie-dollish way.

Evie took her hand off the knife.

"Thank God," Lisa whispered. "I thought we were gonna be stuck with Gerald and Freaky Pinkie all day."

Sam shook his head. "You're the one bringing sweets to the fairies and you're calling Pinkie the freak? I hate to say it, Sis, but you're making her look downright normal."

After another few minutes, they were crossing the brook, which mostly just ran in the early spring and was reduced to a sad little trickle the rest of the year. It was easy to clear in a single step, and even when you missed, you only got wet up to your ankle. Sometimes the brook dried up entirely, but it was always a good place to find red-backed salamanders staying cool under rocks.

Across the brook, the woods opened up, and they could see what was left of Reliance: half a dozen cellar holes lined with stones and crumbling mortar—some stunted lilacs and apple trees, the cemetery and old well. Encircling all this was a low, crooked, broken-down stone wall. The cellar hole closest to the brook was the one they'd seen the lights in the night before, and Lisa headed straight for it, Sammy and Evie in tow.

"Maybe it was swamp gas," Sam said, pacing around, looking at the ground, then up at the trees.

"What?" Lisa asked, peering down into the cellar hole, which looked the same as ever. It was roughly a fifteen-foot square— the footprint of a house that hadn't been very large at all, more like the size of a living room. She remembered the strong feeling she'd had last night as they stood in this same spot—that they were being watched.

"They say that it can glow," Sammy explained. "Make strange lights."

Evie shook her head. Laughed a little.

"Um, hello! Earth to Mr. Science—there's no swamp here!" Lisa said. She loved Sammy. Deep down she did. But sometimes he was so dense it made her head hurt.

"Maybe the gas is escaping from a vent in the ground," he said.

"Maybe," Lisa told him at last. "Why don't you take a long walk and see if you can find it."

Evie chuckled.

Sammy looked totally unfazed. He walked in a circle around the cellar hole but showed no sign of going any farther. His forehead was all crinkled, like that of a fretful old man.

"Hold this, okay?" Lisa said, handing the plate over to Evie while she climbed down into the hole.

"Careful," Evie said, eyes worried, lips trembling a little, as if Lisa was lowering herself into a nest of snakes.

They'd been in and out of this and every other cellar hole hundreds, maybe even thousands of times. Played countless games of hide-and-seek. They'd slain invisible dragons with stick swords and won wars with Vikings. They'd sung that silly "Say, Say My Playmate" song while they chased each other through the village, pretending they each had a house of their own with cellar doors and rain barrels. Reliance was like a second home to them. But today something was different. The woods didn't feel like theirs alone anymore.

The cellar hole wasn't deep—maybe four feet with crumbling stone walls and a dirt floor layered with years of rotting leaves. If Lisa squinted her eyes, she could just imagine the stone walls topped with a wood frame, clapboard siding. A little door and windows. There were old moss-covered bricks on the north side that must once have been a chimney and hearth.

"Do you think this could have been it?" she asked.

"What?" Evie asked.

"Eugene's house," she said. "Our great-grandfather."

She remembered her mother this morning: *Sometimes I see him in each of you.*

Evie nodded. "I wouldn't be at all surprised. Your mom would know, probably. We should ask her."

Lisa looked around the bottom of the cellar hole. Baby trees grew there—poplar, white pine, and clumps of ferns.

"Maybe the lights we saw were like . . . his ghost or something," Evie said.

"Could be," Lisa said, but she didn't think so. It was fairies. Definitely. She was surer than she'd ever been of anything.

"Hey, guys, this is weird," Sammy called, appearing at the edge of the foundation. "I found this just over in those trees." He pointed to the left, near the old well. Lisa folded her arms over the edge of the cellar hole, pushing her belly against the wall, and looked up. Sammy held a half-eaten sandwich.

"Probably from Gerald and Pinkie," Evie said. "Damn litterbugs!"

Sam studied the sandwich, gave it a sniff. "I think it's liverwurst," he said, wrinkling his nose.

The only person Lisa knew who ate liverwurst was Da, and he certainly wasn't in any shape to be picnicking in the woods.

"Weird," Lisa said.

"Gross," said Evie. "I say you chuck it. Some animal will come along and eat it. Maybe. If it's hungry enough."

Lisa let go of the wall and turned from Sam and Evie and the offensive sandwich to study the inside of the cellar hole.

There, in the southernmost corner of the old foundation, right where they might have found little Eugene all alone, squalling in his cradle, Lisa saw a plant growing. It was hung with flowers like a string of bells. The flowers were pale purple with white spots going down their throats. Magic flowers. "I knew it," Lisa exclaimed, clapping her hands together. She leaned down and listened, sure she would hear the sound of tinkling bells.

"Foxglove," Sammy said from up above. "Be careful, they're poison."

Lisa had never seen such a spectacular flower, poisonous or not. And she couldn't believe that anything in those woods would hurt her.

She set the plate of gifts carefully at the base of the plant and then, heart pounding, Sammy hissing warnings, she reached out and touched one of the flowers. It was soft and smooth, like the cheek of a baby.

She could almost hear Eugene's long-ago cry: an infant alone in the woods, left behind.

CHAPTER 9

Phoebe

When Sam and Phoebe pulled into their driveway at nearly three o'clock, Phoebe sighed—she'd never been happier to be home. She'd shower, put on a clean change of clothes, sit down with Sam at their wobbly kitchen table, and figure all this out. Being home and safe and away from the madness at the cabin would put things in perspective.

It was more of a cottage than a proper house, really, and over the last two years, it had become Phoebe's favorite place on earth—the only place that had ever truly felt like home to her.

The house with its high, peaked roof, stained-glass windows, and gingerbread trim at the eaves had charmed Phoebe nearly as much as Sam had. It all seemed too good to be true. And when, after they'd been dating for six months, he asked her to move in, she had no hesitation, though he was the first man she'd ever agreed to live with. Until she met Sam and saw the house, she'd always been determined to have her own space, to keep a certain comfortable distance between herself and her boyfriends. But Sam was different. This house was different. Sam had lived there since college, renting it from an art history professor who had been renovating it. Then the professor's wife got sick and they moved to Boston. He sold Sam the house for half what it was worth.

"Ooh," Phoebe remembered cooing when she first saw it. "It's straight out of a fairy tale!"

But now, as she got closer and saw that the front door was hanging open, it felt more like a scene from a horror novel.

"Stand back," Sam warned, squaring his shoulders, holding the sad little spare car key out in front of him like it was supposed to be a samurai sword.

"Like hell," Phoebe said, staying right by his side. She grabbed a softball-size rock from beside the front steps.

"Guess we didn't just forget to lock up," Sam said, eyeing the front door with trepidation. The dead bolt had been ripped from the wall and the lock in the knob mangled with a screwdriver that had been left hanging there. Phoebe held her breath, kicked the door open with her green boot, and led Sam over the threshold.

The house was trashed: furniture tipped over, drawers and cabinets opened, and everything pulled out. The framed topographical maps were all down, the glass smashed.

"Holy shit," Phoebe mumbled. Still holding the rock, she ran straight for the aquariums at the back of the living room to check on everyone. The aquariums were about the only thing in the house left intact, and all of the residents appeared unharmed. She set down her rock and gently scooped up Horace. The little hedgehog nosed her palm and fingers, searching for treats.

"Hey there, Buddy," she said in the singsongy voice reserved for small animals and babies, stroking his soft quills. "What happened in here, huh?" She held her little pale-bellied hedgie up to her face, wishing he could answer.

"They all okay?" Sam asked. With the exception of the snake, Sam loved the animals, and teasingly referred to them as *Phoebe's menagerie*.

"Seem to be," Phoebe said, setting Horace down in his cage. In the next aquarium, Orville and Wilbur, the two hooded rats, were contentedly snoozing, pink tails curled around their bodies. Jackson the one-eyed ball python was resting half in and half out of his water dish.

The animals had all come from the clinic, given up for various reasons. Horace had badly bitten a boy at a birthday party (why parents would let a group of rowdy seven-year-old boys pass around the hedgehog—who must have been terrified—was beyond Phoebe). Jackson had been rescued from a home with fourteen snakes, half a dozen ferrets, and countless rabbits, all malnourished and neglected. Orville and Wilbur were abandoned when their owner took off for college and his mother refused to take care of vermin.

"Great. It's a comfort to know that the twisted psychos are animal lovers," Sam said.

Phoebe's legs felt like rubber. She wanted to sit, but the furniture was tipped over, slashed open.

Sam stood, dumbfounded, in the center of their living room, looking for the phone. "We shouldn't touch anything. I'll call the police." He went to set down the mail he'd carried in, but the table had been turned over. He dropped the mail down on the floor and that's when he saw it: a small envelope with only his name in neat script on the front. No address or postage. He tore it open.

*I am back from the land of the fairies. Meet me
in Reliance on the next full moon.*

Lisa

They spent the afternoon putting the house back together and taking stock. It didn't look as though anything had been taken. Sam decided it was best not to involve the police. Phoebe argued with him at first, but when he reminded her of their interaction with the cops just that morning, she acquiesced. Who knew what might happen if the police stepped in? And what if that girl had changed her story again? The police might well be on their way at this very minute to arrest Sam and Phoebe.

"I think part of the whole setup this morning was to make us look like really sketchy, criminal-type people. It was a smart move on their part," Sam said. "They know we'll think twice about going to the cops because the police are going to see us as nutty and unreliable, no matter what."

"But we know what we saw," she said. "That woman stabbed Evie! What happened to her? You can't just take off and disappear with a stab wound like that."

Sam shook his head worriedly. "I don't know."

"And who took all our stuff? Cleaned up the cabin like that? Why on earth would anyone go through all that?"

"Hard to say," Sam answered. "The fact that this place was torn apart, too, tells me they're looking for something. Maybe it was just the fairy book they were after, and now that they've got it, they'll leave us alone."

"But who even knew we had the book?" Phoebe said. "Your mom, Evie, and Elliot. The girl on the phone, maybe."

She pulled the memo book from her pocket, wrote: PEOPLE WHO KNEW ABOUT BOOK in her tiny hieroglyphics at the top of a clean page, and made a list.

Sam nodded, rubbing the back of his neck.

"And why take the book?" Phoebe asked.

"Because it was evidence, I guess. It was made by whoever took Lisa. I should have just listened to my mom and brought it to the cops the day we found it."

"You can't blame yourself," Phoebe said.

"I'm not. I just wish I'd at least opened the damn thing."

"So why didn't you?"

"Because, when Evie called that same day, she asked me to promise not to open it without her. She wanted to be there."

Evie. Where the hell was poor Evie? Did whoever did this catch up with Elliot and her?

"Okay, so what now?" asked Phoebe. She opened her little notebook to the next page and wrote THE PLAN.

"Nothing," Sam said. "We just get on with our lives."

Phoebe blew out an exasperated breath. "We can't do nothing!" she said, sitting forward. "Your cousin could be bleeding to death somewhere, held hostage by a bunch of wackos. And whoever that girl in the woods was, she seemed to know things about Lisa. Things only Lisa would know. You said so yourself!"

Sam bit his lip, ran his hand through his hair.

"If all that isn't enough, think about your mom. If there's a chance Lisa might still be alive, don't you think we owe it to her to find out? Christ, this is *her child*, Sam! Your sister."

Sam walked over to the Humane Society calendar hanging

on the wall. "Okay. The full moon is on the eleventh. Friday. Maybe we'll take a ride out to Reliance and see what happens."

"And in the meantime?" Phoebe asked.

Sam shook his head, looked helpless.

"And in the meantime?" Phoebe repeated. "The eleventh is six days away, Sam! Are we supposed to just sit around twiddling our thumbs until then?"

"In the meantime," he said with hesitation, "I guess we try to find out what happened to Evie and Elliot."

"Excellent plan!" Phoebe leaned over and kissed his cheek. "You're very sexy when you get all detective-like."

He rolled his eyes while she opened her notebook again.

THE PLAN
Find Evie and Elliot
Go to Reliance on full moon (Friday)
Make Sam tell me more about that summer

Phoebe knew she should add "Get pregnancy test" to the list, but somehow the idea of writing it down made the possibility of being pregnant all the more real. With all that was going on, she couldn't let herself think about it right now. Later, she promised herself.

Sam went for the phone, punching in the number of the cell phone Evie had given him. He shook his head. "It's no longer in service."

"What about her number in Philadelphia?"

"She never gave it to me."

"Try calling information."

There was no Evie or Eve O'Toole listed in the Philadelphia area.

"Shit," Sam said, "she probably changed her name when she got married. I don't have a clue what Elliot's last name is."

Sam dialed the phone again.

"Hi, Mom," he said into the receiver. "Hey, I was wondering if you could give me Aunt Hazel's number. Yeah, I'll wait. Uh huh. Uh huh. No, we haven't forgotten. See you then."

He hung up. "Got it. And she reminded me about dinner tomorrow night. We're supposed to bring dessert."

Phoebe groaned. She loved Sam's mother, idolized her even, and definitely believed she had the right to know what happened to her daughter, but Phoebe felt intimidated by her clean and cozy house, her home-cooked meals. The slightly disappointed look they'd get when they showed up with a couple of pints of Ben & Jerry's instead of a batch of freshly baked cookies. Phoebe always left Phyllis's house feeling like she'd never measure up and wondering why on earth Sam had chosen her over someone who could bake. Worse still, Phoebe secretly vowed to change. To one day surprise Phyllis with a triple-layer cake with perfect buttercream icing. She could see it so clearly in her head, this Worthiness Cake that would be the most delicious thing any of them had ever tasted.

Phoebe watched as Sam punched in his aunt's number.

"What are you gonna say?" Phoebe asked.

Sam shrugged as he put the phone to his ear, listened to it ring.

"For Christ's sake, don't tell her we just saw her daughter stabbed by some crazy loon in the woods!"

Sam rolled his eyes. "Of course not!" he hissed.

Hazel finally picked up and Sam spent an uncomfortable fifteen minutes on the phone playing catch-up. With the exception of Christmas cards, he hadn't had any contact with her in years. Not since that summer.

"Hazel's a crazy old bat," he'd told Phoebe on numerous occasions. "Drinks like a fish. My mom and she had this big blowout right before Lisa disappeared. They talk now and then but aren't all that close anymore."

The more Phoebe heard about Aunt Hazel, the more she sounded just like her own mother, though she never mentioned this to Sam.

"You never talk about your mother," Sam had remarked once.

"Not much to tell," Phoebe had said, shrugging. "We weren't very close."

Understatement of the goddamn year. But still it was better than saying, *My mom was a miserable lush who had more meaningful conversations with her television than she ever did with any actual living person.*

"They aren't real, Ma," Phoebe said once when she caught her mother talking back to the detectives on TV.

Her mother glared at Phoebe, rattled the ice cubes in her glass, and said, "Who are you to say? You think that something's only real if you can reach out and touch it?" She leaned forward and gave Phoebe a pinch, twisting the skin on her arm.

"Ow!" Phoebe had yelped.

"If that's what you think, you don't know shit, sweetheart."

Phoebe had never flat-out lied to Sam about her mother, but she had definitely withheld crucial information. Like how she died.

She pushed the thought away and focused on watching Sam squirming his way through the conversation with his old alkie

aunt. She waved her hand in a hurry-up-and-get-on-with-it gesture. He nodded.

"The thing is, Hazel," he said into the phone, "I was hoping
you could tell me how to get in touch with Evie and Elliot."

He waited, bit his lip. "Her husband? Elliot?"

He listened again.

"I see," he said, nodding into the phone. "Uh-huh. Uh-huh.
Do you have a number for her there?"

Sam scribbled something on a pad, then thanked his aunt and
promised to be better at staying in touch.

"So," he said after hanging up. "The first weird thing is that
Evie isn't married. The second is that she doesn't live in Philadelphia at all. She's right here in Vermont. Up in Burlington."

"Yeah, I'll say that's weird. Are you going to call her?" Phoebe
asked.

"I'm going to do better than that. I'm going to drive up and
pay her a little visit. See how she's feeling after getting stabbed
and all that. I've got her address." Sam jumped up from the
couch and grabbed the lone key and his worn leather bomber
jacket. "Coming?"

"Damn right," Phoebe said, practically beating him out the
door.

CHAPTER 10

Lisa

Sometimes, when they rode together, Lisa imagined they were attached, two parts of a whole, a Siamese twin girl cemented together where her chest pressed into Evie's back. Evie's black Harley-Davidson T-shirt was damp with sweat while she puffed and grunted, wheezed along like some ancient steam train: *I think I can, I think I can, I think I can.*

You can, Lisa told her with her own breath. *You can do anything you want, as long as you have me.*

Evie didn't have her own bike, but she was the stronger rider, so Lisa perched on the seat holding her feet up, her arms wrapped around Evie's thick waist. Evie stood, legs pumping, feet cranking the pedals, her fingers tight on the handlebars, never touching the brakes no matter how fast they went.

They raced down Spruce to Main Street, Sammy beside them on his BMX bike, going up on curbs and sidewalks, popping wheelies.

When they got to where Main Street forked with Lark Ridge, they took a right, the dirt road following the stream out

past the Tuckers' farm, their wheels humming, crickets singing, the smell of fresh-mown hay in the air. Then it was right
again, on the old fire road, which was little more than an overgrown dirt-bike trail. The air was cool and moist. Twigs lashed
their faces. Lisa held on tight as they hopped and bumped over
stones and roots, fishtailed through sand, dodged a fresh pile
of horse dung. A quarter mile in, they stopped, parked their
bikes against trees, and made their way down the bank to the
whirlpool. It wasn't really a whirlpool at all, but the kids called
it that. It was a place where a curved boulder crossed the creek,
stopping the water enough to form a deep pool. The bottom
was covered in smooth polished pebbles and sand. Minnows
swam there and, if you held still long enough, sometimes they'd
nibble at your toes. Water striders skated across the surface;
brook trout hid in the shadows. The mosquitoes and deerflies
were god-awful, but as long as you stayed in the water, you
were okay.

"Last one in's a rotten egg," Sammy called, peeling off his star
map T-shirt, kicking off his sneakers, and diving into the water
in his shorts. Lisa peeled off her shorts and T-shirt, stripping
down to her bathing suit, which was blue and covered in a light
print of fish scales. Evie called it her mermaid skin. Evie took
off her heavy boots and belt with the knife. She wore her shorts
and layered T-shirts into the water. She didn't own a bathing
suit. Her huge boy's shorts billowed in the water and the shirts
clung to her skin, the edges of her white men's V-neck peeking
out from under the Harley T-shirt. She was a lousy swimmer and
spent most of her time crouched in shallow water.

Sammy dove down to the bottom and popped up, hair slicked

back and nearly down to his shoulders now that it was wet.

"You need a haircut," Lisa told him.

"And you need a reality check," Sammy said, going under, then coming up again and spitting a long stream of water at her. "Fairies!" he said, once his mouth was empty. "How can you actually believe that?"

Lisa shook her head. "How can you not?"

"Because there's no such thing as little green creatures with lacy wings. I hate to be the one to tell you, but Tinker Bell's made up, Lisa. You can clap your hands all you want, but believing isn't going to make them real."

Evie scowled, her arms cutting the water in slow circles around her, making her own little whirlpool. "Maybe they're not like that," she said.

"Huh?" Sammy said.

"I'm just saying," Evie went on. "Maybe they are real, but they're not anything like what we think." She plucked at the front of her T-shirts, pulling them away from her body, but when she let them go, they snapped back into place, sticking worse than ever.

"And what are they supposed to be like then?" Sammy asked.

Evie shrugged. "More like us, maybe. That's what my mom told me once. That it isn't like in all those cutesy little picture books—real fairies look like humans, only they're not. They're like our shadows, she said. Dark. Magic. Here one minute, gone the next."

Sammy laughed as loud and hard as he could. Soon his laughter was mixed with the crashing of footsteps running down the bank.

Lisa turned. "Shit," she said. Gerald and Pinkie. And they weren't alone. Behind them were Gerald's two best friends, Mike and Justin. And a girl Lisa sort of recognized from school—a friend of Pinkie's named Franny. The girl was as pale as Pinkie and had braces.

"Let's go," Lisa said to Sammy and Evie.

"But we just got here," Sammy whined. Lisa threw him a furious look.

"Yeah, stay," Gerald called. "We're all friends, right?" Then he turned to Mike and Justin and said something in his made-up, Minarian language. Lisa caught only the last few words, "Bach flut nah." The other boys laughed.

Gerald could be moderately obnoxious on his own, but when he was around Mike and Justin, he always acted like a total idiot, showing off and saying dumb stuff that didn't make any sense and was supposed to make him seem all impressive and super smart-assy. It was ridiculous, really. Mike and Justin didn't need to be impressed—it wasn't like there was any danger of them ditching Gerald. They were airplane-model-building, computer-gaming geeks, just like Gerald. Three peas in a pod. But for whatever reason, Gerald had to be King Pea. Lisa smiled at this newly thought-up title.

"What's so funny, Nazzaro?" Gerald asked.

Lisa shrugged. "It's just that whenever you speak that language of yours, you sound all phlegmy—like someone with a bad cold clearing his throat." She made her best cat-coughing-up-a-fur-ball noise to accentuate her point.

Gerald's face turned red.

"Hi, Sam!" Pinkie called, waving so hard she nearly fell into the stream. She had on long sleeves, gardening gloves, and a pink baseball hat draped with mosquito netting.

"Hey," Sam said, nodding in her direction. "You coming in the water?"

She shook her head.

Gerald laughed. "She only swims in pools. Can't stand the feel of muck or pebbles under her feet. And the fish and bugs are way too much for her. She's what you call delicate, Becca is. Aren't you?" he asked, looking at his sister. "Then there's all the diseases and parasites, right, Bec? All kinds of nasties floating around in there."

"Oh man, tell me you haven't been showing Becca your parasite book again, have you? That's just cruel," Mike said. He peeled off his T-shirt to reveal a pale white chest that was sunken in at the center, as if someone had crushed his sternum with a baseball bat.

"It's fascinating stuff, really," Gerald said, not taking his eyes off Pinkie. "Amoebic dysentery, giardia, cryptosporidiosis. Then there's the bacterial stuff: cholera, E. coli, typhoid. That water there is teeming with tiny little organisms just looking for a nice warm body to call home." He winked at Pinkie.

Mike gave Gerald a playful cuff on the shoulder. "Don't mind him," Mike said. "He's just a little obsessed with the microscopic world. It's all the research he does for our game. There's nothing in that water that can hurt you, Becca." With this, he took a running leap into it, Justin right behind him. Both boys squealed as they hit the cold water.

"See, Becca, it's safe enough to drink," Mike called, scooping some up in his hand and slurping.

"You're going to be pissing protozoa," Justin teased.

Mike took a second sip. "Amoeba, yum!"

"Actually," Sam said, trying to sound older by lowering his voice, "most microscopic organisms are safe to ingest. The truth is, our bodies are full of bacteria all the time. We've even got E. coli in us, living in complete symbiosis most of the time."

Lisa rolled her eyes. What was this—attack of the geeks?

Franny moved closer to Becca, leaned in, and whispered something in her ear. Becca nodded, then they both giggled, looking at Sam, then away.

Lisa couldn't stand girls like that, no matter what age. Girls who tittered and breathed secrets in one another's ears. Dainty girls who didn't want to get dirty.

"Come on in, man," called Mike. "You only feel like you're freezing your balls off for the first thirty seconds or so."

Gerald took his T-shirt off carefully over his glasses, kicked off his running shoes, and made his way slowly toward the stream, stepping gingerly over stones, as if his feet were ultrasensitive. He stopped at the edge.

"What have we here?" he asked, picking up Evie's belt and knife.

Lisa took in a sharp breath. This was trouble. Bad trouble.

"Looks like a bushwhacker to me," Mike called from the water. "Bach gloon neot?"

Gerald laughed and nodded. "Totally!" he snorted, pushing his dark glasses up his nose.

"Drop it!" Evie snarled from her crouched position downstream.

Gerald unsnapped the sheath, pulled the knife out, and whistled. "Quite a blade on it. Could kill an elephant with this thing, probably. And what is this down by the handle? A little dried blood? Christ, Stevie, what have you been cutting up?"

"Shit, man, maybe it *is* blood," Mike said. "You know what they said about her great-grandfather, how he made some kind of pact with the devil and did sacrifices and shit out in those woods? Maybe Stevie's just following in his footsteps!"

Gerald shook his head. "A pact with the devil? Nah. I heard Old Doc O'Toole was the *son of the devil*. He had powers. Could hypnotize people with his eyes. That's what my mom said. Hell of a family tree you've got, Lisa."

"Enough, Gerald," Lisa warned, swimming toward him.

"I'm just saying. You might be in danger, Lisa. I mean if cousin Stevie is going around like a young psychopath slicing and dicing cats or something, wouldn't you be concerned? Didn't you know that's how Jeffrey Dahmer got his start—cutting the heads off of dogs and cats and impaling them on sticks."

"Eew!" squealed Pinkie.

"No way!" said Franny.

"Yes way," Gerald said. "Totally true."

"Put it down!" Evie growled. She was still crouched, her body a tight ball, the water up to her neck.

"Oh, and are you gonna make me? Not so tough now, huh? Now that I've got your big, bad blade of death here."

Pinkie and her pale friend looked on in silence, both of them frowning. Mike and Justin were treading water, watching. Mike moved closer to shore, walking toward Gerald, water pooling in the well of his sunken chest. "Looks like a sacrificial blade to me, for sure," he called. "I'd be careful if I were you, man. It might have some serious mojo."

Lisa got to the bank and stepped out, moving toward Gerald. "Give me the goddamn knife."

Gerald gave a disgusted-sounding snort. "Not much of a man, are you, Stevie? Getting your pretty little cousin to do your dirty work for you. She is pretty. Don't you think so? I know you do, Stevie."

"Ooh!" crooned Justin from the water. "Stevie has a thing for her cousin? That's so sick!"

Evie stood up, arms rigid at her sides, hands clenched into fists.

Gerald hooted. "Nice swimming trunks!"

Evie's green fatigue shorts hung down to her knees, her belly bulging out above them. Her legs were pale and covered with dark hair. The wet T-shirts clung to her so that you could see the curve of her breasts, even the outline of nipples beneath the bald eagle and flag. The words AMERICAN LEGEND were stuck to her belly, jiggling as she walked.

Mike and Justin laughed. Pinkie let out a little squeal, then covered her mouth and looked away, tittering. Franny did the same.

Evie moved toward Gerald, her eyes blazing, a low growl coming from the back of her throat.

Gerald flinched, then held up the blade, waving it through the air like a conductor's baton or a magic wand.

"And I don't think I've ever seen boobs like that on a dude before. Have you, guys? Maybe Stevie's one of those . . . whatdayacallit?"

"Hermaphrodite?" Justin said.

"Yeah, yeah, that's it. Half girl, half boy. An It."

Evie froze in her tracks, knee-deep in the creek. She crossed her arms over her breasts, her chest heaving as the growl broke apart and her eyes filled with tears. Lisa could see the outline of the key hanging from the bootlace around Evie's neck. Evie's fingers fumbled their way under the neck of her shirt, reaching for it.

It'll save both of us one day.

Lisa had to look away.

"Here you go, It," Gerald said, dropping the knife and heading out into the water, away from Evie.

"Asshole!" Lisa yelled after him.

Evie continued her slow walk to shore, where she stood bent over and dripping as she pulled on her boots. She sheathed the knife and looped the belt around her waist, buckling it with shaking fingers.

Lisa started putting her own clothes on as Evie walked past Pinkie and Franny. Franny gave her an awkward smile. Evie ignored it and began climbing the path up the bank.

"Come on, Sammy," Lisa called.

Gerald said something to Sammy in a low voice. Sammy ignored it, but the other boys laughed.

Lisa shoved her damp, sandy feet into her sneakers and waited for her brother. At last, he was out of the water, pulling on his shirt. "Let's go," she said.

"See ya, Sam," Pinkie said, as they hurried by her, Sam carrying his shoes. He gave her a half wave.

When they got to the fire road at the top of the hill, both of the bikes were still there, but Evie was nowhere in sight.

CHAPTER 11

Phoebe

The one good thing about the chaos of their day was that Phoebe hadn't had much time to obsess about the possibility of being pregnant. But now that they were back in the car, racing up to Burlington on Interstate 89, it was all she could think of.

Once again she toyed with idea of saying something to Sam—but he had enough on his plate at the moment. She needed to know for sure before she talked to him. She'd go to the drugstore and get a pregnancy test. Maybe she could sneak away tomorrow, but if not, it could wait until Monday, when they both went off to work.

Relieved to have a plan in place, Phoebe looked out the window to her left. They were driving through Waterbury, and in the dying light she could see the old state hospital complex with its giant smokestack, the letters vsh climbing up into the sky.

She looked over at Sam driving, his hands on the wheel, eyes on the road ahead. There were so many little things about him she loved: the long, almost feminine eyelashes; the way he licked his lips before answering a hard question; how funny his pale legs with their knobby knees looked each summer when he finally got hot enough to take off his jeans and put on swimming trunks. She loved the raised scar above his collarbone that no one could remember the origin of. Sometimes she'd kiss him there, her mouth covering the thin white line, making it disappear.

What if she was pregnant? Would they keep the baby? Sam had never come right out and said he didn't want kids, but whenever she brought up the idea, his face clouded over and he quickly changed the subject, or sometimes he nuzzled her neck and said, "But you're my family, Bee. You're all I need."

And what about her? Could Phoebe really be a mother? It was such an absurd idea that she found it impossible to visualize. But the alternative, the idea of actually having an abortion, scared her too. Her mother had had an abortion once, when Phoebe was in fifth grade. What Phoebe remembered most was her mother finding out she was pregnant. She'd bought a test, gone into the bathroom, and come out pale and shaking. She didn't look overjoyed, that was for sure. But she didn't seem shocked or surprised, either. What it looked like to Phoebe was that her mother was frightened. Terrified, actually.

"Ma," Phoebe said, "did it say yes?" Phoebe was torn. Part of her secretly wished for a baby brother or sister, but she knew, deep down, wishing to bring a helpless baby into her sorry excuse for a family was just cruel.

Her mother didn't speak, went straight for the vodka, drinking until she passed out on the couch. Phoebe went out to cover her with a blanket before going to bed herself. Her mother stirred, squinted up at Phoebe, and said, "You poor thing, you." Phoebe smiled at her mother, let her raise up her hand with its broken nails and nicotine-stained fingers to stroke Phoebe's hair. Her mother smiled back, said warmly, with love, "I should have drowned you at birth."

Phoebe took a step back, letting her mother's hand fall back down to the couch.

Her mother closed her eyes, murmured softly, "That would have saved you."

In the morning, she made the appointment and went off to the women's health clinic in Worcester. Her ma had acted like it was no big deal—like she'd had a rotten tooth pulled at the dentist. Phoebe knew it wouldn't be like that for her. But shit, she probably wasn't even pregnant, in which case she was running her brain in frantic circles for no reason at all.

She closed her eyes, heard her mother's smooth, low, bourbon-slurred voice in her head: *Ain't no point worrying about what's been or what's gonna be. You just gotta do your best right now. And trust everyone else is doing the same.*

Maybe the only smart thing her ma ever told her.

Most everything else was complete horseshit. Like what she said when Phoebe first told her about the Dark Man.

"There's something in my room," she'd cried, heart pounding, hands sweaty. She was seven years old and they were in the Belcher Street apartment. It was just past midnight and Phoebe had closed her eyes and run from her room, finding her mother in the kitchen. Her ma staggered back against the counter, scrunching her face so that she was looking through one eye and a haze of cigarette smoke.

"What?" she drawled. Her ma had only lived in North

Carolina till she was eight, but sometimes, when she was good and drunk, Phoebe could still hear a southern twang.

"A man," she said.

"And what's he look like, lovie?"

"Dark. Like a shadow."

Her ma looked startled, then smiled. "Where did he come from, this Dark Man of yours?"

"Under my bed. There's a door there."

"You'd best figure out a damn good way to keep it closed. Once the Dark Man comes, he'll be back. And once he gets inside of you . . ." She shivered, turned to pour another drink. "Have a nice big sip of this, lovie. It's like medicine. It'll help you sleep."

Sam?"

He took his eyes off the road and blinked at her.

"Did you ever think Teilo was real?"

He shook his head. "Not then. But I do now. I don't think he was a fairy or anything like that, but I do think there was a guy out there, messing around with my sister."

"And Evie, what did she think?"

"She thought Lisa should stay the hell out of the woods."

"Why did you stop talking to Evie?" Phoebe asked. "I mean, it sounds like the two of you were really close as kids."

Sam turned to look at her, his face lit by headlights of cars from the southbound lane.

"Sam," she said, "we're in this together. You've gotta give me a little to go on here. There are these whole huge chapters of your life I know nothing about."

"You're not exactly an open book," he said.

Touché.

"Okay, I'll make a deal with you," Phoebe said. "You start letting me in and I'll do the same. Shit, I'll even start." Her mind went right to the possibility of her being pregnant, then she jerked it away, let it wander, grasping for something else, some big reveal that would help build a bridge between them because a pregnancy might only tear them apart.

"Okay," she said, latching on to the next best thing. "You're always asking about my mom, and the truth is, I haven't exactly been all that honest. My mom was—well, she was kind of a drunk. Not a well-dressed, martini-drinking socialite kind of drunk, but a drooling, stinking, wake-up-in-your-own-puke kind of drunk. She was a terrible mother. She lied all the time, said horrible things to me, messed with my head. Once I graduated from high school, I got the hell out of there. Didn't go back for anything. Not even the one time she asked me to. Right before she died. She begged me. Said all kinds of crazy shit, but I wouldn't go."

Sam was silent a minute.

"Your mom is perfect, Sam. I just look at her and know you came from someplace good. I was scared that if you knew the truth, if you actually knew the kind of person my mom was, the kind of person I was around her, you'd see me differently. I mean, we're talking about a woman who was such a pathetic drunk that she drowned in her own bathtub with all her clothes on. Shit, they were even on inside out. She couldn't even get that part right."

Phoebe's chin quivered. She shut her eyes tight, thinking about the details she'd left out: all the weird stuff her mother had in the tub with her—kitchen knives, a cast-iron frying pan, nail clippers, a box of bolts and washers. How the landlord had to break down the door when the water from the overflowing tub began dripping into the apartment below. He found her face-down in the tub, the drain plug in, shower running full blast.

Sam reached out to put his hand on her arm. "Phoebe, I'm so sorry."

"No," she said. "I don't want your sympathy or your pity. That's why I don't tell people this shit. It is what it is, Sam. Can't change where you came from, right? Just got to make the best of where you are."

Sam nodded. "I would never think of you differently," he said. "No matter what you told me."

What if I told him about the shadow man? Phoebe wondered. *What would he think of me then?*

"So now it's your turn," she said. "Tell me about that summer. About you and Evie."

He nodded and looked forward again. "Everything changed after Lisa disappeared," he said. "And before. That summer. My mom and Hazel had a big fight. Hazel was taking care of my dad. He'd had this . . . nervous breakdown, I guess, when we were all away in Cape Cod. Anyway, we got back and he'd overdosed. We called 911 and he got his stomach pumped and was okay. Sort of. He wasn't talking or . . . acting normally, but he was alive." Sam bit his lower lip and took in a breath before continuing. "When he got out of the hospital, we brought him home and Hazel was looking after him—she was a nurse, so it made sense. It's not like she didn't know he was at risk for suicide—I mean, he'd tried before, right? His medicine was supposed to be locked up. It was always locked up. But somehow, one night, just before

Lisa disappeared, it wasn't. And he found it and took everything there. He didn't pull through. My mom blamed Hazel."

"Did you?"

Phoebe had rarely talked about her mother, and Sam was the same way with his dad. Phoebe knew almost nothing about David Nazzaro, and the little bits she had gleaned came from Sam's mother, not from Sam. She knew that Sam's dad was a potter and that he'd struggled with bipolar disorder for years. She also knew that young Sam worshipped his dad and would spend hours in his workshop, just watching his father work, studying him really. "I would catch Sammy looking at his dad sometimes and think, 'There he goes again, trying to solve the riddle of Dave,' " Phyllis had told her.

"Nah," Sam said. "I didn't see it that way. But we didn't see much of Hazel and Evie after that. I guess I should have been sad, but I wasn't really. Evie betrayed Lisa big time. She told people about the fairies. Shit, she even showed Lisa's fairy book to all the neighborhood kids. I guess that was the last straw. Lisa stopped speaking to her. I used to think that if Evie hadn't done that, then maybe Lisa wouldn't have gone off to the woods that night. She and Lisa were so close. It was like she lost her biggest ally. And her dad had just taken a shitload of pills and it was pretty obvious he wasn't going to survive. Who wouldn't want to leave all that behind?

"You know what I used to think?" Sam asked, white-knuckling the steering wheel, digging into it with his thumbnails. "That Lisa had it easy. She got to be the one to disappear. She didn't have to say good-bye to Dad or go to the funeral or deal with things after. She got to just slip away, and I was jealous. That's totally fucked up, right?" He looked over at Phoebe, then quickly back at the road. She reached over and stroked his arm.

"No," she said. "Not at all. I would have felt the exact same way."

The address Hazel had given Sam was a basement apartment on Loomis Street, not far from the university. There was a teetering stack of pizza boxes outside the door that led down the stairs.

"This is the place?" Phoebe asked, thinking maybe they'd found a frat house. She remembered the tattoo on Elliot's leg— not a Greek letter but the symbol of Teilo.

"Are you sure?" Sam had asked when she told him about the tattoo.

Phoebe nodded. "Positive."

Whatever was going on, Evie and this guy Elliot were deeply involved.

"This is the place," Sam said, ringing the bell.

They hadn't discussed what they'd do when they found Evie, which suddenly seemed like bad planning. Shouldn't they have rehearsed some lines? Decided on a good-cop bad-cop kind of interrogation technique to break her down, get her to tell them what the hell was going on?

They heard someone coming up the steps, then the curtain in the windowed door was pulled aside and a gaunt-faced woman with bruised-looking circles under her eyes glared out at them. Her shoulder-length dark hair was coming out of its loose pony-tail, the bangs falling across her face.

"What do you want?" she shouted through the door. Her lips were so raw and chapped that they were bleeding.

"I'm looking for Evie," Sam shouted back. "I'm her cousin, Sam."

The woman squinted at them, chewed on a fingernail a minute, considering, then opened the door. She turned her back and headed down the poorly lit stairway before they could say anything more. Sam shrugged at Phoebe and they went in. At the bottom of the stairs, they followed the pale ghost of a woman through another door, which brought them into a living room.

The apartment they found themselves in was small and dark and smelled of mildew and body odor. There were a few narrow rectangular windows that would have given a street-level view, had you been able to look out. They were covered in heavy red cloth that had been stapled over.

The furniture was beat up, the rug stained and worn through in places. There was another stack of pizza boxes by the lower door. Along the ceiling of the living room ran a heavy white PVC drainpipe. Someone in an upstairs apartment flushed a toilet, and water ran through the pipe over their heads. Sam looked up nervously.

"I hope it never leaks," he said.

The woman smiled and sat down in a threadbare upholstered chair. She was average height, underweight in a drug-addict or terminally-ill-person kind of way. She wore a tight-fitting white tank top that accentuated her protruding collarbones and a pair of ripped and faded jeans. Her feet were bare, the nails painted with sparkly blue polish. Around her neck was a chain that looked like something you'd get at a hardware store for pulling a light on with. Dangling from it was an old silver skeleton key.

She had the darkest eyes Phoebe had ever seen.

"So is Evie around?" asked Sam.

The skinny woman laughed, gnawed on an already short fingernail, spit the piece she bit off out on the carpet. "Don't you recognize your own cousin, Sammy?" she asked with a little wheeze. "Did you get a phone call too? Is that why you're here?" Her voice was husky, deeper than Phoebe would have imagined.

Sam just stared at the woman in the chair, blinking like he'd just come out of a dark place into a light one.

"You're Evie?" Phoebe asked.

"Who were you expecting?" she asked.

"Can you prove it?" Phoebe asked.

"Bee . . ." said Sam.

Evie laughed a wheezing laugh that launched her into a coughing fit. Once she recovered, she reached into her back pocket and pulled out a pack of cigarettes. She lit one, blowing smoke out at them. Then she reached back again into her other pocket and produced a small cloth wallet this time. She shuffled through some cards until she came to a Vermont driver's license, which she handed over to Sam. "My name is Eve Katherine O'Toole. Mother's name is Hazel. The last time I saw you, Sammy, you were wearing your favorite shirt: the Superman T-shirt. You'd been in it for days, but no one minded. I remember keeping my eyes on that big red S out the rear windshield of the car, watching it, and you, get smaller and smaller as my mother drove me away." She studied her ragged nails, then took another drag of her cigarette.

"It's her," Sam said. "This is Evie."

"Then who was the other Evie?" asked Phoebe, snapping back from her own memory of Sam in his Superman shirt staring down at her from his bedroom window.

"Other Evie?" asked the woman in the chair. "Jesus Christ, like one of us isn't enough."

"She knew things too," Phoebe said. "She knew about the charm bracelet."

"Lisa's charm bracelet?" this new, skinny Evie asked. "What about it?"

"Do you remember where she got it?" Sam asked.

"Of course I remember." Evie looked disgusted. "She got it for her birthday early that summer. Your mom gave it to her when we were all in Cape Cod for Memorial Day weekend. It had her name on it. Then the next day, we went to this little tourist shack along the waterfront and she picked out the second charm, a starfish. You and I bought eye patches and plastic swords and spent the rest of the trip sword fighting and looking for treasure to bury. We even had secret pirate names. Mine was Captain Evil—I can't remember yours. Something Sammy or Sammy Something. You weren't terribly creative."

Sam looked at Phoebe, nodded, and shrugged. "It's her."

"Okay," Phoebe said. "So if this is Evie, then who the hell was the other woman? And what about Elliot?"

"Elliot?" Evie asked, looking down to crush out her half-finished cigarette.

"Do you know an Elliot?" Sam asked.

"Jesus. I did. I used to date a guy named Elliot. We were kind of engaged."

This was more like it, thought Phoebe. A clue. Elliot was Evie's ex—that was how the impostor knew so much about the real Evie. The pieces were falling into place.

"Do you know where we can find him?" Phoebe asked, suddenly feeling like a clever cop on one of those late-night TV shows she seldom watched. She even reached into her pocket to pull out her notebook so she could jot down any leads. ELLIOT, she wrote.

Evie looked away. "You can't. He's dead."

Now, on top of missing girls, fairies, and changelings, they had ghosts to contend with. DEAD? she wrote.

"You're sure?" Sam asked.

"Yes, I'm fucking sure," Evie said. "I was driving the car when we had the accident."

They drank Mountain Dew—Evie had cases of the stuff—and ordered pizza while Evie told them about her own life in bits and pieces. As she spoke, Phoebe looked from Evie to Sam, seeing one resemblance after another: the dark hair with slight widow's peak, the delicate nose—even their lips were similar. There was no doubt they were related.

Evie told them she'd been an art major in college and was about to have her first big show in a gallery when she and Elliot were in an accident coming back from dinner one night.

"It was late. Maybe I'd had a little too much to drink. Elliot definitely had—that's why I was driving. This deer jumped out into the middle of the road, right in our path, this big old buck—rack of horns as wide as my car. I didn't have time to stop. I swerved, just instinct, you know? We hit a tree."

She bit at a fingernail, working the chewed-off piece around in her mouth for a few seconds before spitting it out. "The passenger side of the car was crushed. The front seat was pushed all the way to the back. I looked over and all I could see were his feet. He had these new black Frye biker boots. But they were all covered in blood and little fragments of glass. I remember think-ing how pissed he'd be, his new boots all messed up like that. It's funny the things you think of."

Evie closed her eyes. "Funny," she mumbled, pushing her thumbs into the upper part of her eye sockets and rubbing hard.

When she opened her eyes, they were red and wet, looking nearly as raw as her lips and cuticles.

"Then I looked out the busted windshield and there, right next to us, was the damn deer. Watching. Totally unhurt. He took off into the woods, his white tail flying out behind him like this big old flag.

"I never did have that art opening. I stopped painting after that. Wound up in the hospital a few times, lost our loft because I couldn't keep up with the rent, *blah blah*. I moved into this little palace."

Now, she explained, she lived on disability checks and only left the apartment once a week, when she took a cab (always the same driver, she said) to therapy appointments.

"Agoraphobia," she told them with a raspy sigh. "You read about it and think it's made up—how scary can stepping out your front door really be?—but then little by little, you become the pathetic person in the story and you have to pay some kid to take your trash out and buy your toilet paper."

Phoebe nodded understandingly, overcome with pity. She tried to imagine Evie cleaned up, a few pounds on her. She was a natural beauty, really: dark eyes and red pouty lips.

"So you don't draw, paint, anything now?" Phoebe asked.

Evie shook her head, played with the metal key on her necklace.

"You know," Evie said, looking up at Sam. "This may sound

strange, but I think my life turned out the way it did because of what I did all those years ago. That summer."

"What do you mean?" asked Sam.

"I betrayed Teilo. The fairies were supposed to be our secret. I knew that. Christ, Lisa made us swear not to tell a soul. But I was the one who showed people the book. And then, a week later . . ."

She didn't finish the sentence. Didn't need to.

A week later, Lisa was gone.

"You said something about a phone call?" Sam said.

Evie nodded. "About a week ago. I thought it was a little girl at first. She was talking so quietly, just a whisper."

"What'd she say?"

"She said, 'I'm back from the land of the fairies. I'll be seeing you soon.' Then she hung up."

"Lisa," Phoebe said.

"It just doesn't seem possible," Evie said. "But who would play a joke like that?"

Sam and Phoebe exchanged a glance.

"So now it's your turn," Evie said. "Tell me about this other Evie. Tell me what made you look me up after all these years."

And so, over pepperoni pizza (Phoebe was feeling nauseous again, so she nibbled tentatively at the crust, claiming that she was too anxious to be hungry) and Mountain Dew, Sam and Phoebe told their story, beginning with the call last week from the woman claiming to be Sam's cousin and ending with the knock on Evie's basement apartment door an hour ago. Evie nodded, asked the occasional question, but mostly just listened until they were through.

"So they got the fairy book?" she asked.

"Yeah, and everything else we brought. Clothes, Phoebe's purse, our digital camera, which had some pictures of this other Evie and Elliot on it—pretty much the only proof we had that they even existed."

"But nothing was taken from your house?"

"Not that we noticed," Sam said.

"He's a tricky bastard, isn't he?" Evie asked. Her face, Phoebe decided, was catlike. The high cheekbones, the pointed chin and large eyes.

Sam shuffled his feet, looked down at them.

"Who?" Phoebe asked.

"Teilo," Evie said with a wheezy sigh. She shook another cigarette from her pack. "I don't know what he's up to, but I wouldn't put anything past him. Be careful. That's my only advice."

Phoebe shook her head. "You're not saying he's a real person?"

Evie lit the cigarette, shook out the match with trembling fingers. "Real, yes. A person? No. He's way more than that. With Teilo, the regular rules don't apply. And nothing is as it seems. So far he's just playing with you. But when he gets serious, you'll know."

CHAPTER 12

Lisa

They crept silently back down to Reliance before breakfast the next morning. The yard and woods were wet with dew, soaking their shoes. Songbirds called out their good mornings from hidden perches high up in the treetops. Evie had spoken very little since she showed up at dinner the night before. She was still in her fatigue shorts and Harley shirt, but they were dry. When Lisa asked where she'd been all afternoon, Evie only shrugged and said, "Around." They didn't talk about what had happened down at the whirlpool. Lisa wanted to, thinking that maybe if she could somehow make a joke about it, then everything would be okay. But this felt too big for any stupid joke and the right words didn't come. All she could think of to say was *I'm so sorry*, but she was sure that would just make everything worse. The best thing to do was pretend it hadn't happened and never mention it again.

What the . . ." Sammy said as he peered down from the edge of the cellar hole. Evie gave a very un-Evie-like girlish gasp.

The chipped china saucer was empty, the glass of Orange Crush drained. And there, beside it on the saucer, was a penny, polished to a shine.

Lisa was sure her heart would explode. She jumped down into the hole and the others followed.

She picked up the copper coin and saw it was an old one, a wheat penny from 1918 with a tiny hole drilled through the top.

"Give it," Evie said, reaching for the coin. Lisa handed it over. Evie brought it close to her face, stuck her tongue out, touched the tip of it against the bright penny.

"What on earth are you doing?" Sammy asked.

"Using all of my senses," Evie explained. Sam rolled his eyes.

Lisa was sorry she'd let them come. It felt all wrong, them being down in the cellar hole with her. The gift was meant for her—she was the one who believed, right?—and if they made fun of it, the fairies might not come again.

"Will you guys quit it?" Lisa asked. She looked up at the trees, wondering if they were being watched. A blue jay gave a scolding cry. A squirrel chattered.

Suddenly the woods seemed full of spies.

"It's an amazingly wonderful gift," Lisa said, her voice as loud as she could make it without shouting.

"I wonder what the hole's for?" Sammy asked, grabbing the penny from Evie, who was holding it up to her ear, listening.

"Mental case," Sammy said.

"Hey," Lisa warned, giving him her most evil look. Evie had suffered enough yesterday. She didn't need any additional ribbing today.

"I meant it in a good way," Sam said. "All the best people

are a little mental, right? Even Einstein." He gave a timid little back-pedaling shrug.

"Wait a sec," said Evie, snatching the penny back from Sam. Her fingers looked thick and clumsy as they held the bright coin. Her nails were chewed to the quick, the cuticles raw. "Look at the year: 1918. Isn't that when the whole town of Reliance disappeared?"

Lisa nodded. "Everyone except for Great-grandpa Eugene."

Sometimes I see him in each of you.

"That can't be a coincidence. Wait till we tell your mom!" Evie said. "And maybe my mom will finally believe us if we bring back proof."

Lisa took the penny back, closing her hand tightly around it. "No. We can't tell anyone. This is something special, just for us. What happens here stays a secret. Okay?"

Evie stared at her a second, her brow furrowed.

"Evie," Lisa said in a pleading tone.

At last Evie gave a tentative nod.

Sam was going to be a little harder to convince.

"I mean it, Sammy," Lisa said. "Say there *are* fairies. The last thing they'd want is for us to bring the whole damn world down here. Then they'd go away for sure. Let's just wait and see what happens before we say anything to anyone. Think of it as a sci-entific experiment. A top-secret one. You can use the scientific method to try to explain it—come up with a hypothesis, collect data, all that."

He scowled a little, then grumbled, "Okay. But I don't think it's fairies."

"Well, what is it then?" Lisa asked.

"My current hypothesis," Sam said, smirking, "is that you've got a secret admirer."

Evie stiffened, jutted out her lower jaw in a bulldog-like way.

Lisa laughed. "Well, there's only one way to find out for sure, right? Tonight, I'm going to come down here on my own. I'll bring another plate of sweets and sit and watch."

"But we've gotta come with you!" Evie said.

"Yeah," Sam agreed. "How am I supposed to gather data to support my theory unless you let us come with you?"

Lisa shook her head. "We don't want to scare them off."

"I don't like it," Evie said. "We don't know who or what we're dealing with. They could be dangerous."

"No," Lisa argued, "if they meant any harm, they wouldn't have left this." She held the penny up, watched the way it caught the morning light, a tiny copper sun of its own.

"What ya got there?"

Lisa jumped, shoved the penny into the pockets of her cutoffs like she was hiding evidence. She turned. Gerald and Pinkie were coming up to the edge of the cellar hole. *Go away!* Lisa screamed inside her head.

Gerald was all in camouflage and Becca had on a pair of pastel pink overalls and a long-sleeved pink turtleneck, which seemed crazy considering how warm it was.

Sammy leaned over and whispered, "Remember my hypothesis? This just backs it up. He wanted to see you find it."

Lisa took a step away from Sammy. She looked over at Evie whose eyes were blazing. Evie was breathing fast, her chest making funny accordion sounds. Lisa had to send Gerald and Pinkie away quickly before things got out of hand.

"I said what ya got?" Gerald called down, peering at them from over the top of his dark glasses. He was right at the edge of the cellar hole now, hands deep in his pockets, jittery, rocking back and forth and rattling his spare change.

"Nothing," Lisa said. She blinked her eyes hard, like maybe she could wish them away. But when she opened her eyes, they were still there. Damn. So much for wishing. She'd have to think of some other more mundane way to make them get lost. But she had to do it tactfully. She didn't want to make them suspicious.

"What are you guys doing out here so early?" Sam asked.

"Nothing. Just out walking. Getting some air. Doing a little bird watching maybe."

"Bird watching?" Lisa raised her eyebrows skeptically. "What, are you an expert on hermit thrushes and warblers all of a sudden?"

Gerald smiled. "No, but it's never too late to learn, right?" He whistled in a birdlike way, looking up at the trees.

"Were you out here last night? Did you leave a little something behind?" Sam asked.

Idiot! Did he really think Gerald left the penny? She shot Sam a shut-up-or-else look but doubted it would do any good.

"Why are you all bundled up, Pinkie?" Lisa asked, changing the subject as fast as possible. "Expecting snow?"

"She's allergic to mosquito bites," Gerald said. "Can't seem to stop scratching, so Mom covered her in calamine and long sleeves. Good thing we don't live where the mosquitoes carry yellow fever or malaria. You'd be a goner for sure," he said, giving Pinkie a wink. "Show them, Bec. Show them what those nasty buggies did to your arms."

Pinkie rolled up her left sleeve to show that her arms were painted pink and underneath were oozing red welts.

"Gross," Evie said.

Sammy nodded. "Mosquitoes are bad this year because we had a such a wet spring." Pinkie smiled at him stupidly.

Good grief. Did freaky Pinkie have a crush on Sam?

"So what was it?" Gerald said to Lisa.

"Huh?" Lisa said.

"I saw something shiny in your hand."

Pinkie nodded her head, shaking her pale white hair; made a funny little smacking sound in agreement. There was something unpleasantly grublike about her.

"It was nothing," Lisa said, reaching into her pocket. "Just my house key." The doors at their house were never locked. Lisa had never carried a house key. She hoped Gerald wouldn't ask to see it.

Gerald looked down at her, shook his head, and adjusted his glasses. "Right, Lisa. Riiiiight." His voice was a whining buzz, not all that dissimilar from the sound a mosquito makes. "The thing is, you're a real crappy liar. So I've gotta ask myself, 'Why wouldn't she tell the truth? What could your good friend Lisa be hiding from you?' So what is it, Lisa? Did Stevie give you a sweetheart ring or something? You and Cousin It going out now?"

Evie moved faster than Lisa would have believed possible, her breath quick and rhythmic, like a train. She grabbed Gerald's left ankle and yanked. He tottered forward, arms pinwheeling as he tried to right himself, then went down into the hole. The fall itself happened in slow motion; it seemed like he hung in the air for ages, flapping his arms helplessly, trying to fight gravity. He landed with a screaming crash right at Lisa's feet.

But the worst noise, by far, was the sound Pinkie made: the high-pitched squeal of a pig having its throat slit.

"Bitch!" Gerald bellowed. "I'll get you for this, you goddamn freak of nature!" He was lying on his side in the dirt, gritting his teeth and panting. Evie was over him, her right hand resting on the sheathed knife hanging from her belt. She unsnapped the leather strap that held the knife's handle in place.

Lisa gently but firmly pulled Evie out of the way. "Enough," she warned Evie, then reached to help Gerald up.

"Get the hell away from me!" he spat. He sat up and she saw his eyes were full of tears. He was cradling his left arm as he stood, and it seemed to be bent up at an awkward angle, like he had a second elbow halfway down his forearm.

Lisa's heart began to beat hard and her mouth tasted like metal. This was not good. Evie was going to be in big trouble.

"Becca, give me a hand here," Gerald said.

Pinkie reached a pink-sleeved arm down, and Gerald grabbed hold with his right hand and squirmed his way up and out of the hole, teeth gritted and making horrible sounds anytime his left arm moved.

"Name's Evie, asshole," Evie said, the knife out of the sheath and in her hand, the blade glimmering.

CHAPTER 13

Phoebe

Tofu mushroom stroganoff. Was there anything more grotesque or stomach-turning on the face of the earth? Chunks of pale tofu and slimy, overcooked mushrooms in a gray milky sauce, served over egg noodles. It was a meal that clearly belonged in a health-conscious convalescent home, school cafeteria, or prison. But to Phyllis, it was good old-fashioned home cooking, vegetarian style.

Sam's mother seemed to have cookbooks full of these hardy vegetarian recipes: stews, dumplings, and casseroles laden with tofu, tempeh, and the much-dreaded seitan. Thick, bland soups served with whole-grain biscuits dense enough to be used as doorstops. Stick-to-your-ribs meatless meals that somehow went with the old-fashioned fifties look of the kitchen—the white metal cabinets, cherry wallpaper, faded yellow countertops, and vintage table with a red Formica top and chrome legs. "My mom's not big on change," Sam had explained.

"Not hungry, dear?" Phyllis asked.

"I'm afraid not. It's delicious, though." Phoebe gave her a warm, thankful, yummy-in-my-tummy smile.

Sam kicked Phoebe under the table.

She stabbed a wide egg noodle dripping with gray goo, forced it into her mouth, and tried to chew without tasting.

"Are you coming down with something, Bee?" Phyllis asked. "You're awfully pale."

"Could be," Phoebe said, setting down her fork, wiping her damp forehead with the back of her hand (was it horribly hot in here?). "There's something going around at work."

It was a lie, but it got an understanding nod from Phyllis, who mercifully removed her plate.

Sam rolled his eyes at Phoebe when his mother wasn't looking.

Phoebe hoped her inability to clean her plate wouldn't mean Phyllis assumed she was too ill for the Vanilla Heath Bar Crunch and Cherry Garcia she and Sam had brought.

"Let me help you with the dishes," Phoebe offered, but Phyllis refused. Did the woman think that because Phoebe couldn't cook she was useless as a dishwasher too?

She loved Phyllis, but Sam's mom definitely brought out all of Phoebe's insecurities and paranoia. Sometimes it was exhausting to be around her—trying so hard, smiling so much. She wished she could just have an oh-well-screw-her-if-she-doesn't-like-me attitude, which she did with most people, but Sam's mom mattered. Growing up with such a shitty mother had led Phoebe to have all these secret fantasies, where she ran away and was adopted into a normal family with a mother who was a mixture of all those perfect classic TV moms: Mrs. Brady, Mrs. Cunningham from *Happy Days*, Beaver's mom. Moms who cooked casseroles. Phyllis was all of that and more.

"I'm just going to put them in the sink," Phyllis said. "They can wait. Let's head into the living room, shall we?"

They followed Sam's mom out of the cheery, stuck-in-time kitchen and into the front room with the furniture that Sam claimed hadn't been changed since he'd been alive. It had survived the years well. Whatever stains there might have been were now artfully covered by pillows, throws, and doilies. The room smelled of the sweet potpourri Phyllis kept in jars. There was a brick hearth, where they lit a fire each Thanksgiving and Christmas, and a mantel covered in framed family photos: Sam's mother and aunt as young girls; Sam's stern-faced great-grandfather who'd built the house. There was the snapshot of young Sam and Lisa that Phoebe had noticed on her first visit to the home years ago. Phyllis had caught her looking and said, "Sam had a sister. We lost her." And Phoebe had pretended that she had no idea, that she had only a vague memory of hearing the story on the news.

Everything about the room, about the whole house in fact, screamed *home* to Phoebe. Not that she was much of a judge.

Phoebe had been brought up in a string of dingy rent-controlled apartments by her single mom, whose idea of a homey touch was a bottle of Lysol that she sprayed now and then to cover up the smell of cigarettes, pot, and general filth and decay. A happy homemaker she was not. The only stroganoff she ever made was with Hamburger Helper, and even that required too much cooking. She was more a SpaghettiOs from the can with Yoo-hoo to drink kind of mom.

Phoebe's friends thought her mom was so cool. Phoebe got to come and go as she pleased, have chocolate cake and Pepsi for breakfast, have her very own cigarette or toke of a joint anytime she wanted. "Your mom is the best!" her friends would squeal when they met up at her place after school to get high. "She's like one of us."

"We're diamonds in the rough, you and me," her mom used say. But Phoebe thought they were more like fool's gold.

Phyllis plopped herself down on the couch next to Phoebe and straightened an embroidered runner on the coffee table. Phyllis was a well-kempt woman in her fifties. She had chin-length gray hair and wore loose linen clothing and Birkenstocks with bright, hand-knit socks. She worked for a nonprofit environmental group raising money, lobbying lawmakers. She'd even been arrested twice: for protesting at an antinuclear event and when she and a group chained themselves to a logging truck trying to stop a clear-cutting operation. When Sam was growing up, his mom would go away on trips to demonstrations down in Washington and he'd be left with the next-door neighbor—a sweet old woman named Mrs. August, whose house smelled like gingerbread and mothballs. After Lisa disappeared, the trips increased. Phyllis threw herself into her work, figuring that if she couldn't save her daughter, she would do her best to save the world from the nukes and chemical plants and people who were, in her words, "raping Mother Earth."

It broke Phoebe's heart to think of Sam and his mother rattling around in the house after Lisa disappeared and Sam's dad died. Phyllis kept Lisa's room just the way it was.

"It was creepy, really," Sam told Phoebe. "To go walking in there later when I was in high school and have everything the same. I was growing up and Lisa was stuck in limbo—a ghost girl haunting her old room, with unicorns on the walls and stuffed animals on the bed."

But Phoebe understood. Phyllis was still waiting for Lisa to come back. And if she did, she wanted things to be just the way Lisa remembered.

Did you reach Hazel?" Phyllis asked Sam.

"Yeah, I did. Thanks," Sam said, looking away. But Phoebe knew Phyllis wouldn't let it go that easy. Sam asks for his aunt's number after fifteen years of not speaking with her and that's not supposed to arouse curiosity.

"How is she?" Phyllis asked, wincing a little, as though asking the question had pained her in some way.

Phoebe glanced over at the girlhood photo of Phyllis and Hazel, both with their hair in pigtails, smiling impishly into the camera. There were no photos of Hazel as an adult anywhere in the house. She, like Lisa, was somehow frozen in time here.

"Okay, I guess. Working in a nursing home. I actually called her because I wanted to get in touch with Evie."

Sam's mother sat up straight, peered at Sam over the top of her small rectangular glasses, which she kept on a chain around her neck. "Evie?" She said it like the name was an unfamiliar one to her: *Evie? Who on earth is Evie?*

Sam cleared his throat. "Yeah. I thought maybe it was time to do some catching up."

Phyllis stared at him. "And did you?"

"Yeah. We did. Phoebe and I had dinner with her. She lives up in Burlington."

Phoebe remembered the pizza and Mountain Dew. Not exactly the white tablecloth dinner Phyllis was probably imagining.

"Is she married?" Phyllis asked. "Any kids?"

Sam shook his head.

"A shame," Phyllis said. "I don't know what it is with you young people. I married your father when I was nineteen."

Sam nodded. Hung his head. He knew where this was going. It was inevitable that she'd bring it up each time they visited.

"Is it so wrong to want to see your children happy? To want grandchildren? Actual children, I mean—not just a snake, a hedgehog, and a couple of rats."

Phoebe bit her lip. She'd been with Sam all day and hadn't had a chance to sneak off to buy a pregnancy test. She'd get one on the way to work tomorrow, do it as soon as she got there. The test would show that she wasn't pregnant, and the worrying would all be over. Hell, maybe she'd get her period tonight and not even need to waste money on the test.

Sam sat up straight, rubbed his hand over his face. "No, Mom. It's not wrong. And I am happy. Bee and I are very happy with things just the way they are."

Phoebe smiled, reached out to take Sam's hand.

Phyllis nodded, frowning. Phoebe understood, even felt bad for her. Sam was her one remaining child—her only shot at grandchildren—and so far, he'd shown no interest in producing any. But in truth, they *were* happy. And this idea that a couple could only be complete and know true happiness by squeezing out a couple of kids just pissed Phoebe off.

"Oh, Phoebe," Phyllis said. "There's something I thought you'd be interested in. Something I'd like your help with."

Excellent. She was changing the subject. This got them off the when-are-you-going-to-settle-down-and-get-married-and-start-pumping-out-babies hook. For now anyway.

Phyllis reached into the pocket of her pants and pulled out a small drawstring bag.

"After you found that fairy book up in the attic last week, I went up and took another look around in there. I sat for a while, remembering how Lisa used to spend hours up there, playing."

Sam nodded, looked away.

"Anyway," Phyllis continued, "I found this shoved back between the joists, tucked under the insulation at the very edge."

Sam leaned forward, frowning. But his mother handed the bag to Phoebe, not to him, as if she was suddenly more worthy of her trust than her own son was. Phoebe took it, opened it slowly, and peered in.

"Teeth," Phyllis said. "From a large animal. Must have been some treasure of Lisa's. I was hoping maybe, with your work at the clinic, you might have some idea of what animal they're from."

Phoebe pulled one out. It was brownish yellow. Large. The tooth felt strangely heavy in her hand.

Sam peered at the tooth with a look of revulsion.

"I don't know," Phoebe admitted, dropping it back into the bag, wiping her hand on her jeans. "But Dr. Ostrum or Franny might. I can bring the bag in to work and ask."

"That would be great," Phyllis said. "I'd appreciate it. I know it doesn't really matter, won't help with anything, but I'm curious."

Phoebe took the bag of teeth, held it tight in her hand.

"Have you done anything with the fairy book?" Phyllis asked.

"No," Sam lied. "Not yet."

"It should probably go to the police. It is evidence, after all. I have the names of the two detectives we dealt with if that'll help. I don't even know if they're still around anymore, but it would be a starting place."

"Sure," Sam said. "If you could write them down, that would be great."

Phyllis excused herself. Phoebe flashed Sam a what-are-we-supposed-to-do-now look. Sam shrugged. Whispered, "We can't exactly tell her it was stolen, can we?"

"No," Phoebe agreed. "But we can't keep lying to her forever."

"Not forever," Sam said. "We'll hold off until we have some idea of what's actually going on."

Phoebe nodded, clutched the strange little bag of teeth, and wondered if they'd ever be able to make sense of any of it.

"They were his first gift, I think," Sam said, nodding at the bag in her hand.

"What?"

"The teeth. Lisa woke up one morning and found them on her pillow. We thought she was tricking us, that she put the teeth there herself. But now I think the son-of-a-bitch actually came into the house while we were all sleeping and left them on her pillow. Can you imagine? Who would take a chance like that?"

Someone who knew he wouldn't be caught, Phoebe thought as she shook the bag, rattling the teeth like dice.

CHAPTER 14

Lisa

Lisa had been thinking about it and had decided that maybe all of the tests she'd given herself over the years—holding her breath until she turned blue, making herself face angry dogs, touching bloody meat—maybe all of this was just training. It was a way to teach herself to not let fear get in the way. Preparing her to one day go into the woods and meet the fairies, no matter what might happen.

"Tell more of the story," Evie begged, licking her lips like she was hungry. "About the sisters. They'd just left the castle, right?"

She was trying to distract Lisa, to make her forget about going alone into the woods. The very woods Lisa had just caught Evie coming out of, which was its own weird mystery. Evie had snuck off on her own after dinner, and an hour and a half later Lisa spotted her stepping into the yard from the woods. Lisa wondered if Evie was starting to believe and was looking for the fairies herself.

"What are you doing?" Lisa had asked.

"Nothing," Evie said, not looking her in the eye. "Come on, it's freezing out here. Let's go in."

Now they were back in Lisa's room, getting sweatshirts because the night had grown cool. Once Evie had on her baggy gray pullover, she grabbed her sketchbook and flipped open to a drawing she'd been working on for the past two days—the cellar hole with the foxglove in the corner. Only in Evie's rendition each flower had a horrible skeleton face at the end.

"Okay," Lisa said. "But only if you tell me what you were just doing in the woods."

Evie gave a frustrated sigh. "Scoping it out. You know, making sure it looked safe." She scribbled hard, shading in the bottom of the cellar hole.

Lisa nodded, but somehow she knew Evie wasn't telling the truth. She couldn't believe Evie would lie to her. But then again, she couldn't believe Evie had hurt Gerald so badly either. Over and over, Lisa had replayed the way Evie had stood over his crumpled body, taking out her knife. What would have happened if Lisa hadn't stopped her? How far would she have gone? Lisa shivered. It was up to her to keep Evie under control, to make sure she didn't hurt anyone again. But now she was worried that somehow she might be losing her influence over Evie.

"Come on, Lisa, the story!" Evie said.

"Okay already. They were on horseback, remember?" She touched the teeth in her pocket, remembering her strange dream.

"Yes," Evie said, setting down the sketchbook and closing her eyes. "Riding fast through the woods." She reached under her shirt and pulled out the key, holding it tight.

"Away from the dark, cursed castle," Lisa said. "They rode

all night. And then they came to a river. It was deep and wide. They looked for an easy way across but couldn't find one. Then a frog hopped out of the water and spoke. He said, 'If you can answer my riddle, sisters, I'll get you across.'

" 'Very well,' answered the dark sister.

" 'What holds water but is full of holes?' asked the frog, smiling slyly.

"The pale sister moaned. 'Cursed frog. It's impossible. Nothing with holes can hold water.'

"But the other sister said, 'Not so fast. It's a sponge. A sponge holds water and is full of holes.'

"And so the frog hopped along the shore to a little grove of trees where he showed the sisters a hidden boat."

"A sponge!" Evie exclaimed. "You're the most clever storyteller in the history of the planet!"

Lisa smiled. "I'll tell you more later. I've gotta get down to Reliance."

They headed out to the yard, where Sammy was waiting. "You still going down there?" he asked, peering apprehensively into the dark woods.

Lisa nodded.

"Take this," Evie said, pressing her sheathed hunting knife into Lisa's hand. It was heavier than Lisa expected.

"No," Lisa said, handing the knife back. "I don't want to scare them. And remember what my mom said? About how they don't like iron? So probably they don't like knives and stuff."

"I've got a bad feeling about this," Evie said, looking uncharacteristically nervous. "I don't think you should go. Not on your own."

"Don't worry," Lisa said. "Besides, you just checked it out your-self, right? Made sure there were no booby traps or an angry army of little green men waiting to tie me up and steal me away?"

Evie snorted, rolled her eyes.

"What if Gerald and Becca come back?" Sam said. "I think they're the only thing you might have to worry about down there."

"It's not me they're pissed at," Lisa said, looking at Evie. "And Evie's got the knife."

"We'll be here in the yard waiting," Evie said. "Any trouble, you yell as loud as you can. We'll hear you." She and Sammy had their sleeping bags out. Lisa's was beside them, an empty chrysalis.

Lisa slowly made her way down the hill and stepped over the brook, wondering if there'd be a frog waiting to ask her a riddle, and across to Reliance. The moonlight cast shadows of the trees with their leaves blowing—they looked like shaggy monsters writhing on the forest floor. Suddenly the whole landscape re-minded her of one of Evie's drawings.

Fighting the growing urge to run, she walked up to the edge of the cellar hole, sure she heard footsteps behind her. She held her breath, listening.

"Sam? Evie?" she called.

Silence.

She was sweating in spite of the cool breeze.

"If you two are following me, I'll wring your necks. Skin you with Evie's knife."

In the fairy tales, the girl gets nothing unless she takes a chance.

Carrying the plate of treats, Lisa carefully lowered herself down, landing in roughly the same place Gerald fell. She thought of the awkward angle of his arm when he got up.

"I hope he's okay," she said out loud. And she did. He was just a dork who had found someone even lower on the social food chain than him and couldn't resist taking advantage. He shouldn't have said those awful things to Evie, but he didn't deserve a broken arm.

In the corner of the old cellar hole, next to the foxglove, Lisa placed the plate with a glass of Orange Crush, a couple of cherry Life Savers, an unwrapped Devil Dog. She could barely see the rough shapes in the dark—sweet, shadowy offerings.

Lisa crab-crawled backward across the dirt floor, keeping her eyes on the treats. Then she settled herself against the rough stone wall across from the plate, looked up at what little she could see of the stars through the trees. She zipped her red hooded sweatshirt up tight, touched the bag of teeth in her pocket. Then the penny, which she'd attached to her charm bracelet.

1918. The year everyone in the village went missing.

Except for little Eugene.

People don't just disappear without a trace like that.

Lisa yawned. She was tired. Bone tired. That was one of Aunt Hazel's expression, one she always thought was funny—bones couldn't get tired. At least she didn't think so. But hers felt tired now. She let her eyes close. If anyone came into the cellar hole, she'd wake up.

A few seconds (or was it minutes? hours even?) later, she opened her eyes. Footsteps. Getting closer. She told herself she was hearing things, it was just that overactive imagination she was famous for.

"Hello?" she called, her own voice a strange crackle in the dark.

"Eugene?" she said, tentatively.

What if there were ghosts? What if everyone who'd disappeared in Reliance was still trapped there in some way? Maybe that's what the lights were.

Twigs cracked. Feet shuffled through the leaf litter, but she couldn't tell if they were moving closer or farther away.

She closed her eyes. Said the four most comforting words she knew: "Once upon a time."

An incantation.

Protect me. Open the door and let me go someplace else.

She held her breath, stood slowly, peeking up at ground level. Maybe it was just Gerald after all, pissed at Evie and looking for revenge.

But there was no one there.

Just her ears playing tricks on her. Maybe the footsteps were part of the dream she'd been having, something about teeth and keys and doors.

She was about to climb out and head for home when a scream filled the woods, bounced off the walls of the cellar hole, through the trees—a scream so loud she was sure that not one human being could be making it. Surely the woods, the animals, even the soft beams of moonlight were all screaming together.

CHAPTER 15

Phoebe

It had been a Monday like any other, putting aside the fact that Phoebe had spent every free moment telling her boss, Dr. Ostrum, and Franny, the clinic's head tech, about her strange weekend, hoping to make some sense of it all. And telling the story kept her from thinking about the unopened pregnancy test in her purse. She'd promised herself that she'd do it before she went home. She had to.

She'd stopped at O'Brien's Pharmacy on her way to work. Not wanting to dawdle and draw attention to herself, she'd snatched up the most expensive test, figuring quality mattered in a case like this. The woman behind the counter was heavyset, with dyed orange hair sticky with hairspray. Her eyebrows seemed to be missing, but she'd drawn some on with a matching orange pencil. She'd worked at O'Brien's for forever, but her gardenia-scented perfume seemed particularly cloying today.

"All set, hon?"

Phoebe nodded and plunked the test down on the counter. The woman scanned it.

"Eighteen eighty-nine," she announced. Her nails were coral pink with little rhinestones stuck on.

Phoebe reached into her purse for a twenty.

"Aren't you Sammy Nazzaro's girl?" the woman asked, scrunching up her face.

Phoebe froze, unsure how to answer. If she said yes, then word of her having bought a pregnancy test might filter down through the grapevine so that Sam would know by suppertime.

Phoebe shook her head, smiled lamely, and looked down, handing over the money she owed. She flashed onto the dozens of times she'd stopped in here with Sam in the last three years, picking up toilet paper or Tylenol or shampoo. How many times had this very woman waited on them, mentally cataloging their purchases, assessing, judging? She cursed herself for not driving to an anonymous big box store in another town.

The cashier squinted at Phoebe and made a clicking sound with her tongue. "Just as well," she said, turning to the cash register, then back again to give Phoebe her change. "Cursed, that family is. Stillborn babies, missing girls, suicides. And that old man, Dr. O'Toole"—she gave a dramatic shiver—"he was like the grim reaper himself. There used to be a little song all us kids sang about him."

Phoebe said, "Oh?" in what she hoped was a politely uninterested way, as she stuffed her change into a pocket and grabbed the bag, already half-turning to leave.

But she continued, her singsongy voice high-pitched and harsh at the same time:

> *Don't get sick, don't miss school,*
> *'Cause your papa will call for Doctor O'Toole;*

He'll eat your heart, he'll tie you to the bed,
He'll put bad dreams inside your head.

She paused to giggle and shrug. Phoebe shrugged back, heading for the door as quickly as she could without actually running.

"Have a good one!" the woman called.

Phoebe, Franny, and Dr. O. were gathered around the reception desk just before closing. Phoebe was shutting down the computer and getting ready to turn the phones over to the answering service. The floors were swept and mopped, giving the office its familiar pine-scented disinfectant smell. The seats in the waiting area had been wiped down; the brochures on heartworm, obesity, flea control, dental care, and pet health insurance straightened.

"But why would they go to the trouble of faking a stabbing? That seems a bit much, doesn't it?" Dr. Ostrum asked.

"It was a sure way to get them to chase her," Franny said, taking off her lab coat and yanking her unruly brown hair loose from its ponytail. "If the goal was to get them out of the cabin for a while. You should never underestimate what people are willing to do to get what they want. For whatever reason, they wanted something you guys had packed in your stuff."

Franny was a local. She'd gone to school with Lisa and Sam, was in Sam's grade. When they all got together for drinks, Franny and Sam talked about what became of old classmates, of the gym teacher with the harelip, of the time the football team lost a bet and they all came to school in drag.

Phoebe nodded. "There was an old book. The one Lisa claimed to have found in the cellar hole that summer. *The Book of Fairies*. They took that along with everything else."

Dr. Ostrum pursed her lips, shook her head. She was in her late fifties, a petite woman with short silver-white hair. She reminded Phoebe of a bald eagle, though she would never say that out loud. It was more than the gray hair—there was something dignified about her sharp features and perfect posture. She never lost her cool and was completely poised in every situation. And perhaps the best thing about her, the thing that made Phoebe absolutely devoted to Dr. O., was that she thought Phoebe was smart. She never once looked down on her for not having a college degree, never suggested that Phoebe improve herself by taking adult education courses. She listened to Phoebe's thoughts and opinions, let her run the office the way she thought best. And when Phoebe had a good idea, Dr. O. praised her for it, made her feel appreciated. It was different from any job she'd ever had.

"Do you think the government might be involved in this somehow, Bee?" Franny asked. "I always wondered if they had something to do with Lisa's disappearance. Like maybe she and Sammy stumbled across some military secret in the woods or something."

Phoebe admired Franny's powers of deduction but not her paranoia. In Franny's world it was us against them, and the best way to survive was to live under the radar. She believed the government had spy cameras in people's homes and workplaces, was monitoring every phone conversation and keeping track of every citizen's credit card purchases. Franny had no credit cards or bank account. "They can't trace you with cash," she said. She used disposable cell phones and tossed them every few months, and she rented a post office box at a Mailboxes & More store three towns away. Franny and her husband, Jim, lived in an off-the-grid house they'd built themselves that was powered by solar panels, a windmill, and a generator. They had an underground gas tank, a cellar with enough canned and dry rations to last two years, a hidden fallout-proof bunker with walls made of two feet of reinforced concrete, and guns and ammo enough to supply a small guerrilla group. Franny and Jim said they were only preparing "just in case," but on the few occasions Phoebe had visited what they referred to as "their compound," Phoebe got the sense that it was something they were eagerly awaiting.

"It just all seems a little over the top. A little theatrical," Dr. O. said about Phoebe's weekend adventures.

"I agree," Phoebe said. "Whoever these people are, they have a flair for the dramatic."

"This is like one of those crazy Missing Persons stories from TV," Franny said. "A woman disappears for fifteen years, only to return and send everyone's lives spinning out of control."

"But not many missing people claim they were living in the land of the fairies," Phoebe said.

"I don't know about fairies," Franny said, "but something weird is going on in those woods. A whole town disappearing like that all those years ago. Plates of food on the tables. Cows unmilked in the barns."

Dr. Ostrum shook her head. "That's not what happened," she said.

"What do you mean?" Phoebe asked.

"I'm afraid it's not the story of intrigue people like to believe. If you really do the research, you'll see that the truth is the town dried up slowly, like any other. People packed up and left to go where the work was. They moved closer to the railroad, the quarries, better pasture land for the animals. But that's dull and doesn't make for a good story. So over the years, people embellished it, turned it into this eerie legend. The mysterious disappearance of the town called Reliance."

"But Sam's mother said that's what happened. Her grandfather was found out there," Phoebe said.

Dr. O. shook her head. "Come on, Phoebe. What's more likely, that he was left by fairies—*fairies!*—or that he was a child someone had out of wedlock, maybe an orphan, a regular old abandoned infant in the days before access to birth control, much less safe, legal abortion? Stories passed down in families aren't always the truth. You know that."

"I still say there's something creepy about those woods," Franny said. "And what about the Lord's Prayer carved into the rock on the way into town? I heard the guy who did it was trying to protect Harmony from what was out in those woods."

Dr. O. shook her head, laughing. "Just another story," she said. "And even if it's not, the man who did it was obviously too caught up in the stories himself."

"What about all the fairy stuff?" asked Franny. "And what about Lisa? A little girl doesn't just vanish like that."

"No," Dr. Ostrum agreed. "Of course not. Someone—some real, tangible person—took her. No doubt someone who took advantage of her gullibility and superstition. There are evil forces at work here, but I'd say they're definitely the human kind—as much as that lacks romance. I think the best thing you can do, Phoebe, is leave all of this alone. Tell the police about the note, the phone call, the impostors at the cabin, your stolen things, all of it. Let them sort it out—that's their job. Someone's playing games with poor Sam, and it's not right. But the longer you play along, the harder it's going to be to extricate yourselves."

Phoebe nodded. "I guess you're right."

"Oh, almost forgot, here," Dr. Ostrum said, handing the little velvet bag of teeth to Phoebe. "I took another look. Horse. Definitely horse." She put on her coat and headed for the door.

"Thanks," Phoebe said, tucking the little bag into her purse next to the unopened pregnancy test.

They called their good nights to each other, and Dr. O. made her way across the parking lot and started her Saab. As Franny was about to go out the door, Phoebe called out, "Wait a sec, would you?"

"What is it?" Franny said, turning back.

"Have you ever done one of these before?" Phoebe asked, holding up the pink and white cardboard box that held the pregnancy test.

Franny's eyes grew wide and her mouth made a little O shape, but no sound came. Just her breath, which seemed strangely loud.

"It's just that I never have and I'm a little freaked out," Phoebe said. "I was hoping you would stay."

Franny dropped her jacket and purse, bolted the door, and flipped the CLOSED sign. She came behind the desk and enveloped Phoebe in a big hug. "Let me see that thing," she said, reaching for the box and reading the instructions. "Can't get much more simple. Pee on the stick, wait three minutes. If a plus sign shows up, it's positive."

Phoebe nodded, taking the box back. "I guess I'll go take care of step one, then."

Franny held on to her arm. "Are you sure, Phoebe? Wouldn't you rather do this at home with Sam? Does he even have any idea?"

Phoebe shook her head. "No. I need to know for sure before I say anything."

Franny nodded. "Go pee, then come back out here. We'll wait together."

It was the longest three minutes of Phoebe's life. "Is it time?" she kept asking.

Franny stared down at her watch, refusing to let Phoebe peek until the time was up. "Now," she said at last, and they hurried, jostling against each other, into the bathroom where the plastic stick rested on the back of the toilet. And there, like crosshairs in the little window, was a bright blue plus sign.

Phoebe got home at six after stopping at the grocery store, where she discovered she'd somehow lost the list. She had to muddle her way through, relying on her Swiss cheese memory. (Was it eggs they needed or milk? She bought both. And ice cream. Three different kinds. She thought about adding a quart of pickles to the cart, bringing it home and making her own special sundae in front of Sam, telling him that way.) While in the store, she wandered down the baby aisle, studying the diapers, creams, wipes, spoons, bottles, formulas, and little jars of food. As she looked at the stocked shelves, she realized how totally unprepared and clueless she was. Who even knew there were special brushes for cleaning bottles? Or at least seven different kinds of formula to choose from? Was soy-free better? And who gave their baby goat's milk formula? ORGANIC, it said.

That would definitely be Sam's choice. But wasn't breast-feeding better than all of that? She was suddenly aware of her own breasts aching, feeling huge and swollen. A mother. She was going to be a mother.

She'd sobbed when she first saw the plus sign, then denial hit hard and fast. "Tests can be wrong," she'd said to Franny.

"No," Franny told her. "False negatives, yes. But it's impossible to get a false positive with these things. Trust me."

They'd sat down and talked it through. Phoebe was going to go home, cook Sam a wonderful dinner, and tell him.

"But he doesn't want a baby!" she'd howled. "What if he thinks I'm trying to trap him?"

Franny reached over and stroked her hair. "Bee," she'd said, "this is Sam you're talking about. He's one of the kindest, smartest, most understanding people I know. And he loves you like crazy. It's going to be okay. Just go home and tell him. You'll work it out together."

So Phoebe stopped at the store to pick up ingredients for spaghetti and salad, one of Sam's favorite meals. She threw a bottle of merlot into her cart, a couple of gold candles that seemed like good luck. She'd make a romantic dinner, give him a little wine, and tell him about the baby.

When she finished shopping, she was starving, so she went through the McDonald's drive-through and scarfed down a quarter-pounder with cheese, fries, and a chocolate shake. It seemed crazy to eat when she was about to make dinner, but all she'd had for lunch were some saltines and a Granny Smith apple. She had to find a way to do better—she was eating for two, after all. Maybe she should have picked up some prenatal vitamins at the store.

She sat in the parking lot finishing the last of her shake with the motor running. Sam hated McDonald's and was a vegetarian for the most part, so Phoebe kept these little trips to herself. She was always careful to throw away all the packaging so she wouldn't get a lecture about how she was supporting an evil corporate empire intent on poisoning the world. When Sam did eat meat, he insisted it be organic, local, cruelty-free (a term that made no sense to Phoebe . . . they'd killed the animal, right? How was that not cruel?).

Sam's truck wasn't in the driveway. Balancing grocery bags, she unlocked the door and carried everything in. The answering machine was blinking and she pushed PLAY, still balancing the groceries in her arms. The first message was from Sam. The tree service he worked for was clearing a lot and he said he'd be home late.

The machine beeped a second time and Franny's voice came on: "Hey there, Bee. I just wanted to tell you I love you and I'm thinking of you. If you need anything, just call. Oh, and I thought of something you might be interested in. There's this girl, Becca Reynolds. She was in the same class as me and Sammy. I was kinda friends with her, but mostly because I felt sorry for her. Anyway, she and her brother lived two houses down from Sam and Lisa. They hung out a lot. They moved away just after Lisa disappeared, down to Massachusetts, I think. Anyway, I just ran into Becca the other day—she's moved back to Vermont and is working in the floral department at Price Chopper over in St. Johnsbury. I thought maybe you and Sam might want to talk to her. Who knows—she might remember something from the time Lisa went missing. As I recall, she was all into the fairy stuff, went around telling everyone that she'd seen the Fairy

King herself. Anyway . . . I hope everything goes well tonight. I know it will. Let's get together soon, huh? Maybe Friday after work? Let me know."

The third message was from Evie.

"Sam?" said a quavering voice into the machine. "They were here. My place is trashed. They hit me over the head. I'm afraid they'll be back. I don't know what to do. If you get this, please—" There was a little wheezing breath, then the line went dead.

Phoebe dropped the grocery bags, grabbed the phone, and punched in Evie's number. She let it ring twelve times before giving up and trying to get Sam on his cell. It went right to voice mail. "Damn!" she said. Sam had either left his phone in his truck or was out where there was no service. She slammed the phone down and scrawled a quick note to Sam.

> *Gone to rescue Evie.*
> *(Play phone message)*
>
> *Love, Bee*

CHAPTER 16

Lisa

A light bobbed down the path through the woods.

"Lisa? Lisa! Where are you?"

"Here," she called, her voice small and flat. She clung to the damp stone wall of the cellar hole, watched as the light moved closer.

She'd been unable to move out of the hole since hearing the scream, terrified of what might be out there. But now they were coming to rescue her.

Suddenly the light was in her face. Bright. Blinding. Interrogation light. She put up her hands to shade her eyes.

"Are you okay?" It was Evie's voice, wheezing and frantic. "We fell asleep. God, I'm so sorry! I heard you scream. That's what woke me. What happened? Jesus, get the light off her face, Sam."

Lisa listened to Evie try to catch her breath—she must have run all the way down from the yard.

"It wasn't me," Lisa said, putting her hands back down. She looked up and saw Evie and Sam at the edge of the cellar hole, two pale faces peering down, making her feel like a tiger in a pit at the zoo. "I didn't scream." Lisa saw that Evie had her hunting knife clenched in her hand.

"Well, who the hell did, then?" Evie asked, sheathing the knife.

"I don't know. I couldn't tell what it came from," Lisa admitted.

She squinted past her brother and cousin, scanning the dark woods for any sign of movement.

"Fisher, maybe," Sammy said. "Or an owl."

"That was no damn owl," Evie said, sounding a little spooked as she looked around the woods, then back down at Lisa. "Come on. Let's bug out. Go back to the house." She held out her hand.

"What's that?" Sam asked. The beam of the flashlight was pointed at a little nest of cut ferns down in the cellar hole, right beside Lisa. In it, like a strange, misshapen egg, was a cloth bundle wound round and round with string.

"Give me the light!" Lisa said, reaching up.

She scanned the corner and saw that the plate of sweets was empty, the cup drained.

"Damn it!" she snapped. How could she have missed it? She couldn't believe she'd let herself fall asleep.

She turned the light back down on the ferns and picked up the bundle. The cloth was worn and dirty—white or beige once, now stained brown. The string was thin and waxy.

"Bring it up here," Evie instructed, holding out her hand to help Lisa out of the hole. "Lemme see," Evie said, grabbing for the bundle, but Lisa held it tight.

"No," she said. "I'll open it."

Tucking the flashlight between her tilted head and shoulder, Lisa went to work untying the string. Evie moved so that she was toe to toe with Lisa, her head bumping Lisa's as they both looked down.

"Careful," Evie warned. Lisa stopped what she was doing, suddenly frightened by what might be inside. More teeth? Some other body part?

What had the scream in the woods been? Was whatever it was still out there, watching?

Pushing the questions from her head, she went back to work untying the strange egg-shaped bundle.

Lisa finally got the string off and slowly opened the stained, worn cloth. Inside was a round silver medal with the words SAINT CHRISTOPHER PROTECT US around the edge. In the center was a picture of a man with a staff and beard carrying a child on his back.

"Is he stealing the kid?" Sammy asked, leaning in for a closer look.

"No, dummy," Evie said. "That's Christ. Look at the halo. He's carrying Christ across a river. Don't you know the story?"

Sammy shook his head.

"This guy, Saint Christopher, he's the patron saint of travel. You're supposed to pray to him and stuff when you take a trip. Carrying this is supposed to bring good luck if you get on a plane or a boat or something."

"How do you know all this?" Lisa asked. No one in their family was even slightly religious. When she'd once asked if she and Sammy had been baptized, her parents had laughed like it was the most ridiculous question in the world. When she told them that Gerald and Pinkie said she wouldn't get into heaven if she wasn't baptized, they laughed harder still.

"Not everyone believes in God and heaven," Da had explained. "The people who do tend to think that they're right and anyone with different beliefs is wrong."

"Well then, what do *we* believe?" Lisa asked. Da looked at Lisa's mom, who smiled.

"That organized religion is the opiate of the masses," her mom said.

"Huh?" Lisa said.

"That people should be educated enough to make their own choices," Da said.

Lisa's mom snorted. "Right," she said. "I'm sure that'll happen any day now, honey. And the sky will rain pink lemonade and we'll have snow made of big, puffy marshmallows."

Lisa looked down at Saint Christopher, then at Evie. "Well?" she said. "What makes you an expert on saints all of a sudden?" She hated when Evie knew something she didn't. Lisa was the one who read all the time. Evie got F's in school, never went to the library.

"I go to church sometimes," Evie said at last, looking shy about it, like it was a secret and she shouldn't have told.

Lisa stared up at her, perplexed. She didn't know what was weirder—the idea of Evie going to church or the fact that Evie had kept this a secret from her.

"What, with your mom?" Lisa asked.

"No," Evie said. "Don't say anything to her, huh? She'd kill me. I go by myself. There's one about two miles from our house. Sometimes I get on my bike and ride down. They have doughnuts after."

"So what, you're getting in good with God for doughnuts?"

As soon as she said it, she knew she shouldn't have. She was just pissed that Evie had kept a secret.

"Forget it," Evie said. "Let's just get back to the house." She turned away and started toward the hill through the darkness. Lisa and Sam followed, Lisa holding the flashlight in one hand, the Saint Christopher medal in the other.

"Well," Sammy said, as they walked along. "One thing's for sure—if the medal is supposed to protect you when you travel, it was found by the wrong person. Lisa never goes anywhere."

At that moment, from the dark woods off to the left, came another voice, a girl's voice edged with panic.

"Did—did you see him?" They all froze.

Lisa pointed the beam of the flashlight toward the voice and spotted Pinkie, partially hidden behind a tree.

"See who?" Lisa asked.

"The bogeyman," Pinkie said.

"What do you mean?" Evie asked, moving slowly toward Pinkie, who was cowering behind the tree.

"You stay away from me," Pinkie said. "You busted Gerald's arm, you know? We were at the hospital for hours. My mom's real pissed—she had to miss work and everything. She might get a lawyer and sue your asses off."

Evie stopped. Took a step back.

"Becca," Sam said, stepping close enough to touch her, "what are you doing out here? What did you see?"

"I wanted to know. I see you down here all the time. I wanted to know what the big secret was. I watched tonight. I was there at the edge of your yard. I saw Evie go into the woods. Then Lisa. So I waited. Then I came down and saw."

"Saw what?" Sam asked.

"I'll take you to where he was," Pinkie said, pushing off from the tree and walking off to the left, deeper into the woods. They walked in silence for a few minutes, following Pinkie.

There was light up ahead.

"I don't like this," Evie said.

Lisa reached out and took Evie's hand, which was cool and clammy. Evie's breath whistled in her chest.

Becca led them to a clearing. A pink flashlight was lying on the forest floor casting a beam of dim light, the batteries low.

"He was right here," Pinkie said, swiveling her head around, squinting into shadows. She reached and picked up her flashlight, giving it a shake, trying to make it brighter.

"Who?" Sammy asked.

"The bogeyman."

"What did he look like?" Evie asked.

Pinkie was silent a moment, thinking. "Like a man made of shadows," she said at last.

"What about his face?" Sammy asked.

"He didn't have a face," Pinkie said.

Lisa shivered.

"No face," Evie said. "Right . . ."

"But he was wearing a cap," Pinkie said.

"A cap?" Sammy asked.

"Yeah, you know, like a baseball cap."

Evie laughed. "The bogeyman's a baseball fan, huh? What, does he play shortstop?"

"I know what I saw, *Stevie*," Pinkie spat. "I screamed, dropped my light, and ran away as fast as I could."

Lisa nodded, relieved to finally know where the horrible scream had come from.

"Know what I think?" Evie asked. "I think you're making all this crap up."

Pinkie didn't say anything. She picked at her arm, making one of the mosquito bites bleed.

Lisa looked away. Something on the ground behind Sammy caught her eye and she walked slowly over to it.

"Lisa?" Evie called as Lisa moved away from the group, casting her flashlight at the object on the ground. "You find something?"

"No," Lisa said, her voice sounding small as she forced the lie out. She turned out the flashlight and bent down to pick up the faded, paint-splattered object in the grass. She'd know it anywhere. Lisa hid it under her sweatshirt and walked back to the others, heart racing.

"You okay?" Evie asked, putting a hand on Lisa's shoulder, making her jump.

She nodded. "I just want to go home."

"You got it," said Evie, glancing around the woods. "Let's bug out before Pinkie the Spy here thinks up any more crazy bullshit."

Lisa followed them, crossing her arms over the object in her sweatshirt.

It was Da's Red Sox hat.

CHAPTER 17

Phoebe

Evie's door had been forced open; the wooden frame was splintered as if it had been hit hard with a battering ram. Phoebe took a deep breath, pushed the door in with her fingertips, and saw that the stairs were dark. She groped around for a light switch. Her fingers found one and flicked it. Nothing happened.

She left the stairway and went back to the Mercury, where she grabbed the heavy metal Maglite from the trunk. Sam had put it there along with a few tools, some road flares, and an emergency silver space blanket. Sam believed in being prepared.

"This would sure be a lot easier if you were here," she mumbled. If she found out later that he was pounding back beers with some of the guys from work while she was out risking her life to save his cousin, she'd kill him.

"Here goes nothing."

Holding the flashlight with both hands like a weapon, she made her way down the stairs into Evie's dark cave of an apartment.

Evie hadn't been exaggerating. The place was trashed—the same interior decorating team who'd visited her house over the weekend had come to Evie's. A horrible thought occurred to her: Had she and Sam led them here? What if they'd been followed from their house Saturday night?

However they got here, the scene looked all too familiar. Chairs were tipped over, the upholstery sliced open and stuffing pulled out. The television was smashed. Books and papers were scattered. Phoebe found another light switch and tried it: nothing.

"Evie?" Her voice trembled as she called in just above a whisper. "You here?"

Nothing. Not so much as a murmur. Then, all at once, came a roaring sound from above. Phoebe gripped the flashlight like a baseball bat and crouched down, ready to pummel whatever came at her. But there was only the gurgle of water. Someone in the apartment above had flushed the toilet.

Phoebe gave a weak laugh to comfort herself.

Holding the light out in front of her, she made her way through the kitchen, where dishes and glasses lay shattered on cracked linoleum. Then she moved down the hallway. On the left was the bathroom. The shower curtain had been ripped down, the mirror on the medicine cabinet smashed. To her right was what she guessed to be Evie's bedroom. The door was opened just a crack. It was covered with red paint—not blood, definitely not blood, Phoebe assured herself. It was rough, slapped on in a hurry, but in a second she recognized it. The same symbol Sam found on their car when they made it out of the woods.

Teilo, Sam had whispered. *The King of the Fairies.*

Phoebe held her breath and gently toed the door open, swing-ing her body into the door frame, pointing her light like a gun, secretly wishing it was one.

And what was it she thought she'd see? A fairy? Tinker Bell, she could handle. The bastards behind what happened to them at the cabin were another matter. But she saw no movement, no sign of life, human or otherwise.

The mattress was overturned and eviscerated. Feathers from a down comforter covered the floor like fluffy Christmas snow. Magazines and books were scattered, as were clothes. A small chest of drawers stood empty, all the drawers pulled out and smashed to useless splinters. The sliding doors to the closet were closed, and from behind it Phoebe heard a small thump, then a dragging sound.

Phoebe froze, listening.

Her mind flashed to the sounds she would hear at night as a kid, the scuttling and scraping beneath her bed. She'd lie with her head under the pillow using all of her power to try to convince herself that it was just her imagination. Then, eventually, she'd need air and she'd lift the pillow slowly, tell-ing herself that she'd keep her eyes closed, but she always looked. And he was always there. Standing at the foot of her bed.

There was another muffled thud from inside Evie's closet.

Cold sweat beaded on Phoebe's forehead.

She used to think it was her mother's fault. That he only came into houses with drunk mothers who never checked on their daughters; that maybe it was really her mother he was after and he was just waiting for Phoebe to fall asleep so he could go get her ma.

She told herself that maybe it was all just her imagination. Maybe she was going nuts. One time her ma drank so much, she hallucinated cockroaches everywhere. Maybe it was like that.

But she knew it wasn't true.

And what did she think now, at thirty-five? Now that she was supposed to know better?

There was another thump from inside the closet and Phoebe's bowels felt icy.

You're way too old for the bogeyman, she told herself.

She raised the flashlight, counted to three, and jerked the door open.

Evie was there, crouched on the closet floor among mismatched shoes, dressed only in bra and panties. She still had on the silver chain with the old key dangling from the end. Her lips quivered, and her narrow face was flushed and wet with tears. She had feathers from the comforter in her tangled hair. Her left eye was nearly swollen closed. In her hands she held a small handgun, which was pointed directly at Phoebe's chest.

Phoebe moved the light out of Evie's eyes and cast it back at her own face.

"Evie," she said in her calmest voice, "it's me, Phoebe. I'm here to help. Put down the gun."

There was no relieved recognition in the other woman's eyes. The gun stayed pointed at Phoebe's chest, the hand that held it trembling.

Phoebe licked her lips, took in a breath. If Evie shot her now, even if it was an accident, she'd be killing two people. What was she thinking coming here? It wasn't just her life she was putting in danger. What kind of mother-to-be made choices like that?

"They came," Evie whimpered. "They said they'd be back."

"Then we better get moving, okay?" Phoebe whispered. "I'm going to take you someplace safe. Just put down the gun and we'll get you dressed and be on our way, okay?"

Slowly, reluctantly almost, Evie lowered the gun. She looked so broken there, crouched on the closet floor in her underwear. Bones and tendons bulging out, making her look more like a puppet than a flesh-and-blood person. Phoebe held out her hand.

"I've got you," she said, helping Evie up. "You're safe now."

W here have you been?" Sam demanded. Then, as she walked through the door, his eyes fell on his cousin.

"Evie? What the hell happened?" he asked.

"Didn't you get my note?" Phoebe asked, pushing past Sam to get some ice from the kitchen. "Didn't you play the message on the machine?" She wrapped the ice in a clean dish towel.

"I didn't see any note," Sam said. "And there were no messages on the machine. I got home an hour ago, saw the groceries still in bags in the kitchen, ice cream melted, and I was worried sick. I tried to get you on your cell, but you left the damn thing on the kitchen counter. I've called everyone we know. I was about to call the cops."

Phoebe came back into the living room and looked for the note, checked the machine, and saw the message had been erased.

"I don't understand," she said.

"Teilo," Evie said, shaking her head. "This is all his work."

Surely no one had come into the house, taken her note, and erased the message. Phoebe must have erased the message herself by accident. And the note . . . shit, there was no explaining the note. She knew damn well she'd left it there.

"I think," Phoebe said, turning back to Evie, "that you should start at the beginning. Tell us everything that happened. But here," she said, handing the ice over, "put this on your eye first. Maybe it'll get some of the swelling down."

She hadn't tried to talk to Evie about the attack. She had grabbed Evie some jeans and a T-shirt and got her out of the apartment and on the highway. Evie rode curled up in the back-seat in a fetal position, a jacket over her head. Phoebe heard Evie counting backward from one hundred over and over. She glanced in the rearview mirror to see Evie's whole body trembling under the jacket.

"I was home. Right . . . duh," Evie said, hitting herself on the head lightly with the hand that wasn't pressing the dish towel full of ice to her eye. "I'm always home. I mean, where else would I be?" She was still shaky, but less so. She licked her chapped lips and looked around the apartment with her one good eye, which fell on the aquariums. "What the hell's all this?" she asked. "Lab rats or something?"

"Phoebe's menagerie," Sam explained. "Home of the broken and neglected. A biting hedgehog, a one-eyed snake, and a couple of rats no one but Phoebe could love."

"No shit?" Evie said, stepping toward the tanks. "You've really got a hedgehog in there?"

Phoebe nodded. "I'll introduce you to him later. In the mean-time, you were telling us what happened at your place?"

"Right," Evie said, taking a seat on the couch. "I was watch-ing some crappy infomercial on TV—you know, do our program and you'll lose thirty pounds, have more self-confidence, and have beautiful people lined up at your door begging for a date. I was sitting in the recliner and must have dozed off. The next thing I know, I open my eyes and it's dark. No TV. No lights. And I have those heavy curtains on my windows, so it's not like much daylight is gonna sneak through there."

Phoebe nodded, remembering how dark the apartment had been, how none of the light switches had worked.

"And the room is . . . full of people." Evie's unhurt eye was wide, panicked at the memory.

"How many people?" Sam asked.

"It felt like ten, but it may have been just three or four. I don't know. They were moving fast. Really fucking fast. Like other-worldly kind of fast."

Phoebe remembered how fast the old woman had run, shedding clothes and years until she was young.

"So what? Are you saying fairies trashed your place?" Sam asked.

"No," Evie said, looking down at her ragged fingernails. "These were no fairies. Not like what we saw when we were kids, anyway. No twinkling little lights. These were people. And they meant business. They clobbered the shit out of me before I could get up from the chair. I barely fought back. I was out cold after the second punch. When I came to, I was still in the chair but stripped down to my underwear. And they had all left. Except for one. I heard this voice calling down from the top of the stairs. *We'll be back*, he says. And I'm thinking, hell no. Then I guess I must have fainted again or something. When I came to, I called you guys. Then I remembered the gun I keep in my closet, inside my left winter boot. I got it just after Elliot was killed—intended to use it to off myself, but I never had the guts. Pathetic, right?" She looked at Phoebe as she said this.

No, Phoebe shook her head. She wanted to take the other woman in her arms, rock her, find a way to fix what was broken.

"Anyway," Evie said, chewing on a nail, spitting the little sliver she'd bitten off onto the floor, "I crawled into the closet, found the gun right where I'd left it, and just stayed put. I was too terrified to do much else."

"Did you get a look at any of them?" Sam asked.

"No. It was dark. And like I said, they all moved so fast."

"What do you think they were after?" Phoebe asked.

"I don't know, but whatever it is, they sure didn't find it. I can't go back there. Shit." She put down the towel of ice and glanced over at Phoebe, her eyes frantic and little-girlish. "What am I going to do?"

"You'll stay here," Phoebe told her. "With us. As long as you need. As long as it takes us to get to the bottom of all of this."

Evie gave her a relieved smile, and Phoebe reached out, took her hand, and squeezed it. Evie's fingers were bony and cold. "You must be starving," Phoebe said. "I'll go fix us all some dinner. Make yourself at home."

W hat were you thinking?" Sam whispered when he came up behind her in the kitchen. Phoebe was putting on water for pasta. "She can't stay here."

Phoebe couldn't believe her ears. She set the pot down, turned up the flame. "She's your cousin, Sam. She's got nowhere else to go."

"But we don't have room. We hardly know her." This was not the Sam she knew. The Sam who was happy to let old college friends he hadn't seen in years crash at their place whenever they were passing through.

Phoebe gave him a puzzled look. "But, Sam—"

"The woman is obviously a fucking basket case," Sam said.

There was an awkward little coughing sound, and they both turned toward the doorway of the kitchen, where Evie stood, leaning against the frame. Her bony shoulders were hunched, her left eye weepy and swollen.

"You're right," she said to Sam, her jaw clenched tight. "I'll go. I can call my mom. Maybe she can drive down and get me."

"No," Phoebe said quickly. "You'll stay with us. We could use your help trying to make sense of all this. You were there that summer."

She wasn't letting go of this link to Sam's past. Evie was the one person other than Sam who might have some actual insight into what happened to Lisa. And the truth of it was, she really liked Evie. She wanted to get to know her, to help her. Evie didn't have anyone else, and Phoebe remembered all too well what that was like. Before Sam, she didn't have anyone. Not anyone who could be counted on.

"This Teilo guy seems to think you're connected, Evie," Phoebe went on. "We all seem to have something he wants. We've got to band together if we're going to get our heads around all of this." She looked at Sam, but he looked away, opened the fridge, then slammed the door shut.

"You forgot to buy beer," he said. "I'll go get some." He stomped out of the kitchen, looking neither Evie nor Phoebe in the eye.

"Sam?" Phoebe called, but she heard the front door close. Then the engine of his truck started in the driveway.

"Son of a bitch," Phoebe mumbled. She couldn't believe Sam would act this way. Not sure of what else to do, she turned back to the cooking, grabbing an onion from the hanging basket above the sink. He'd never walked out on her like that. This is exactly what she would have expected from the other guys she used to date—the lowlifes whose big idea of communication was asking if she wanted to get high first or just go straight for the bedroom.

"I should go," Evie said. "Sam obviously doesn't want me here."

Phoebe sliced into the onion and shook her head. "He'll come around. I'm sorry he's being such a jerk. He's just a little overwhelmed right now. He doesn't deal well with change, and a lot has happened in the past few days."

And all this was without even mentioning the baby. What was going to happen when she told him?

Her eyes began to water, and she wiped at them with the back of her hand. Goddamn it. She was not going to cry. Phoebe did not cry. Not in front of people.

Evie moved to stand next to her.

"I used to like to cook," Evie told her. "Back when Elton and I . . ." Her voice trailed off.

Elton? Who the hell was Elton?

She must have been flustered, Phoebe told herself. Because surely, if he was the great love of her life, she wasn't going to forget that his name was Elliot, not Elton, right?

"Sam and I both hate cooking," Phoebe confessed. "We'd live on takeout if we could."

"If you want to shop, I can definitely do the cooking. There aren't any grocery stores that deliver up in Burlington, so I lived on whatever the pizza guy could bring—I'd be glad never to see another pizza box."

"Deal," Phoebe said.

Evie reached for the loaf of white bread on the counter (it was Phoebe's—Sam only ate organic sprouted wheat bread). "May I?"

Phoebe nodded. Evie slathered a piece of bread with butter, then spooned sugar onto it. It was a treat Phoebe hadn't had since she was a kid.

"Want one?" Evie asked with a mischievous smile.

"Absolutely."

It was so good, they each had a second slice.

CHAPTER 18

Lisa

W ere you in the woods last night?" Lisa whispered to Da before breakfast the next morning. He was still on the couch in his ratty old pajamas. He just stared straight ahead, a little bit of spit leaking out of the corner of his down-turned mouth. He didn't even seem to notice she was there.

"I found your Red Sox cap," she said. Still nothing.

What exactly had Pinkie seen? A no-faced bogeyman with Da's cap? It didn't make any sense. She'd gone to Da's studio in the garage and found the coveralls but no hat. The garage was unlocked, as always. Anyone could have come in and taken the hat. But why?

Was it possible that Da had gotten up himself and went shuffling off through the woods like a zombie?

Her mom and Aunt Hazel were in the kitchen having one of their whisper fights while Hazel made breakfast. Lisa heard only a few words: *Too much. Remembers. Too far.*

They'd been fighting like this for days now. The longer her dad stayed sick and silent with no sign of getting better, the tenser things became. Now she heard her mom questioning Hazel about the medications and if she was sure she was giving them right. Their whispers had escalated into near shouts.

"Would you rather hire a nurse? A stranger?" Hazel snapped.

Lisa's mom mumbled something Lisa didn't catch.

"Then let me do my job," Hazel said.

After a minute, Lisa smelled something burning.

"Is something on fire?" Lisa yelled from the living room.

"Shit!" Hazel yelped. Then there was a banging and the sound of water running.

The chaos in the kitchen was interrupted by a loud rapping knock at the front door. *Weird*, Lisa thought—it was only a little after seven. Lisa's mom came through the living room to answer it, looking frazzled and annoyed but taking a breath and smiling before opening the door. After a quick greeting, she went out onto the front porch, shutting the door behind her. Lisa got up and leaned around the edge of the couch so she could see out the window. Gerald and his mother were on the porch. Gerald had a cast on his arm. He stared down at his feet, said nothing. His mother was doing all the talking, her voice loud, her arms gesturing in tight little patterns as they cut through the air. Lisa knew Gerald's dad had left them a few months ago and his mom worked full-time waitressing at Jenny's Café, plus cooked and cleaned and made sure Pinkie got to her oboe lessons. Now she had to deal with the fact that some neighborhood kid had busted her son's arm. Not just any kid, but Evie.

And what, if anything, had Pinkie told her about what she saw in the woods last night?

Gerald ran his foot along the peeling paint on the floorboards while his mother went on and on. She was a skinny woman with bleached-out hair and bad teeth. She had on her blue waitress-ing apron and clunky white shoes. Lisa watched her own mother nodding, arms folded tight over her belly. She didn't seem to be saying much. At last they said their good-byes and Lisa's mom came into the house, her face tight.

"Does anyone know where Evie is?" she asked.

"Sleeping. In my room." Lisa answered.

Hazel came out of the kitchen, wiping her hands on a dish towel. "What's she done now?" she asked.

"It seems there was some trouble in the woods yesterday. But don't worry," Lisa's mom said. "I'll take care of it. You just see to breakfast."

"But I—" Hazel started to say, and Lisa's mom flashed her a look that made her snap her jaw closed.

Lisa listened to her mother's footsteps climb the stairs. A door opened, then closed. Her mother began to yell. It was hard to make out just what she was saying, but Lisa caught the gist of it: Evie had crossed the line. Lisa's mom had never had much patience for Evie—she was quick to lose her temper with her and to chastise Hazel for letting Evie run wild the way she did.

Evie began to yell back, and then there was a crashing sound. Lisa headed for the stairs, thinking she'd do whatever she could to keep Evie from getting into any more trouble. Evie would listen to her. Lisa was on the first step when Hazel grabbed her shoulder.

"Better not," Hazel said.

"Maybe you should go up. Just see if they're okay?" Lisa's voice sounded whiny and desperate. She wasn't sure who she was more afraid for up there—her mother or Evie. She remembered the way Evie's hand went for her knife when Gerald was down on the ground.

"Your mother has it under control, I'm sure," Hazel said.

Lisa nodded, went back over to the couch.

Everything around her was all topsy-turvy. And there was Da in the center of it, looking peaceful and oblivious. Lisa wanted, more than anything else, to join him there.

"What's it like where you are, Da?" Lisa asked. She gently put her head against his. His skin was hot and he smelled yeasty, like sourdough bread.

"Your father's right here with us," Aunt Hazel said. She had his pills in a little plastic cup in one hand, a glass of water in the other. Hazel looked tired. More disheveled than usual. And Lisa smelled the sweet, sickly scent of booze coming from her. What kind of person poured themselves a drink at seven in the morning?

"It doesn't even seem like he can hear me."

Hazel smiled. "Oh, he hears you. He knows everything that's going on. Don't you, Dave?" Then gently, carefully, she parted his lips, put the pills on his tongue, fed him a sip of water.

"Swallow now, Dave," she said. "That's it. Good boy."

"Could he get up on his own? And go for a walk or something?"

Hazel shook her head. "No. But he'll be able to soon, isn't that right, Dave?"

The water dribbled down his chin, and one of the pills came with it. Hazel gently poked it back into his mouth.

Lisa stood up, turned away from the wrecked creature who only vaguely resembled her father.

And she stopped then, right there, closed her eyes, and made herself remember three things she loved about him: the way he talked in a bad Italian accent when he cooked spaghetti and meatballs every Friday night, the song about Lydia the tattooed lady he'd sing when he was shaving, the way he called her Beanpole.

"You keep growing like this, you're gonna shoot straight up into the sky, Beanpole," he'd told her, tousling her hair. "The clouds will sit on top of your head like dusty old wigs."

"Maybe I'll meet a giant up there," she'd said.

"Are you kidding? You're going to *be* the giant!"

She'd laughed, called out "Fee Fi Fo Fum!," sending Da running through the house, she chasing after him, making the floorboards shake with her heavy footsteps.

But already, it all felt made up. Invented somehow. Like something from a story that began *Once upon a time*.

She opened her eyes just in time to catch Evie charging down the stairs, across the hall, and into the kitchen. Her face was red, wet, and swollen-looking.

"Evie? Wait!"

"Leave me alone!" Evie snapped, heading out the side kitchen door and into the yard. Lisa stood at the sink, looking out the window above it, watching Evie run for the woods, for Reliance.

Lisa waited around most of the day, but Evie didn't come back. Lisa went in and out of the house, paced around the yard, picked some strawberries in the garden that was choked with weeds, and ate them for lunch. The yard had turned into an overgrown field—cutting it had always been Da's job. Sometimes Sammy would help, but he hadn't been able to get the mower started.

"Where's Evie at anyway?" Sammy asked when he caught Lisa playing solitaire at the kitchen table.

Lisa shrugged. Sam got a peanut butter sandwich and went back up to his room to do whatever it was he did up there—read, experiment with his chemistry set, watch his ant farm.

It was a little before suppertime when Lisa finally decided to go look for Evie. She headed across the tall grass of their backyard and into the woods, which seemed dark and cold. Every sound made her jump. Twigs cracked. Birds shrieked. Everything seemed to be warning her to leave. Run now. She heard a strange bird call, something unfamiliar and sad—a sound that went right to her belly and stayed there.

"Evie?" she called out.

This was silly. There was no need to be such a scaredy-cat. She took a deep breath and walked slowly, showing the woods she wasn't afraid.

She wound her way down the hill toward the brook, but there were more sounds than just birds and running water. Voices. From up ahead. She stopped just before the brook, ducked behind a big sugar maple, heart pounding. On the other side of the brook, Evie was talking with Gerald. Not shouting or going for his throat but actually talking. Weird. Evie was shouldering her black knapsack, which looked full and heavy. Gerald's arm was strapped up in a sling, the lower part wrapped in a thick plaster cast. His fingers jutted out from the end of the cast, swollen and purplish. He was nodding at whatever Evie was saying. Pinkie was standing off to the side like a little guard dog, with her lower jaw jutting out. She was picking at a bug bite on her hand, making it bleed.

"Why should we believe you?" Pinkie asked.

Evie mumbled something Lisa couldn't catch. She took off her backpack, handed it over to Pinkie who unzipped it. Pinkie and Gerald peered inside.

"Just do what I said and you'll see," Evie said.

Gerald took the backpack, awkwardly sliding it onto his good shoulder with one hand.

Evie nodded at them, then walked away with a funny duck-footed swagger, her big work boots snapping twigs, crushing ferns and saplings. Lisa hid behind a tree, holding her breath while Evie crossed the brook and walked by, not five feet from where she stood.

Gerald and Pinkie watched her go, then they turned to go back into the woods, toward Reliance.

"I think she's full of crap," Gerald said. Lisa's fingers clawed at the bark of the tree she was hiding behind. What was Evie doing with these two? "She's just trying to make us look like idiots," Gerald continued.

"But just think," Pinkie said, her voice all soft and dreamy. "What if she's right?"

CHAPTER 19

Phoebe

Cognitive therapy for the agoraphobic patient?" Franny waved the page that had just come out of the printer. "What on earth is this for?"

Usually, when Phoebe used the computer and printer at work for personal stuff, it was to look up her horoscope or print some word scrambles to do on her lunch break. It was a habit she'd picked up from her mother (one of the few, thank God), who always said word puzzles kept the mind limber and that it was a proven fact that people who did them were less likely to get Alzheimer's. Her ma could sit on the couch all day, TV tuned to talk shows and soap operas, tumbler of booze in one hand, a pencil in the other, as she worked her way through the puzzle books she'd picked up at the checkout line. It was the most constructive thing her ma ever did.

Phoebe wasn't much of a reader, but she liked a good puzzle. There was something deeply satisfying about making sense of all the jumbled letters, turning them into a word or sentence you could actually read.

"I mean," whispered Franny, leaning down so that their shoulders were touching, "shouldn't you be researching baby names or something?" She gave Phoebe a conspiratorial smile, and Phoebe felt a split-second ache—a wish that her mother were here so she could share the news of her pregnancy, ask her advice on names. But then reality hit and Phoebe knew that even if her ma was alive, she was the last person on earth Phoebe would confide in or ask for bits of motherly wisdom.

This was, after all, the woman who went down to Florida on the back of some loser's Harley when she was five months pregnant with Phoebe, cranked on amphetamines, shooting pool at roadside dives.

"It was the closest thing to a family I ever had," her mother explained wistfully to Phoebe years later.

"Was he my father?" Phoebe asked.

Her mom laughed. "Al? No!"

"Then who was he? My father?"

Her mother's eyes narrowed as she focused on some faraway object Phoebe couldn't see. "Your father was just some drifter who dumped me as soon as he heard I was knocked up. Left without a trace."

"But you must have known something about him? What was his name? Where was he from?"

Her ma shook her head. "His name's not important. It's not like you can go look him up. He wasn't from anywhere, Bee. He moved from town to town picking fruit and tobacco, emptying trucks. He went where the work was or wherever there was a pretty lady to buy him a drink. He was a looker, that's for sure. Handsome in an old-fashioned movie star way." Her mother smiled, then shook her head. "Then I met Al. God closes one door, opens up another. Al and his biker friends, they took me right in. They called me Mama Bear. They gave me that tattoo I have on my chest. The little heart. It was for you. I wanted something with your name, but I didn't know who you were yet, so I had them write the letter S. S for sweetheart."

Phoebe had grown up thinking the botched and blurred tattoo was supposed to be the S for Superman.

"Weren't you afraid of hepatitis? AIDS? And did you even wear a helmet on the motorcycle?" Phoebe asked.

Her mother laughed. "Sometimes, my little sweetheart, you've just gotta live. Feel the wind in your hair."

Phoebe blinked at Franny and shook her head. "Sam's cousin Evie," she explained, putting away the little memo pad she'd been taking notes in. "She's been staying with us this week."

"And she's agoraphobic?"

Phoebe nodded.

"No kidding? Is she on meds?"

"No. She's tried them but says they just made her worse. The pills just gave her one more thing to be anxious about."

"God, I kind of remember her from when we were kids. She'd come visit sometimes. Kind of a chunky kid. Bad asthma. People were mean to her. Real mean. It's horrible, the things kids do to each other." Franny shivered. "So what's she like now?"

Phoebe thought for a few seconds. "Careful. Guarded. Hard to get to know, but I think she's warming up to me. She seems less panicky around me anyway."

Phoebe had written off to good old-fashioned anxiety the fact that Evie had gotten Elliot's name wrong. Here was a woman with a true disorder in a totally unfamiliar environment—of course she's going to misspeak. And since then, she'd called him Elliot several times, no hesitation.

With Sam working overtime at the tree service and Phoebe's hours at the clinic cut back for summer, she'd spent a lot of time alone with Evie. She'd bought Evie some basic toiletries along with new pants and T-shirts from Walmart (another place of mass consumption that Phoebe adored and Sam didn't approve of).

When they were together, Phoebe did most of the talking. Evie listened, smiling as if everything that came out of Phoebe's mouth was vaguely amusing to her. And Evie was in love with the animals, especially the python, which she took out and draped around her neck daily. She even made little salads for the rats and hedgehog.

When she wasn't fawning over the pets, Evie spent her days reading and cleaning the house. At night she cooked. Evie seemed to love the comfort foods Phoebe had grown up with and had stopped eating entirely when she got together with Sam. Phoebe bought Hamburger Helper, Kraft macaroni and cheese, white bread and bologna. One night they ate peanut butter and fluff sandwiches, giggling like girls. Sam rarely shared dinner with them—either coming home late or claiming he'd already eaten and wasn't hungry. He did little to hide his revulsion of the new food in the house.

He'd pick up the boxes, reading the list of ingredients out loud. "Sodium tripolyphosphate, yellow five, yellow six, monosodium glutamate. Jesus, do you have any idea what this stuff is? What it does to your body? Those artificial colors cause cancer in lab rats, did you know that?"

"Good thing we're not lab rats," Phoebe shot back, diving into her dinner with relish.

Phoebe knew it shouldn't bother her, that Sam was only concerned about her health, not trying to be a holier-than-thou food zealot, but the pregnancy hormones made it hard for her to keep her emotions in check.

When he was finished making some harsh judgment about their dinner, he'd head into the office to use the computer. He was spending hours alone online every night, creeping into bed at one or two in the morning. Phoebe would wake up startled and look at the clock on the bedside table, which also held a glass of water, pencils, memo pads, the strange little sack of horse teeth, and the word-puzzle books she'd do until she fell asleep.

"Are you just coming to bed now?" she asked last night when she'd caught him, sure that she'd felt him beside her just moments ago, his body warm, his breath slightly faster than her own.

She must have been dreaming.

"Yeah," Sam said, settling into bed beside her. "I was on the computer."

"What are you working on?" Phoebe asked.

Sam shrugged. "Nothing. Just messing around."

So what, you and Sam are running a kind of halfway house now?" Franny asked.

Phoebe remembered what Sam had said when Evie first noticed the pets: *Phoebe's menagerie. Home of the broken and neglected.*

"You're going to try to cure this cousin?" Franny asked.

Phoebe shook her head. "I just want to help. This poor girl has nobody else."

But the truth was, she did want to cure Evie, didn't she? It was her nature to take what was broken and try to fix it. A shrink would probably tell her it was because she'd spent her whole childhood wishing she could fix her ma but being completely helpless. This deep-seated kind of masochistic need to keep trying again and again to get it right and actually save someone. Isn't that, on some small level, what drew her to Sam? She fell in love with people's frailty, their brokenness. But the deeper she delved into the things that made Sam broken, the more she wondered if it was possible to fix him. Would Lisa's return make things all right? If they traveled to Reliance tonight, as they were planning, and met her there under the full moon, would Sam somehow be whole again?

Fixing Evie seemed more realistic. Especially now that she had a road map. The key, according to her research, seemed to involve desensitizing her. She would start small, encourage Evie to take baby steps: going out on the porch to get the mail. Then to the driveway. Then down the driveway to the street. Before Evie knew it, she'd be walking around the block.

"So she and Sam are pretty close then?"

Phoebe shook her head. "Not at all. They were when they were kids. They spent every summer together. But now they're like strangers. Sam's really pissed that Evie's staying with us. He's being kind of a prick."

Kind of? The very fact that Phoebe felt the need to down-play just how bad Sam had been acting worried her. The truth was, Phoebe was horrified by Sam's behavior toward his cousin, which ranged from practically ignoring Evie to flat-out, no-holds-barred animosity. In the past five days, Sam had pulled away from Phoebe and turned into someone she hardly recognized.

"Maybe he's scared," Franny said.

"Scared?"

Franny shrugged her shoulders. "Just a guess. I'm not the one reading all the psychology stuff online." She gave Phoebe a wink.

"Maybe," Phoebe said.

Just this morning, when she'd cornered Sam about why he was being so cold to his cousin, he said there was a lot Phoebe didn't understand. They were still in bed, speaking in hushed tones.

"Like what?" she'd asked.

Sam hopped out of bed, pulled on his jeans. "There was something going on between Lisa and her that summer."

"What do you mean?" Phoebe had asked.

"I don't know. They were together all the time, whispering. Wearing each other's clothes. They started locking the door to their room." He sat on the edge of the bed lacing his boots.

"I don't think that's so weird, Sam," Phoebe had said, pulling the covers up to her chin. "They were twelve and thirteen. They were just being girls."

Sam shook his head. "There's other stuff, too."

"What stuff?"

Sam looked away. "Nothing. Forget it. All I'm saying is that Evie shouldn't be trusted. I don't like you spending all this time alone with her." He stood and went for the door.

"What—is she supposed to be some deviant or something? Dangerous even? Because of the kid you remember her being at thirteen? I look at her and you know what I see, Sam? A broken woman. I don't know what's sadder—the way she is or the way I see you treating her."

Sam slipped out of the room without responding.

I think," Phoebe said, turning back toward Franny, "it's that Evie reminds him of Lisa. Of what happened to her. Sam has spent years building this wall around that part of his life. Now Evie's come in with a big old sledgehammer."

Franny made a note in a chart and put it on the desk to be filed. "Poor thing," she said, and Phoebe wasn't sure which one of them she was referring to: Sam or Evie.

"So how'd he take it?" Franny asked.

"Huh?" Phoebe said.

"Sam," Franny said. "He's over the moon about the baby, right?"

Phoebe bit her lip. "I umm, haven't exactly told him yet."

"You what?" Franny took a step back and gave Phoebe a puzzled look. "Why on earth not?"

"It's just that we've been a little preoccupied, you know, with Evie staying with us. And remember that crazy card we got? Tonight's the night we're supposed to go meet his long-lost sister in Reliance."

"Are you going? Out into those woods?"

Phoebe nodded. "That's the plan. I doubt anyone will show up though. Dr. O. is probably right—someone's just messing around with Sam. But still, we have to check it out, don't we?"

"You want me and Jim to come with you? We could round up some of our friends, too. It might be safer to go in with more people. And to be armed, maybe."

Phoebe shook her head, knowing that if there was even the faintest chance that Lisa might be waiting for them out there, the last thing in the world they wanted to do was scare her off with a parade of kooky survivalist types with guns. "Thanks anyway. I think Sam and I will be fine."

"It'll be a good opportunity for you to tell him about the baby."

Phoebe nodded. "Things have been so damn crazy. There just hasn't been a right time."

Franny shook her head. "If you keep on waiting around for the perfect time, Bee, he's not going to find out till you're in labor! You've gotta tell him. Now. Tonight."

Phoebe nodded. "I will," she promised.

Franny and Dr. Ostrum were both in an emergency surgery. Mrs. Laluk's cat, Queenie, had swallowed a four-foot piece of ribbon. Phoebe checked her watch. Only three-thirty. An hour and a half until closing time. She was itching to get out of there, get home, and go with Sam to Reliance as soon as it got dark. She pulled a mirror out of the backup purse she'd been using and touched up her lipstick. It seemed stupid really, carrying a purse for just her lipstick, notebook, keys, and cell phone. She was going to have to accept the fact that her wallet was gone for good and get a new one. The stuff they'd had taken from the cabin wasn't just going to miraculously show up. She'd have to go to the DMV and stand in line for a new license. She picked up the phone to call Sam again, then set it down.

She'd tried calling Sam on his cell phone four times so far to check in, make sure the plan was still on, but he didn't pick up. She'd left three messages and he hadn't called back. It was one thing to be rude to his cousin, but closing Phoebe out was inexcusable. And it made telling him about the pregnancy damn near impossible. Her thoughts were going in circles as she skimmed over the agoraphobia printouts, unable to concentrate. She put the printed pages in her bag and dug out her little memo pad.

She grabbed a pen and wrote:

CLUES & LEADS

She chewed on the end of the pen, thinking, then wrote:

> *Mass plates on fake Evie's car*
> *Notes from Lisa? Looks like Lisa's writing.*
> *Evie's apartment trashed—why?*
> *They knew about Elliot—how?*
> *Man in the cabin must know something—go back and talk to him?*
> *Changeling girl: Amy Pelletier, Castleton State College*
> *A girl named Becca who might remember something—CALL HER!*
> *Reliance: legends. What happened to all those people? Does it have anything to do with what happened to Lisa?*

Pleased to have come up with some actions she could actually do right now, Phoebe pulled out the phone book, found the number for Castleton State College.

"Yes, I'm trying to reach my niece. She's a student there. There's been a family emergency and it's very important that we get in touch with her. Her name is Amy Pelletier."

"I'm sorry, ma'am, it's against our policy to give out any kind of information about a student."

"But I'm family! And this is an emergency."

"The best I can do is take a message and see that it gets to her. What's the student's name again?"

"Pelletier. Amy Pelletier."

Phoebe heard keyboard tapping.

"I'm sorry. We don't have an Amy Pelletier registered here."

"Are you sure?"

"Positive. Not an active student, and she's not listed as an alum either."

"Thank you," Phoebe said. She shouldn't have been surprised. She herself had once had a fake college ID she used at bars when she was nineteen—it was easy enough to get. The girl could be anyone from anywhere.

Phoebe turned to the computer and did a search for Reliance, Vermont. Not much turned up. A few brief mentions here and there. And then, an excerpt from an out-of-print book called *Lost Vermont: An Historical Perspective*.

> *Little is known about the village of Reliance. All that remains are the foundations and cellar holes of several homes and barns, a church and blacksmith shop. A small stream runs along the western edge. In the northwest corner is a small cemetery, the names and dates on the stones illegible. In 1918, according to local legend, the entire population of the town (approximately forty) disappeared.*

"Duh," Phoebe said out loud. She clicked around uselessly for another five minutes or so, then gave up.

Next, Phoebe looked up the number for Price Chopper in St. Johnsbury, dialed it, and asked for the floral department.

"Hi, I'm looking for an employee named Becca?"

"You got her. Who's this?"

"This is going to be a little out of the blue, but I'm a close friend of Sam Nazzaro's. I was hoping I could ask you a couple of questions."

"Seriously? How did you find me here?"

"Franny Hunt told me she'd run into you at work."

"Is this about Lisa?" Becca asked, her voice much more animated. "Have they found Lisa?"

"No," Phoebe said. "I was wondering if you could tell me about that summer. I understand you and your brother were friends with Lisa, Sam, and Evie."

God. She sounded like some TV cop. And a really bad one at that.

Becca laughed. "Not Evie. No one liked Evie. No one but Lisa. But I'm sure Sam told you all that already. I bet he told you how close the two of them were. Like little love birds. Kinda sick, actually."

"Uh huh," Phoebe said. She was taking notes in her memo pad: *Love birds. No one liked Evie.*

"I'm also guessing there are things he hasn't told you. Lots of things."

"Like what?" Phoebe asked, drawing a question mark in the margins.

"Does he know you're calling me?"

"No, I swear. Franny told me you were friends. That you might be able to tell me something new. I won't tell Sam we talked. I promise."

"Sammy Nazzaro. God, I haven't thought of him in ages. We moved out of town that fall—right after Lisa disappeared. I think my mom was trying to keep us safe—out of those woods. And away from that family."

"Sam's family?"

"Evie broke my brother Gerald's arm that summer. Did Sammy tell you?"

"No," Phoebe admitted.

"Evie, she was nuts. One time she tried to convince us that her blood was green. That she was some kind of alien or something. 'I'll prove it,' she kept saying, then she goes and jabs herself in the thigh with her big old freaking hunting knife. Shit! Her blood was red as red could be. The girl was crazy. Certifiable. But it ran in the family. Everyone in that house was wacko."

"They were?"

Phoebe heard Becca cover the phone and say, "Yeah, I know. I'm going on break."

"If this isn't a good time . . ." Phoebe started to say.

"It's fine," Becca said. "Call me back on my cell phone in two minutes. I'll be outside on break."

Phoebe scribbled down the number Becca gave her in her memo pad, waited two minutes, and called. Becca picked up after the first ring.

"Where were we?" she asked.

"You said everyone in the family was crazy."

"Uh huh. Well for starters, there's Sam and Lisa's dad, right? He was an odd one. Moody as hell. He almost never left the house, a real recluse. He offed himself that summer. He'd tried before, but they had found him in time."

They were both silent a few seconds. Phoebe guessed from the way Becca was breathing that she had a cigarette going.

"Then there was their grandma, their mom's ma," Rebecca continued. "She was nutty as could be. Lived with her father all her life until she had the stroke. No wonder her husband left. Her dad was a creepy old man, that's what my mother always said. The town doctor, but half the folks went to the next town because they didn't want his cold hands anywhere near them. Now Sam and Lisa's mom, Phyllis, she turned out okay. But Hazel drank like a fish, hid bottles in the garage and the shrubs. Sometimes Gerald and I would find them and take a sip. Real rotgut, bottom-shelf stuff. It's no wonder she was such a drunk. Growing up in that house. Getting pregnant so young."

"You mean with Evie?"

"Nah, this was before Evie. She had the baby at home. Her grandfather delivered it. Stillborn, that's what they said. But people in town, my mother for one, they say they heard a baby crying in that house for some time after."

"So what happened to it?" Phoebe asked.

Rebecca sighed. "Don't know. Maybe it really did die eventually. Maybe creepy old Grandpa sacrificed it to the dark lord and drank its blood."

Phoebe shivered.

"Just kidding," Rebecca said. "Probably the lucky kid got adopted into some other normal family."

"What about Lisa?" Phoebe asked. "What was she like?"

Becca was silent a minute. "Everyone said she was just imaginative. But there was more to it than that. She saw things. Heard voices. She said the trees and birds and frogs and shit all talked to her. Would you say a girl like that's just imaginative, or would you think she needed some hardcore psych meds?"

Phoebe nodded, even though Becca couldn't see her. "So what do you think happened to her?"

"I think what I've always thought. Teilo came for her and took her to the land of the fairies."

"Seriously?" Phoebe said.

"Look," Becca answered, "I gotta go. I shouldn't even be talking to you. If he finds out . . ."

"If who finds out?" Phoebe asked.

"Forget it. You want to know what happened to Lisa, you ask Sammy what he saw in the woods that night."

"But Sam wasn't in the woods," Phoebe said.

Becca laughed. "You ask him how he got that big old scar on his chest," she said, then hung up.

CHAPTER 20

Lisa

Were you spying on me?" Evie's breath was hot on her cheek. Lisa had just come out of the woods after watching Gerald and Pinkie head down to Reliance with the backpack Evie had given them. Evie had been lying in wait in the tall grass, and as soon as Lisa got into the yard, Evie pounced, tackling her. Now Evie was on top of her, pinning her down.

"No, I wasn't spying," Lisa said, struggling to get a breath. "I just went for a walk." Evie was sitting on her stomach, leaning over her chest. She held Lisa's arms up above her head. Evie outweighed Lisa by at least a good thirty pounds. She wasn't going anywhere. The key on a string dangled down from Evie's neck, hitting Lisa's face.

"Bullcrap. You were following me."

"I didn't even know you were out here. Now get off me!"

Evie's grip tightened on Lisa's arms.

"Please?" Lisa begged. "I'm kinda suffocating here."

Evie rolled off her.

"I think you should stay out of the woods. Quit going down to that cellar hole," Evie said. She took out her knife and started to use it to cut one blade of grass at a time, making a neat little pile.

"Why?" Lisa asked, squinting at her cousin. "Don't you get it? Whatever's going on down in Reliance is the most magical thing that's ever happened to me, to any of us. Don't you want to figure out what's happening here?"

It wasn't like Evie to want to give anything up or leave any mystery unsolved. Evie wasn't acting much like Evie these days. The old Evie would have clobbered the crap out of Gerald before conspiring with him in the woods.

But then again, no one in her family was being very normal. Maybe there was a spell on all of them. A curse from a wicked witch.

"Because this is getting too weird. At first I thought it was just someone playing a joke, you know? But now I'm thinking it's kind of creepy. And what if it's like . . . like a trap or something?" Evie turned, continued adding to her grass pile.

Lisa laughed. "It's not a trap," she said.

"How do you know?" Evie asked.

"Because they wouldn't do something like that."

"They?"

"The fairies," Lisa explained.

Evie shook her head. "Jeez-us!" She stabbed the knife hard into the lawn so that only the handle stuck out. "This isn't one of your freaking stories, Lisa. This is real life."

"Exactly," Lisa said. "And that's why I keep going back. Because this is really happening. They're down there. And before the summer's over, I'm going to find a way to prove it."

"Just say you're right," Evie said. "Say the fairies are real. What if it was them that made that whole town disappear?"

"Exactly!" said Lisa, excited that Evie was finally starting to get the importance of what was happening.

Evie shook her head, pulled the knife out of the ground, and wiped the dirty blade off on her sleeve. "If they did that to a whole town, just think what they could do to one twelve-year-old girl."

Lisa took a breath, watched Evie clean her knife. The fairies weren't dangerous. How could Evie think they were?

"You shouldn't be down there alone," Evie said.

Maybe it wasn't that Evie was worried or scared about what was happening in Reliance. Maybe she was just jealous.

"Okay," Lisa agreed, crossing her fingers behind her back. "We'll go together next time."

"Promise you won't sneak off on your own?"

"Promise."

Evie put her knife in its sheath and lay down on her back in the grass beside Lisa. She blew out a long, dramatic breath.

Lisa turned to Evie. "I think it's sweet that you want to protect me," she whispered. "But I don't really need protecting." She felt Evie's body stiffen beside her. Lisa pushed herself up on her elbow and studied her cousin. Evie's body seemed all wrong to Lisa. Her forehead too broad, her nose too small for her round face. It was like Evie was put together from a bunch of mismatched parts.

"Evie?"

"Yeah?"

"I heard my mom yelling at you earlier. About Gerald. It sounded bad."

Evie chomped on her lower lip and shrugged. "It wasn't too bad, I guess. Aunt Phyllis said I'd gone too far. And that I need to stay away from Gerald. His mom's real pissed. His arm's broken in three places." She gave the tiniest hint of a smile.

Lisa nodded, thinking her mom's warning must not have sunk in at all if Evie was already having secret meetings with Gerald.

"Has your mom said anything to you lately? About my dad, I mean?"

Evie was quiet a minute, staring up at the sky. "Nah," she said at last.

"What do you think? About Da? Does he seem any better to you?"

"I don't know, Lisa."

"That's bull. Tell me the truth, Evie. This is me."

She sighed, turned onto her side, inching a little closer to Lisa. Her breath smelled sweet and fruity. "He seems the same, I guess. No better, no worse."

"He's like a zombie," Lisa said. "Some days I look at him and I don't think he's inside there at all. I talk to him, get right up in his face, and whisper in his ear, and he just looks right through me."

She thought of the Red Sox cap she'd found in the woods—the one Pinkie's bogeyman had been wearing. Was it possible Da had gotten up? If it wasn't him, who'd taken his hat?

"It's like he's an empty husk," Lisa continued. "I don't know if it's the sickness or all the medicine they've got him on."

Evie chewed her lip, considering. "A little of both, probably. But he's in there, still. I can tell."

Lisa shook her head. "I feel like I don't have a dad at all anymore." As soon as she said it, she realized it was a dumb thing to say to Evie, who'd never known her dad. No one even knew who her dad was. When Hazel got pregnant at sixteen, everyone had their theories—it was a married man with a family of his own;

she was raped; it was the retarded janitor in the nursing home where she worked weekends; it was one of the male residents of the home. Lisa had grown up hearing everyone around her discuss it in hushed conversation: her parents, the people in Jenny's Café, even old ladies who volunteered at the town library—they all wondered who Evie's father might be.

"I'm sorry," Lisa told her. "That was a dumb-ass thing to say."

Evie shook her head. "Don't worry about it."

"Do you ever think about it?" Lisa asked. "Who your dad might be?"

She didn't answer.

"Evie?"

"No one would believe us if we told."

Lisa sat up. "So what? You're saying you know who he is? She told you?"

"Forget it," Evie said.

"Evie." She put her hand on Evie's arm. "You're not allowed to keep secrets from me, remember? Especially not something this big."

Evie frowned, plucked up a handful of grass. "There's a lot you don't know," she said.

"So tell me," Lisa said. Lisa crossed her fingers, showed them to Evie. "We're like this, you and me. Remember?"

Evie closed her eyes. "Remember what I said about how I started going to church?"

"Yeah."

"There's this picture there, in stained glass. It's the Virgin Mary. She's got on that blue robe, and her face is all serene and peaceful. But you look down, and there, under her bare foot, is this huge snake. And she's holding it there, crushing it."

Lisa nodded. She couldn't imagine where Evie was going with this, but she wanted her to keep talking. Maybe it would be like a ball rolling downhill—once she started, she'd just keep going, faster and faster, until everything was out and there were no more secrets.

"Sometimes when I'm there, I just scrunch down in the pew and stare at that window. And you know what I'm thinking? I'm thinking—I know how that feels. The snake is like . . . like evil, like secrets, and she's trying to hold it there, to crush it. And maybe she can, 'cause she's Mary, she's the mother of Jesus, but who am I? I'm nobody." Evie's eyes were full of tears.

"Evie," Lisa said, reaching out to stroke Evie's unruly hair. "If you'd just . . ."

"Bioluminescence!" Sammy appeared at their feet, a jar of fireflies in one hand, a net in the other.

"What?" Lisa said, furious that he'd interrupted them. Now Evie would never talk. Evie sat up, rubbing her eyes hard, blinking at Sam.

"Fireflies. Glowworms. Deep-sea marine life. Maybe there are other insects that can do it. Something that hasn't been discovered yet. Maybe that's what we saw in the woods."

He was studying the fireflies in the glass mason jar, blinking green lights.

"What we saw wasn't fireflies!" Lisa snapped. "Or any distant cousins of fireflies."

"Right," Sam said. "Because fairies are the logical choice. Why not leprechauns?"

Evie laughed and said, "Yeah, like the Lucky Charms guy. Magically delicious."

"Would you get serious?" Lisa scolded.

Evie nodded and said, "I'm so serious. This is big, Lisa. *Really* big. Maybe it is the wee folk and they've come to take you to a pot of gold at the end of the rainbow!"

Lisa couldn't believe this was the same person who'd just been telling her about the stained-glass window.

Sammy started singing a horrible, chortling rendition of "Somewhere Over the Rainbow" while Evie quit laughing long enough to gasp, "Stop! You're going to make me pee myself!"

"Would you guys quit it!" Lisa yelled. They only laughed harder, both their faces bright red.

"You're just jealous," Lisa said, but they were too busy making fun to even hear her.

She turned away from Evie and Sam, looked at the old penny and the Saint Christopher medal on her bracelet. It didn't matter what the others thought. Maybe these gifts had a purpose, a reason. Maybe they told a story. Or maybe they were something she'd need at some point—magic charms. Talismans.

There was one thing she was sure of—she was ready to take the next step. And Evie and Sam weren't going to be a part of it.

That night, once she was sure Evie was sound asleep, Lisa snuck back out to the cellar hole on her own and left a note folded neatly under a pile of sugar cubes.

I want to meet you. Please.

CHAPTER 21

Phoebe

JUNE 11, PRESENT DAY

We're on our own tonight," Evie called from the kitchen when Phoebe came through the door, drawn in by an intoxicatingly sweet smell.

"I baked a cake," Evie said. "From that Betty Crocker mix you got. I was going to make pasta, but since it's just you and me, I thought maybe we could skip the pasta and go right for the cake."

"Where's Sam?" Phoebe asked, doing her best not to sound pissed off or disappointed. She headed into the kitchen, watched Evie (who was wearing the python draped around her neck like a scarf) spread blobs of canned vanilla frosting onto the pink, strawberry-flavored cake. Just looking at it made Phoebe's teeth hurt. But the idea of cake for dinner sounded perfect. It was something Sam would never consent to. And the food they cooked at home was always so wholesome—it was nice to take a little break. Even when they went out, it was often to the vegan place Sam loved where everything tasted like paste and she'd once had the misfortune of ordering macaroni and "cheese," not realizing it would be spelt noodles covered in mashed tofu and white beans.

Cake for dinner probably wasn't the best thing for the baby, but it was better than nothing, right? And these days, with her stomach the way it was, she was just grateful that anything at all appealed to her, even if it was pure sugar.

"He left a message on the machine. He's working late, then having dinner with his mom."

Phoebe felt herself stiffen. Sam ate regular dinners there once a month, and when he did, he always brought Phoebe along. Did this mean he'd go straight to Reliance on his own from there? Was he going to tell his mother the truth about everything? Confide in her now that he'd pretty much shut Phoebe out.

"Great," she said, a fake smile plastered on her face. "All the more for you and me."

Phoebe allowed herself one beer even though she knew she shouldn't. She justified this by telling herself that she might not be keeping the baby anyway. Not with things with Sam the way they were. But if they were to make a choice, *that* particular choice, they'd have to move quickly, which meant she needed to take the first step and tell him she was pregnant. But how, with him being so distant? What was she supposed to do—leave him a cell phone message? An e-mail? A note tucked under the wiper of his truck?

"This is really good," Phoebe said, diving into her second piece of cake. "Wait until Sam hears what he missed. He's probably suffering through one of his mom's tofu casseroles right now," Phoebe said. Idiot. How could he just ditch her like that? On this of all nights.

She reached into the pocket of her khakis and touched the little bag of teeth. It was silly, really, keeping it with her. But she felt like it somehow tied her to Lisa. Like if she held on to it, maybe she'd stand a chance of finding out the truth. Phoebe didn't consider herself a superstitious person, but she believed there was more to this world than meets the eye. And carrying around a few ancient horse teeth for luck couldn't hurt, could it? When she'd called Sam's mom to report what Dr. Ostrum said about the teeth, Phyllis had thanked her. Phoebe offered to drop them off, and Phyllis said, "No need to bother, dear. Why don't you keep them? It seems a fitting addition to your odd little collection."

If the teeth were a treasure of Lisa's, then Evie might remember them. Maybe she'd even know the story behind them.

Phoebe pulled the bag from her pocket, placed it on the table.

Evie pushed back in her chair, nearly losing her balance, as if Phoebe had just dropped a severed limb onto the table.

"Where did you get that?" Evie looked at Phoebe with fear and suspicion.

"It was Lisa's," Phoebe said.

"I know," Evie said. "The teeth. All those ugly yellow teeth. They were the first gift he left for her. Before she even knew who he was. He came into her room and left them on her goddamn bed."

"He?"

"Teilo. Where'd you get them, Phoebe? Was it Sam? Did he have Lisa's teeth?"

"They're horse teeth. Old horse teeth."

"I know what they are," Evie said. She was breathing faster

now, struggling a little with each inhalation. "But I don't think you do. You shouldn't have them, Phoebe. Anything of Teilo's, it's full of magic. Bad magic. It links you to him. Do you understand?"

Phoebe nodded, put the teeth back in her pocket. "I don't believe in magic," she said.

"You will," Evie said.

They ate in silence, forks scraping against plates. Their chewing seemed unnaturally loud.

Sorry I freaked out like that," Evie said as she stood to clear the table. There was only one square of cake left, and they'd decided to save it for Sam. "The teeth always kind of creeped me out. And I wasn't expecting to see them again. I thought Lisa had them with her when she left. The teeth and the charm bracelet. The two things she was never without. Her goddamn gifts from the fairies." Evie set the dishes back down on the table, reached into her pocket for her cigarettes. Phoebe knew she should stop her, knew Sam would throw a fit when he came home and smelled cigarette smoke, but what was she supposed to do? It wasn't like she could tell Evie to step outside to light up. "So where'd you get them, Phoebe? Did Sam have them?"

"No. Of course not. Why would Sam have had them?"

"I don't know. I thought maybe you could tell me. He was the last one to see her that night. And I always thought . . ."

"What?" Phoebe asked, sounding more defensive than she'd meant.

"That he knew more than he was saying."

Phoebe considered this, wondering if Sam knew something more about Lisa's disappearance. Mr. Lisa-was-taken-and-there's-nothing-we-can-do-about-it-so-let's-all-just-get-on-with-our-lives. Was it possible he was keeping something from them? Some secret he'd been carrying for fifteen years but which was slowly, steadily clawing its way to the surface? It would certainly help explain why he was acting like such a freak lately.

She remembered her conversation with Becca: *there are things Sam's not telling you.*

"I know it's been hard on you two with me staying here," Evie said.

Phoebe shook her head. "Not at all." She managed another smile, which she sensed Evie saw right through. Evie pushed the hair back out of her eyes.

"Been awhile since I've visited the salon," she said apologetically.

"I could cut it," Phoebe said, worried she'd sounded a tad too enthusiastic. "I mean, if you want me to. I cut Sam's hair. And do some of the grooming at the clinic—not that I'm comparing you to a poodle or anything, but I can handle a pair of scissors."

"I'd love it," Evie said. "Do whatever you want. When I was a kid, I let my hair get so badly tangled once that my mom had to shave me bald. Some people have the head for it. Mine's all lumpy. Lisa said it looked like a stubbly potato."

Phoebe laughed. "No potato haircut. I promise."

They pulled the kitchen table to one side. Evie grabbed a chair and Phoebe fetched the scissors.

"So what's the story with this?" Phoebe asked, touching the key dangling from the chain around Evie's neck.

"Lisa gave it to me. She told me this story that summer about two sisters who went on an adventure with a magic key that was supposed to save them. She said this was the key."

Phoebe walked around Evie, trying to visualize how to turn the dark tangled mop of hair into something a little more stylish.

"Wanna know the crazy thing? I've worn it every day since. I guess I somehow had this idea that one of these days I'd get the chance to use it—that maybe this dumb key was going to help me save Lisa. Stupid, huh?"

"I don't think it's stupid at all."

"I thought you didn't believe in magic," Evie said.

"I don't. But I believe in hope." She went back to studying Evie's hair, wondering where to begin.

"Full moon tonight," Evie said, as if Phoebe didn't know.

"Yeah," she said.

"Do you think he's going to go?" Evie asked. "To Reliance?"

"I have no idea," Phoebe admitted. "We were planning to go together, but he hasn't said anything about it in days. Maybe he's decided to just let the whole thing go. To try to forget about it. He's kind of perfected it to an art over all these years, so why change anything now?" She bit her lip, thinking she'd said too much. The beer had gotten to her, made her feel warm and open. She ran her fingers through Evie's hair, deciding to start at the front.

Sam's warnings echoed in her head: Evie shouldn't be trusted. There was something going on with her and Lisa that summer.

"Sam wasn't always this way, you know," Evie told her as she started cutting.

"What way is that?"

"Closed down. When he was a little boy, he was this fresh, bright-eyed kid—excited all the time, talking nonstop about whatever came into his head. He couldn't keep a secret if you paid him. Until the fairies came." Evie's face darkened.

"So you were there for all of it?" Phoebe asked, tugging at Evie's bangs, shortening them by several inches with one quick snip of the scissors. "What was it like? When they first came?"

Evie closed her eyes, smiled. "First, there were the bells. It was dusk, and we were supposed to be back in the yard before dark, but we followed Lisa over to the other side of the hill. We heard these bells, like wind chimes almost, this tiny tinkling sound coming from Reliance. Lisa saw them first. Little dots of light, flitting from one place to the next."

"What? Like lightning bugs?" Phoebe asked. She worked carefully to trim the hair around Evie's left ear, noticing that it was pierced in three places but that she wore no earrings.

Evie shook her head. "Not at all. It was little white lights, bright and dancing from leaf to leaf, branch to branch, chasing each other down into the old cellar holes. We chased after them, but they all disappeared.

"Lisa knew just what they were. 'Fairies,' she said. She was so excited. The next day, we were back in the cellar hole leaving them gifts. Lisa said that maybe then, if we left presents, they'd let us see them."

"And did they?" Phoebe asked, pausing to step back and assess the back of her hair before she continued cutting. She decided to try to do some layers in the back—something Sam never let her do. Evie's hair was beautiful really, now that it was combed and clean. It was thick and had a natural wave.

"No. Not Sammy and me anyway. It was Lisa they wanted. She was the one Teilo came for." Evie's face twitched a little. Phoebe tried to imagine what it must have been like to be the odd girl out. The one not chosen by the Fairy King. And if Evie and Lisa were as tight as Sam suggested, then it must have been horrible to have Lisa choose the Fairy King over Evie.

"So you never saw him? Never heard him?"

Evie shook her head, which Phoebe grabbed with both her hands, reminding Evie to keep still while she was cutting. "Only Lisa. She said she was the chosen one."

"But how do you know she wasn't making it up? Or that this Teilo wasn't just some weird pervert hiding in the bushes pretending to be the King of the Fairies?"

Evie sighed and was quiet a moment. Phoebe worked the scissors across the back of her head.

"I don't, I guess. I mean, we were a little doubtful—Sammy especially. But she was so . . . so caught up in it. Giddy. And she came out of that cellar hole with these little trinkets, gifts from Teilo. They were proof."

"But they were just everyday objects, right? A coin, a Catholic medal? Nothing otherworldly about that."

Evie brought her fingers to her lips, chewed on the nails. "I guess not," she said at last. "We were kids, Phoebe. Lisa told us the fairies were real, that their king came, and there was no point arguing with her. I guess you had to know Lisa for that to make sense. She was so stubborn. And more than that. She was sort of enchanted. Exactly the kind of person the King of the Fairies might come for."

Evie said this with an expression that was both wistful and slightly bitter.

Phoebe had worked her way back around to the front, facing Evie and trying to make the right side match the left.

"So what do you think happened to her then?" she asked.

"I think"—Evie hesitated, closed her eyes, then opened them—"I think she went with Teilo."

"What? To the fairy kingdom? Come on, Evie! You can't tell me you really believe that."

"Maybe we'll find out tonight."

"Do you think it's really possible," Phoebe said, stepping back to admire the finished haircut, "that Lisa's still alive? That it could really be her?"

Evie brushed the hair off her shoulders and stood up.

"The biggest lesson I learned that summer, the one I've carried with me my whole life, is that anything is possible."

Phoebe smiled at her, reached out her hand to take Evie's, which was cool and clammy.

"Do you really believe that?" Phoebe asked.

"Absolutely," Evie said, smiling.

"Then come with me," Phoebe said.

She led Evie to the front door.

Evie pulled away from her, her face sweaty and panicked. "I can't," she said.

Phoebe took her hand again. "Just one step out the door. I'll be right there with you. One step, Evie. Remember, anything's possible."

Evie bit her lower lip, closed her eyes, and held her hand out to Phoebe. Phoebe opened the door and they stepped through together. They stood on the top step leading down to the driveway, the rising moon lighting up their faces.

"Open your eyes," she said in her calmest voice.

Evie did.

"See," Phoebe said. "You did it." Evie locked eyes with her. At first, Evie looked frightened, then for just the briefest second it was as if a shade lifted and Phoebe could see someone else in there. Someone brave, sure of herself. More confident than Phoebe herself, even.

And just then, Sam came wheeling into the driveway in his pickup. The shade slammed shut and Evie clawed at Phoebe's hand, sucking in air with a wheezing fish-out-of-water gulp. Sam jumped out of the cab, face flushed.

"I'm on my way to Reliance," he said. "You coming?"

CHAPTER 22

Lisa

In all the stories, it's the same. The girl is ordinary. The girl is dull. But she is kind, has a good heart. Maybe she's got a wicked stepmother. Maybe her stepsisters are fat and ugly and have dresses much fancier than hers. Maybe her father's taken her deep into the heart of the forest and left her there.

Lisa knew her own story started just like theirs: *Once upon a time.*

Once upon a time there was a girl who could talk to the animals. A girl who lived next to a village where all of the people had disappeared. All but her great-grandfather, a tiny squalling baby left behind, tears and snot running rivers down his pink piggy face. His blood was in her veins. The salt inside it lucky somehow.

And she was a lucky girl. She knew that now, more than ever. Because she'd been given a magical gift, something straight out of a fairy tale: a book written by the King of the Fairies himself.

Y ou put the book there yourself," Sammy said.

"How can you say that?" Lisa demanded. "Just look at it! Look how old it is."

"You told us you wouldn't go back there on your own," Evie said. "You promised!" Her voice crackled, and for the first time ever, Lisa thought Evie might swing out and hit her. She waited for it, bracing herself, but Evie stood still, her breathing getting louder and louder.

Lisa had found the book down in the cellar hole that morning: a gift wrapped in wide green leaves, bound with thin vines, a purple foxglove with a spotted throat on top.

The note she'd left the fairies was gone.

Lisa had opened the package and found a book inside with a worn and tattered green cover. The paper looked old, the cover stitched on with heavy black thread. She ran her fingers over the letters on the cover: *The Book of Fairies.* Above it, a strange symbol painted in gold—an upside-down number 4 with a circle at the bottom.

She opened the book, squinted in the early morning light to make out the words. Flipping through, she found sections called "Fairy History," "Fairy Legends," "Fairies and Humans." At the end of the book there was a page that began, *If you wish to cross over to the land of the fairies. . .*

There was a recipe for fairy tea that involved steeping the flowers and leaves of foxglove, adding honey, and letting the mixture sit for several days.

Lisa had closed the book and climbed out of the cellar hole, heart pounding because she knew that now she had it: proof that the fairies existed.

That's easy to fake," Sammy said. "Stain the paper, singe the edges. You've taken this fairy crap too far, Lisa."

"So I went to the trouble of writing the book myself, making up page after page, carefully putting it all down in handwriting that looks nothing like my own? Right. Come on, Mr. Logic. Be logical, would ya?"

Sam shook his head.

"Just look at the book, Sam. It's full of all kinds of stuff. The King of the Fairies, his name is Teilo. He's been here a long, long time. And I know what we have to do next. It says right here in the book what we have to do if we want to meet him."

Evie's face twisted into a pained expression. "What?"

"We just have to promise him something—you know, to prove we're taking it seriously. And he'll grant our wishes. And let us see him. Can you believe it? Can you believe how lucky we are?"

Sammy shook his head. "What I can't believe is how nuts you are. No way am I promising anything to one of your invisible friends!"

"What do you think, Evie?" Lisa asked. "You'd do it, wouldn't you? He's offering to grant us any wish, and to let us see him."

"Oh great. Ask her," Sammy said. He stormed off through the tall grass, which moved like waves in the wind.

"I think we should tell people about the fairies," Evie said, making a determined bulldog face with her lower jaw jutted out. "Show them the book."

"No," Lisa argued. "The book says we have to keep all this a secret. If we tell, they'll go away and never come back. And if we don't keep it a secret, bad things might happen."

Evie raised her eyebrows. "Bad things?"

"I don't know exactly, but the book warns not to cross them. The fairies can grant wishes, bring good luck, but if you get on their bad side . . ."

Evie shivered. "But Lisa, if there is this whole other race of beings living on the back of this hill, that's like the greatest discovery of all time. And this, right here," she said, shaking the book, "this is proof! We could be famous all over the world."

"I don't want to be famous," Lisa said, snatching the book back from Evie.

"What do you want?" she asked.

Lisa thought a minute. "I want to know what it's like there. On the other side. In Teilo's world."

And maybe, she thought, maybe this book is the key. Maybe the fairies have a potion that could bring Da back. There were directions at the end for crossing over to the Fairy Realm, weren't there? Would she ever have the guts to follow them? The courage to leave behind everything she knew and loved?

"Promise me," Lisa said. "Swear you won't breathe a word of this to anyone."

Evie nodded solemnly.

"And think about what I said. With one little promise to Teilo, we can get anything we ask for."

Evie chewed her lip.

"If you could wish for anything," Lisa said, "no matter how big, how impossible, what would you wish for?"

Evie didn't answer. She kicked at the ground with her huge work boot. Lisa hugged *The Book of Fairies* to her chest.

The question hung in the air between them like a golden bubble, all shiny and radiant, neither of them daring to answer out loud.

CHAPTER 23

Phoebe

JUNE 11, PRESENT DAY

I thought she couldn't go outside," Sam said, eyes straight ahead on the road.

"She can't. Couldn't. I'm trying to help her, Sam. I've been doing some research on agoraphobia."

"Great, Bee. That's just great." He gripped the wheel tighter, rubbed it hard with his thumbs. The cab of Sam's truck was tidy—no crumbs or food wrappers. His travel mug with the Vermont Public Radio logo was resting in the cup holder. Phoebe knew without opening it that the glove box was neat and organized—insurance and registration on top, manual and maps underneath. Hers was stuffed full of leaking ketchup packets, napkins, and receipts.

They traveled in silence a few minutes, passing the Maple Hills Credit Union and Al's Quality Southern Used Cars. Phoebe wondered what they'd find when they got to Reliance—if it was really possible that Lisa would be there, waiting. The full moon was just up over the mountains, bright and reddish. Like blood, Phoebe thought, then stopped herself. Raspberries, she decided. Currants.

Cranberries maybe. The moons all have names, she knew, but which one was this? The planter's moon? Strawberry moon?

She touched her belly.

Tell him, she begged herself. *Open your goddamn mouth and speak.*

She reached over and took his hand, which rested on the shift lever. She gave it a squeeze. "I love you, you know," she said. He grunted, kept his eyes on the road.

It was no secret that everyone had expected Sam to do better than a woman like Phoebe. And she sensed that some—Sam's mother in particular (though Phoebe knew Phyllis would never come right out and say it)—blamed Phoebe for Sam's apparent inability to live up to his potential. He'd gone to college after all, studied philosophy and art, and yet here he was cutting trees for a living. Phoebe herself was no great success story, having barely graduated from high school, then taken a string of low-wage service jobs, scooping ice cream, waiting tables, answering telephones. When they had dinner with his college friends and they all got to talking about French philosophers and politics, her mind went numb.

"Well, what do you think, Bee?" some well-meaning girl in natural fiber clothing would ask. Phoebe would shrug or give some totally inconclusive answer that made everyone in the room look at her with their isn't-it-a-shame-bright-Sam-ended-up-with-a-complete-dolt looks. Then, if she'd had enough to drink, she'd play it up, act like some dumb hick—cussing up a storm, saying "ain't" and dropping the g's at the end of words: *I ain't foolin'*. Sam would roll his eyes, amused and irritated all at once, but he never really got why she did it. She was not from their world and never would be. Sam said it didn't matter—that he loved her for who she was, but she knew better. One day he'd wake up and realize she was ten years older and light-years behind. And telling him she was pregnant could be viewed as just a sad and desperate attempt to hold on to him, to get him to commit to a relationship that was obviously beneath him.

"Pathetic," she mumbled out loud.

"What?" he asked.

"Nothin'," she said, dropping the g on purpose, slouching down into the seat.

They were coming into Harmony now. Sam's headlights illuminated the Lord's Prayer rock.

Sam turned right onto Main Street. They passed the general store with the neon CLOSED sign lit. The letter board in front of the Methodist Church said STRAWBERRY FEST SAT 9–1. SHORT-CAKE, PIES, MRS LAROUCHES WORLD-FAMOUS JAM!

"Thanks," Phoebe said, sitting up straight again, fiddling with her trucker belt buckle for luck with all this, "for coming to pick me up. I thought maybe you'd gone alone."

Sam didn't respond. Just drove in silence, chewing his lower lip—a boyish gesture that reminded Phoebe of Evie. Then she remembered Evie's description of Sam.

Excited all the time, talking nonstop about whatever came into his head. He couldn't keep a secret if you paid him. Until the fairies came.

They turned onto Spruce Street.

"So what's the plan?" Phoebe asked.

"Plan?"

"You're not going to park near your mom's place, are you?"

They were just passing it now. The lights were all out, the curtains drawn. Phoebe remembered little Sam's face in the upper window all those years ago. The girl in pink asking, "Are you here to see the fairies?" She remembered the glove she'd been shown—the leather stained, an extra finger sewn on with heavy black thread.

"Nah. I thought I'd circle around and park along Rangley Road. We'll have to cut through the woods, but I think we can find our way."

And what'll we do if we find her? she wanted to ask.

Sam had a flashlight, but it did little good. The woods were thick, dark, and impenetrable. The moon above them seemed nearly as bright as the sun, but little of the light was able to make it through the thick canopy of leaves above. Phoebe held on to the back of Sam's T-shirt, sure that if she let go, she'd be left behind, lost.

"Are you sure this is right?" Phoebe asked, her ankle slamming against yet another rock. She hated what a girly girl she acted like sometimes when she was with him. *Brave strong man, please put my simple mind at ease and reassure me that you've got it under control.* It made her want to gag.

"No, Bee, I'm not sure. I think so."

"It feels like we're lost."

Sam gave an exasperated sigh. "We're headed in the right direction. The hill is in front of us, and Reliance is somewhere on this side of it. I've never come at it from this direction before. And Christ, I haven't been here in fifteen years! Things have grown in a little since then. It looks totally different."

If he'd had a map and compass, Phoebe knew he'd be checking them now.

"You never came back? After Lisa disappeared?"

He stopped walking, sighed. "Not really. I tried a couple of times, but it felt all wrong. Like trespassing." He started walking again, the beam of the flashlight moving from tree to tree. Paper birches stood like ghosts. An owl let out a chortling cry.

"Barred owl," Sam said, because that was the thing with Sam, wasn't it? He was always teaching her things, filling her head with these golden nuggets.

She thought of the owl he'd carried in to the clinic, limp and full of buckshot. Sam's arm was a mess of cuts and scratches from the owl fighting him, not understanding he was trying to save it. He still had the faintest scar by his right elbow, if you knew right where to look.

She thought of Becca's advice: *Ask Sam what he saw in the woods that night. Ask him how he got that big old scar on his chest.*

Had Sam really been out here the night Lisa was taken?

What had he seen?

"It's hard to imagine a town ever having been here," Phoebe said, looking around at the dense forest.

What she was really thinking was, it's hard to imagine that she'd ever been anywhere near there. Hard to imagine herself at twenty, being led through the woods by a girl in pink with scabby arms. Hard to believe any of it was real—the yellow police tape, the strange six-fingered glove inside the paper sack.

She had her secrets. Sam had his. And it seemed like it was too late to start fessing up now.

"It was a long time ago," Sam said. "And it was hardly a town by today's standards. More like a little village. Half a dozen houses, some barns, a blacksmith shop, and a church. There's an old well out here, too. We have to be careful where we step."

Great, Phoebe thought. As if she could even see where she was stepping.

She thought of the rumors about Reliance: the whole town being swallowed up, people losing dogs, the music and voices people said they heard from deep in the woods.

Was it possible for a place to be evil?

Were there really doors to other worlds?

It didn't seem likely, but the idea caught in her brain like a hamster in a wheel spinning around and around.

"So what exactly are we looking for?" Phoebe asked.

"Rocks. Some big squarish pits in the ground, where the foundations of the buildings used to be. That's about it."

"Jesus," Phoebe said. "I don't think—"

"Shh!" Sam hissed, coming to a dead halt, making Phoebe run into him. "Listen."

Gripping his bunched-up shirttail with one hand, wrapping the other around his chest, she clung to him, listening. The owl was silent now. She heard crickets. The high-pitched trill of a toad. But there was something else off in the distance, something that didn't belong.

"Bells," she said. Sam's body grew rigid.

"This way," he said, and he took off quickly, breaking her hold, the T-shirt slipping out of her hand.

"Wait," she hissed, scrambling behind him, her eyes on the swath of light cutting through the darkness as he ran.

Her toe caught a root and she nearly lost her balance, saving herself by blindly reaching out and grabbing a spindly tree that bent with her weight. The beam from Sam's flashlight was farther ahead now, a shimmering mirage through the trees.

"Sam!" Phoebe called. "Slow down!" She pushed off and

fumbled slowly through the darkness, feeling her way. She shuffled her feet carefully, feeling for stones and trees, her arms swinging in great arcs in front of her as she struggled to keep her eyes on Sam's light, now farther away than ever.

The bell sound got louder.

She remembered Sam's words: *We saw something.*

But what?

And what would she see when and if she finally caught up with him?

And what, she wondered in a moment of blind panic, would she do if she never caught up with him? If she got to Reliance and found him gone? His flashlight and shoe left behind at the bottom of an old cellar hole.

"Sam," she moaned. "Please."

Don't leave me.

She touched her belly.

Don't leave us.

Phoebe stumbled forward, branches clawing at her bare arms and face, as she moved toward the sound of the bells, toward the faint light dancing on the trees. It looked greenish. Was it Sam's flashlight? Or something else?

Up ahead, the forest was brighter, glowing and shimmering. She moved toward it, saw that the trees were thinning. She remembered the stories she'd heard of the green mist in Reliance, how some people claimed they'd seen a man walking out of it.

Once more, she caught her foot on a rock and stumbled, but this time there was nothing to stop her fall.

"Shit!" she yelped. She'd skinned her elbows and bashed her left knee hard against something. Looking around, she saw there were several tall, thin rocks jutting out of the ground around her. But these weren't just rocks. They were gravestones.

"Sam!" she called, scrambling desperately to her feet.

The little cemetery was at the edge of a small clearing, the moon bright above her, illuminating the landscape. A breeze blew, and the shadows of the trees played in the moonlight at her feet. About ten yards to her left was Sam, holding the flashlight, pointing it down. She ran to him, carefully avoiding holes, ditches, mounds of rock, and trees.

"Sam!" she said throwing her arms around him, his back still to her, damp through his T-shirt. Sam. Her Sam. He wasn't lost forever. She peeked over his shoulder, saw that the beam of the flashlight was pointed down, into a cellar hole lined in rocks. There, crouched in the corner like an animal caught in a trap, was a woman with a pale face and dark, tangled hair. She stared up, eyes round, black, and hollow. Around her neck was a string of bells with a ratty old fabric pouch tied on at the bottom.

"Lisa?" Phoebe breathed the word and the woman smiled but didn't answer. She reached up and continued shaking the bells.

PART II

The Shadow People

If you receive a gift from the fairies, treasure it. Know that no matter how ordinary the object may seem, it is infused with fairy magic. Guard this object with your life. Tell no one where it has come from.

When you are in possession of such a gift, you and the fairies are bound.

Phoebe

Do you think it's her?" Evie whispered. She was standing with Phoebe and Sam in the kitchen. The girl from the cellar hole was in the living room eating her third bowl of corn flakes with a quarter cup of sugar sprinkled on top. Before that, she'd finished off the leftover strawberry cake.

"I don't know," said Sam, opening a bottle of beer. "It could be. But then again I was fooled by that woman at the cabin pretending to be Evie. What do you think?" he asked, turning to his cousin.

"I'm not sure," Evie said, chomping on her chapped lower lip, peering anxiously through the doorway into the living room where Lisa sat on the couch, noisily slurping milk out of her bowl. "It could be. But her eyes aren't like I remember."

If anything, Evie seemed frightened of the girl. She kept her distance, looked down or away when the girl glanced in her direction. And was Evie so wrong? There was something spooky about the girl. Even the animals picked up on it, all of them panicking in their cages, as if a dog had come in.

"Shit, Evie. Nothing about her is anything like the Lisa I remember. But does that mean it's not her? I don't know. And if it's not her, who the hell is she and why's she going around pretending to be my sister? If it is her, where's she been all these years? And don't either of you dare so much as mention the freaking land of the fairies."

"But Sam, the letter she left," Evie said.

"There are no fairies!" Sam said. "It's all some made-up bullshit meant to lure little girls off and scare thickheaded people who don't know any better." Sam looked furious. "Let's get real, huh?" he said, looking right at Evie. "If this is Lisa, how are we going to find out?"

Phoebe guessed that the young woman they picked up was in her late twenties or early thirties, but there was a phantom-like quality about her that made her seem ageless. She had scraggly long dark hair and black jeans with holes in the knees. She wore a baggy lace-up blouse with long sleeves that looked like a leftover from a pirate costume. On her feet, which were caked with filth, was a pair of cheap drugstore flip-flops. Her skin was sallow and her teeth were in bad shape—yellow, brown in places. She carried nothing. Around her neck was the string of little brass bells, and tied at the bottom was a dingy cloth bag. The whole ride home, she hummed to herself and played with the bells around her neck. So far, she had ignored all their questions.

"I just don't know, Sam," Evie said. "I wonder if maybe we should call your mom."

"No!" Sam shouted. "The last thing she needs is for us to get her hopes up and then find out it's a hoax."

"I just thought," said Evie, "that since she's her mother and all, she might know, might have some mother's intuition or whatever."

"We're not calling her," Sam said. "Not until we're sure that this is really Lisa."

"But how are we going to find out?" Phoebe asked. She agreed that going to Phyllis right away was a bad idea, but she wasn't sure where they should start.

Sam groaned. "This is ridiculous! There's got to be some way to find out."

"There's DNA testing," Phoebe suggested.

"That could take forever," Sam said. "There must be something we can do now. Something we can ask her that only Lisa would know."

Evie cleared her throat. "I don't know that she'd be able to answer. She hasn't been all that cooperative so far. We don't even know that she's capable of speaking."

"Well, we've gotta try," Sam said, leading the way out of the kitchen into the living room. The girl from the woods was rocking in her chair, smiling into her empty bowl.

"Would you like more cereal?" Phoebe asked.

The girl shook her head. Tangles of matted dark hair fell across her face. Phoebe thought of stories she'd heard about feral children, boys and girls raised by wolves. Myths, surely.

"What's your name?" Sam asked.

She clicked her spoon against the side of the bowl. *Tap, tap, tap.* Maybe she was trying communicate with Morse code.

"If you're really Lisa, then where have you been all these years?" he asked.

She tapped so hard, Phoebe was afraid she'd cracked the bowl. Then she stared down at the dregs of milk and soggy cereal crumbs.

"Say something, damn it!" Sam snapped in a tone that gave Phoebe chills. He was up on his feet, leaning toward their guest.

The girl dropped her spoon and growled at Sam, showing her teeth like an angry dog. Sam backed away.

Evie, who was still hovering in the doorway to the kitchen, flashed Sam a holy-shit look.

"Lisa," Phoebe said, placing her hand gently on the girl's arm. She didn't have a clue whether or not this was really Lisa, but for now, the girl needed a name, so she went with the obvious choice. "It looks like you've had a long, hard journey. Would you like a hot bath and some clean clothes?"

Lisa shrugged. Her lips hadn't relaxed completely after the growl, and she was left with a little lopsided sneer.

"Why don't you come with me," Phoebe said. "I think you'll feel a lot better. Then we'll get you off to bed. It's very late."

Lisa nodded and stood up, following Phoebe. When she was nearly out of the living room, she stopped and turned back to Sam. "I think I'd like my bracelet, first," she said in a child's unsure voice.

"What?" Evie demanded.

Sam stared, openmouthed like a fish out of water, gulping at air. "Bracelet?" he stammered.

"I gave it to you the night I left. Made you promise not to tell. Don't you remember, Sammy?"

Sam lurched forward and hurried out of the living room toward the kitchen.

"Sam, what's going on?" Phoebe asked. She and Evie had followed him into the kitchen and were now watching as he balanced precariously on a wobbly wooden stool, going through the top cupboard where they stored things rarely used: a crusty old bottle of molasses, kosher salt, cooking wine. The girl hovered in the doorway, smiling.

Sam pushed the sediment-filled bottle of wine aside and pulled out a dusty box of blue-tipped kitchen matches. The box looked as if it had been there since long before they'd moved in. Did they even make blue-tipped kitchen matches anymore?

"Here," he said, climbing down, wiping the dust off the cardboard matchbox on his faded Green Mountain Club T-shirt.

He took a step toward the girl and opened the matchbox. His fingers gently pushed through the layer of matches on top and pulled out a small bundle, wrapped in crumpled white tissue paper. He carefully held it in his palm and unfolded the paper. A tarnished bracelet stared up at them.

"You said you didn't know what happened to it," Phoebe said, her voice sounding thin and papery. "I asked you when we were back at the cabin."

There are things Sam isn't telling you.

She looked to Evie, but Evie's eyes were focused on the bracelet.

Sam worked his fingers over the charms. Lisa's name. A starfish. A Saint Christopher medal. An old wheat penny.

She still couldn't figure out why a fairy would leave such human gifts. Wouldn't acorns, flowers, and pretty stones make more sense?

"You've had it all these years," Evie said, sucking in her bottom lip. "We all figured she must have been wearing it when she went missing. She had it on that night at dinner. She never took the thing off."

Sam held the bracelet out to the girl, who smiled, took it, and clasped it on her bony wrist. She touched the *Lisa* charm and let out a little laugh that sounded more like a sigh.

Phoebe drew a bath, dumping some lavender bath salts in.

"I love the smell of lavender," she told the girl. "Some people think it's an old lady smell, but to me, it's just so soothing. Sam's mother," she hesitated, wondering to herself if she should have said *your mother*, "gave us these little sachets of it and I put them in my drawers. Sam says that's an old lady thing to do, but when I open the drawers, it smells like summer year-round."

Lisa undressed, leaving her ratty clothes in a pile on the floor. Phoebe took in a sharp breath, heard herself, then forced a warm everything's-okay smile.

Lisa was stick-thin, her bones clearly visible under her pale skin. It wasn't only the emaciated look that got to Phoebe, but the tattoos. The girl (and Phoebe clearly thought of her as a girl, even though she was an adult) was covered in tattoos: line drawings of stick figures, strange letter-like symbols. Lisa stepped forward, lowered herself slowly into the steaming tub. There, between her shoulder blades, was Teilo's mark—the same tattoo she'd seen on Elliot back at the cabin. It didn't seem possible that their night at the cabin had happened only one week ago.

"I'll just take these things and wash them," Phoebe said, her voice trembling a little. "I'll bring in something cozy for you to sleep in. And I'll get a bed made for you. You can have our room—it's the most comfortable. Sam and I can sleep in the office. We've got an air mattress."

Lisa didn't respond. She was opening and closing her hand under the water, looking down at her fingers as if they didn't belong to her. She'd kept the bracelet on and fiddled with the charms, studying them, mumbling something under her breath. Phoebe gathered up the things: stained, baggy white panties, tattered black jeans, lace top that was torn in places and full of leaves and pine needles from the forest. Beneath all of this was the necklace of bells, which she wrapped inside the filthy clothes so they would stay silent.

Phoebe left the bathroom and dumped the clothes on the living-room floor in front of Evie and Sam.

"You should see her," Phoebe said. "You can practically count her bones. And she's covered in tattoos. Including Teilo's mark. It's between her shoulder blades."

Sam gave a shiver.

"Jesus," Evie said.

Phoebe started going through the pockets of Lisa's jeans and found only two dimes and a nickel. "I told her I'd wash these, but I think we'd be better off throwing them away."

"It's all she's got," Sam said. "I say we wash them."

Phoebe nodded, thinking, *This is more like it. This is the Sam I know.* She picked up the necklace. She felt the cloth bag tied at the bottom. "There's something inside." Her fingers untied the drawstring that held the bag closed. She pulled it open and turned it upside down, giving it a shake.

Four things fell out onto the floor: two pieces of colored chalk (one blue, one yellow), a key on a string, and a plastic laminated card that Sam immediately snatched up and studied.

"What is it?" Phoebe asked.

"A library card. From the Aldrich Public Library over in Barre."

"Does it have a name?" Evie asked, leaning in for a better look.

"There's a signature on the back. It says Mary Stevens."

"Who the hell is Mary Stevens?" Evie asked.

"No idea," Sam said. "But there's one thing I know for sure. No one else knew I had that bracelet. Only Lisa and me."

CHAPTER 25

Lisa

Has anyone seen my sewing basket?" Lisa's mom asked. The others were all finishing up breakfast, but Phyllis was walking around the house flapping Da's rainbow trout pajama top.

"Not me," Lisa said. The others all shook their heads. No one had seen it. Her mother was now clutching the pajamas to her chest as though the fish beneath her fingers were live trout struggling to get free. She looked thinner to Lisa, more fragile. More disturbing was the fact that she kept losing things: her gardening trowel, the kitchen shears, and now her sewing basket.

"There's a button missing," Phyllis said, plucking at the fabric. "I thought I could mend it. I thought I could do this one thing . . ." Her voice trailed off.

"Dave's got plenty of other pajamas," Hazel said, putting a spoon of corn flakes to his mouth. He kept his lips closed tight and she bumped the spoon against them gently, coaxing them open and sliding the cereal in. Milk dribbled down his chin.

Phyllis stared at her. "I think I'm well aware of how many sets of pajamas my husband has. But what you might not be aware of, Hazel, what only a wife would know, is that this is his favorite pair!" She charged out of the kitchen.

Sammy watched his mother leave with his jaw open, like a cartoon boy about to speak in a big white bubble, but no words came.

Evie finished her cereal with a slurp and burped hugely. It was just like her to try to lighten the mood by being stupid on purpose, but really it was just plain gross.

"Maybe," said Hazel in an unsure voice, "maybe one of you should go help Phyllis find her sewing basket." Her hand shook a little as she reached for her mug, took a big sip of coffee that was so heavily laced with brandy that Lisa could smell it from across the table.

"I'll go," said Lisa, eager to get away from Evie, who was now making more repulsive sounds as she picked her teeth. Lisa got up and followed her mother upstairs. The door to her bedroom was locked.

"Mom?" she called, knocking.

There was no answer.

But she knew what to do. She'd find the missing sewing basket, leave it outside her mother's door. It wasn't much, but it was one small thing she could do to restore order to the world, to make her mother a little happy. She started in the hall closet and found linens, extra rolls of toilet paper, unopened bottles of shampoo, but no sewing basket. She checked the guest room, where Hazel was staying, which smelled sweet and boozy. Opening the drawer of the bedside table, Lisa found a bottle of brandy and some Valium. No sewing basket. Were you even supposed to mix alcohol and Valium? Hazel would know. She was a nurse, after all.

Under the brandy and pill bottle was a paperback book. Lisa picked it up. It was one of Hazel's cheesy romance novels with a hunky guy on the cover, holding a swooning woman in his arms. Fairy tales for adults, that's what these were. Evie said some of them had dirty parts, scenes where the relationships were consummated in sometimes steamy ways. It made Lisa's stomach hurt to think about. But still, she was curious. She flipped through it. Near the middle, she found a photograph tucked between the pages. Lisa pulled it out and blinked hard at it. Da was in the picture, looking young and happy. No eyeglasses, no crow's-feet or worry lines on his forehead. His hair was longish and shaggy. Standing in front of him, wrapped in his arms, was a girlish, thin Hazel with perfectly coiffed hair and a little wry smile on her face.

Lisa's face felt tight. Her head began to pound.

Where had the picture come from? And what was Hazel doing with it now, hidden like this? Lisa realized right away that she didn't want to know the answers to these questions. The best thing to do was to get rid of the picture, make sure no one else ever found it.

She crumpled the photo, jammed it into her pocket, and threw the book back in the drawer.

Standing up, Lisa glanced out the window into the backyard. There was Evie, casting a quick glance back at the house before slipping into the woods with her backpack on. The same backpack she'd given Gerald.

Pleased to have something to distract her from the photo, Lisa took the stairs two at a time, racing through the kitchen and out the door into the yard.

By the time Lisa caught up to Evie, she was down in Reliance, talking with Gerald and Pinkie. Lisa crouched behind a nearby tree. There weren't any good trees in the clearing where the cellar holes were, so she had to hang back and couldn't hear well. A mosquito buzzed around her face, landed on her ear. She swatted at it, missing. The air felt soggy and gray. The sky was darkening, threatening to rain at any second.

Once again, Lisa watched as Evie took off the backpack and handed it to Gerald. He nodded at her, said, "Thanks, Stevie," but she didn't seem to mind. She didn't raise a fist or reach for her knife, or even so much as flinch. She just backed away slowly, looking humble and defeated. This was *so* not the Evie Lisa knew. Evie did a slow shuffle-walk toward home, looking more like a strange hunched-over gorilla than a girl.

Were they blackmailing her? Swearing they'd get her in trouble for breaking Gerald's arm if she didn't pay them? But what did Evie have to give them?

Determined to get to the bottom of this one way or another, Lisa waited until Evie was back up the hill, then took off after Gerald and Pinkie. They were walking in the other direction, deeper into the woods. If they kept going, they'd eventually hit Rangley Road, which ran along the back side of the woods. If you went left on Rangley, you'd reach Hill Road, which brought you back into the center of town. Were they just taking the long way home?

"What are you two doing to Evie?" Lisa demanded once she'd caught up with them. The forest was more grown up down here, and there were no clear paths. The ground felt damp and spongy under her feet.

Gerald and Pinkie turned, surprised. They were standing in a cluster of ferns.

"We're not doing anything," Gerald said, adjusting the knapsack with his good arm. His cast was decorated in little drawings and scribbles—airplanes and cartoon faces and a huge, swirly BECCA signature done in pink marker. There was a skull and crossbones, which might have looked tough and cool on someone else's arm, but on his, it just seemed dorky. As Lisa studied the drawings on the cast, her eye was drawn to one of the cartoon faces. It was thin, vampire-like, with dark circles under the eyes. Evie's work, no doubt.

"What's in the bag?" Lisa asked.

"None of your beeswax," Pinkie said. She had a spot of blood on her left check from a mosquito bite. There was a chintzy little toy compass pinned to her shirt.

"You two are messing with my cousin, so that makes it my business. Now are you gonna let me see what's in the bag, Gerald, or do I have to figure out a way to make sure your other arm gets broken?" Hanging out with Evie so much was rubbing off on her.

"Jeez!" Gerald, said, adjusting his glasses. "You can look already. Fine." He shrugged the bag off and held it out to her. Lisa opened it and peeked inside, holding her breath.

It wasn't money, the family silver, body parts, or drugs.

It was food.

Peanut butter and jelly sandwiches. Apples. A package of pink cupcakes swiped from a box in their pantry at home. A can of cling peaches in heavy syrup.

"What the hell is all this?" Lisa asked.

"A picnic," Gerald said, smiling.

"Not for ants, either," Pinkie added.

"Why did Evie give you all this?"

Gerald shrugged his shoulders. "'Cause we looked hungry, I guess." He laughed and added something in his ridiculous made-up language, a long series of half-swallowed sounds.

"What?" Lisa demanded. Her head spun. She hated to be the one left in the dark. How could Evie do this to her?

"Nothing," Gerald said, snickering to himself. His hair was greasier than ever, and the pimples on his forehead looked painful. Pinkie giggled along with him, though Lisa was sure she had no clue how to speak a word of Minarian.

"I don't know what kind of hold you two have over Evie, but whatever it is, you need to quit messing with her. If you don't, there will be consequences."

Gerald laughed, shook his head. "Consequences, right," he said. "You don't have a clue."

Pinkie gave a twitchy little smile and said, "You think you're so special, Lisa. But I'm special too." She rubbed at the spot of blood on her cheek, smearing it. Then she touched the little compass, peering down at it as she jiggled the needle.

"Good for you, Pinkie. Good for you." Lisa turned to walk back home. It was starting to sprinkle.

"She told us, you know," Gerald shouted after her.

Lisa stopped, turned back to face them. "Told you what?"

The drizzle picked up and the rain began coming down in huge, heavy drops.

Gerald was putting the backpack onto his shoulder. His bangs were already plastered to his head. "About the cellar hole," he said, the words nearly drowned out by the rain pounding down on the canopy of leaves above them.

Lisa took in a deep breath and held it as she turned away from Gerald and Pinkie and kept walking, rain pelting her. *Act like it's no big deal. Don't ask what Evie told them. Act like it doesn't matter.*

But it did matter.

Evie had betrayed her.

CHAPTER 26

Phoebe

Phoebe was digging around in the office closet, looking for the air mattress, when she found Sam's old green knapsack stuffed deep in the back corner, under a trash bag full of shredded bills to be recycled. Odd. Sam kept his hiking and camping gear in the front-hall closet. She pulled the bag out, realizing from its shape and weight that there was something inside. She dropped it on the desk, then went to the doorway to listen. She heard the faint splash of Lisa in the bath. In the living room, Sam and Evie were talking about whether or not they should take Lisa to see a doctor.

"Just think it through, Sam," Evie said. "They'll want to know her name. Your relationship to her. Shit, they'll probably call the cops. I'm not saying it's a bad thing. I'm just wondering if maybe we should hold off. Find out what we can on our own first."

It was strange to hear Sam and Evie getting along so well—relying on each other in a whole new way. It almost didn't matter if the girl turned out to really be Lisa—she'd brought Sam and Evie together again and that seemed like an incredible gift.

Phoebe eased the office door shut, went over to the desk, and hesitated over the knapsack. It was Sam's. And obviously he hadn't wanted her to see whatever was inside.

What if it turned out to be an early birthday gift and she ruined the surprise?

But what if it wasn't?

Once more, she thought of what Becca had told her on the phone: *There are things he's not telling you.*

The sliding closet door was open, and she was sure she saw the slightest hint of movement in the back left corner. She blinked. Impossible, she told herself. *There's nothing there.* Heart thudding, she stepped to her right so that she was directly in front of it. She kicked at the trash bag full of shredded paper. Then, taking a deep breath, she pulled the winter coats aside.

Nothing.

Of course it was nothing. What had she been expecting?

Shaking her head at her own foolishness, she went back to the desk, unzipped the bag slowly, and peeked inside.

It was stuffed with papers. She reached in and pulled them out, fanning them out on the desk. Printouts from the computer were mixed up with sheets of legal paper full of Sam's perfect penmanship.

"Son of a bitch," said Phoebe, lowering herself into the chair in front of the desk. Her legs felt shaky, like the entire earth had shifted under her and the ground itself was not to be trusted.

Here, at last, was the answer to the mystery of what he'd been doing on the computer each night.

In Sam's neat script were strange stories, notes in the margins saying what source they'd come from, books and website addresses.

*In twelfth-century Suffolk, England, a boy and a girl appeared
at the opening of a pit in the earth. Their skin was green and
they spoke a strange language. The boy died. In time, the girl
learned English and was able to explain that they had come
from an underground world she called St. Martin's Land.*

*A common story in Scottish witch trials between 1550
and 1670: A woman meets a man dressed in black or green.
He asks her to be his servant, offers her something in return
(sometimes the gift of clairvoyance). He has sex with her and
often leaves a mark on her.*

*The Scottish Ballad of Tam Lin: A young maiden picks a
rose at an abandoned castle. A handsome man in green ap-
pears. He lies with her and she becomes pregnant. He tells
her he was once a mortal man, captured by the Queen of the
Fairies. Now he's a changeling, moving between two worlds.*

The more Phoebe read, the more unsettled she became. These
were not the sweet, winged fairies Phoebe remembered from the
stories when she was young. These were dark, brooding, supernatural beings with the power to shape-shift, to read minds, to
lure innocent young girls away.

But Sam didn't believe in any of this. He'd been adamant
about that. He was the voice of reason. The map and compass
guy whom Phoebe knew she'd never get lost with.

The next sheet of paper was a printout that Sam had high-
lighted and put stars around:

*Boston, 1919: A young woman named Jenny Hobbs was
arrested after drowning her infant son in a wash pan in her
rented room. When questioned by the police, she told a*

peculiar story. She claimed the child was only half human. His father, she insisted, was the devil himself, a shadow man without a face who claimed to be King of the Fairies. When asked where she had come from, where she met this man, she refused to answer, saying only a small village up north. "No one there anymore," she told police. "The fairies took them all away." Miss Hobbs was later committed to Danvers State Hospital, where she came down with pneumonia and died.

Phoebe ran a trembling hand through her hair. Had Jenny Hobbs come from Vermont? From Reliance?

She read over another sheet of notes Sam had taken:

The ability to shape-shift? To appear as a human or an animal? My dreams of the dark whispering man.

Phoebe stabbed her finger at that line. *I thought you said you didn't dream, Sam.*

Her heart pounded. She thought of the trapdoor beneath her childhood bed, the shadow man she'd known but of whom she never spoke.

Don't think about that.

Did Sam have his own shadow man too?

She went on reading:

A journey to the fairy realm is like a shamanic journey—few who go come back. Those who do are often mad. (Da?) Or gifted—clairvoyant, seers, masters of prophecy. Sometimes, a person is taken and a fairy changeling left in their place. Ugly, sickly. There are stories of humans going into the fairy

world where they spend a day, but when they return, a hun-
dred years have passed here and everyone they know is dead.
Would Lisa still be a young girl? Is it possible that ten years in
our time might only be ten minutes over there?

The world of fairies is the reverse of our world, like a photo
negative.

Some say fairies are the dead. Like ghosts stuck in their
own world. If Lisa returns, will she be alive or dead? Human
or fairy?

To protect yourself from fairies: carry things made of iron,
stay in or near running water, ring bells, carry a four-leaf
clover, and wear your clothes inside out.

For a split second, everything dropped away—there was a
rushing sound in her ears, and the words on the page seemed
to pulse with a sickly rhythm. The description the landlord and
police had given her of how her mother had been found—*An ac-*
cidental drowning, they'd said. *Blood alcohol content of .35.* Drunk,
of course, beyond drunk—why else would you get into the bathtub in inside-out clothes, with a bunch of frying pans, knives,
and assorted junk-drawer hardware, and leave the shower running full blast?

Just a creepy coincidence, Phoebe told herself.

But what if. . .

Phoebe stopped herself cold and went back to Sam's notes.

The fey are masters of disguise: people, plants, animals.

They can appear as anyone or anything, often appearing
as just what the human was hoping to find.

(The fake Evie and Elliot? The old woman/girl?)

"Bee?" Sam called from the living room.

"Yeah?" She scrambled to stuff the papers back into the bag.

"It sounds like the water's draining out of the tub. I think she's done in there."

"Coming!" Phoebe called, stashing the knapsack back where she'd found it.

"What are you doing?" Sam asked. She turned from the closet to find him standing in the doorway behind her, filling it.

"Looking for the air mattress."

"It's in the front-hall closet," he said, "under the sleeping bags. I'll get it set up. I think you better get into the bathroom with some clean clothes."

"On my way," Phoebe said, keeping her eyes on the ground, scared that if she looked at him, he'd know what she'd found. If he didn't already.

She went to their bedroom to find something for Lisa to sleep in, her mind racing. The framed owl above their bed glowered at her.

She grabbed a pair of sweatpants and a T-shirt from her drawer, knowing they'd hang on the skin-and-bones creature in the bathtub, the words from Sam's notes haunting her:

They can appear as anyone or anything, often appearing as just what the human was hoping to find.

CHAPTER 27

Lisa

I found something in the woods," Sammy said. He was out of breath, dressed in his bright yellow rain slicker, plastered with mud and leaves. His shorts, sneakers, and socks were soaked. He stepped through the open garage door, out of the rain. Water pooled at his feet.

Evie and Lisa were sitting on the dirty, grease-stained floor of the garage. Behind them was Da's kiln, throwing wheel, and shelves of glazes, brushes, and half-completed projects. The front of the garage was where they kept tools, gardening supplies, and junk that didn't have any other place to go. As far as Lisa knew, the garage had never actually been used for a car—there was no room for one with all the other stuff in there.

Evie had her overalls on and was trying to get the mower going. She had taken it apart, pretending to know just what she was doing. There was a blade here, a filter there—nuts, bolts, and screws scattered everywhere across the stained cement floor. Lisa was pretty sure that Evie would never get it back together right. One of Evie's greatest faults was that she always thought she was way smarter than she actually was.

The whole time Lisa had been watching Evie mess with the poor defenseless lawn mower, she'd been stewing over what Gerald had said: *She told us, you know. About the cellar hole.*

What exactly had Evie said?

Lisa touched the charm bracelet, imagined Evie, Gerald, and Pinkie having a good laugh about crazy Lisa and the fairies. Poor pathetic Evie trying to seem cool by telling them all her secrets, trying to turn Lisa into the outsider Evie herself was so used to being.

"What'd you find?" Evie asked, wiping grease-stained hands on the bib part of her overalls.

"I think I'd better show you," Sammy said. "Both of you. And I think we should bring your knife, Evie. And maybe some other weapons. Just in case."

"Whoa there," Evie said. "What the hell did you see? A rabid wild boar? Bigfoot?"

"It's pouring out," Lisa said. The rain was pelting off the driveway, running in rivers down to the road.

"So go get raincoats, whatever. Just hurry!"

"Okay, okay already." Evie dropped the wrench with a clang and used the side door to get into the house. Lisa followed her to the front hall, where they grabbed rain slickers.

"What do you think it is?" Lisa asked as she zipped her coat and pulled up the hood.

"I don't know," Evie said, shrugging into her coat. "But whatever it is, it's gotta be good. It takes an awful lot to get Sammy this worked up."

Lisa nodded. Maybe he'd found another gift. Or something bigger. Like a door.

If there was a door, would they go through? Lisa knew her answer. She wouldn't hesitate. But Sammy and Evie—no, she didn't think so. They didn't have it in them. Lisa would be on her own.

When they got back to the garage, Sam had a wooden baseball bat and the rusty machete Da used to hack back the raspberry brambles at the edge of the yard. "Let's go," he said, thrusting the baseball bat at Lisa, leading them out into the rain.

The rain drummed on the top of Lisa's hood and seemed to be coming from all sides, working its way down her face and neck, soaking her shirt. It ran through her open cuffs and up her sleeves, giving her arms goose bumps. The baseball bat was slippery, and she gripped it tightly in both hands to keep from dropping it.

"Hell of a day to declare war," Evie complained.

They trudged down the hill, slipping and sliding on wet leaves and mud.

"Hurry!" Sammy urged.

They crossed the brook, which was twice the size it had been earlier that morning, the chocolate-colored water looking angry and wild. Instead of leaping over it, they had to wade through. Their feet were soaked anyway, so it didn't matter. The water was freezing, and the bottom of the brook was lined with slippery rocks. Lisa almost went tumbling down but caught her balance just in time, using the baseball bat like a cane.

Once they crossed the brook, Sam led the way through Reliance. They passed the cellar holes, skirted the cemetery with its worn stones. After they'd moved out of Reliance, the trees got thicker, but Sam seemed to be following a little path Lisa had never noticed before. A deer trail maybe. Lisa thought she recognized the place where she'd caught up with Gerald and Pinkie earlier.

She told us, you know. About the cellar hole.

Evie followed behind Sam, hunting knife drawn. Lisa kept her eyes on Evie's back, feeling, for the first time in her life, that maybe she didn't know Evie at all. If Evie was conspiring with Gerald and Pinkie, what else was she capable of?

"Just what did you see?" Evie asked Sammy again.

"Shh!" Sam hissed, finger over his lips, eyes wide open. "We're almost there."

Da had taken Lisa duck hunting once, and this reminded her of that day. How she walked quietly behind him, ears and eyes alert to any movement, all her senses on overdrive. And then, like now, she was afraid. Then, she was worried about doing something wrong, scaring the ducks, disappointing Da in some profound way. Now, she was just plain scared. Sammy's fear was contagious. And it didn't help that the one person she'd always counted on had turned out to be a two-faced trickster. She gripped the baseball bat tightly and walked on, her eyes on Evie's back.

Sammy led them through a tight stand of maples, the path (if it even was a path) weaving in and out and seeming to go in circles. Lisa wondered if he was trying to get them lost on purpose. At last he stopped. Using the machete as a pointer, he showed them what he'd brought them to see.

There, in the midst of a dense thicket, was a small clearing— saplings had been cut, low-growing shrubs and plants flattened to the ground. In the center of the clearing was a thick bed of freshly picked ferns with a worn gray blanket on top. At the edge was an antique-looking pair of brass binoculars and a piece of rope coiled like a snake.

"What the hell is this?" Evie said.

"Shhh!" Sammy hissed, looking wildly around, warning them that whoever stayed here could be close by, watching.

Evie nodded, stepped into the clearing, picked up the blanket. There was nothing under it but a pile of crushed ferns. She grabbed the binoculars, wiped the rain off the lenses, and peered through them.

"What are you doing?" Sammy whispered frantically. "Get out of there!"

"I can see your nose hairs," she said, pointing the binoculars right at Sam.

"Come on," Lisa said. "Let's go." Then her eyes fell on something buried in the nest of ferns: a tan circle. She reached down, pulled back the ferns, and saw what it was.

Sammy gasped as Lisa picked it up. "Mom's sewing basket," he said.

Lisa nodded. She held up the dripping basket. The thread inside would be ruined; the needles, if not dried out, would rust.

"But how'd it get out here?" Sammy asked.

Lisa kicked through the nest of ferns, and her foot made contact with something hard. Setting down the basket and bat, she reached in. A can of peaches in heavy syrup.

Evie dropped the binoculars, looked down at the peaches, and said only, "Weird."

"No kidding," Lisa said, studying Evie's face, daring her not to admit that she'd given Gerald and Pinkie a bag with a can of identical peaches just a couple of hours ago.

"I say we bug out before whoever's been hanging out here comes back," said Evie.

Lisa grabbed the bat and her mother's sewing basket, following Sam and Evie back toward home.

"Maybe it's Lisa's Fairy King," Sam said as they made their way through Reliance.

"Maybe," said Lisa, even though she was thinking there was no way. "We should come back later, find some good hiding spots, hunker down and wait to see just who it is."

And catch Gerald and Pinkie doing who knows what. . .

"I don't know," Evie said.

I bet you don't.

"I think I got soaked enough for one day," Evie said

It took Lisa the rest of the afternoon to talk Evie and Sam into returning—Sam was genuinely scared of getting caught, Lisa could see. Evie had one lame excuse after another. They only agreed once the rain finally stopped. But when they made their way back to the clearing after supper, the blanket, binoculars, and can of peaches were gone.

"Weird," Evie said again, kicking at the crushed ferns with her giant work boot. On the way back, Evie talked a mile a minute, laughed too hard at things that weren't funny. She seemed strangely giddy.

Relieved, thought Lisa. *She seems relieved.*

CHAPTER 28

Phoebe

They were back in the cabin, and the old woman was there, doing a strange puppet dance, sticking out her tongue, which turned into a snake.

Sammy, Sammy, weak little Lamb-y! Hiss, hiss. The wink of a small, reptilian eye.

Then Phoebe was back in her childhood bed, the wooden frame painted white, the headboard with its carved daisies. She'd decorated it with stickers—scratch-and-sniff ones that the scent had worn off of long ago. Tangerine. Toasted marshmallow. And her favorite, the one with the monkey holding the banana that said, *I'm bananas for you*.

She heard the scrabbling and scraping of the door under the bed being opened, hinges letting out an endlessly long, low creak. She tried to sit up, to scream, to stop it somehow, but she was frozen in place. At last a shadowy figure slipped out from under the foot of the bed, slinked along the edge of the room by the baseboard heaters that clicked and groaned all night long.

"You're not real," she managed to whisper. "This is a dream."

He started to laugh. It was a wet, choking laugh. His mouth was open, his teeth gleaming like little white daggers.

Phoebe's eyes flipped open, heart hammering, the taste of blood in her mouth—she'd bit her cheek. She wasn't at the cabin or her old bed at all but in her very own house, on the floor of the office, next to Sam. The blanket was pulled up tight around him, even covering his head. She'd never known anyone who slept as deeply, as surely, as Sam did. The air mattress had deflated, leaving them on the floor. A crash came from the bedroom where Lisa was sleeping. The sound of breaking glass. Sam slept on.

"Sam!" she said, putting a hand on his shoulder.

But maybe it wasn't his shoulder. Maybe it wasn't Sam under there at all.

The thought came so quickly, with such strength, that she jerked her hand away.

A chill worked its way through her body, and there was another loud thump from the bedroom.

"Whatisit?" Sam's familiar voice mumbled from under the sheet.

She touched him again, pulling the covers off. Sam. Of course it was Sam. Her imagination was going strange places these last few days.

"Something's happening in Lisa's room."

"Lisa?" he said sleepily, then sat up, listening. Phoebe opened the door of the office, walking on shaky legs, turning left down the hall, through the living room. She glanced over at the row of aquariums where the animals were going on with their evening routines: the snake was digesting the frozen mouse she'd given him earlier; the hedgehog was dozing; the rats were chewing on toilet paper rolls in their cage, building a new nest. Evie groaned and shifted on the couch, buried in covers despite the warm night (Christ, maybe this was some inherited thing). She looked like a sleeping ghost.

Phoebe paused in the kitchen long enough to grab the large maple rolling pin Sam's mom had given them for Christmas last year—a sad attempt to bring out some hint of domesticity in Phoebe, some underlying need to make a good piecrust that Sam's mother was sure was just buried deep inside her somewhere. Phoebe had never made a piecrust in her life, and the only pie she made involved a premade graham cracker crust, a box of chocolate pudding, and a tub of Cool Whip. No baking necessary.

Rounding the corner into the dark bedroom, she brandished the rolling pin in both hands, like a stumpy baseball bat held high.

"Lisa?" She squinted into the darkness, struggled to make sense of the shadowy scene before her.

There were signs of a struggle. The covers had been thrown off the bed. The ceramic lamp from the bedside table lay in ruined pieces on the hardwood floor. The window was open, and Lisa was in the process of crawling through it, but because of the bookshelves in front of it, she was having trouble. She seemed stuck on her belly, kicking her legs in Phoebe's borrowed sweatpants like a swimmer.

Sam came in, flipping on the overhead light. Lisa continued to flail her legs, trying to wriggle the rest of the way through.

"Come back in, honey," Phoebe said, setting the rolling pin down on the bed, leaning to lay a hand on Lisa's back. Then Sam was there, grabbing hold of Lisa's waist, hoisting her from the window and back into the room. She didn't seem to fight him; her body went limp in his arms as if she were a giant doll.

"What are you doing?" he asked, once he'd set her down on the bed, closed and locked the window.

Lisa was out of breath, eyes darting from the window to the open door like a trapped animal searching for the easiest route of escape.

"Teilo," Lisa said, lips trembling.

"What about him?" Phoebe asked, placing a reassuring hand on Lisa's shoulder.

Lisa pointed at the closet door opposite the bed.

There in black paint was Teilo's mark, still wet and dripping.

"He was here? In the room?" Sam asked, opening the closet door, peering under the bed.

Under the bed. He came from under the bed.

Shut up, Phoebe told herself. *Enough.*

Lisa nodded. "We're all in terrible danger," she said. It was not the voice of a woman but that of a frightened little girl. The same voice Phoebe had heard on the phone telling them where to find the fairy book. There was no doubt in her mind.

Phoebe pulled Lisa close and embraced her. "It's okay," she said, sure that if she pulled too tight, she'd easily crush the life out of this poor, skinny girl.

"What's going on?" Evie stood in the doorway, cocooned in her blanket, blinking in at them like a worried owl.

"Teilo was here," Phoebe said, releasing the girl but continuing to stroke her hair. "He was after Lisa." She looked at Sam, asked, "What are we going to do?"

Sam shook his head. "I don't know. But one thing's for sure—they know she's here now. She's not safe with us. We'll have to find another place for her."

Phoebe nodded, looked at her watch. It was a little after four.

"I'll put on some coffee. In a while, I'll make a call. I know a place where she'll be safe."

Sam drove with both hands gripping the wheel. They were on a seldom-used dirt road near the state forest. It was a bright, clear morning, and they had the windows open, letting in damp woodsy smells. Sam's pickup was bouncing along, Lisa between Sam and Phoebe, straddling the gearshift. The radio was on a talk show, but it was turned so low that all Phoebe could hear was the dull hum of voices like far-off insects. Sam often kept the radio on low, afraid that if he turned it off entirely, he might miss something.

They passed a run-down trailer with a rusted swing set out front. A little girl wearing only a pull-up diaper and an Elmo T-shirt was passing trash to her daddy, who was burning it in an old oil drum. The little girl waved at them through a cloud of noxious smoke. Phoebe waved back, thinking, *If these people can be parents, we sure as shit can*, then feeling guilty for it.

Phoebe had her memo pad out and had written:

> *How did Teilo get in? The window? How did he know where she was? Are we being watched?*

"So," Sam said, looking over at Lisa, "are you ready to tell us who you really are?"

"Sam!" Phoebe scolded. When was he going to learn that the cut-to-the-chase approach was going to get him nowhere with this girl?

"I'm Lisa," the girl between them said, looking up at him.

Her eyes were brown, the pupils huge, making her whole eyes seem cartoonish and black. In spite of the long bath in lavender the night before, she gave off the heavy scent of damp earth. She raised her head high and spoke. "I am Lisa, Queen of the Fairies."

"Where have you been all these years?" he asked.

"The land of the fairies."

Phoebe scribbled *Land of Fairies?* and circled it.

Lisa looked at her notebook, at the tiny rune-like scribblings. "Did they teach you to write like that?" she asked.

"Who?"

"The fairies?" Lisa said.

Phoebe shook her head. "I taught myself. What are they like?" Phoebe asked. "The fairies."

Lisa smiled. "You know how sometimes, you catch the faintest hint of movement in the corner of your eye, then you blink and it's gone? That's them."

Lisa let out a raspy cackle that turned into a hacking cough.

"Sometimes," Lisa continued, coughing fit over, "they come to you in dreams."

Sam gripped the wheel so tight Phoebe was sure it would crack.

"Sam?" she said, putting a hand on his shoulder, but he shrugged her off. "You okay?"

"Fine," he said.

"Ain't got no rain barrel, ain't got no cellar door, but we'll be jolly friends, forever more," Lisa sang softly. Phoebe thought of the old woman in the woods, shedding her clothes, her hair.

She touched the bag of teeth in her pocket. Wondered if she should show them to Lisa, see if she recognized them.

Horse teeth.

Bad magic, Evie had warned.

"Their driveway is the next left," Phoebe said, closing her notebook. "Where all the NO TRESPASSING signs are." Sam took the corner too fast, sending Phoebe slamming into Lisa. "Sorry," Phoebe said. Lisa smiled.

The driveway was bordered with trees—a rough, narrow trail that just seemed to get narrower as they crept along. The trees were so close together that nothing green grew on them except up top, the canopy so thick that no light came through. NO TRES-PASSING, warned the signs. BEWARE OF DOGS. As they got closer to the house, the signs, now hand-painted, grew more menacing: TURN BACK NOW; USA OUT OF VERMONT; OWNER ARMED; ATTACK DOGS ON PREMISES.

Ahead, they saw the buildings: house, barn, and workshop. A metal windmill turned in the air above the house, reminding Phoebe of something a child would build from a giant Erector set. At the south side of the house were a forest of solar panels, a satellite dish, and a radio tower.

"Pretty bird," Lisa said.

"What bird?" Sam asked, looking up at the sky. "I don't see any bird." His voice was crackling with frustration.

"I think she means the chickens," Phoebe said. A small flock of colorful speckled hens pecked at the dirt in front of the house. Sam grumbled something Phoebe didn't catch, stopped the truck behind Franny's Subaru wagon, and cut the engine. As he and Phoebe put their hands on the handles to open the doors, the dogs were on them. It was impossible to tell how many at first: a pack of enormous beasts, shiny black and brown, hackles raised, teeth bared, drool flying as they ran circles around the truck.

Franny and Jim bred Rottweilers, and Phoebe could never keep track of the latest updates: who'd had puppies, how many were sold, how many were kept. Most of the barn was taken up by kennels, whelping pens, an indoor agility course.

The front door of the house opened and Franny stepped out. Her straw-colored hair was pulled back in a braid, and she had a morning glory print apron on. Jim sauntered out of the open workshop door in coveralls, wiping greasy hands on a rag. He was a gangly man with a large Adam's apple and constant five o'clock shadow.

Franny whistled, and all the dogs froze, turned their great, blockish heads her way. She did a hand signal that looked like she was writing the letter Z, then closed her fist. The dogs took new positions—one posted by the driver's door, one by the passenger's, one at the front of the truck, and one at the rear—and sat quietly. Three more formed a rough semicircle between the truck and house.

"I think we can get out now," Phoebe said.

"Are you sure?" Sam asked. Phoebe opened her door and stepped out, giving Franny a quick hello hug.

"Thanks so much for agreeing to this," Phoebe said.

"No problem at all," Franny told her. Jim appeared by her side, grinning, disheveled, looking like a mad scientist. The left arm of his glasses was being held on with a safety pin. His eyes were bloodshot and his teeth yellow. "I'm converting the old Mercedes diesel so that it'll run on vegetable oil," he told Sam, who had stepped tentatively out of the truck but still held on to the door, as if he might decide to jump right back up in the cab. "French fry fuel. I've got gallons of the stuff from a couple of local restaurants." Jim had a funny habit of sticking his head forward when he spoke, which made his neck seem very long and turtlelike.

"Very cool," Sam said, eyes nervously watching the dog that was just two feet to his left, holding statue still.

"This is Lisa," Phoebe said, holding the door open, waiting for Lisa to join them. Lisa didn't move. Franny walked around, stuck her head in, and whispered something to Lisa that made her smile and nod, then held out her hand. Lisa took it, and Franny helped her from the truck.

Phoebe knew she'd done the right thing. Lisa would be safe here.

"If anyone shows up out here, we'll know it," Jim told Sam. "I've got cameras and infrared sensors all around the perimeter. At the first sign of any trouble, we'll take her into the bunker. It's underground. Completely out of sight and pretty much impenetrable. We've got supplies in there to last a year—food, water, weapons, a toilet, and shower." There was a glint in his eyes that gave away how much he was loving this.

The cameras and infrared sensors were a surprise to Phoebe, though not a complete shock. Who the hell were they expecting?

"Come on," Jim said, giving Sam a hearty pat on the back. "I'll show you the work I'm doing on the diesel." Jim led Sam toward the workshop, one of the dogs staying right at Jim's side.

Phoebe followed Franny and Lisa into the house, through the mudroom, and into the kitchen, which was hot, steamy, and sweet smelling.

"I'm making strawberry jam," Franny said, moving to the stove to stir a large, steaming pot. The counter was covered in canning jars of various sizes, rubber seals, and lids. Franny's kitchen was enormous and old-fashioned: there was a wood cookstove and a

heavy maple table that did double duty as workstation and gathering place. Cast-iron pans hung from hooks on the rough-hewn
beams that ran the length of the ceiling. Simple open shelves
lined each wall and were full of jars of dried beans, rice, canned
tomatoes, herbs, and spices. To get water at the sink, you had to
use a red-handled pump.

Franny scooped a small amount of the hot strawberry goo into
a ceramic bowl, sliced off a thick piece of homemade bread, and
spread the jam on top, passing it to Lisa.

"It's still a little runny," she said, "but I sort of think it's best
when it's warm and runny, don't you?"

Lisa nodded, diving in like she was starving. She smiled while
she ate, jam leaving sticky stains around her mouth.

They visited a few minutes, making small talk about the office
and the weather. Then Franny walked Phoebe to the door while
Lisa spooned jam onto her third piece of bread and gulped strong
tea with hot milk and honey.

"She'll be fine here, Bee," Franny promised. "I won't let her
out of my sight."

Phoebe knew it was true. There was no safer place for Lisa
than right here. But still, she hated to leave her.

"If she says anything . . . anything at all about where she's
been, or her past—"

"I know. I'll pay close attention. You know me, I've got a
mind like a steel trap. I'll remember any detail she tells me and
report straight back to you. If it seems important, I'll call you
right away. Promise."

Phoebe thanked her and turned to go, but Franny grabbed
her arm, drawing her back. "Did you tell him yet?" she asked,
her voice low.

Phoebe shook her head. "Today," she said. Franny scowled. "I promise."

Phoebe left, casting one quick glance back at Lisa, who sat hunched over the kitchen table, mouth and face grotesquely red, reminding Phoebe a little too much of coagulated blood.

CHAPTER 29

Lisa

Dave, you're being unreasonable," Hazel was saying. Da was lying on the couch, mouth firmly closed. Hazel was holding out a glass of water and two pills. "The medicine's helping, Dave. Call it a blessing, call it a curse, but it's doing its job. Do you want to end up back in the hospital?" Hazel asked. "Is that what you want?"

Lisa had just come in from the yard where she'd been drying out the sewing basket as best she could, thinking things over and coming up with a plan. The first thing she was sure of was that bringing her mom the still-damp basket and explaining where she'd found it would send the household into a tizzy, which was the last thing she wanted. So she snuck upstairs and stuck the sewing basket on the bottom shelf of the hall closet, behind a pile of towels, then headed back down to the kitchen.

The house was warm and bright and familiar. Lisa stood peering into the living room, where her mother and aunt were fussing over Da on the couch. Behind them, on the mantel, a photo of the two of them as young girls watched their backs, smiling out at them from another time. Lisa saw only the vaguest resemblance between the grinning girls and the grown women who stood hunched over and tired, worried lines on their faces.

"Dave, please," Lisa's mom said. She was hovering at the edge of the coffee table in her creamy silk pajamas.

Lisa stepped into the living room, and her mom caught sight of her and shooed her away.

"What are you kids still doing up?" she asked, her voice high and tight.

Lisa shrugged, moving back into the kitchen. "It's summer, Ma. And it's only nine o'clock."

"Well, go on up to bed. And in the morning I want the three of you up early to make me a new pie."

"Pie?"

"Yes, pie. Strawberry pie. To replace the one that mysteriously disappeared from the kitchen counter."

"But we didn't . . ."

"Up to bed. No arguments," Lisa's mom said.

"What's going on?" Sammy whispered when he stepped into the kitchen.

"Mom's upset about her missing pie."

"I didn't even know there was pie," Sam said.

"Probably Evie. Or maybe there never even was a pie."

"Huh?" Sammy said, scrunching up his face.

"Forget it. Look, I have something to tell you. Something important. You head out to the yard. I'm gonna go get Evie and we'll meet you there. We have to be quiet and play it cool, though—Mom's pretty wound up and she wants us all in bed."

"What—you want me to face the wrath of Mom?" Sammy said. "No thanks. I'm going to bed."

"It's important, Sam," she said. "Please."

Sam rolled his eyes, but Lisa knew she'd won. He trudged out through the kitchen door into the yard.

Lisa peeked back into the living room. Hazel was shoving the pills at Da again. He pushed her hand away, then abruptly leaned forward, grabbed the corner of the coffee table, and flipped it. A stack of magazines, plates of toast crumbs, and cold tea went toppling onto the floor. It was the most Lisa had seen Da move since he got home from the hospital. Part of her cringed, but another part wanted to cheer him on.

"That's it, I'm calling the doctor," her mom announced, stalking toward the kitchen. Lisa bolted out of the room, down the front hall, and up the stairs, taking them two at a time, her pink and silver sneakers barely touching the carpeted treads. When she got to her room, she flung open the door and gasped, actually gasped, like a girl in one of those horror movies Sam and Evie loved.

What she saw was herself. Only not really her at all. This was a chunkier, Frankenstein-girl version of herself. Maybe it was a little like what the two little girls peering out of the photo might see in the living room now—themselves, only totally different.

But this was not some future Lisa she'd glimpsed through time and space—this was an impostor.

Evie was standing in front of the mirror dressed in Lisa's hooded red sweatshirt. She had on the black witch wig Lisa's mom used last Halloween, and the hair hung down over her face, the red hood pulled up snug over the top of her head. She was wearing a stretchy black pair of leggings of Lisa's that were too small and made Evie's legs look all sausage-y. Evie's feet were bare and her toenails were painted with blue glitter polish, just like Lisa's.

"Um . . . what are you doing?" Lisa asked, noticing that over the strange Lisa costume, Evie had on her thick leather belt, the hunting knife in its sheath strapped against her right hip.

"Nothing." Beneath the curtain of fake polyester hair, Evie's face turned lobster red and her breath got whistley.

"Okay," Lisa said, though nothing was okay at all. She took a step backward, feeling dizzy. "Okay," she said again, trying to convince herself everything was A-OK. Perfectly normal. The world wasn't going crazy around her. "Sammy's waiting for us outside," she said at last, turning away. "Oh and my mom's all upset about the pie."

"What pie?" Evie asked as Lisa backed out of the room, shutting the door behind her.

Downstairs, as she walked through the kitchen, she heard her mom on the phone. "Yes, noncompliant," she was saying. "But it's not only that. He believes we're trying to poison him."

CHAPTER 30

Phoebe

They were in Sam's pickup, heading toward home. Phoebe had her little notebook out and stared down in disbelief at what she'd just written:

Willa. Jasper. Zoe. Cooper.

She snapped the book closed. She wasn't even sure they'd be keeping the baby, and here she was naming it. Totally delusional. Not so different from her own mom after all. The apple doesn't fall far from the tree. And sometimes the apple is just as fucked up—all bruised, full of worms, scarred with blight.

She knew that's what she was most afraid of, deep down. Not Sam's rejection of the idea of parenthood but her own fear of being as shitty a mom as her own mother had been.

We're diamonds in the rough, you and me.

She thought of her last conversation with her mother, two days before she died.

"Come home," her ma begged. "I need you. *He* needs you."

"He?" Phoebe had asked, wondering what scumbag her mother was shacking up with now.

"Your Dark Man, lovie. He's here. He's waiting for you."

"You're drunk," Phoebe said. "Call me when you sober up. If you sober up." Then she'd hung up and never heard from her mother again. Two days later, the police called.

Accidental drowning.
Blood alcohol content of .35.
Clothes inside out.

"Did your mother often do dishes in the bathtub?" the detective had asked.

"Dishes?" Phoebe said.

"There were some pots and pans in the tub with her. Knives and flatware, too."

Your Dark Man, lovie. He's here. He's waiting for you.

Sam," Phoebe said, looking up. "You don't think all this fairy stuff could be real, do you?"

Sam nodded, downshifted, gears grinding. "Of course not," he said, face in a tight grimace.

She wanted so badly to tell Sam that she'd found the backpack in the closet, ask him if really believed any of it. But she didn't want to be accused of snooping, prying, meddling. Sam obviously wanted to keep his research a secret, so be it. He'd tell her when he was ready. Wouldn't he?

Just like she was going to tell him about the baby. Damn.

"Franny mentioned something earlier this week," Phoebe said. "That you and Lisa were friends with a couple of kids who lived nearby. She said one of them, the girl, believed the fairies were real. Even went around saying she'd met the King of the Fairies."

Sam nodded robotically. "Gerald and Pinkie."

"Pinkie?"

"It was a nickname. Her real name was Becca, but she was always dressed in pink—it seemed like she didn't own anything in any other color."

He looked back out the windshield.

Pinkie.

Phoebe remembered the little girl in pink who had led her into the woods that afternoon. *Are you here to see the fairies?* The girl who'd shown her the paper bag with the strange six-fingered glove inside it. Pinkie. It must have been.

"So you were friends? You, Lisa, Gerald, and Pinkie?"

"Honestly, we were kind of at war with them that summer. Gerald had a big crush on Lisa, but he hated Evie. He called her Stevie. Humiliated her."

"And Evie put up with all that?"

Sam laughed harshly. "Not exactly. She broke his arm."

Phoebe was silent.

"You think you know Evie. That you're doing this good deed, trying to help her. But I'm telling you, Bee, she can't be trusted. You don't know what she's capable of."

Over a dinner of wonderfully starchy white-flour pasta topped with sweet sauce from a jar, Sam went over the plan.

"We'll go pick up Lisa tomorrow. Then we'll drive over to Barre with her, see if anything there sparks any memories. We'll take her into the library, see if they can tell us anything about this Mary Stevens person. It's not much of a clue, but it's all we've got."

The phone rang and they all jumped. "I'll get it," said Sam, heading for the living room.

Phoebe listened to Sam say, "Yeah? What? Uh huh. Uh huh." Then he mumbled something she didn't catch.

"Something's still bothering me," Evie confessed, voice low. "I can't believe Sam's had that bracelet all these years." Evie sucked in her bottom lip. "We all figured she must have been wearing it when she went missing. She had it on that night at dinner. She never took the thing off."

Why would she? Phoebe wondered. If it was her most treasured possession, why leave it behind?

Two ideas came to mind: that Lisa suspected something bad might happen to her and she wanted to leave behind a clue; or she had it on the night she went into the woods for the last time, and Sam somehow got hold of it. Which would mean he was involved. Evie was looking right at her, and Phoebe sensed the other woman was somehow reading her mind. Phoebe felt her throat tighten. "You don't think—" she started to say.

Sam burst into the kitchen and Phoebe jumped a little, hating herself for it. This was her boyfriend. Her great love. The father of her child.

"She has a baby," Sam blurted out.

"What?" Evie said. "Who?"

He knows, Phoebe thought. He learned about the pregnancy.

Maybe the fake Evie had just called him on the phone and given her up.

"Lisa," Sam said. "That was Franny. She noticed the front of Lisa's shirt was all wet, then realized her breasts were leaking milk. Lisa told her there was a baby. Just a few weeks old. When Franny asked where it was, she said it was back with his father—in the fairy world."

"Holy shit," Evie muttered, eyes huge.

"If the people who have been after us have that baby, we need to go to the police," said Phoebe, shuddering.

"Okay," Sam said, nodding.

"Not so fast," Evie said. "Let's think this through."

"What is there to think through?" Phoebe asked. "We've got some psychopaths who've kidnapped a baby. If this is really Lisa, then we're talking about your niece or nephew, Sam. We've gotta find that baby."

"Exactly," Evie agreed. "But I think we have a better chance doing it on our own. If Teilo gets wind that the cops are involved—and he will find out—he'll take that baby where we'll never find it. Or worse."

"But I—" Phoebe said.

Evie cut her off. "Think about what happened with the police back at the cabin. You two turned out looking like the criminals, remember? He's clever. He'll always be two steps ahead of us."

"So what are we supposed to do?" Sam asked.

"Follow your original plan," Evie said. "Take Lisa to Barre. See what you can find out. Lisa is the key here. She's carrying clues around in that jumbled head of hers. We just have to make sense of them. Cops are going to scare her to death. And trust me, they hear the first *whisper* from her about the fairy world, and bam, social work and psych are involved, and she's hospitalized and drugged to the gills, no good to anyone, least of all the baby. We're Lisa's *family*, Sam. We can get through to her."

Sam bit his lip. "Okay," he agreed. "But if we don't turn up anything on our little field trip to Barre, we call the police."

D o you think we should tell your mom?" Phoebe asked. "Maybe even bring Lisa by?"

It was nearly eleven and they were back in their bedroom. Phoebe was changing the sheets, taking off the ones Lisa had slept on and putting on a pale blue set. Sam shook his head as he kicked off the old hiking boots he wore everywhere.

"Not yet, Bee." He took off his watch and set it on the little table next to his side of the bed. The book he'd been reading was there, too—some horribly depressing book on global warming his mom had given him for his birthday.

Sam stood shirtless, his curly hair disheveled and slightly sweaty. Phoebe studied the scar on his chest, wondered if she'd ever learn the truth about it.

He turned his back to her, pulled off his jeans, letting them drop to the floor. "Not until we know for sure. And I'm still not convinced. Something just doesn't feel right about all this."

"Maybe your mother would know. Some people say mothers have a kind of intuition, a connection to their kids that never goes away."

Sam grunted.

"That's what I've always heard, anyway," she said. "I was reading somewhere recently that mothers and babies can identify each other just by smell. Isn't that amazing?"

"So what are you suggesting?" he asked. "You want my mother to give this girl a great big sniff all over to see if she's Lisa? Christ, Bee, we're not a pack of wolves." He climbed into the freshly made bed and turned off the light on his table. Phoebe's own bedside light had been smashed to pieces during Lisa's struggle with Teilo. She'd replaced it with an old metal gooseneck lamp from the office.

"That's not what I'm saying at all! Lisa was her baby. Her only daughter. They must have had a strong connection. Just like you would if it were your kid we were talking about."

How could she be such a coward? It wasn't just her baby; it was Sam's too. He had to know the truth. Especially now. If Teilo had taken Lisa's baby, wouldn't he come for theirs too?

It's now or never, she told herself. "Sam, I—"

"But I don't have any kids," he told her. "I'll never have kids." His eyes were closed, his face calm.

Phoebe clenched her hands into tight fists. "Never?" The word came out high and tight.

"It's never been anything I've wanted." Sam's voice was sleepy, drifting. "It's just not in the cards, Bee."

And just then, she thought she felt the tiny baby move inside her, give a kick in protest, pound on the walls of her uterus, to say, *Like it or not, I'm here.*

Can't sleep?" Evie asked. She was in the kitchen, warming milk on the stove, spooning honey into it.

Phoebe shook her head, sure that if she spoke, she'd burst into tears.

"Me neither," Evie said, smiling. "No worries, though. It's my personal belief that all the best people are insomniacs." She sprinkled cinnamon into the milk, then reached for two mugs. "Try this." Evie filled a mug with steaming milk and passed it to her. "It's what my mother always gave me when I couldn't sleep."

Phoebe took a sip. It was warm and sweet and perfect. She took another long gulp, feeling it warm her. Had her mother ever made her warm milk? She'd given Phoebe NyQuil to help her sleep (and poured herself a slug for good measure). Half a Valium now and then. An ounce of brandy, which tasted like poison, but her mother promised it would chase the nightmares away. Her mother, who spent her last years in some hideous public housing unit, trading disability checks for frozen dinners, generic cigarettes, and booze.

Sometimes you've just gotta live, sweetheart. Feel the wind in your hair.

For the millionth time that day, Phoebe wondered what kind of mother she'd be and if she was genetically programmed to be lousy at it. She imagined some hidden switch flipping somewhere in the back of her brain the day her baby was born, the fucked-up-mommy switch inherited from her mother and grandmother, along with her curly hair and narrow hips.

Jesus. A tear ran down her nose, dripped into her mug of warm milk.

How could she have even considered keeping the baby?

Little Willa or Jasper didn't stand a chance.

"Phoebe?" Evie said, placing a hand gently on her arm.

"Do you think you could drive?" Phoebe asked.

"I—I don't know. I remember how. But it's been a long time. And there's the little detail that in order to drive, I'd have to leave the house. Go out there." Evie gestured toward the door, her hand trembling a little as if the devil himself was waiting for her there.

"Forget it," Phoebe said, touching her forehead, then pressing hard, massaging it in little circles. She was so shitty at this—asking people for help. She'd spent her whole life trying not to need anyone's help, prided herself on her independence. "It's just that I need a ride. I can get myself there, but someone else has to drive me home and there's no one I can ask. No one I want to ask. There's Franny, but she can be so judgmental."

"Phoebe, I—"

"I'm pregnant." She spit the words out like bits of metal, sharp against her tongue.

Evie took in a breath, then nodded, her face calm.

"Sam doesn't want a baby," Phoebe continued. "And besides, it doesn't matter. I'd be a lousy mother anyway. And it's not like Sam and I have any chance at all of making it. I don't know what we're doing even trying." The tears were coming hard and fast and she was gulping for air.

"Oh, Phoebe," Evie said, pulling Phoebe to her. Evie held her tight, and she cried harder, her tears soaking the shoulder of Evie's T-shirt.

"Bee?"

Sam was at the edge of the kitchen in his boxers, squinting at them, his face one big sad question mark. "Why didn't you tell me?"

So this was how it was going to be. No romantic dinner with candlelight and wine. She could practically hear Franny scolding her, saying, *This is why you should have told him the minute you found out.*

"Oh God, I'm sorry, I tried," Phoebe sobbed, stepping away from Evie. "I was waiting for the right time, but Franny was right—there's no such thing as the right time."

His face grew more puzzled. "Franny knows?"

Phoebe tried to calm down, took a few ragged breaths.

"I should have come to you first, I know. But things have been so hectic. So complicated. I'm scared, Sam. I'm scared that whoever took Lisa's baby will want ours too."

Sam stared at her, his eyes glassy.

"Sam? Say something."

"You remember, don't you," Evie said, looking at Sam, her own eyes wide and panicked. "What we all promised Teilo?"

Sam said nothing.

"What?" Phoebe asked.

Evie cleared her throat. "All of us—Sammy, Lisa, and I—we each promised to give our firstborn child to Teilo."

Phoebe felt the air in her lungs escape. She felt light-headed. The baby inside her, the size of a lima bean, she imagined.

Sam's firstborn.

"You did *what?*" Phoebe said, the words taking every ounce of effort to form. She looked at Sam pleadingly. It was a tell-me-it-isn't-true look, but he didn't meet her gaze. "Sam?" she said, stepping backward, stumbling over a chair. She turned and ran from the room.

"Bee!" he called after her, but it was too late.

She got to the office, bolted the door.

Phoebe took in a breath.

Firstborn. Sam promised Teilo his firstborn.

Just as Lisa had.

CHAPTER 31

Lisa

Where's Evie?" Sam asked when Lisa met him out in the yard.

"She's, um, changing," Lisa said. She tried to push the image of Evie's legs stuffed into her too-tight pants out of her head.

"What's this big important thing you wanted to tell us?"

"Let's wait for Evie."

"Is it about Da?" Sam asked. "'Cause if you know something, you should tell. I'm old enough. I'm sick of everyone thinking I'm not old enough."

"No," Lisa said. "This isn't about Da. I've got a deal for you. I think you'll like it."

Evie sauntered out into the yard, dressed in her own clothes—baggy overalls, big shitkickers on her feet.

She didn't say a word or make eye contact.

They all three plopped themselves down in the tall grass, bending it, making little nests for themselves.

"Okay, I know you guys are getting a little sick of all this talk about the fairies and the cellar hole. Sam, I know you don't believe me. And Evie, I know you want me to stay away from there."

They both nodded in agreement. Lisa couldn't see their faces in the dark, only their silhouettes. Evie started ripping at the grass. Sam sat perfectly still.

She waited. Sam and Evie leaned a little closer. She could hear them breathing. Crickets chirped. Lightning bugs flickered.

"So here's the deal. You two sign papers promising your first-born to Teilo, and I'll never mention him again. I'll drop the papers off in the cellar hole and wait. If he doesn't come tonight, I'm done. I won't go down there, I won't leave any gifts, I swear I'll never talk about the fairies again."

Sam laughed.

"Wait, firstborn? You mean, like, firstborn *child*?"

It sounded so ridiculous when Sam said it, Lisa thought she might lose her resolve. But she called upon the strength of the fairies and replied quietly, with dignity.

"Yes. Precisely. Firstborn child."

"Lisa," Evie said, "you're kidding, right? You wouldn't really promise . . . something like that? Or ask us to?"

"Come on," Lisa said, growing impatient. "What have you got to lose? Who knows if any of us would ever even have kids. You don't believe in any of it anyway, Sammy. And Evie, if you do this, I promise I'll just drop the whole thing."

Sammy and Evie were silent.

Lisa reached into the back pocket of her jeans, pulled out the three pieces of paper and pens, and handed Sammy and Evie one.

"Are you sure about this?" Evie asked, picking up her pen.

"If your Fairy King doesn't show up, you won't go down there anymore? You swear?"

"Not after tonight," Lisa said.

Sam snickered, filling out his paper.

"Don't forget to write down your wish too. Then sign it."

"Do I seal it with a drop of blood?" Sam asked, folding his note into a paper airplane and aiming it straight for Lisa's head.

Lisa rolled her eyes.

"So do you ever wonder?" Evie asked, once she was finished folding up her paper into a tight little rectangle. She recapped the pen using her mouth, making it all gross and slobbery.

"Wonder what?" Lisa said. She took Evie's paper and the pen, careful not to touch the cap.

"Why you? I mean, no offense or anything, but why are you the one getting the gifts and the book? If he really is the King of the Fairies, he could have any girl on earth, right?"

Lisa shrugged her shoulders. Evie walked back toward the house. Lisa listened for the door but didn't hear it slam.

"I think Evie's jealous," Sam said. "She wants a chance to go at it with the Fairy King."

"That's sick," said Lisa.

"Nah," Sammy said. "What's sick is you two believing all this crap. I hate to say it, Lisa, but you're getting to be as crazy as Da." Then he was gone, too, leaving Lisa feeling like she'd been punched in the gut.

She entered the woods and made her way toward Reliance, heart pounding as she descended the hill and jumped the brook, walked through the spindly trees, smelling the rich loamy smell of the woods. Her plan had worked! It didn't matter what they thought: they'd have proof soon enough. She was on her way to meet the King of the Fairies—the very thought of it made her feel giddy and light, like a balloon bouncing around, needing to be tied down so she wouldn't float away.

As she approached the cellar hole, Lisa heard a voice talking, then shouting. She held her breath, listening.

"I know you can hear me! You don't belong here. Leave Lisa alone!"

Lisa crept closer, squinted in the darkness until she made out a figure in overalls and big work boots.

Evie. It was just Evie. She must have circled back and gone into the woods without Lisa noticing.

"What are you doing?" Lisa asked as she approached Evie.

"Lisa," Evie said. "This is a huge mistake. You don't get that now, but you've gotta trust me."

"Trust you?" Lisa said. "Why should I trust you?"

Evie looked as if she'd been slapped in the face. "Because—" she stammered.

"Because why?" Lisa asked.

"There's so much I could tell you. So much you don't know. I thought it would ruin everything, but now . . ."

"What I do know is that you've been sneaking around with Gerald and Pinkie, telling them about the cellar hole," Lisa said, stepping away. "How am I supposed to trust you when you've been blabbing away about the one big secret I've ever asked you to keep?"

Evie took a step forward, gave Lisa a pleading look. "I did it to protect you."

"Protect me? How is telling my biggest secret to those jerks protecting me?"

"Look, I can't explain it all right now. But I will. Soon, I promise. Come on. Let's get out of here—just you and me. We'll take the stupid papers we filled out and burn them. I know where Mom keeps the keys to her car. I can drive a little, enough to get us far away from here, from the hill and Reliance. From all the bullshit."

Lisa couldn't believe what she was hearing. Evie was actually asking her to run away?

"And where are we supposed to go?" Lisa asked.

"Away. Like those girls in the story you've been telling. We get on a horse or in Ma's old busted-up Caddie, and we ride. We ride until we run out of gas, until the car breaks down, then we walk. We jump a train. We hitch. Whatever. We just go. Now. Before it's too late."

Lisa stared at her cousin. "Too late?"

Evie clenched her jaw and looked down at the ground. She pulled the key on the cord out from inside her shirt. "All of this is my fault. But I can stop it. I can save us." Evie let out a wheezing, raspy breath. "I have to tell you something," she said, hanging her head down, looking guilty.

"Look," Lisa said, "if it's about tonight, what I saw in my room, forget it. It's okay. I don't mind. You can borrow my stuff anytime you want. Really."

"But that's not—"

"It doesn't matter," Lisa told her. She touched Evie lightly on the arm. "This thing with the fairies, Evie, it's huge. And it's so wonderful. Do you understand how lucky we are? We can get whatever we wish for. They may be able to help Da. Don't you get it, Evie? I want you to be a part of it too. And if Sammy's right, if there are no fairies and Teilo doesn't come, then I'm done with all this. Promise." Then she reached down and took Evie's hand, entwining her index finger with Evie's. "We're like this," she said. "And nothing's going to take that away."

Evie nodded.

"You go on now," Lisa said, gently pushing Evie away. "Back to the house. I'm gonna drop off our papers."

Evie headed back up the hill, her feet crunching the ground beneath her.

Lisa went right for the cellar hole and pulled the papers out of her pocket. Hers was on top, so she looked at that one first.

> *I, Lisa Nazzaro, promise my firstborn to Teilo, the King of the Fairies. My wish is that one day I can come visit the land of the fairies and see it with my own eyes.*

She hesitated over the others, then broke down and opened them, deciding Teilo wouldn't mind. Sam's was simple: *I, Sam Nazzaro, promise my firstborn child to the fairies. My true wish is that Lisa gets a clue and stops jerking us around with all this fairy crap.*

Duly noted. Lisa folded it back up.

Then she opened Evie's.

Evie's wish sent a little electric warning through Lisa's body. There, in Evie's messy childish scrawl, were these words:

> *I, Eve Katherine O'Toole, do promise my firstborn child to Teilo, King of the Fairies.*
> *My wish is that Lisa never learns the truth.*

Now, hours later, Lisa understood the truth: the King of the Fairies was not coming for her. She'd waited in the cellar hole half the night with her notes, calling Teilo's name like some pathetic schoolgirl with a crush. Stupid. She'd done what she was supposed to: she'd promised the King of the Fairies her first-born, even convinced the others to do the same. But he hadn't come. Maybe the fairies had looked inside her and decided she was unworthy. She grabbed a handful of her hair and yanked it hard. "Idiot!"

Maybe she should have waited longer, but she couldn't make herself. Each minute that ticked by was just further proof that Sammy was right—Teilo wasn't coming. Maybe he didn't even exist at all.

Now, cold, tired, and utterly defeated, she had to go back to the house and keep her promise. She had to find a way to act like this thing with the fairies had never even happened. She wasn't allowed to ever mention it again. Or go down the hill into Reliance.

Worse still, she'd have to listen to Sammy saying, *I told you so.*

Sure everyone was asleep, Lisa let herself in the kitchen door. She was creeping up the stairs when something stopped her. Voices. She held her breath, listening.

One of the voices was Da's.

But Da hadn't spoken in over two weeks.

She listened harder. This was definitely Da's voice. And someone else. Lisa tiptoed back down the stairs, straining to hear through the heartbeat hammering in her head. Was she imagining the voices?

When Lisa peeked around the corner from the kitchen, she saw it wasn't her imagination. There was Evie, crouched on the floor, talking with Da in the living room. And Da was talking back.

But what were they saying?

And why was Da talking to Evie when Lisa herself, his own flesh-and-blood daughter, had been trying to get him to speak for the past two weeks?

Lisa heard the words *her*, *she*, *too late*, and *never again*. Then, clear as could be, she heard Evie say the words, "Please, Dad."

The kitchen light came on.

"Lisa?"

She spun to see Aunt Hazel in her shabby flannel nightgown. Her hair was going every which way and she reeked of brandy. "It's nearly three in the morning," she said. "What are you doing up?"

Lisa couldn't think fast enough to answer. Her head swam.

Dad. Evie had called Da Dad.

Hazel marched past Lisa, leaving a trail of brandy fumes, and threw on the living room light switch. Evie was hiding behind the recliner, but Hazel spotted her instantly. "What's going on here, Evie?"

Evie's cheeks blazed red.

Then Hazel looked at the couch. "Dave?"

But Lisa's father was no longer on the couch. There was only a damp pillow and balled-up cotton blanket covering the large indent on the cushion where his body had been for the past three weeks. Lisa followed Hazel through the living room into the office. Her father was seated at the desk, the phone in his hand.

"Who are you talking to, Dave?" Hazel asked, hurrying into the room.

She took the phone from his hand, said, "Hello? Anyone there?" into it, then shook her head and hung up.

"We need to get you back in bed, Dave. And you children, upstairs, now!" Hazel pointed to the stairs with a shaking hand.

Evie?"

As soon as they'd gotten back to the bedroom, Evie had turned off the lights and crawled into her sleeping bag. Lisa got into bed but knew she'd never be able to sleep.

"Yeah?" Evie said. She was just a disembodied voice in the darkness of Lisa's bedroom. A voice from down below.

Lisa struggled to keep her thoughts straight.

"I heard you just now," Lisa said. "I heard you call my father Dad."

Evie was silent a moment. "You know why?" she said at last. "Because he thought I was you. You know how messed up he is from all those medicines they've got him on."

"What did you say to him?" Lisa asked.

"Nothing," Evie said.

Lisa turned, facing the wall, her mind racing.

"So I take it your Fairy King never showed up," Evie said.

"No," Lisa mumbled.

"Then you're done with all of it? Like you promised?"

Lisa nodded in the dark and spoke through the hard lump in her throat. "Like I promised."

Lisa woke up in the morning to the sound of bells, not the gentle tinkling of the fairy bells but something far more ominous. Ringing, chiming, one loud whine that went on and on, getting louder. A great whirling vortex of sound. A siren. She stumbled out of bed to the window, tripping over Evie in her sleeping bag.

"What?" Evie shouted, sitting up. Then she heard the sound and crawled out of the sleeping bag, joining Lisa at the window.

Outside, everything looked hazy in the early morning light. Two men were wheeling Da on a stretcher into an ambulance. His eyes were closed. He had an oxygen mask covering his nose and mouth. Lisa's mother got in with him. She was still in her pajamas, which was all wrong. Her mother would never leave the house in her pajamas. Aunt Hazel was coming back into the house, her face tight as a statue's.

PART III

Say, Say My Playmate

If you wish to cross over to the fairy realm, it needs to be done on Midsummer's Eve.

For at least three days before, take no solid food. Drink only water sweetened with honey and tea made from the flowers and leaves of foxglove.

On Midsummer's Eve, journey into the woods alone, near midnight. Bring nothing with you. Tell no one you are leaving.

Stand inside a circle of thirteen stones, close your eyes, and call out to the King of the Fairies. Tell him you are ready and that you come willingly. Then wait for him to take your hand.

CHAPTER 32

Phoebe

She was back in her childhood bed with the white wooden headboard. *Beds are like boats*, she was thinking, smiling as she navigated her way using the glow-in-the-dark stars on her ceiling. The bed was moving, rocking on the waves. Gradually, horribly, it dawned on her that it was not the ocean that caused her bed to sway. It was something below trying to get out: pushing, thrashing, clawing his way up from the trapdoor under the bed where she'd piled books and toys and suitcases full of clothes, thinking that might keep her safe. At last, he pushed through. A shadow slithered to the far corner of her room, then back toward her. It made no sound.

She wanted to run, but her legs were frozen in place, the covers heavy as lead. As the figure moved closer and lifted his head, she saw that it was Sam.

"Shit!" she yelped, sitting up on the half-deflated air mattress to find bright sunlight streaming through the window.

Home. She was home. Not in her own bed beneath the watchful eyes of the owl but on the office floor.

Double shit.

She replayed the events of the night before in her mind and felt sick to her stomach.

Squinting at the clock, heart still hammering from the dream, she saw it was a little after eight. Sam was thumping around in the kitchen making coffee. The water ran; the grinder whirred. Hearing the chirps of the cordless phone being dialed a few minutes later, she opened the office door, listened carefully, and realized right away that he was talking to his boss.

"Something's come up," he explained. "A family emergency, and I won't be in for a couple of days. I'll give you a call if it's going to be any longer. Uh huh. Thanks, man."

Phoebe quietly closed the door and waited, holding her breath, sure that at any moment she'd hear him come down the hall, knock softly. Maybe he'd even have a cup of coffee for her. They'd talk about the baby. He'd say he was sorry. He'd promise to keep her and the baby safe.

Just as she was expecting, she heard Sam's footsteps come from the kitchen to the hall. Then he stopped and grabbed his keys, which jingled in his hand. He hesitated a moment, not three feet from her door, then turned and walked the other way.

"Sam?" she called, but he didn't seem to hear.

She couldn't believe he would just leave her like this.

And if he wasn't going to work, where was he off to?

Phoebe pulled on her jeans and green boots, ran a hand through her sleep-tousled hair, and hurried into the hall. Sam's truck started in the driveway.

Phoebe grabbed her purse and keys.

"Where're you going so early?" Evie asked. She was watching from the living room, still cocooned in blankets on the couch.

All Phoebe could see of her was her face with its enormous dark eyes. And the key necklace, on top of the covers.

"To see what the hell Sam's up to," Phoebe said, hurrying toward the front door.

Evie nodded. "Be careful," she said, and Phoebe got a chill.

At first she was sure she'd lost him. She knew he'd turned left out of the driveway onto Lang Street, but did he go left on River or right? She looked right and saw no sign of his truck. The road to the left took a sharp bend, so it was impossible to see very far. She took a chance and went left and soon had him in sight.

She kept her distance, making sure there were always at least two cars between them. As they drove out of town, this got harder because the traffic thinned. He was heading toward the state forest. He could be going for Lisa, maybe to take her to Barre on his own now. He turned down Harrington Road, which took him away from Franny and Jim's and into the heart of the state forest with its vast network of hiking trails. Where the hell was he going? There was nothing out this way. Nothing, nothing, and more nothing. Phoebe hit the brakes, wondering if she dared follow. There were no cars between them now. Maybe he was going to take a little impromptu hike to clear his head. That seemed a very Sam-like thing to do.

But then, Sam hadn't been acting like himself lately, had he?

She moved her foot from the brake to the gas and rolled slowly after him.

They passed a small pond, a stand of sugar maples, and a Christmas tree farm. The road twisted and turned like a drunken snake. Phoebe clawed at the wheel with her thumbnails. Every now and then, she caught sight of his taillights and slowed. At least she hadn't lost him yet. If he turned down a side road or driveway, she'd have no way of knowing. Each time she came to one, she hit the brakes, glanced down the road, and, seeing no sign of Sam's red pickup, continued on.

The houses were few and far between. Seasonal cabins, mostly. A few year-round dwellings for hardy souls.

She passed a run-down trailer on the right. There were cars up on cinder blocks, an oil tank outside on bent legs. And there were Christmas decorations up—strings of ragged lights, a tattered reindeer flag, and a big shiny plastic sign on the door that said SANTA IS COMING. A warning.

And who was Santa anyway, Phoebe thought, but the king of the elves? Elves—first cousins to fairies.

"Idiot," she mumbled to herself. The road dipped down, then leveled. Phoebe wished she was back home at the kitchen table, drinking a cup of hot coffee, instead of out here on a wild-goose chase. Evie would get up and they'd have cinnamon toast with mountains of sugar.

Up ahead, she caught up with Sam just enough to see him turn onto a side road. She followed, creeping along. She passed a U-Haul in front of a small gray house. Two guys in dirty T-shirts were loading a couch into the back of it. Up ahead, Sam was pulling his truck into the driveway of a small ranch three houses down on the left. Phoebe slammed on the brakes, put her car in reverse, and backed up so that she was hidden by the U-Haul.

The house whose driveway Sam had pulled into was set back from the road and had sickly yellow vinyl siding and a tidy yard. And in the driveway, right in front of Sam's truck, was the black Jeep with Massachusetts plates.

"Holy shit," Phoebe said, rubbing her eyes like a stupid comic book character who can't quite believe what she's seeing. And she felt more like a character in a comic book or film than her true self—surely this wasn't her real life, her real boyfriend and father of the baby she carried inside her.

"What's your daddy up to?" she asked, placing a protective hand over her belly.

She sat and watched in a dumbfounded stupor as Sam approached the front door and knocked. The door was answered by the bearded man who had called himself Elliot back in the cabin.

Phoebe slouched down in her seat. The fake Elliot stood talking with Sam for a minute. Then the girl who played Evie appeared in the doorway in a midriff-exposing halter top. There was no hole in her side or thick bandaging. She was intact and unhurt.

Sam seemed agitated. The more he talked, the louder his voice got. Phoebe unrolled her window all the way, straining to hear.

She caught Sam saying *baby*. Elliot shook his head, rubbed his face worriedly. Then the fake Evie said something Phoebe couldn't hear.

She couldn't risk moving any closer. Elliot shook his head, said something that made Sam relax. Then, a few seconds later, Sam was laughing.

She had to do something. Call someone. But who? The police—no, she'd sound like a crazy person. How could she possibly explain? Sam was involved; involved in what, exactly, she couldn't say.

She grabbed the phone and dialed her home number. Evie picked up.

"You're not going to believe who Sam is talking to right this minute," she said.

"Who?" Evie asked, sounding half-asleep.

"The fake Evie and Elliot! He drove right to their goddamn house, and they're all chatting away like the best of friends. The girl's got a short shirt on, exposing this totally perfect belly—not a mark on her. Shit! He just went inside with them. What the hell is going on, Evie? Who are these people?"

Evie was silent a minute. "I think you better get out of there," she said, sounding suddenly awake. "Don't let them see you. Get out of there and come back home. We'll sit down and figure out what to do next. Okay?"

"Okay, but I want to make a stop first. I want to check on Lisa and tell Franny not to let Sam and his merry bunch of goons come anywhere near her."

B̶ut how could Sam be involved in whatever happened to Lisa?" Franny asked. "This is his own sister we're talking about. And her baby!"

They were sitting at Franny's kitchen table sipping jasmine tea with honey from heavy ceramic mugs. Lisa was outside picking strawberries with Jim. Phoebe could see them through the kitchen window. Lisa was wearing overalls and a T-shirt. She looked lost in Franny's clothes, and she had the complexion of a vampire. How could such a skin-and-bones woman give birth to a baby? Phoebe couldn't believe that it would have been born healthy. She pictured the baby out there now, malnourished, sick, needing medical attention.

"I don't know," Phoebe admitted. "None of it makes any sense.

I can't believe he might have been involved with what happened at the cabin—I mean, what would be the point of all that? It seems like a hell of a show to put on just for my benefit. And when I think for even a second that he might have had anything to do with taking Lisa's baby . . ." Her voice broke and she blinked back tears. "He didn't say anything when he found out I was pregnant, Franny. And then I find out he's promised his firstborn to the fairies! What other secrets is he keeping?"

"I've known Sam practically his whole life, Bee," Franny said, putting a comforting hand on Phoebe's arm. "He'd never put a child in harm's way—his or anybody else's. The idea of him being involved in some crazy criminal conspiracy just doesn't fit. But he obviously knows more than he's been letting on, right?"

Phoebe nodded, took a sip of tea. It seemed impossible that her life had spun so far out of control these last days. That the love of her life, the guy who cried at the death of the wounded owl, had become one of the bad guys.

"He may be into this deeper than I ever imagined," she said. "When I talked with Becca, she said if I wanted to know what really happened to Lisa, I should ask Sam what he saw in the woods that night and how he got the scar on his chest. So he was there! And he saw what happened. Shit, he might even have been a part of it!"

Franny slammed her mug down and stood up quickly, reached for Phoebe's hand. "Come on," she said.

"Where are we going?" Phoebe asked, spilling tea down the front of her shirt as she was jerked to her feet.

"Becca knew Sam was in the woods that night."

"Yeah?"

"Which means she must have been there too."

CHAPTER 33

Lisa

This is the worst day of my life. Period."

Evie smiled. "Did you mean to do that? Isn't that kind of a pun or something?"

Lisa threw a pillow down at Evie, who teased, "Missed me."

They were in Lisa's bedroom with the door locked.

"What's going on in there?" Sammy asked, pounding at the door.

"Girl talk," Evie said. "Buzz off."

"Have you heard anything?" Sammy asked through the door. "From Mom or Aunt Hazel?"

"Um, you can hear the phone ring as well as we can, right?" Evie said. "Why don't you go watch for them in the driveway."

Lisa rolled over and looked at the clock. It was nearly four. All they'd heard was the one phone call from her mom this morning saying that Da was in a coma. He'd taken a lot more pills this time.

"But he's gonna be okay, right?" Lisa had asked.

There was a long pause. "We're not sure," her mother had said.

"I want to see him!"

"You can't, sweetie. He's in intensive care. No one under sixteen is allowed in."

"But I . . ."

"Rules are rules, love. I'll call again when there's news."

Evie spent the morning upstairs by herself, while Sam and Lisa played hand after hand of rummy. Evie came downstairs and made them all tuna melts, which she burned. Lisa couldn't eat a single bite.

"Come on," Evie had said. "I know my cooking sucks, but you gotta eat."

"Stomachache," Lisa said, her abdomen twisting and cramping.

Later, when she went into the bathroom, she found brown stains on her panties.

"I think there's something wrong with me," she'd told Evie.

"No, dummy," Evie had said. "It's your period."

"My period? But isn't blood supposed to be red?" This wasn't how it was supposed to happen. Her mother should be there, welcoming her to womanhood. And she was supposed to feel like a woman—not a helpless kid who couldn't even go visit her dad in the hospital. Her belly had cramped and she bent forward, grimacing. No one had told her it was going to hurt like this.

"Trust me," Evie had said. Then she rummaged around in the bathroom closet and found a box of pads. "Get some fresh underwear and put one of these on. Then take three Advil."

After, they'd locked themselves in Lisa's room and Evie told her that she'd been getting her period for almost a year now.

"But how could you not tell me something like that?" Lisa asked.

Evie shrugged. "Maybe there's lots of stuff I don't tell you."

"Like what?"

"Forget it." Evie looked away. "Let's go see what Sammy's up to, huh?" She stood up and unlocked the door.

"Evie?"

Evie stopped, her hand on the knob.

"There's something I want to show you. Something I found in your mom's room." Lisa went to her bookshelf and pulled out the dictionary. The old photo of Da and Hazel was right where she'd hid it. After crumpling it up, she hadn't been able to throw it away. So she smoothed it out and stuck it in the M's.

Misery.
Misfortune.
Mishap.

She held it out to Evie. "Is this part of the secret?" she asked. "Your mom and my dad—they were together once, right? Is he your dad too?"

Evie took the photo and stared down at it, her brown eyes darkening. "You shouldn't have been snooping around in her room!" she said.

"It's true, though, isn't it?" Lisa asked. "We're sisters, right?"

The door was pushed open.

"Sammy!" Lisa snarled, turning to see that it wasn't Sam but her mother stepping through the door. Her mother's eyes were red and puffy with dark circles under them.

"You're back! What happened? How's Da?"

Don't say he's dead. Please God, don't let him be dead.

"No change," her mother said. "They said they'd call if there was any news." Then her eyes went to the photo in Evie's hand.

"Where did you get that?" Lisa's mom hissed.

"Lisa," Evie said.

"Give it to me," Phyllis demanded, snatching the photo from Evie and ripping it up right in front of them. "What's done is done," she said, staring at Evie with a venomous look.

"Lisa got her period," Evie said.

Phyllis looked like Evie had slapped her.

"What?" she said, studying Lisa. "Is this true?"

Lisa nodded. She wasn't sure what to expect: some motherly wisdom, a hug, or maybe some kind of you're-a-woman-now congratulations. But her mother's face just got paler. Then she swallowed hard, smiled, and said, "You two go on downstairs now. Or go outside and get some air. Sam says you've been locked in here for hours."

They played another round of rummy while Hazel threw together a tuna noodle casserole.

"We had tuna for lunch," Evie whined.

"Well, you'll just have to have it again, won't you?" Hazel said. "Has anyone seen the cream of celery soup?"

"No," they all chimed.

"And the cookies," Hazel said. "I just bought a brand-new package of those chocolate peanut butter chunk ones you love so much, Sammy. Don't tell me you ate the whole bag!"

Sam shook his head. "I didn't even see them. Ask Lisa. Maybe she took them for her Fairy King."

Lisa glared at him across the table. She'd kept her end of the deal. She hadn't mentioned the fairies all day. And now here he was, blabbing away.

"What?" Hazel asked, turning from the counter to face them.

"She's been leaving all kinds of treats for him. Soda and cookies. And he left her stuff, too, right, Lisa? Show her your charm bracelet. Tell her about the book."

"Book?" Hazel's face got all pinched-looking. "What book?" She looked right at Evie when she said it. Evie looked away.

"*The Book of Fairies*. It's got all kinds of crazy stuff in it. She so obviously made it up herself. Fairy King my ass!" Sammy said.

Something inside Hazel snapped. Lisa could almost hear a popping sound fill the kitchen. "Enough! We do not talk like that at the table. Go to your room!"

"But I—"

"Now!" she snarled. "And Evie, you too. I want to talk to Lisa alone."

Sam headed upstairs and Evie slunk outside.

"You've got some explaining to do," Aunt Hazel said once she and Lisa were alone. Hazel got right in her face, her hundred-proof breath nearly knocking Lisa flat. "What's all this about a fairy book?" Hazel's eyes were bloodshot and frantic.

"It's nothing," Lisa said, shrinking. "It's . . . it's a story I made up."

Hazel took an unsteady step back, shaking her head in an I-don't-believe-you way.

Hazel reached out, grabbed Lisa's wrist, studied the bracelet. "Tell me the truth, damn it!" She was twisting Lisa's wrist so hard it brought tears to Lisa's eyes.

Lisa shook her head firmly and tried to yank her hand away,

but Hazel had it in a firm grip. "I made it all up. Really. I left the gifts there myself."

Hazel let go of her wrist. Her mouth was working like she was saying something, but no words came out.

Lisa slowly backed away from Hazel and went to look for Sammy, but he wasn't in his room. When she left his bedroom, she heard her mother and Hazel having one of their whisper fights downstairs. Lisa snuck down the steps, tried to listen in. All she caught was the end. Her mother saying, "Just go. Now!"

And Hazel grabbed her bulky purse, crammed full of tissues, romance novels, and expired coupons, got in her car, and took off, tires squealing.

"Mom?" Lisa said. Her mother was standing at the stove, making tea. "Is everything okay?"

Her mom gave her a vacant stare, like her eyes weren't focused on anything at all. "Fine," she said at last, forcing a painful-looking smile.

Hazel came back from her trip just as they were sitting down to dinner. Sammy was heaping casserole on his plate. Lisa took only a little salad. Evie hadn't shown up yet—no one had seen her all afternoon.

"Well?" Phyllis said, glaring at her sister.

Hazel shook her head, then fixed herself a tumbler full of milk and brandy, bypassing the tuna casserole completely. She went and said something to Phyllis in a low voice. Lisa, who was sitting beside her mother, caught only one word: *Gone*.

Did she mean Da? Had he died? And here they were eating stupid tuna casserole?

Hazel took a seat at the table and nursed her drink. Her hands shook each time she took a sip.

"Have you heard anything more about Da?" Sammy asked. "Are you going back to the hospital?"

Neither Phyllis nor Hazel responded. They were both staring off into space.

"It just seems like someone should be there," Sam said. "You know, in case he wakes up or something."

Or dies, Lisa thought, hating herself for it.

He's not dead, he's not dead, he's not dead, she told herself, concentrating with all her might. She pictured him coming home from the hospital, giving her a big hug, saying, "Hiya, Beanpole."

"I'm going back to the hospital later," Phyllis said, pushing food around on her plate. Hazel kept working on her milky drink. No one spoke. There was only the sound of forks scraping plates.

Evie burst in through the kitchen door, shouldering her knapsack. Her face was red and sweaty, and her chest wheezed.

"You!" Phyllis snarled, leaping up from the table and stepping toward Evie. In a low voice, she hissed, "What have you done?"

Lisa held her breath, waiting. What was Evie in trouble for this time?

"I'm sorry," Evie said. "I didn't know this would happen."

Lisa's mom leaned in and whispered something Lisa didn't catch.

Evie looked like she might cry. "I know, but he promised—"

Phyllis slapped Evie across the face, so hard it knocked Evie off balance. Lisa flinched and held her breath. Evie backed slowly out of the kitchen, head down, sobbing. When she got to the door, she turned and ran.

CHAPTER 34

Phoebe

How do you even know she'll be here?" Phoebe asked as they pulled into the Price Chopper parking lot.

"I don't," Franny said. "But if she isn't, I bet I can talk whoever's there into telling me how to get in touch with her. I'll play the long-lost-relative card." Phoebe had seen Franny in action and knew the Price Chopper employees didn't stand a chance.

They made their way past rows of shopping carts, through the automatic doors and the vestibule full of gum-ball machines and the claw game full of ugly stuffed animals and plastic jewelry. Phoebe flashed back to her job at the Crazy Cone when she was twenty, the constant mechanical beep and song of the video games, the kids who came in, pockets heavy with quarters, hoping for a high score or for the biggest, best prize.

"There she is," Franny said, heading past the display of freshly baked cinnamon buns toward the floral department. A woman with a green smock was trimming rose stems. She lifted her face and Phoebe inhaled sharply and grabbed Franny's sleeve, jerking her back.

"What?"

"That's Amy Pelletier—the girl from the woods! The one who played the old woman and ran naked onto the golf course." She tugged on Franny's arm, dragged her out of the store.

"Are you sure?" Franny asked, stopping at the rows of green plastic shopping carts on the sidewalk outside. They hadn't moved far enough away and the automatic door kept opening and closing with an angry hum.

"Positive!"

Franny scowled, which she often did when she was thinking hard. An elderly couple walked past them into the store. Then a woman with a baby in a pink pig sleeper complete with a snout built into the hood. "Come on," Franny said at last, turning to head back into the store.

"What are you doing?" Phoebe's voice was frantic. Becca was just a girl, but the stunt at the cabin made her seem . . . otherworldly. Like a true changeling. A person who could turn from old to young, who could stab another with a corkscrew without injury. Who knew what else she was capable of?

"Do you want to figure out what's going on here or not?"

"I do, but what makes you think she's even going to talk to us?" Phoebe asked.

"Oh, she'll talk. If she doesn't, we'll make a scene. If she wants to keep her job, she'll cooperate."

Phoebe followed Franny into the store and toward the floral department. Becca caught sight of them, immediately put down the sharp beaklike pruners, and took off her smock. She spoke briefly to an older woman behind the counter, then headed right for them.

"Let's go outside," Becca said. "I could use a smoke."

For the first minute, they all just stared at one another, no one knowing how to get started. Becca took long, hard pulls from her Marlboro Light.

"I don't get it," Phoebe said. "How did Sam not recognize you?"

Becca smiled. "It's been a long time. Our family moved down to Massachusetts a few months after Lisa disappeared. Would you recognize the adult version of some kid you knew when you were ten?"

Phoebe was silent, trying to remember kids she'd known back then. She'd never had close friends, no one she'd ever invite home. There were girls she talked to in school, girls she got paired with for gym and science projects, but no one special. Even now, they were all faceless, nameless.

"Well, I barely recognized you," Franny admitted. "And you and I were pretty good friends for a while there. If it hadn't been for your name tag, I wouldn't even have been sure enough to come up and ask."

Becca nodded.

"So when did you move back to Vermont?" Franny asked.

"After I finished high school. I moved up to Burlington, waited tables there. I kind of stayed away from this whole area, too many crazy memories. But they found me. *He* found me."

"He?" Franny said.

"You can't run from the Dark Man."

A sharp chill ran down Phoebe's neck. She took in a sharp breath and exhaled slowly.

"Dark Man? I think I saw that movie. He was a vigilante superhero, right? All scarred up and tormented. Or maybe you're talking about the Man in Black—Johnny Cash?" Franny laughed, but the others didn't. "No? So what are we talking about, the devil or something?"

Becca shook her head. "You don't understand."

"Tell me about what happened at the cabin," Phoebe said. "Why would you do it? And who are the others? Did you all plan it with Sam? How long did he know?"

"Whoa!" Becca said, holding up her hand with the cigarette in a smoky slow-down gesture. "That's a lot of questions."

"So start with the first . . . the most important," Franny suggested. "Why?"

Becca studied the burning ember at the end of her cigarette.

"If you don't start talking, we're going right to the cops," Franny warned.

"I'm sure Alfred the constable would love to meet the true Amy Pelletier," Phoebe added. "At the very least, you'd have a hell of a lot of explaining to do. And I'd bet it's against the law to present false ID to cops."

"Okay," Becca sighed. "I'll tell you whatever you want to know. But then we're done, right? You don't come back and bother me at work. You don't tell anyone you talked to me. Deal?"

Phoebe nodded.

"So back to the original question," Franny said. "Why do it? How'd you get involved in this mess?"

"Because Teilo asked me to." Becca dropped her cigarette into a can of sand next to the building that was already overflowing with butts.

"Teilo?" Franny said.

Becca nodded. "The King of the Fairies. He contacts me

sometimes. Asks me for favors. But it's not like asking really, 'cause no one ever says no. That's how come I ended up moving back here, getting this shit job. He wanted me close by." She lit another cigarette with a pink Bic lighter—the one remaining vestige of her old nickname.

"How does he contact you?" Franny asked.

Becca's eyes darted around the parking lot. She lowered her voice. "Leaves me notes. Calls me on the phone."

"From fairy land?" Franny asked, raising her voice. "Is that a long-distance call or what?"

"I don't expect you to understand," Becca replied, her voice dripping with contempt. "He walks between the worlds. Sometimes in human form. Sometimes he comes in dreams. Or as an animal. He's a magic man."

"What does he look like when he's human?" Phoebe asked.

"Tall. Dark hair. He has six fingers on each hand."

"Well *that's* pretty distinguishing," Franny said. Phoebe shot her a look.

"What about his face?" Phoebe asked.

"He always wears a mask. If a human looks upon the true face of a fairy, they'll be driven mad."

"How convenient," Franny said.

"The others at the cabin—the fake Evie and Elliot—who were they?" Phoebe asked.

Becca sucked on her cigarette, held the smoke in her lungs, and closed her eyes. Then she exhaled and opened her eyes only halfway, squinting at Phoebe. "You'll leave them out of it, right? If I tell you, you won't go hunt them down?"

"Not if you explain everything," Phoebe said.

"It was my brother, Gerald, and his girlfriend, Trish."

"So you go through all this hoo-ha at the cabin for what exactly?" Franny asked.

Becca looked around nervously. "It was all Teilo's plan. He told me what to do. He said we had to take all your stuff, especially the old fairy book. Make it look like you were never there. Make you think you were going crazy."

"And who was the old man?"

"Just the guy who owned the cabin. Someone Gerald knew from work or something. We gave him five hundred bucks, told him we were playing a prank on some old friends, and he agreed to go along with it."

"Gerald and his girlfriend—does Teilo contact them too, ask them for favors?" Phoebe asked.

"No," Becca said firmly. "I do. They're all caught up in this mess because of me. Me and Danny."

"Danny?" Phoebe said.

"My son. He's five. His uncle Gerald adores him." She reached into her front pocket and pulled out a little cloth coin purse that was stuffed full of cards and money. She rummaged through and pulled out a tiny photo of a little boy with dark hair and freckles. "That's my little man," she said, touching the boy's cheek as if he was actually there, then tucking him carefully back into her wallet.

"So, what—you threaten to not let Gerald see Danny if he doesn't do what you ask?" Franny asked.

Becca shook her head. "It's not like that. Gerald and Trish, they do it to keep Danny safe. To keep him with me."

"Safe from whom?" Franny asked, but Phoebe knew the answer.

"Teilo. If I don't do what he asks, he'll take Danny. I couldn't live without my son." She looked pleadingly at Phoebe. "You know how it is, right?"

Phoebe took a step back. "Yes, I mean, no. I don't have kids. But I can imagine."

"Danny's dad got killed in a bike accident two summers ago. Danny's all I've got."

"So let me get this straight," Franny said. "Some crazy, mutant, child-stealing, six-fingered guy—whose face you've never even *seen*—gets you to do things by threatening to steal your child. And what, take him away to live in a big old tree with the Kee-bler elves?"

Becca shook her head frantically. "Look, you don't know, okay? You haven't seen what he's capable of. He has . . . powers."

"Do you know how to get in touch with Teilo?" Phoebe asked. "Where to find him?"

Becca shook her head. "It doesn't work that way. Teilo finds you. I've told you enough already. Too much. But in case you haven't figured it out, you can't hide. If you've still got some-thing he wants, you can't win."

Phoebe touched her stomach. There was no way he was get-ting Sam's firstborn.

"What do you know about Lisa's baby?" Phoebe asked.

Becca looked at her blankly. "Lisa? Is she back?"

"You tell us," Franny said.

"I haven't seen Lisa since that summer. But Teilo, he told me she's been with him. But then she ran off. Once you live with fairies, you can't come back to the human world. That's what Teilo says."

The cell phone in Franny's bag rang.

"Look, I gotta go," Becca said, tossing her cigarette butt on the ground and grinding it out with her foot. "Remember our deal, okay? We're done."

Franny answered her phone, listened a minute, then said to Phoebe, "Sam's at our place. He's trying to take Lisa." Turning back to the phone, she said, "Jim? Don't let him take her. Do whatever you have to do. We're on our way." She dropped the phone in her bag, said, "We've gotta fly."

Becca was halfway back into the store, but Phoebe caught up with her, put a hand on her shoulder, got her to turn around.

"Was Sam really in the woods that night? When Lisa disappeared?" Phoebe asked, remembering what had brought them to Becca in the first place.

"Ask him," Becca said.

"I will. But first, I'm asking you," Phoebe said.

Becca smiled. "He was there. Gerald and I, we went into the woods because Evie told us Teilo was going to open the door to the fairy world. Sam was there too. And Evie."

"And Teilo? Did you see him?"

She nodded.

"Was it the first time you ever saw him?" Phoebe asked.

"Nah," Becca said. "Gerald and I had seen him a bunch of times. Evie told us where to find him. She gave us stuff for him—food, presents—offerings, I guess. We'd bring it to him in the woods and he'd give us gifts—junky stuff like old coins, a silver spoon. He gave me a toy compass once. God, I loved that thing."

"Wait," Phoebe said. "Evie did that? She knew who he was? Where to find him?"

Becca nodded. "The first I saw him I was by myself in the

woods. I thought he was the bogeyman. I was scared shitless. Then the next day, Evie comes to me, explains that it wasn't the bogeyman. She tells me and Gerald that the King of the Fairies is living down in Reliance and whatever we do, we have to keep it a secret. She drew us this little map showing us where to find him. You find Evie, the real Evie, and ask her. She can tell you all about Teilo."

CHAPTER 35

Lisa

Phyllis stood statue-still, her hand raised, frozen in place right where it had slapped Evie's left cheek. Sammy stared, wide-eyed as an owl. Phyllis had never struck any of them, had never so much as threatened a spanking. How many times had she or Da said it when Sam and Lisa and Evie were little, intervening over a disputed toy? "We don't hit in this house." Calmly and firmly, a reminder, a statement. And it was true—even drunk, Aunt Hazel never lost her cool.

Hazel drained what was left of her drink, setting the empty glass down on the table with a thud. Lisa pushed her chair back, the metal legs scraping across the linoleum floor. She scooted past her mother, keeping her eyes averted, and jogged out the door after Evie.

"Lisa!" her mother called, snapping out of her trance. "Come back!" But Lisa kept on going. She searched the yard and saw no sign of Evie. It was just starting to get dark. Racing around the house to the driveway, she saw her bike was gone, and there, in the distance, was Evie, riding toward the center of town.

"Evie!" Lisa cried. "Wait up!"

The bike wobbled as Evie stood and pumped the pedals faster.

Lisa sprinted after her, leaping over cracks in the sidewalk, her feet in their pink and silver Nikes flying across the ground.

Evie. Poor Evie. How could Lisa's mother have done such a thing?

"Please! Wait!" Lisa cried, panting, but Evie was out of earshot.

Evie. Her half sister. How long had Evie known? Had she known that Dave was her father her whole life, watching as he showered Lisa with gifts and hugs and funny songs while Evie stayed off in the shadows, the unacknowledged daughter? God, it was so unfair! And Da? Did he know? How could he live with a secret like that?

She remembered what Evie had told her back in Cape Cod: *Things are going to be different when we get back.*

Lisa didn't understand what had happened in the kitchen, but she was sure it had something to do with Da.

The questions piled up in her mind as she ran faster, harder. Up ahead, she saw a gathering of kids outside the general store. They were hanging out on the porch eating ice cream and drinking sodas. And there was Evie as their center, holding something in her hands. Lisa's bike was parked against the side of the building, the spokes gleaming in the bright floodlights illuminating the front of the store. Behind the kids, a blue bug light lured mosquitoes in, zapping them with a horrible little sizzle.

Lisa slowed to a walk, trying to catch her breath before climbing the steps to the porch. In the window were lottery signs, a neon Budweiser light, and a taped-up poster for a lost dog. HAVE

YOU SEEN BRUNO, it said in a childish, messy scrawl. WE MISS HIM. Below it, a photo of an old yellow Lab and a phone number.

Lisa climbed the steps, trying to identify all the kids. Gerald was there, holding a cream soda in his good hand. And Pinkie with a strawberry sundae cup. Her friend Franny was beside her with a matching sundae cup. Mike and Justin were beside Gerald, both wearing Little League uniforms that had an ad for Tucker's Body Shop on the back. They had on green caps and cleats. There were two other boys there, who Lisa vaguely knew but couldn't name—older, also in green baseball uniforms. Backpacks and baseball gloves covered the two benches.

There, in the center, was Evie, with the gang of kids circled around her.

"I don't know, Stevie," Gerald was saying. "Are you sure this is real?"

"Positive," Evie said. "Just look at it."

Gerald leaned down and Lisa came up behind him, getting a strong whiff of dirty hair and body odor. She peered over his shoulder to see what Evie was showing them.

There, opened up in Evie's hands, was *The Book of Fairies*.

"How could you?" Lisa blurted out, shoving past Gerald.

"Lisa?" Evie blinked. The left side of her face was red and swollen-looking. "I just thought people should know. I'm tired of all the secrets."

"You've ruined *everything*," Lisa said, almost in tears, her voice shaking. She couldn't believe that just a few minutes before she'd been chasing Evie to comfort her. "Why would you do this? Why? Just to seem cool to these idiots?"

Lisa saw it so clearly: Evie, the odd girl out, tired of never being special, desperate for attention, willing to do whatever it took to get people to notice her. It was pathetic.

"Hey, who you calling idiots?" one of the older boys said, squaring his shoulders. He had the faint beginnings of a mustache and tiny, rodentlike eyes.

Lisa ignored him. "I kept my stupid promise. And you did this. It says right there in the book, Evie. It says we have to keep it a secret! Or else." Lisa snatched the book from Evie, held it tight to her chest.

"Or else what?" asked Pinkie, her pale face all scrunched up, stained with strawberry sundae. The others were silent, holding on to the sodas and ice creams, waiting to see what might happen next.

"Lisa," Evie began, "I—"

"You were pissed off that the fairies came for me!" Lisa interrupted. "That I was chosen and you weren't. Kind of like with Da, right? I'm the daughter he sees. You're just no one. The fat cousin nobody can stand."

Evie took a step back, cowering like she'd been hit again.

Gerald snickered into his hand, covering his mouth, looking more nervous than amused.

Lisa turned and jumped down the steps, grabbed her bike, and pedaled toward home, one hand steering the bike, the other clinging to *The Book of Fairies*. She pumped the pedals as fast she could, trying to race away from everything had that just happened. She wished she could ride hard enough and fast enough to leave it all behind. Escape the whole stupid town, her whole life. She dumped her bike in the driveway and ran straight for the woods.

Her promise to Evie and Sam didn't count anymore. Not after this.

She made her way quickly but quietly to Reliance, stopping every now and then to listen and make sure she wasn't being followed.

The only sound was her feet in the leaves and twigs on the forest floor—*crunch, crunch, crunch*. She found the cellar hole and sat with her legs crossed, back pressed against the wall. Yogi posture.

Her back ached and she had horrible cramps. She couldn't believe she was going to have to go through this misery every month—what was so hot about "being a woman" anyway?

She closed her eyes, then called out. "Teilo? Are you there? Everything's such a mess," she sobbed. "Da's in the hospital and I think he really might die. Evie's a traitor. She took the book and showed it to people. I'm so sorry. I know you trusted me or you wouldn't have left it." She was crying hard now, leaning forward, sobs wracking her. "Teilo? I know you're there. I believe in you. I've always believed."

And then she heard it: a rustling in the leaves that turned to footsteps, coming her way.

CHAPTER 36

Phoebe

When they got back to Franny's, they found Sam sitting at the kitchen table drinking coffee with Jim. They were laughing about something. Jim was smiling a goofy, brown-toothed smile and Sam seemed perfectly at ease.

"Where's Lisa?" Phoebe asked.

Jim nodded toward the living room. "Watching TV. She loves that cooking channel. Can't seem to get enough of it. Crazy, 'cause she doesn't seem to enjoy food all that much. Just sweets. Never seen a grown woman eat like that. It's like she's a god-damn honeybee or something."

"Bees don't eat honey," Franny said. "They eat pollen and make the honey."

Jim shrugged his shoulders. "Pollen, honey, nectar—whatever. She's more like a bee queen than a fairy queen, that's all I'm saying."

Sam nodded. "A bee queen isn't born a queen, you know," he said. "She's made. The workers choose an unborn bee, tend to it, stuff it full of royal jelly. No one knows how they pick the next queen. They just do."

Everyone was quiet. Sam and his damn lectures.

How did Teilo pick Lisa to be his queen—the one he stole away?

"We need to talk," Phoebe said, looking at Sam.

"Let's give these two some privacy," Franny said, putting her hand on Jim's shoulder. Jim started to stand.

"No," Phoebe said. "I want you to stay."

Sam nodded. "Stay," he said, and they all sat down. Jim leaned back in his chair and looked out the window, seeming disappointed that he hadn't been dismissed. Sam fidgeted with his coffee cup, turning it, plucking at the handle. Then he looked at Phoebe and began.

"I'm sorry about last night, Bee. I've been a real asshole lately—I know that. This thing with Lisa, it's turned everything upside down and made me question not just who she is but who *I* am. It threw me into this huge existential crisis. But you know what I've come to realize, Bee? That whoever I am, whatever my greater purpose is, it's nothing without you." He reached across the table and took her hand, giving it a squeeze. "And the baby, well, it must be meant to be or it wouldn't have happened, right? And maybe that's it, Bee. Maybe that's our greater purpose. To be the most amazing parents we can be. To just love each other and this little baby."

Franny wiped tears out of her eyes, beamed at Phoebe. Phoebe stared at Sam. He was telling her everything she wanted to hear, and yet it left her with a sick feeling in the pit of her stomach.

Jim, who'd been looking increasingly awkward, stood up. "I gotta go feed the chickens," he said, loping out of the kitchen, sticking his head into the living room. "Want to help me with the pretty birds, Lisa?"

She came bounding after him like a kid and followed him out the front door into the yard.

"I have something to tell you," Sam said, his eyes glinting with excitement. "I solved part of the mystery. Remember how yesterday, you asked me about my old friends Gerald and Pinkie?"

Phoebe nodded.

Franny opened her mouth and said, "Becca? We just . . ." and Phoebe gave her a gentle shut-up kick under the table.

Sam continued. "Well, just for the hell of it, I decided to look them up. I thought maybe they might remember something I didn't. Pinkie—err, Becca—wasn't listed in the phone book, but Gerald was. Turns out he lives over in Groton. So I decided to pay him a surprise visit. And you'll never guess who Gerald turns out to be . . ."

"Elliot," Phoebe said.

"Right!" Sam gave a surprised cry. "And his girlfriend played Evie."

"Trish," Phoebe said.

Sam pushed his chair back. "How did you know?" he asked, looking at Phoebe like she was the criminal.

"I'll tell you in a minute. What else happened with Gerald and Trish?" Phoebe asked.

"They said they did what they did to save some little kid, that if they didn't follow this guy's orders, he'd take Pinkie's little boy."

"And you believed them?" Franny asked.

Sam nodded. "Yeah. At first I thought it was complete shit, then they showed me pictures of him, told me their story."

"What about Lisa's baby?" Phoebe asked. "Did they say any-thing about that?"

"No. But they said Teilo was looking for Lisa. Sounds like she left him. Just ran off or something. He's desperate to get her back, told them to find out anything they could about where she might be. That's why he sent them to the cabin. Oh, and to get the fairy book. And anything else we might have saved from that summer. Now it's your turn. Tell me how you knew about Gerald and Becca."

Phoebe looked at Franny, who shrugged. What did she have to lose by telling him?

"I found Pinkie. Or rather, Franny did. She works at the Price Chopper over in St. Johnsbury. We just got back from visiting with her. She told me pretty much the same story you just did. She also said that Evie was the one who introduced her and Gerald to Teilo that summer."

And that you were in the woods that night.

"No shit?" Sam said. "I knew it! I was positive she knew more than she was saying. She knew who he was?"

"Sounds like it," Phoebe said. "Or, at the very least, she knew how to find him. She was bringing him gifts—food and stuff."

Sam nodded. "Food kept going missing that summer—jam, pie, sandwich stuff. I bet Evie was taking it to him. He was hiding out there in the goddamn woods the whole time and she knew it!"

Franny scowled. "But who is this Teilo guy? And what's he done with Lisa's baby?"

"That's what we're going to find out," Sam said. "Come on," he said to Phoebe. "Get Lisa. We're going to Barre. See if we can find anyone at the library to tell us who Mary Stevens is. And see if anything sparks any memories for Lisa."

"What about Evie?" Phoebe asked. "Shouldn't we talk to her? See what she really knows about Teilo?"

"She'll be there when we get back. It's not like she's going anywhere," Sam said.

I had a secret room in a secret garden," Lisa said. She was in the backseat of the Honda. Her voice was barely a murmur. It was unclear if she was talking to anyone in particular. "The walls were bright with flowers. I slept in a bed of lace. On the full moons, Teilo and I would walk through the orchard. We'd laugh and dance. He'd speak to me in the secret language of the fairies. He'd kiss my arms but never my lips. A fairy kiss is poison. It can put you to sleep for a thousand years."

Phoebe closed her eyes, leaned back against the passenger seat, wishing she could sleep for just a few hours. Her body was sore and stiff from a night spent tossing and turning alone on the office floor. To make matters worse, she had a headache coming on and didn't have any aspirin. She wondered if she was even supposed to take aspirin or if it might hurt the baby. The world seemed full of dangers now that she was pregnant: mercury in tuna, hot tubs, beer, secondhand smoke, over-the-counter medicine. Not to mention crazy baby-abducting fairy kings.

She glanced over at Sam, who had his eyes fixed on the road ahead, his hands gripping the wheel tightly, just where they should, at the three and nine o'clock positions. Safety Sammy.

She wasn't an idiot. Back at Franny's, Franny had pulled her aside just before she left with Sam and Lisa to say, "Are you sure he's telling the truth? I mean, what if he knows you spotted him and he's just covering his tracks?" Franny was the queen of paranoia, but she had a point.

Phoebe wasn't sure. Not of anything anymore.

"What does Teilo look like?" Phoebe asked sleepily.

"I don't know," Lisa said.

"How can you not know," Sam interrupted. "You saw him, didn't you? Christ, if you had a kid with him, he must have shown himself to you."

"He never appeared as himself. He was always in disguise."

Phoebe's guts went cold as she remembered what Becca had said about Teilo wearing a mask.

"You've got to be kidding," Sam muttered.

"If a human being looks upon the true face of a fairy, they'll be driven mad by the pure beauty," Lisa said.

"Jesus! I'm being driven mad right now," Sam grumbled, gripping the steering wheel tighter. "Do you know where the baby is, Lisa? Do you have a clue where we could start looking?"

"Don't you remember, Sammy?" she asked. "He was promised to Teilo. My firstborn. Evie's. Yours. They were all promised to Teilo."

Sam clenched his jaw. Phoebe reached out and took his hand, and he turned, gave her a weak smile and a little squeeze of the hand that was meant to be reassuring.

"You're really okay with this?" she asked. "The baby, I mean."

Sam nodded. "Of course I'm okay with it. It's just going to take a little getting used to. I'm kind of still in shock."

They were coming into Barre on Route 14, and Sam took a left at Hope Cemetery, then another left, which took them up through a residential neighborhood of twisting roads, then led them down a hill, past a playground, and toward downtown. Just after a blinking traffic light, Sam turned left into the library parking lot.

"Here we are," he said. "Everybody out."

"The hall of faces," Lisa said dreamily.

"What?" Phoebe asked.

Lisa giggled, put her hand over her mouth.

They crossed the grass and walked around to the front of the large, two-story gray brick building. The front of the library looked very grand to Phoebe: two polished granite columns stood on either side of the doorway; large stone steps led up to it. Above the doors, an ornate carving in stone of a torch.

"Beautiful building," Phoebe said.

Sam nodded. "Classical Revival," he said. It was yet another display of his seemingly unending knowledge that both made her proud and made her feel very small. Maybe if she had gone to college she would have learned about building styles and understand what Classical Revival meant. They could have intelligent discussions about things like rooflines and columns. Phoebe touched her belly and felt suddenly light-headed. She'd skipped breakfast yet again. She was supposed to be filling her body with healthy, baby-growing food, taking prenatal vitamins, drinking milk and shakes with protein powder. Instead, she'd gulped down half a cup of black coffee at Franny's that now churned in her stomach. She was one hell of a mommy-to-be.

Sam grabbed one of the double doors and held it open, shepherding Lisa and Phoebe inside. They walked through a beautiful entryway with long curving staircases to the right and left. On the walls around the stairs were portraits—serious men and women painted in oil, scowling down from heavy, ornate frames. A hall of faces.

They walked through the entryway and found themselves in the reference area. A homeless-looking man with a long gray beard and stained army fatigue coat was reading *Popular Mechanics* and chewing on a large wrapped Tootsie Roll. He looked up from his magazine, nodded in their direction. A kid in a black T-shirt, jeans, and combat boots was on the computer and an old man in golf clothes was reading the paper.

They continued on, to a small dark room of stacks. Phoebe looked up and saw that the floor above was glass. She saw a shadow move across it, quick and dark, like an animal. Her body was covered in warning gooseflesh.

The smell of old books filled her nostrils, and, feeling dizzy, she tried taking deep breaths through her mouth. They stepped out of the small room of books and were at the circulation desk.

A woman with a long gray braid and silver and turquoise earrings looked up from the computer, smiling.

"May I help you?"

Sam produced the tattered library card from his pocket, but the librarian didn't have a chance to look at it before she caught sight of Lisa.

"Mary!" she cried. "I've been thinking about you. How are you? How's the baby?"

Lisa smiled shyly, looked down at the floor.

"She's Mary Stevens?" Sam said, showing the librarian the card. She nodded.

"I'm her brother, Sam," he said. "And it's been a while since she's been in contact with her family. We're trying to figure out where she's been living. Did she show you ID to get the card?"

The librarian shook her head. "I'm not sure. All that's required is a piece of mail with a name and address on it."

"So would you have her address?" Sam asked.

The librarian looked at him skeptically. "Is that all right with you, Mary? If I tell him?"

Lisa nodded.

"Is the baby all right?" the librarian whispered.

"I hope so," Sam told her.

"She started bringing him in a few weeks ago. The sweetest little thing. Hardly made a sound. Such a good baby."

"Here it is," she said, peering at the computer. "Mary Stevens. Huh. That's odd."

"What is it?" Sam asked.

"It's just a post office box. We're not supposed to give a card with just a post office box."

"Thanks for checking," Sam said, discouraged by the dead end.

"Did she ever come here with anyone?" Phoebe asked. "Other than the baby, I mean."

"Sometimes there was a woman who'd come to get her at the end of the day. We always figured she was Mary's, you know, caregiver. She was so gentle with her. She'd just whisper in Mary's ear and she'd get up and go."

"Do you know who she was?" Sam asked.

"No. And I haven't seen her lately. She's maybe thirty or so. Kind of average height. Dark hair and eyes. Thin. Really thin . . . Eve! That's what Mary called her. Her name was Eve."

CHAPTER 37

Lisa

JUNE 15, FIFTEEN YEARS AGO

Keep your eyes closed," a voice whispered. A male voice, raspy and musical as a woodwind instrument. It sounded as if he was speaking from just above her, but through some sort of tunnel. "If you open them, I'll go away forever."

Lisa nodded. Did as she was told. Her skin was buzzing with the relief that it was finally happening. He was here.

"Do you understand?" he asked, his voice whispery and light, like wind through dry grass. "I mean it. Keep. Your. Eyes. Closed."

Lisa nodded. Her face felt tight and sticky from the tears drying on it.

"Good girl," he said. "Good, good, good girl."

The air was suddenly sweet, heavy with the scent of flowers she could not name. The smell caught in the back of her throat, made her feel dizzy. She was sure that if she stood, she'd fall back down.

She held up her wrist, the charm bracelet jingling a little. "I got your gifts. The penny and the medal and the book. Thank you."

He said nothing.

"You're a fairy, right?" Lisa asked.

There was quiet laughter.

"Are you Teilo? King of the Fairies?"

Silence. If she concentrated hard, she could hear him breathing. His smell was so strong and sweet, like honeysuckle, only richer. Her head spun. She was afraid she might faint or fall asleep. Her eyelids felt heavy, glued shut. She couldn't open them if she wanted to.

"Yes," he said at last. "Fairy King. Lizard King. King of Rock and Roll. Queen Bee *buzz-buzz-buzzing* in your ear. Everything and nothing. That's what I am."

What if Evie was right? What if this was a trap and the King of the Fairies was going to steal her away or cast a spell on her so that she'd sleep for a thousand years?

She found she didn't care. He was here, and it was the most amazing thing that had ever happened to her. He was more real to her than anything else in her so-called real life back at home. He had come, just as he promised.

And she knew then what she wanted. She was more sure of this than she had ever been of anything.

"I want to cross over," she told him. "I read the book. I know what to do—I'll fast and make the tea. Midsummer's Eve is next week. Please, Teilo. Please say I can come with you!"

He was quiet. The leaves rustled. Was he leaving? Doing a little dance? She wished she could open her eyes, but she remembered what it said in *The Book of Fairies*: if a human being looks upon the true face of a fairy, they'll be driven mad.

Maybe that's what happened to Da. Maybe he came down here, to the back side of the hill, and met a fairy. And if that was true, then maybe they could fix him. If she crossed over, went into their world, maybe she could find a way to convince them to make him well again.

"Please, Teilo. I want to come with you. To your world. I've never wanted anything so much. I feel like I've been waiting my whole life for this, like it's my destiny. Please say yes, Teilo. Please."

His breath made a funny, jagged sound. "Yes," he said at last. "Yes."

She smiled, felt glittery and golden, a shiny bauble of a girl. She was fulfilling her destiny, like a girl in a fairy tale. Leaving behind the shoddy mortal world of lies and betrayal, of being misunderstood and mistreated.

"How do I know I'm not dreaming?" she asked, her voice sounding far away to her own ears. Like someone else was saying it from the end of a long, narrow hallway. "Or imagining all this, like Sammy thinks. How do I know you're even real?"

She felt a hand reach down and touch her shoulder, give it a squeeze. She reached her own hand up and took his.

"Eyes closed," he warned, his breath warm on her ear.

She took his hand in hers, felt his fingers long, cool, and dry. She studied each one with her own fingers, thinking this is what it's like when you're blind. Thumb, pointer, middle, ring, pinkie, pinkie.

She counted them again to be sure.

It was true. There were six.

CHAPTER 38

Phoebe

Evie!" Phoebe said as they hurried back down the steps of the library. "Is Evie Teilo?"

Lisa giggled vacantly.

"Evie's pretty clever, but I somehow doubt she was able to make Lisa pregnant," Sam said.

"Then who?"

"I don't know. But whoever it is, Evie's protecting him. She's deep into this and has been all along. Agoraphobic my ass."

Phoebe couldn't believe she'd let herself be fooled. She'd felt sorry for Evie, tried to help her. She'd even confided in her about the pregnancy! "We've gotta go talk to her," Phoebe said.

They jumped back in the car and pulled away. Phoebe looked out the window as they drove past an auto repair shop, the back side of a run-down apartment building, where an old woman in a turquoise sunhat was sitting in a plastic lawn chair, sipping from a forty-ounce bottle of beer. She stuck her tongue down inside the bottle neck each time she took a gulp. Phoebe's stomach churned. She remembered the old woman at the cabin, could almost hear her chortling refrain: *And we'll be jolly friends, for-ever more*.

The old woman who turned out to be Sammy's childhood friend, Becca, who was convinced Teilo was going to take away her son. Becca, who told her Sam had been in the woods that night. *There are things he hasn't told you.*

"What did you see, Sam?" Phoebe asked, thinking the question, saying it out loud without meaning to.

"I didn't say anything, Bee."

"No. *See*. What did you see, that night in the woods? The night Lisa disappeared?"

"I wasn't in the woods," he said. "I was home. In bed."

Lisa laughed again, said happily, like it was a game, "Time to tell the truth, Sammy!"

"I'd say it's long past time," Phoebe said. "Becca said she saw you in the woods that night. She told me to ask you how you got your scar. Now please, Sam, tell me what really happened that night."

He gave a deep sigh. "Okay, but it won't help. I didn't see what happened to Lisa or anything." His words were crisp and defensive.

"Start at the beginning," Phoebe said. "When did you go into the woods?"

"Just after Lisa gave me her charm bracelet and left my room. I got up and went after her. I mean, how could I not? She made me promise not to, but she said she was leaving forever. Crossing over to the goddamn fairy world." He stopped, looking at Lisa in the rearview mirror and biting his lip.

"So you went after her," Phoebe said, encouraging him to continue. He'd kept this story secret for fifteen years—now that he'd started, she was going to do everything she could to get him to tell it through to the end.

"I thought I could stop her." His voice cracked and faltered. He shook his head. "It was stupid, really. Me thinking I had that kind of power."

Phoebe put her hand on his arm. "You were ten, Sam. You did the best you could. What happened once you went into the woods?"

He nodded, continuing, his voice more hesitant now. "I spotted her by the brook. She was wearing her red hoodie." He pinched his lips together tightly, as if he was trying to keep the rest of the story in.

"Did she see you?" Phoebe asked.

"Yeah. She took off running. I chased her for fifteen minutes, crisscrossing through the woods, going farther and farther from home, from Reliance. It was pitch-black. Darker than dark. I don't remember ever being afraid of the woods like I was that night. I felt like . . . like the whole forest was against me somehow, helping to protect Lisa. I got snagged on trees, tripped, fell over things, got all banged up. When I finally caught up with her, she turned and swung at me." Sam clenched his jaw, still staring straight ahead, like he could see the whole scene through the windshield. "Then I saw she had a knife."

"What?"

Sam nodded. When he continued, his words moved quickly, running together. "I jumped back but not fast enough. She got me with the tip of it, right over my collarbone." He flinched a little, as if his body remembered the shock of the blade cutting into him.

He let go of the steering wheel with his right hand and moved his fingers under the neckline of his T-shirt, reaching in to touch his scar.

"Lisa stabbed you? I don't get it."

"Yeah, neither did I." He took in a breath, and Phoebe watched as his face, his whole body actually, changed. He didn't look like a scared guy with his defenses down anymore. He looked furious. His face colored; every muscle in his body seemed to tighten as he gripped the steering wheel so hard Phoebe was sure he could break it. "Then I saw that it wasn't Lisa at all. It was Evie." He spat out the name like it had left an acid burn on his tongue.

"Evie?"

"Yeah. But she was dressed like Lisa. She had on a wig and everything."

"But why would Evie want to hurt you?"

"She was mad. Furious. 'It's only you!' she said. She was wheezing real bad, just sucking at the air. Could barely talk. With her asthma, it must have nearly killed her to run as hard and fast as we had that night."

"But why was she dressed like Lisa? And why run from you, then stab you?"

"I asked her what the hell she was doing, and she said, 'Saving Lisa.' She told me I'd ruined everything. 'If Lisa's gone forever, it's your fault, Sammy!' she said."

"So you didn't see Teilo?" Phoebe asked.

Sam laughed an are-you-kidding laugh. "No. I didn't even believe there was a Teilo back then. Shit, Bee, I thought Evie and Lisa were nuts. And I didn't trust Evie. I thought maybe Lisa had talked her into dressing up, leading me on some wild-goose chase."

"But why?"

Sam's body relaxed again, and he sank down low in his seat,

so low that he looked like a little kid peering out over the top of the steering wheel at the road before them. He bit his lip, which trembled a little. "I guess I always thought she really wanted to leave. And Evie helped her." He rubbed his eyes with the palm of his hand. "We weren't enough for her, Bee. We'd all failed her in this really profound way. My father with his suicide, me not believing her, Evie betraying her, Mom and Hazel acting crazy. She chose another life."

Phoebe remembered the little boy in the Superman shirt who had gazed down at her through his bedroom window with such absolute sorrow. She saw that same face now as he drove, his eyes focused on some unnameable place in the distance. "What happened next, after Evie stabbed you?"

Sam sat up straight and glanced at Lisa in the rearview mirror. She was holding very still, listening. "Evie ran down to the cellar hole, and I followed her, but there was no one there. No Fairy King. No Lisa. Just me and Evie. 'We're too late!' Evie said. She was crying, frantic, screaming Lisa's name over and over. Lisa! Lisa! Lisa!" His voice rose and fell. "We should have stayed. We should have woken up the whole neighborhood, searched the woods. But we didn't. I didn't, anyway. I thought Evie was hamming it up, still trying to trick me. Do you know what I did? I went back home to take care of my stupid cut. It wasn't even all that deep. I washed it out, put a bandage on. Then I went back to my room and tossed and turned all night. I think part of me knew she was really gone, knew what a fucking coward I was."

They were silent for a long moment. Phoebe thought of a dozen things to say to offer comfort, but they all seemed empty and useless.

"There's one thing I still don't get," she said at last. "How did Pinkie know you were in the woods that night?"

"I saw her when I was coming out." Sam's voice was evening out, sounding more like matter-of-fact Sam. "She and Gerald were going in. They saw I was hurt, but I didn't tell them what happened."

"And where was Evie?"

"She stayed in the woods, looking for Lisa. I heard her sneak back into the house just before dawn."

"And you never told anyone else you were in the woods that night? Your mom? The police? You never said anything about Evie stabbing you?"

Sam shook his head. "The next morning, when it was pretty clear Lisa was really gone, Evie and I talked it over. She convinced me that it wouldn't do any good to tell. That it would just make us both look like we were involved in some way—that we knew more than we were saying."

Sam looked over at Phoebe, blew out a long breath. "I know it sounds crazy, and to this day I can't say exactly why I went along with her. I mean, this was the girl who'd just stabbed me! On some level, I believed what Evie said that night—that it was somehow my fault that Lisa was gone. I felt guilty. I thought admitting that I'd been in the woods would make me seem even guiltier." He shook his head as if at his own stupidity.

"Jesus, Sam, you were only ten years old, a little boy! Your sister had disappeared, your dad was dying, and you were scared shitless. Of course you went along with whatever she said."

Sam didn't reply. Phoebe could tell from his face that the guilt had stayed with him—he'd been carrying it around for fifteen years, wondering if Lisa might still be here if he'd done things differently that night. Phoebe leaned over and gave him a hug, kissed his cheek. "Thank you," she said, "for telling me what happened."

"I should have done it ages ago. It's just, when you keep a secret for so long . . . it just gets stronger, you know? Harder to tell."

Phoebe kissed him again. "I know exactly what you mean."

They were on the Barre-Montpelier Road, passing Kinney Drugs and Blockbuster. The McDonald's Phoebe snuck off to for her quarter-pounder with cheese fix. Her stomach growled. She opened the glove compartment and found some stale saltines, and gobbled them gratefully.

"What if she was telling the truth?" Phoebe said, mouth full of crackers.

"Huh?" Sam said.

"What if Evie was really trying to save Lisa? Maybe that's why she showed the book to people. She wanted to get everyone's attention because she knew something bad was happening and she wanted to stop it."

"We'll be jolly friends, forever more," Lisa sang.

Sam shrugged his shoulders. "I don't know, Bee. Why was she dressed up like Lisa that night?"

Phoebe thought a minute. "A decoy. So they'd take her instead. That's why she had the knife out. She thought you were Teilo grabbing her, thinking she was Lisa."

Lisa giggled. "Eeny, meeny, miney, moe," she said.

Evie?" Phoebe called, but as soon as she stepped inside, she knew the house was empty.

They'd found the front door of their house wide open, Teilo's sign painted on it.

On the floor of the living room was Evie's key necklace, the chain broken. She bent down and picked it up, remembered Evie saying, *I thought you didn't believe in magic.*

She didn't, did she?

Phoebe picked up the key and went to the aquariums. Orville and Wilbur were sleeping. The hedgehog was nibbling on a nugget of food. The snake stared out at her with his one milky eye.

"What did you see?" she asked him. "Where did Evie go?"

Phoebe's head was pounding.

"Evie!" Sam called.

Phoebe found Sam and Lisa in the kitchen. There was a dirty cereal bowl and coffee cup in the sink, which seemed to be the only proof that Evie had been there at all.

Sam put his hand on Phoebe's shoulder. "She's not here, Bee."

Now the question was, did she go on her own or was she taken? Phoebe clasped the old skeleton key in her hand. She didn't think Evie would have left it behind. Unless she wanted them to think she'd been abducted.

Phoebe ran a hand through her hair. *Think,* she told herself. *You like puzzles; you should be able to figure this out.* But the clues she had made no sense: Who was the six-fingered man? What was his relationship to Evie? And why had Evie introduced Teilo to Pinkie and Gerald, whom she hated?

She thought of Becca's warning and shivered: *You don't know what this guy is capable of.*

She wondered if it was possible that they were truly up against some dark, child-stealing, shape-shifting being.

Right, Phoebe told herself. *And next thing you'll be thinking is that he comes out of trapdoors under kids' beds.*

"Lisa?" Sam said, his voice as gentle as he could make it. "Do you know where Evie is? Where have they gone?"

"Don't you see?" Lisa said. She still smiled vacantly, but for the moment, at least, she seemed to be addressing Sam directly, like a real person, not a figment of her imagination. "There's nothing you can do to stop it. I tried. I thought if I came here, I'd be safe. I thought we could save the baby."

"It's not too late," Sam said.

"My baby, yours—they were promised. The firstborn, Sammy. Don't you remember?"

Sam's face twitched. His eyes looked wild with panic. And for the first time since all this began, Phoebe truly understood.

"Oh my God," Phoebe said. "You believe."

Sam shook his head, slowly, gently, the smallest of gestures that betrayed the truth.

"This is why you didn't want children, isn't it? You didn't want Teilo to take your firstborn like he took Lisa. You've believed all along, even if you tried to convince yourself it wasn't possible, that there's no such thing as fairies."

"No," he muttered.

"I found the bag of papers in the office, Sam. I know what you've been reading up on. I saw the notes about your dreams. The Dark Man, Sam? It's Teilo, isn't it?"

"They're just dreams."

"Maybe," Phoebe said. "But what if they're not?"

And maybe the shadow man I met when I was a kid was real. Maybe he's watching me still.

A nightmarish thought occurred to her then: Teilo had chosen her too; picked her, for whatever reason, to deliver Sam's firstborn. Maybe it was Teilo who orchestrated their meeting, bringing Sam and her together.

"It's not possible," he said.

"Yeah, and just last week you said Lisa coming back was impossible, but here she is. What if there is a King of the Fairies, Sam, and he's like those fairies in those notes you took? A shape-shifting, immortal, evil son-of-a-bitch who wants our baby next?"

Sam swallowed hard, looked down at the floor. "That's crazy, Bee."

"Why do all that research, then? Why write all that stuff down?"

"Because I believe that whoever is behind this—*they* believe that the fairies are real."

"So you don't believe?" Phoebe asked.

"No," Sam said firmly, but he wouldn't look her in the eye. He reached out and put a hand on Phoebe's belly. "Our baby is going to be fine. No one's going to take her."

"The O'Tooles have fairy blood in their veins," Lisa said. "That's what Teilo says."

"Oh my God," Phoebe said, slumping down into a kitchen chair. She'd had enough. Enough of all this. She didn't care anymore if the fairies were real or not. She just wanted it to be over.

"Call it a blessing, call it a curse," Lisa said. "That's what the guardians say."

Sam gave Lisa an astonished look, as if she'd just opened her mouth and let a flock of birds fly out.

"Grab the keys," Sam told Phoebe. "We're gonna take another little road trip."

CHAPTER 39

Lisa

JUNE 20 AND 21, FIFTEEN YEARS AGO

Maybe Sleeping Beauty was in a coma.

Maybe that's what a coma was, a magic spell some evil witch casts. She waves a wand, makes a potion, pricks you with a needle, hands you a poison apple all shiny and red that you can't help but take a bite of.

But a spell can be broken.

Da could be saved. Lisa knew this deep in her heart even as she listened to her mother and Hazel talking about how the doctors thought it would be best to turn off all the life-support machines. Even as they said Da was gone, Lisa knew he wasn't. Not really.

Lisa had been fasting for days. She cleverly hid food in her napkin at dinner. Evie, who was always watching, spying, caught her and scowled but never said a word. Lisa had to be careful with her mother and Hazel too—they'd been watching her like sister hawks. And though she was staying out of the woods, she'd seen her mother and Hazel going in and out of the woods several times, often at night, with flashlights. It was just plain weird. It was like seeing sharks living life on land, breathing air, drinking piña coladas.

Following the recipe in *The Book of Fairies*, Lisa made tea from foxglove flowers and stems and honey and kept it in a mason jar under her bed. She'd scoured the neighborhood looking for the flowers and finally found a patch in the badly neglected garden behind Gerald and Pinkie's house. She'd picked them all, doubting anyone would notice. The tea was sweet but bitter and burned her mouth and stomach, giving her horrible cramps and diarrhea.

She remembered what Sam said when they found the first foxglove flower: *poison*.

But she trusted Teilo. And she wanted so badly to go with him, away from this place, these people. To see what it was like on the other side.

"Lisa," Evie said when she caught Lisa sneaking a sip of the tea. "I know what you're doing. I read the damn book. Do you have any idea what that stuff does? I looked it up. Digitalis. They make heart medicine out of it. It can kill you, Lisa. You've gotta stop."

But Lisa wasn't speaking to Evie, Evie didn't exist to her anymore, so she put the lid on the jar, turned, and walked away. Evie didn't understand. And besides, she was just jealous, really. Pissed off that she wasn't the one chosen by the King of the Fairies.

"What has he done to you?" Evie called after her. "Is he screwing you? Telling you you're his queen?"

Lisa froze, then turned and looked at Evie.

"He's not who he says he is," Evie said.

Lisa squinted her eyes, making Evie smaller and smaller, until she was all gone.

Lisa crept down the hall to Sammy's room. The fasting and tea were making her light and floaty, giving everything a fuzzy look and sound. It was like being underwater. She felt as if she were swimming through a green sea into her brother's room.

"Lisa?" Sam said, blinking, sleepy. "What time is it?" He squinted at his digital clock—11:35.

"I'm going to cross over," she told him. "To save Da."

"What?"

"I'll be able to fix things from over there. They have special medicines, plants and stuff. And magic. I'll be able to use magic, Sam. But the thing is, if I go, I won't be able to come back, not ever."

Sam blinked his eyes, not sure if he was dreaming. "You're not making any sense," he said at last. "And your eyes look funny."

She smiled, handed him the bracelet. "You have to hide this, Sammy. Promise. Never tell anyone you've got it, okay? And you can't follow me, understand? You can't go where I'm going."

He nodded. Lisa leaned down to kiss him. She was going to miss her logical, Mr. Science, everything-can-be-explained brother. And maybe, just maybe, once she was gone, he'd finally get that there were some things that couldn't be explained so easily; that there was more to this world than meets the eye.

"Think of me," she said because it seemed like something a girl in a fairy tale might say. Think of me. Remember me. Love me. Turn me into a story you tell again and again. The sister who was good as gold and became a queen.

Lisa crept down the stairs, through the dark kitchen, out into the night. She flew across the yard, stomach cramping, body light.

What would they think when they found her gone? Or would she be gone? Would it be like Da in the coma? Her body left behind, resting in a glass coffin, while her spirit goes to live with the fairies. Or would they put a changeling in her place—some unkempt sullen girl who won't comb the leaves out of her hair, who growls instead of speaking?

She turned to look back at the house one more time before heading into the woods. It was only a black silhouette, two lights on like eyes. Then one went out with a wink.

Think of me.

She entered the woods, crept along the path. Her stomach was clenched into a fist. So tight and hard, she imagined a baseball-size rock down there—a knuckleball straight to the gut.

She and Sammy dissected a baseball once. They peeled back the carefully stitched, smooth white skin and found a tight ball of yarn inside. Must have been close to a mile of it. And then, at the very core, a rubber ball. They sliced it in half with their mom's best filleting knife and found a perfect circle of cork inside.

"It's like the earth," Sammy told her. "All these layers. The white leather is the crust, then the mantle, the outer core, and the inner core."

Lisa snorted, then smiled at her little brother. "Maybe you're right, Sammy. Maybe the earth is full of secret string and a red rubber ball that no one knows is there."

The hunger was gone. Her body was empty and clean.

She'd been throwing up for days. And sitting crouched over on the toilet, feeling like her guts were spilling out from one end or the other.

"Your body is a vessel," *The Book of Fairies* told her. "You have to empty the vessel to come to our world. Once you cross over, you can eat and drink all you wish. Sugar cakes. Sweet dumplings made from violets, honey, and morning dew."

She's tired. So tired. Light and floaty. Like if she took a deep breath, she might just leave the ground.

The world had a fuzzy edge. Everything radiated with halos of pale green. Her eyes and body were adjusting, getting ready for her new life in the fairy realm.

She gathered rocks as she walked, filling her pockets, balancing a pile in the crook of her left arm. When she got to the cellar hole, she crawled down, laid the stones out in a careful circle.

She crouched in the dirt in the bottom of the old cellar hole— the place where it all began—a circle of thirteen stones around her. Cold sweat beaded on her forehead, and her heart was playing a crazy rhythm she felt from her chest to her throat—fast, slow, fast, like a horse that didn't know if it wanted to run or limp. Her stomach was cramping. She'd swallowed a secret world of string.

Secret world.

Secret. World.

A body was a vessel and a vessel was something that could be full or empty. It's also something that can travel. A vase or a boat.

Which was she?

Both and neither.

The only thing she was sure of was that it was time to go.

"Teilo," she called, voice shaking. "I'm ready."

She waited. Silence. The forest was holding its breath. She inhaled deeply through her nose. Smelled dirt. Worms. Something damp and rotten.

Then she heard footsteps. Was it just one person walking or more? She closed her eyes. Listened. They were coming her way. Quickly at first. Then slowly.

"Teilo?"

"Do you come willingly?" Teilo asked, his words floating somewhere out in the darkness above her. He sounded out of breath. Anxious. The words had a strange rasp to them that she didn't remember from her first meeting with him.

"Yes," she told him, her heart pounding up into her throat. "Yes."

"Then come," he told her. "Come be my queen."

A gloved hand reached down and took hers, and keeping her eyes clamped tight, she let herself be lifted out of the old cellar hole. Her left shoe came off, and she smiled because it didn't matter. Back in the human world, it would matter because they were her favorite pair of pink and silver Nikes, which she wore laced but not tied, and the left one had a purple lace and the right one was pink. But she was leaving all that behind. It was a symbol, the sneaker. Her English teacher, Mr. Milne, would be impressed that she'd thought of this. Especially now, as she traveled to another world.

She was floating, being pulled into the world she'd dreamed of visiting since Teilo first came to her three weeks ago.

When her feet were back on solid ground, she gripped the

hand tighter and opened her eyes and was sure, at first, that they were playing tricks on her.

She had not crossed over at all, and the face that looked back at her was all too familiar.

"What are *you* doing here?" Lisa demanded, trying to pull away, but her hand was being held in a viselike grip. Everything was glowing greener than ever. She twisted and pulled, slamming her bare foot down on a sharp rock. The pain radiated up through her leg, centering in her stomach. She was sure she was going to throw up.

"No!" she yelped. This was all wrong. This was not what was supposed to happen.

"Teilo!" she cried, knowing he couldn't be far, desperate for him to come rescue her, take her the rest of the way.

She could hear her heartbeat in her ears, feel it in her throat. And there, somewhere far off behind that sound, someone was calling her name. Someone was moving through the woods, down the hill, calling "Lisa! Lisa! Lisa!"

"I'm here!" she started to yell back, but the other gloved hand covered her mouth, pressing hard. She gagged on the taste of dirty leather. The inside of her lip was jammed against her front teeth. Her mouth filled with blood, warm and metallic, sharp as a blade on her tongue.

The greenish face moved closer to her, blurred and scowling. "Shh!" A whispered hiss as her hand was pulled and twisted, jerking her forward. "I'm going to take you to Teilo, but we haven't got much time."

PART IV

The Fairy Kingdom

It is true that sometimes we may take a human over to the fairy world and leave a changeling in his place. How do you know a changeling? Dark eyes and pale, yellowy skin. It will be a sickly child who seems to eat and eat but gains little weight. Often, they die in childhood. But sometimes they survive and adapt to the world of humans. Sometimes so much so that they don't remember who they truly are. Until we call on them. When they're around their own kind, they remember. They always remember.

CHAPTER 40

The Girl Who Would Be Queen

The room he brought her to was green and pink and smelled like sweet flowers, but there was something acrid, tangy, and biting just underneath.

"This is your home now," he said.

The walls were made of flowers. Hundreds, thousands of blooms bursting with color. It was like living inside a valentine. X's and O's. Hugs and kisses. I love you. You love me. Soon we'll be married under a cherry tree.

There was another girl in the room. She guessed the girl was her age, maybe a little older. Her hair was also dark and wild. She had tattoos up and down her stick-thin arms. There was a bump on her belly.

She didn't know much about pregnant girls, but this one looked like she could have the kid any second. If she watched for long enough, she could see the baby moving around inside its tattooed mama. Pushing on her belly, making the skin bulge and ripple, like a monster that couldn't wait to get out.

She tried to leave the room, but the door was bolted on the outside.

"Hey!" she shouted, pounding on the door. "Come back. You can't just leave me here like this!"

She turned to the tattooed girl in desperation. "He can't do this! This is against the law."

"They're keeping us safe," the girl said.

"From what?" she asked.

The pregnant girl laughed.

"Who are you?" she asked.

The pregnant girl looked up, her eyes two black holes. "I'm Queen of the Fairies," she said.

"But Teilo told me *I* was going to be queen."

"He lies."

CHAPTER 41

Phoebe

JUNE 13, PRESENT DAY

They'd been driving for over an hour and were within five minutes of Aunt Hazel's house in the far northeast corner of Vermont. Phoebe was hunched over a map with a flashlight. Lisa
rode silently in the backseat.

Sam had already explained the impetus for the trip.

"That *call it a blessing, call it a curse* thing Lisa said one of the
guardians used. It's a saying Hazel used all the time."

"So what? Now your kooky old aunt Hazel is supposed to be
the one who took Lisa? It doesn't make sense."

"I'm just following a lead here, Bee. And Hazel's the one
person from that summer we haven't talked to yet. I think it's
high time we paid her a visit."

Now, studying the map and seeing how close they were,
Phoebe was getting nervous. "Shouldn't we call or something?
Let her know we're coming?"

"If she knows anything, she'd be more likely to talk if she's
caught off guard. Give her time to prepare and she could make

up just about anything. Or get so completely blotto on booze that she'd be out cold by the time we got there."

"Okay," Phoebe agreed. She turned to Lisa in the backseat. "So tell us about these guardians. Who were they? What was their role?"

"The guardians kept us safe."

"Who is 'us'?" asked Sam.

Lisa didn't answer. Instead, she said, "One of the guardians, she'd tell us stories. Lessons, she called them. About the fairies. About how important what we were doing really was. How special we were. How lucky."

"Lucky," Sam mumbled through clenched teeth. "Right."

"Stop!" Lisa cried from the backseat.

Sam hit the brakes hard, sending all of them jolting forward, straining their seat belts. He scanned the dark road in front of them, then turned and scowled at Lisa. "What?"

There was no deer, no kid on a bicycle. Phoebe saw nothing but the dirt road ahead of them and trees on either side.

Then Lisa was out of the car, running across the dirt road and into the trees. She'd left the car door open. The dome light was on and a repeating chime dinged over and over, warning them about the open door.

"Jesus!" Sam muttered. "Lisa! Get back in the car."

He pulled over to the side, and he and Phoebe got out and hurried off in the direction Lisa had run.

"Lisa?" Phoebe called. Sam broke into a run, Phoebe right behind him, following a narrow path through the trees. The moon had risen, big and bright, casting the woods in a cool blue glow.

The path opened up, and they found themselves in a grove of wild, sprawling trees with branches like gnarled hands and fingers. The branches were heavy with sweet-smelling white flowers. Some of the petals fell, drifting through the air like magic snow.

Phoebe was no nature girl, but she recognized apple trees when she saw them. They were in an old, abandoned orchard. The overgrown, unpruned trees were spaced evenly apart in neat rows.

Lisa was sitting on a stump, rocking and humming. Her arms were wrapped tightly around herself and she was smiling.

"Sometimes we'd dance here," Lisa said, eyes closed, a blissful smile still on her face.

"Who would? You and Teilo?" Phoebe asked.

Lisa nodded. "On full moon nights. He'd take us here."

"Wait," Sam said. "You mean right here, to this place?"

Lisa was up off the stump, walking, dancing through the trees, touching the branches, laughing. It was the first time since Phoebe had met her that she actually seemed happy.

Sam and Phoebe followed. The branches from the overgrown trees reached out and scratched their faces, caught on their clothing. Sam was right behind Lisa, but Phoebe was exhausted and having a hard time keeping up. It seemed to Phoebe that she'd spent entirely too much time running through trees this past week. She'd had enough of dark, creepy forests and was thinking that she'd much prefer wide-open spaces. When this was over, she wanted to go to the ocean. Or the desert. Someplace with endless horizons where you could see what was coming for miles. No surprises. No trees with branches like claws reaching for you. No place for shadowy figures to hide behind.

Up ahead, Lisa and Sam had stopped and were looking down at something on the ground.

Lisa turned and continued on, singing a song just under her breath.

Say, say my playmate, come out and play with me.

Sam stayed frozen, eyes fixed on the ground. Phoebe came up behind him, saw that there, under a great, gnarled apple tree, were four wooden crosses inside a large circle of rocks.

I cannot play with you. My dollies have the flu.

A crude cemetery—something a child might do for pets. The earth above one of the markers was freshly turned. And it was a huge rectangle, way too large to be anyone's pet.

"What is this?" Phoebe asked, a chill working its way from the ground, up through her feet and legs, settling finally deep and low in her belly. Sam shook his head slowly, not taking his eyes from the ground.

"Lisa," Phoebe said, turning to see that the other woman had disappeared into the darkness. She listened but couldn't hear the singing anymore. Sam stepped away from the circle of graves.

"This way," he called back. "I see lights through the trees."

"I'm right behind you."

The orchard ended abruptly and they found themselves at the top of a hill in a newly mown field. Lisa was running down it toward the house at the bottom. Sam and Phoebe chased behind.

The lights in the house were blazing, casting the yard around the house in a welcoming glow.

"It's Aunt Hazel's," Sam said. It was an old white farmhouse with a metal roof and sagging porches. There was a circular gravel driveway with one old car parked in it—a big, boxy Cadillac.

Lisa reached the house and got down on all fours to peer into a low, rectangular basement window. Phoebe and Sam raced to catch up with her. There were broken, rusty nails hammered here and there around the edges of the basement window, like someone had tried to keep whatever was inside from coming out.

But it hadn't held them.

Sam reached forward, pulled the window open, and, feetfirst, lowered himself through it until he was gone.

CHAPTER 42

The Girl Who Would Be Queen

Trolls. Ogres. Goblin babies, not meant for this world. That's what the queen gave Teilo. And he raged. Called her a dirty human girl.

"I could crush you in an instant," he said. "Grind you like salt. If you don't give me a son soon, I will make the other girl my wife."

He took the creatures off. At first they cried. Then they didn't.

The queen cramped and bled. Her nipples leaked.

The girl's heart broke for the queen. And she understood her role now: she was a handmaid. Her job, Teilo said, was to tend to the queen, be a companion. Try to keep her happy.

"You will get your turn one day," he promised.

She washed the queen's soiled rags in the bucket. Held her while she slept.

"I want to go home," the queen whimpered.

"I know," she told her queen, rocking her gently. "Me too." But the truth is, she hardly remembered home anymore. It was a faraway place. Made up, like something from a fairy tale. A place she had been *once upon a time*.

CHAPTER 43

Phoebe

Following Sam, Phoebe lowered herself down through the open window, scraping her back against the wooden frame. She hoped like hell she hadn't scratched herself too badly on the rusty nails. Did they give tetanus shots to pregnant women?

She landed with a not-so-gentle thud and saw that they were in a dimly lit room with cinder-block walls. Lisa came through next, lowering herself down without a sound. Above them a single forty-watt lightbulb gave a dull glow. Covering the walls were pictures cut from magazines and books, held up with yellowing tape: flowers of every shape and color. Lilacs and lilies. Sweet peas and daffodils. Flowers from formal gardens and weed-filled roadside ditches. There was a twin mattress on the floor in the corner, piled high with dirty blankets. Two stained pillows were at the head. Next to it, a five-gallon plastic bucket and roll of toilet paper. The walls, between the taped-up flower pictures, were full of chalk drawings—lines, circles, dashes, Teilo's mark. She saw Lisa's name written in tiny scrawl, just beside the bed. Next to it, another name, in different, more bubbly writing: *Gabrielle*.

Phoebe blinked hard, tried to focus.

"There was another girl here with you," she said to Lisa. "They'd taken someone else. A girl called Gabrielle."

Lisa flinched a little at the name.

"Phoebe," Sam called from the doorway. He held a heavy, open padlock in his hands, taken from the hasp on the frame. There was also a sliding bolt outside the door.

"Oh my God," Phoebe said. "This is it, isn't it, Lisa? This is your room in the garden?"

Could it be? The place Lisa had been kept, year after year? Taken by whom? Old drunk Aunt Hazel? It didn't make any sense. But Phoebe felt strangely relieved to know once and for all that they were dealing with real people, not shape-shifting fairies who could get inside your dreams.

Lisa smiled, touched one of the taped-up flowers, bending the corner a little.

"Once upon a time," she said, "there were two little girls out wandering in the forest. They met a wicked man."

Sam slid the lock back into the hasp and walked across the cellar, past the furnace and water heater. Phoebe followed, green boots creeping over the damp cement floor. There was a dusty exercise bike, piles of newspapers and magazines, cardboard boxes. A tall bookcase rested against a wall, stuffed full of paperbacks, mostly romances. The bookcase looked slightly askew. Lisa went right up to it, grabbed the edge, and pulled.

"Lisa!" Phoebe yelled, sure the case would come toppling over, crushing her.

Instead, the bookcase swung out, its left edge held with heavy hinges. It opened like a door.

"Sam, look!" Phoebe called.

Behind the swinging bookcase was a heavy wooden door with a cut-glass knob. Phoebe turned the knob and pushed, but the door was locked. She glanced at the keyhole below the knob, then, taking a chance, reached into her pocket and took out Evie's necklace. The key slid right into the hole and turned easily.

Lisa gave it to me. She told me this story that summer about two sisters who went on an adventure with a magic key that was supposed to save them. She said this was the key.

Phoebe opened the door and stepped inside.

The room was small but tidy. There was a high rectangular window, like in the flowered room. A twin bed rested in one corner, neatly made with a green wool blanket on top, tucked in so tightly Phoebe was sure you could bounce a quarter on it. A wooden bookcase was stuffed full of books on the occult, mythology, and fairies.

Next to it, a small desk. On it, an old red leather-bound diary, a stack of notebooks, a blank pad of paper, a pen and pencil, and a small microcassette recorder. There was an antique-looking pair of brass binoculars. Sam picked them up. "Son of a bitch," he said.

"Sam? You okay?"

"We found these in the woods that summer. He was there. He was watching us the whole time!"

Taped to the wall above the desk were sketches of a girl Phoebe recognized from the family photos at Sam's: Lisa. A young Lisa, smiling, laughing, stars in her eyes. Lisa in a hooded sweatshirt. Lisa in a summer dress, the straps loose on her narrow shoulders. The drawings were done in pencil and charcoal. Phoebe looked from the drawings to the older, haggard version of Lisa, who stood beside Phoebe smiling down at her younger self. It was impossible to believe this was the same person. It wasn't just the sallow skin, the worn expression. It was as if the shape of her eyes had changed. Just how much could sorrow reshape a person?

"Sam, look," Phoebe said, holding out the diary.

"Teilo's?" he asked.

"No. It belongs to a girl. No dates, but listen to this:

> *Early Summer, 10 years old*
> *Dear Diary,*
>
> *Today, Sister and I met the King of the Fairies! Mother says we're lucky girls, that when she was little, she could see him too.*
>
> *Grandfather smiled, went back to reading his newspaper. Sometimes when Grandfather smiles at me, my throat feels like there's an invisible noose around it, and as the corners of his mouth go up, the rope gets tighter.*
>
> *People in town say we shouldn't play back there. That those woods are haunted. An evil place where the Devil dances.*
>
> *The King of the Fairies is no devil. He's very handsome. That's what Sister says anyway. It was so dark, and at first, he made us close our eyes. When we opened them, he was standing against a tree, and at first it was hard to see where the tree ended and he began. But as we looked longer, harder, we could make him out.*
>
> *But it was a little like that game you play in the dark—the one where you stand in front of a mirror, chanting Bloody Mary until you see something, then*

*you wonder if you really saw it at all, or if it was just
your imagination.*

What I saw was this:

*A man with the blackest eyes I'd ever seen. Like oil,
all reflective and glimmering. His hair is long and dark.
His breath is sweet at first, like flowers, but then horrid
and rank. He speaks in riddles. Sister loves riddles. He
wears a cloak colored like tree bark, and when he wraps
it around himself, you can't see him at all.*

*He's called Teilo and he says he's lived here a long,
long time.*

"Jesus," Phoebe said, closing the diary. "Who is this guy?"

"I don't know," Sam said. "But the diary sure isn't Lisa's. She didn't have a sister."

"So he went after other girls too," Phoebe said.

Sam opened a chest of drawers, exposing neatly folded men's briefs, white T-shirts, jeans. Sam reached into the back of the top drawer and pulled out a white face mask and a pair of black leather gloves.

"If you look upon the true face of a fairy, you'll be driven mad," Sam said, holding up the mask.

Phoebe picked up the gloves. "Look at the fingers!"

Six. There were six fingers on each hand.

"Who the hell is he?" Sam asked.

"He calls himself Teilo, the King of the Fairies," Lisa said. "But he isn't really."

Sam was going through the bookshelf. Lisa stood in the doorway, looking in with worried eyes. Phoebe opened the diary, flipped ahead a couple of pages, and read another entry:

Middle of Summer, 11 years old
Dear Diary,

Sister says she's going to marry Teilo.

I was angry at first. Not because I actually expected him to choose me over her or because I even wanted him to. It's just that Sister has changed so much since he came. She's become so serious. Each day, I feel her pulling away from me and getting closer to him.

So when she said she was getting married, I was silent.

"Don't be a mope," Sister said.

Later, when we went to the bottom of the hill, Sister told Teilo I'd been sulking all day. He laughed. "Don't worry," he said. "You can both be my brides."

Sister says we can live here forever, all three of us.

"Aren't we the luckiest girls on earth?" she asks.

When we got back to the house, Grandfather asked, "Why the long face?"

"Because I'm one of the luckiest girls on earth," I told him.

He laughed, throwing back his head. His teeth are perfect squares, whiter than white, like a mouth full of sugar cubes. His breath smells like dirt and minerals, like the inside of a cave.

He wrapped his cool fingers around my wrist like he does sometimes. It's like he's checking my pulse. Wanting to know if I'm alive or dead. Sometimes he just holds me like that awhile, his strong bony fingers encircling my wrist like a handcuff, and if I try to pull away, he just grips me tighter.

"Figured out who it belongs to yet?" Sam asked.

Phoebe shook her head. "No, but it's damn creepy."

She closed the diary and picked up the small recorder, saw there was a tape inside. She rewound it to the beginning, then pressed *Play*.

"Tell me a story," a girl said. Another girl giggled.

The first girl cleared her throat and said, "Here she is, ladies and gentlemen, for your listening pleasure, the world's greatest storyteller, Lisa Nazzaro." There was the sound of clapping, then another giggle.

Phoebe glanced over at Sam, who looked like he'd been hit with an arrow.

On the tape, Lisa said, "You're too much, Evie."

"Just tell the damn story."

"Once upon a time," Lisa began, "there was a poor peasant girl. Orphaned, she lived on her own at the edge of the woods. She came to town to gather rags and food scraps. Sometimes the townspeople would take pity on her and give her some soup. A slice of bread. A shiny coin. Mostly, they were cruel. They called her Rag Girl. But what none of them knew, including the girl herself, was that she was really a princess."

"Ooo," moaned Evie. "Will there be magic in the story?"

"There always is," said Lisa. "What fun is a story without magic?"

CHAPTER 44

The Girl Who Would Be Queen

On full moon nights, the man who called himself Teilo came for both of them. He wore a mask. Black leather gloves and jacket.

"Shh!" he warned. "We don't want to upset the guardians."

It was a game. It was us against them. The guardians were overprotective, Teilo said. They didn't approve of him visiting his girls.

"But how could they keep me away?" he asked. "A way. Where there's a will, there's a way. Up, up, and away!"

He led them through the small opened window, took them to the orchard. They all held hands and danced in a circle. The queen threw back her head and laughed. "I think," said Teilo, "that you each grow more beautiful every day. The fairy world suits you."

They both knew it was a lie but smiled anyway. They knew they looked washed out, had tangles in their hair, sores on their lips and in their mouths. Moth-girls who never saw sunlight, never washed in a tub, only a bucket with a sponge. Girls who lived on white bread and sweet sugary Kool-Aid that had a bitter aftertaste and made them sleepy. Their teeth were rotten. Their breath, rank. They bruised easily, like old fruit.

Once, they were dancing and a voice from the trees called out, "What are you doing?"

"Nothing!" shouted Teilo. "Mind your own business, Evie!"

Evie stepped out of the shadows, looked at the girls. She looked tall and brave and very, very angry. "You're not supposed to talk to them! They shouldn't even be outside," she said. "I'm telling Mom." She ran back to the house.

"We'd better get you girls home," Teilo said. "The ball's over. Time to turn back into pumpkins. Pretty little, pretty little pumpkins in my pumpkin patch."

That night they heard a lot of shouting outside their locked door. The voices were muffled but furious, and they caught only a few words here and there:

Dangerous. Ruined. Teilo. Who do you think you are?

Then hammering, as nails were put into the outside of their little window.

They held each other there in the dark, shivering on their thin mattress.

Teilo didn't come to visit again for a long, long time. But Evie did. She warned them. "Don't talk to him," she said. "He isn't who he says he is. They're all a bunch of liars. The only one you can believe is me. If you trust me, if you're patient, I'll get you both out of here one day. I swear it."

CHAPTER 45

Phoebe

JUNE 13, PRESENT DAY

Phoebe carried the diary out of the hidden room, flipping through pages as Sam searched the rest of the basement.

> *End of Summer, 11 years old*
> *Dear Diary,*
>   *Sister says we have to make a deal with Teilo.*
>   *It seems like whatever I do, however hard I try*
> *to break away, he's there. Even when I don't go see*
> *him, when I make excuses to Sister, he's there in my*
> *dreams. He's always there.*
>   *I have my own secret name for him. I call him the*
> *Nightmare Man.*
>   *Sometimes in the night, I wake up screaming.*
> *Grandfather comes into my room, gives me a bitter*
> *tablet to place under my tongue. "Excitable child," he*
> *calls me as he encircles my wrist with his fingers. Then*
> *he asks, "What did you dream?"*
>   *"I don't remember," I tell him and he gives me this*

horrid little smile. Sometimes I wonder if maybe my
pulse is telling him a story, beating out words in some
kind of code that only Grandfather can understand.

"So what's the deal we have to make with Teilo?" I
asked Sister when we were on our way into the woods.
Lately, when we go there, I feel like everything is
alive—like the trees have eyes and ears and we have to
be very careful about what we say and do.

"If we promise him our firstborn," Sister explains,
"he'll give us what we wish for most in the world."

What I wish for most is that we never met Teilo.

If I said that out loud, something terrible would
happen to me. I just know it.

Phoebe skimmed ahead.

Mid-summer, 12 years old
Dear Diary,
Sometimes I wonder if Sister's making all this up. I
don't know how she could, but still, I wonder. . .
I wonder if a person can bring something to life by
wishing it. But why would you wish for something
dark? Something evil?

Phoebe skipped ahead again, and found an entry that made
her heart sink like lead into her stomach.

"Oh my God, Sam," she said. "I know whose diary this is."

Sam turned away from the boxes of books and papers he'd
been going through. "Whose?"

"Listen:

Midsummer, 13 years old
Dear Diary,

I am in love. And the best part is . . . he loves me
too! We're keeping it a secret, though. Grandfather
says I'm not allowed to go out with boys and that if he
ever catches me with one, I'll never leave the house
again. Grandfather says boys only want one thing.
But he's wrong about David. David has promised
to take me away from all of this, as soon as I turn
eighteen.

He works at the general store, but he goes to high
school. He's an artist. A potter.

The other day he gave me a gift: a blue bowl with a
mermaid painted at the bottom.

"It's too pretty to eat out of," I told him.

I filled the bowl with water, made it ripple, and the
mermaid seemed to come to life. Then a crazy thing
happened, a thing that made me wonder if I was going
mad. I looked into the bowl and saw the mermaid's
sweet face turn angry and horrid—it was Teilo's face
looking back. Then I heard a laugh, felt cold breath on
my neck. He was standing behind me. Only when I
turned, he wasn't there.

I told Sister about this later. She demanded to know
where the bowl had come from, and when I told her,
she got quiet.

"David loves me," I told her. "He says that when
he's done with high school, when I'm old enough,
we'll get married. We'll move far away. California
maybe."

*I left out what I was thinking. Away from Teilo.
Away from you and Grandfather.*

*Sister just smiled, said, "You think you can leave
that easily?"*

Phoebe closed the book and looked up at Sam. His face was
pale. "It's my mother's," he said.

Phoebe nodded. "And I don't know who or what Teilo is,
but your Aunt Hazel's been involved with him for a long, long
time."

Sam turned from the boxes, jogged over to the steps.

"Stop," Lisa said as Sam stepped onto the rough wooden basement stairs. "We're not allowed up there. It's dangerous."

"Bullshit," Sam mumbled, taking the stairs two at a time.
Phoebe tucked the diary in her back pocket and followed him.
Lisa hung back, muttering, "Not safe, not safe, not safe." An
incantation.

Phoebe wondered what they would find up there—the King
of the Fairies? A doorway to another world?

She flashed back onto the dream she'd had back in the cabin:
the hand reaching into her belly, pulling back the door of flesh,
muscle, and skin.

She thought of the tiny graveyard in the orchard.

"Sam?" she said, voice quavering. "Maybe it's time to call the
police?" He didn't show any sign of having heard her and hurried
up the last steps. Phoebe stayed right behind him. And behind
her, Lisa tentatively followed, mumbling, "Not safe," again and
again.

The door opened into an ordinary kitchen with laminate
countertops, a peeling linoleum floor, slightly sticky underfoot.

Empty cups, bowls, and gin bottles littered the counter. Phoebe surveyed the room and felt a horrible sense of familiar unease—this was so much like one of the kitchens of her childhood, reeking of spilled booze and sour milk. There was a large spray bottle of Raid on the cluttered table. Phoebe shuddered. It was as if she'd gone back in time to when she would walk through the kitchen and find her own mother passed out on the living room couch. And now, like then, she felt she was a meek little girl, powerless to other people's demons.

"Sam?" The word was little more than a moist puff in the air. She wanted to leave this place. To run as fast as she could and not look back.

Sam turned left, walking through the dining room into the living room.

Phoebe covered her nose and mouth and walked over to the sink. Among fossilized pots of orange macaroni and cheese and SpaghettiOs were baby bottles and half-empty bags of curdled formula. Phoebe's stomach clenched. She couldn't bear the thought of a tiny infant being in a place like this, cared for by a woman who obviously could barely care for herself. She put a hand on her stomach and made a silent promise: *I will keep you safe. I will keep things like this from ever happening to you. You will grow up in a clean house, eating wholesome, organic, Sam-approved food.*

"Sam," Phoebe said, holding one of the bottles up. "The baby was here." He looked over and nodded grimly.

She dropped the bottle of curdled formula and followed Sam into the living room.

Both rooms were cluttered and filthy: stacks of junk mail, books, and magazines covered the table and floor. Ashtrays were overflowing. Afghans that had no doubt once been bright and cheery hung over the furniture tattered and stained. The lights were on, but there was no sign of life.

"Hazel?" he called out. There was no response.

"Sam," Phoebe asked, eyeing yet another bottle of gin on the coffee table, this one half-full. Next to it, a ring of condensation, still damp and glistening. "When was the last time you were here?"

"When I was a kid. Before Lisa disappeared."

Lisa had followed them into the living room but stood with her back pressed against the wall, eyes open wide, hands clenched into fists, fingernails digging into her palms.

"You okay, Lisa?" Phoebe asked. Lisa showed no sign of having heard her.

Sam climbed the mottled brown and orange carpeted stairs in the living room. The wall was covered in school photos of Evie. There she was in first grade, pudgy and freckled, smiling for the camera. Then later, in fifth grade, the freckles faded, the smile replaced by a scowl. In her high school graduation picture, she was tall and lean with close-cropped hair and piercing eyes.

The light in the hall was on. They passed reprint landscapes in cheap frames, a plaster handprint Evie had done when she was seven. Phoebe placed her own hand over it, fingers working their way into the grooves Evie's hand had left behind.

Where *was* Evie?

What was happening to this family's girls and women?

The first bedroom, Hazel's, was empty. A bed was covered in a flowered quilt. There was a *Reader's Digest* on the night-stand and a small television. There were some dirty clothes on the floor: a stained nightgown, a faded pair of enormous pink briefs with the elastic sprung. Phoebe looked away, embarrassed.

Sam went across the hall to the second bedroom. "Jesus!" he yelped. Phoebe ran in.

"Evie's room," Sam said.

There was a twin bed, neatly made. Next to the bed was a desk. Above it, a poster of a tarot card: the Hanged Man.

Phoebe's skin felt cool and damp, like she'd just entered a cave.

"Look familiar?" Sam said, pointing at the image. It showed a man hanging upside down by his foot, his leg crossed, his hands bound.

"Teilo's sign," Phoebe said, instantly recognizing the rough shape the man's upside-down body made.

There was a scattering of notebooks on the desk. Sam picked one up, thumbed through it, scowling. Then he set it down, picked up another. "They're all full of writing, but I can't decipher it. It looks a lot like your chicken scratch, Bee." Sam gave her a quizzical look.

"Let me see." Sam handed the notebook over, and she flipped through it. "A lot of people use their own form of shorthand. It just makes writing faster," she explained.

"And makes it so other people can't read it," Sam added.

"Right, she was definitely trying to keep whatever she wrote a secret," Phoebe said, "but I can read this just fine."

"You can?"

"It's pretty simple, really." She held the book out for him to look at. "See these dots—they stand for the word *the*. She's dropped most of the vowels, used phonetic spelling. And she's simplified some of the letters, like leaving the A's without the line across. And this squiggle here," she said, pointing at the page, "is a G. The word is 'talking'."

Sam squinted at the notebook. "You can actually read it?"

"Sure," Phoebe said. "She's talking about the fairies, Teilo, a magic door in Reliance." She set down the notebook and picked up another, an earlier one, the cover worn and faded.

"Okay," Sam said. "So we know Evie was helping Teilo, but who the hell is he? He sure doesn't pop out of a secret door in the woods. Who lives in that room in the basement?"

Lisa stood in the doorway, as if she was afraid to step over the threshold. She laughed a high, nervous laugh.

"I don't know, but Evie definitely does," Phoebe said, a knot forming in her stomach. "But I'm not sure she was always on his side." She pointed at the notebook. "Listen to this, it's from fifteen years ago, in August:

> " 'They're keeping her so doped up she doesn't know where she is. It kills me to see her like this; it's like being gutted. But I know it won't last. It's just for a short time. I sneak into her room at night, curl up next to her, and tell her I promise I'll get her out. I bring her little treats: chocolate, colored pencils, bubble gum. One day, I'll find a way to break the spell. We'll get on our horses and ride away from here. I'll use my magic key and save us both.' "

Phoebe remembered what Lisa had said, that Evie was the one who let her go. But why had it taken fifteen years? What was she up against?

Phoebe looked up at the hanged man poster above the desk. What struck her most was his expression of perfect calm. Here he was, hung upside down, looking completely at peace, a yellow halo glowing around his head, making him seem saintly, enlightened.

She glanced back down at the notebook, flipping ahead until something caught her eye. "Listen to this," she said.

Evie had taken notes from a book called *Tarot for Beginners*:

> "'The hanged man suspends serenely upside
> down, having let go of all worldly attachments.
> The hanged man has perspective obtainable only
> by someone who is free from everyday reality.
> He is an outcast who appears to be a fool, but in
> reality, he is the most enlightened of them all. He
> understands change is coming and has opened
> himself up to it completely. It's a card about
> surrender. About being suspended between the
> worlds.'"

He walks between the worlds.

It's a card about surrender.

As she set down the journal, her eye caught on the pile of books underneath the notebooks. Phoebe held up a thick hardcover in a transparent library slipcover: *Understanding Agoraphobia*. "Looks like maybe Evie was doing a little research." Getting ready to play the role of the poor, terrified cousin who can't leave her apartment. Phoebe flipped through. Tucked between pages of the book were two snapshots, one of the house Phoebe and Sam shared.

"She was watching us," Phoebe said.

The other was a childhood photo of Evie, Sam, and Lisa on a beach. Evie's arm was around Lisa. They were all three smiling into the camera. Phoebe caught the glint of Lisa's brand-new charm bracelet on her left wrist. Sam and Evie held plastic pirate swords. Off in the corner of the photo, between the kids and the ocean behind them, a blurry figure was lurking. "Who's that?" she asked Sam, pointing at the photo, wondering if it was an actual person or just a trick of light.

"No one," Sam said. "There wasn't anyone else there."

Behind them, from a room down the hall, a door closed.

They all froze, looking at each other.

"He's here," Lisa said.

Phoebe looked up at the Hanged Man and stumbled a little, suddenly light-headed, as if she herself were upside down. Her stomach churned, and a wave of nausea overtook her. She hurried from the room, down the hall in search of a bathroom, making it just in time. She vomited, rinsed out her mouth with lukewarm water, looked at herself in the mirror. For just an instant, a nebulous figure moved across the mirror, behind her. She spun. No one. Nothing.

"Shit," she mumbled, gripping the sink. She thought she felt the baby twitch inside her, her own little divining rod telling her something was terribly wrong.

She walked on shaky legs out of the bathroom and saw there was one more room across the hall, the door closed. She crept slowly up to it, placed her hand on the knob, turning it gently, pushing the door open. The room was warm, sweet smelling but with a sour undertone.

"Oh," she said, not meaning to speak, the sound escaping anyway. In front of her was a pretty white bassinet, a changing table stocked with diapers, powder, wipes, diaper rash cream. On the edge of the table, a bottle of formula. Phoebe touched it—still warm.

"You're too late," a voice told her. It was gravelly, unfamiliar. The hairs on the back of Phoebe's neck stood up. She tried to make herself turn around but found she was frozen in place, as in a nightmare.

CHAPTER 46

The Girl Who Would Be Queen

He made them both pregnant this time. He was getting his son, one way or another.

They talked about escaping. When the babies were born, they were going to take them and run.

"They'll never let us," the queen said. She'd been there longer. She'd lost hope long ago.

"I know people," she told the queen. "There are places where we would be safe. Sometimes there are happy endings," she said. Hansel and Gretel pushed the witch into the oven, took her treasures, and found their way back home. Sleeping Beauty was woken with a kiss.

They didn't see Teilo much. They continued to hear arguments through the flowered walls. Angry words saying things like "How could you?" and "I trusted you!" and "You've ruined everything."

The girls waited. Their bellies grew. To pass the time, they told each other stories.

Once upon a time there was a little girl. And she had a little curl. Coal black hair. Dark eyes. She lived with her mother and father and brother on the edge of a forest. She ate oatmeal for breakfast and called it porridge. She had a shelf full of books and a silver comb and mirror that were magic. She had a secret hiding place in the attic. She went to school. Learned the golden rule. Loved her English teacher, who taught her things like what a metaphor is and how every story, if you look at it right, is a circle with a beginning, middle, and end.

She had a cousin named Evie, who said, "Don't go into the woods anymore."

And Evie was right. She should have listened.

CHAPTER 47

Phoebe

Who is Teilo?" Sam demanded. Hazel stood in the center of the nursery, holding a large glass of what smelled like straight gin with ice. She was short and chunky, with black tousled hair streaked with grey. Her cheeks were rosy and covered with thin spidery red veins, her eyes dark. She wore a pair of stretchy navy blue pants, stained at the knees, a white cardigan, and fleece slippers. *House clothes*, Phoebe's mother would have called them. Phoebe saw an instant resemblance to Phyllis, only this was a ravaged version—the dark sister who stole children away.

"Do you really need to ask that?" Hazel asked, her words a slurred, drunken hiss. "After everything you've seen? You of all people should understand the truth, Sammy." She waved her drink in his direction, some of it spilling over the edge.

"What truth is that?" Sam asked. "What I understand is that you kept Lisa here. Made her think she was with the fairies. It was *you*. You and some mysterious six-fingered rapist who lives in your goddamn basement! Who is he, Hazel?"

"I did what I did because I *had* to. I did it to protect my children."

"Evie?" Sam said. "How in the hell did stealing Lisa protect Evie?"

Children. She'd said children.

Phoebe remembered what Becca had said about Hazel having a stillborn baby that everyone in town heard crying.

"He's your son," Phoebe said. "Teilo is your son."

Hazel chuckled, sounding more like a dainty Mrs. Claus than a psychotic kidnapper. "No. Gene is Teilo's son."

"Who?" Sam asked.

"The Dark Man," she said. "Teilo." When Hazel said the name, a shadow crossed her face. She took a long sip from the glass of gin, hand trembling.

She's afraid of him, Phoebe thought.

"But who the hell is Gene?" Sam asked.

"Your cousin," Phoebe explained. "Evie's older brother."

"Evie doesn't have a brother." Sam shook his head firmly.

Poor Sam. Sometimes he was too smart for his own good. By the time his brain analyzed and processed, he was half a step behind.

"Why?" Phoebe asked Hazel. "Why keep him hidden?"

"He walks between the worlds," Hazel said. "Half human, half fairy."

"I have fucking *had* it with the fairy shit!" Sam exploded. "Where's Lisa's baby? What have you freaks done with him?"

"I said, you're too late," Hazel said calmly, smoothing at a crease in her stained pants. "They've taken the baby."

"Where?" Sam asked. "What are they going to do to him? Lock him up in another secret room in someone's filthy basement?"

Hazel flinched a little, then smiled, showing crooked, stained teeth. "No. They'll take him to Teilo. In time, he'll be joined by another, a human girl not yet born who will be raised by the fairies. Together, they'll change the world."

"This is insane," Sam said. "You can't actually believe all this."

"It's the prophecy. And it's all coming true. Ask her," Hazel said, looking at Lisa. "She knows the truth. She's seen the future." Hazel looked down into her glass, closed her eyes, and took another deep swallow.

Sam shook his head. "Lisa barely knows her own name anymore."

Hazel laughed. "You still think this is Lisa?"

Phoebe's mind ran in circles, then something clicked into place, like tumblers in a lock.

"Let me guess, she's a *changeling*? Jesus!" Sam said. "Hazel, you pulled all this insane fairy crap from your own sick, twisted mind and brainwashed Evie. You kidnapped your own niece. And on top of it, you've got a secret son who never sees the light of day? What the fuck is the matter with you?"

Hazel shook her head. "I didn't want to believe either, at first, Sammy. But then I saw the truth. Sometimes I wish . . . I wish things had turned out differently. But they didn't. And you can't run from your own destiny. You can't hide from Teilo, no matter how hard you try."

"Where have they taken the baby?" Sam said, raising his voice and speaking slowly, annunciating each syllable. "Where is Teilo?"

"Where do you go when there's nowhere else to go?" Hazel said, rocking back on her heels. "Home, Sammy. You go home."

The Girl Who Would Be Queen

Teilo got what he wanted, what the dreams and prophecies promised: a boy child with thick dark hair, the palest skin, eyes like chestnuts, a mouth as red as any ruby. He smelled like warm summer rain. And the only time he seemed to stop crying was when her nipple was in his mouth. He rolled it around in there like a sweet cherry, then clamped down tight and went to work. Queen cow, pumping out milk, walking the halls with the baby howling, one of the guardians telling her to shut him up. Then another guardian hissed, "You shut up before Teilo hears you and fries up your skin for breakfast! That's the prince you're talking about."

Things were tense since Teilo's son was born. There was arguing all the time. Evie fought with the guardians, who then fought with the man who called himself Teilo but wasn't really.

Her own baby had been stillborn. She must have come too early. She was perfect in every way, though. Ten fingers. Ten toes. A head full of damp, curly hair.

A week later, the queen's baby, the perfect son, came. The queen had a hard labor, much worse than her own. There was so much screaming. So much blood. The guardians, they tried to stop it. "We should get her to a hospital," Evie said. She was yelling, begging. And she was crying. Actual tears.

"No," said her mother. "Teilo would be furious."

So they let her die.

Lisa, her name had been. Queen of the Fairies.

She'd heard the guardians talking. They said they had no use for her anymore.

"She's got a loose screw," one said. "A fucking mental case, that one is. Not even the kid's mother. Just a wet nurse plucked at random off the street because Gene thought Lisa was lonely. So he brings her a fucking crank addict? How's that for a play-mate for the Queen of the Fairies? Disgusting!"

"Too late now," the other said. "It's your fault, really, when you look at it. It was your job to keep Gene under control. She's serving a purpose now, feeding the baby. When we don't need the girl, we'll get rid of her. And take care of any evidence."

Evidence.

Evidently.

Eventually.

Fucking mental case.

Once upon a time, there was a girl who thought she was special, but really she was just dumb. A bad girl who skipped school, stole her mother's cigarettes and brandy. She left home at sixteen, looking for something more. She lived on the street. Learned to make a buck however she could. It was funny what some guys would pay for. Funny strange, not funny ha ha. That was a saying her ma used to have. Sometimes she missed her ma.

Mostly, she didn't. Each day on the street was like panning for gold: you never knew what you'd find, who'd turn up.

He was dressed all in black, not much older than she was. His hair was dark and slicked back. He had a goatee. His boots were spit-shined so that you could look down and see the reflections of streetlights and clouds. He was a magic man, he told her. He gave her a twenty just for a smile. That's when she saw his gloved hands, each with an extra finger.

The next day, he came back with a pack of smokes, a handful of pills, bright and colorful as candy.

"What would you say if I told you there was a whole parallel world beside ours and that the beings who lived there controlled our destiny?"

The girl laughed.

"You know how sometimes, sometimes when you're just sitting there, you catch this movement in the corner of your eye—just a shadow, really—and you blink, sure you imagined it?"

She nodded. She knew exactly what he meant. It happened to her all the time.

"That's them," he said.

She took out a smoke and lit it.

"People like you and me, we get that the life people are living is really an illusion, don't we? Smoke and mirrors, hiding the real deal. The steal of a deal. That guy coming out of Banana Republic with a seventy-dollar shirt. The woman with her grande half-caff latte. They don't have a clue. But you and I, we know different."

The girl blew smoke at him, smiled. "So what, exactly, are you saying?"

"I'm saying I can show you the truth. I can take you away from all this and change your life forever."

Now the girl was just tired. And she wasn't a girl anymore. She's what—in her twenties? Thirties maybe even. Time meant nothing in the fairy world. Her body hurt. Her teeth ached. She lay in bed at night and heard voices no one else seemed to hear. They'd get loud, then soft, but stayed steady, like a pulse. A strange heartbeat in her ears. Lisa's babies. Hers. Lisa's voice saying, "I lived next to a town called Reliance. My brother, his name is Sam. If I ever get out of here, he's the first one I'll find."

When they started the baby on formula, she knew it was over.

Evie came into her room one night, said, "You need to go. Now."

Evie had been so kind to her these last weeks. She snuck her and the baby out when the guardians were away. They went for rides in the country. Evie took her to a library in the afternoons, even let her check out books. It was far away, a place where no one would recognize them.

But now Evie was panicked as she pried open the window and helped her through.

"Where will I go?" she asked.

"As far as you can," Evie whispered.

She pulled herself through and ran. But it wasn't her own life she was running toward. It was Lisa's, the girl who was Queen of the Fairies. Because somehow, after their years together, she knew Lisa's life better than her own. It was more real to her—more vivid and sparkling and full of hope than her own past.

Once upon a time there was a girl named Lisa who lived in a house with her mother, father, and brother, Sammy. They all loved her very much. She ate oatmeal for breakfast and called it porridge. Her father was very sick and she thought she could save him. She was a good girl.

Good girl.

Good girl.

CHAPTER 49

Phoebe

So what you're saying," Phoebe said, "is that there really is no Teilo."

"Right," said Sam. He was speeding along through dark and twisting roads, hurrying back toward Reliance, hoping like hell the baby would be there. "He's just a figure in some fucked-up fairy tale my mother and Hazel believed in, a story their own mother told them. They passed it down to their children. Hazel was a little . . . unbalanced, and took the story too literally. She came to really believe it, and then there was the pregnancy. I'm guessing that's what put her over the edge." Sam paused, took a breath. "Maybe she was raped," he said, shuddering. "And, to deal with it, she convinced herself that it was Teilo's baby. She hid him away, raised him with this crazy belief that he was of fairy blood. Some families have shit like cancer and heart disease passed from one generation the next—we've got malevolent stories."

It made sense in an awful way. A legend passed down from one generation to the next that made each child feel special, like they were part of something much larger, much more magical than the mundane world of friends and school and rock collections. *There are fairies on the back side of the hill. Your great-grandfather was really a changeling left to pass as a human infant in a crib.*

Didn't everyone want that? Have a secret longing to be more special than the guy next door? Didn't everyone secretly wish there was another world you could find a doorway to, step inside, and become a queen?

Phoebe could understand that longing.

She had spent her whole life being nothing special. The girl who fell between the cracks. Who barely got through school, didn't show much promise. The daughter of a drunk who wasn't destined for any sort of greatness.

There was some part of her—some desperate, pathetic part, dying to be special—that wished it was true that Teilo really might have chosen her to give him Sam's firstborn.

Phoebe swallowed hard, feeling like she had a golf ball stuck in her throat.

Phoebe remembered what Dr. Ostrum had told her—that the people in Reliance hadn't vanished overnight, it was a slow drying-up, people moved on to other places. But that didn't make for a good story. Every town needs a mystery or two, she'd said.

"So who is the father of Lisa's baby?" Phoebe asked.

"It's gotta be this cousin, Gene," Sam said. "Shit, I bet he was there that summer, hiding out in the woods, masquerading as the Fairy King! We found a bed of ferns one time, a blanket and those brass binoculars."

"Oh," Phoebe said, relieved that they were talking about an

actual person, not a mythical being. But then she remembered the dark shadow she'd seen pass behind her in the bathroom at Aunt Hazel's. Thought of the nightmares.

"I still don't understand," Phoebe confessed. "Everything that happened at the cabin, the other Evie . . ."

"I think all hell broke loose when Lisa ran away," Sam explained. "I mean, they'd kidnapped her, held her against her will for years, used her for some fucked-up incestuous breeding project where they were trying to make some crazy fairy prophecy they'd probably made up themselves come true. Lunatics! They knew she'd come to us. And they knew that the fairy book linked them to the kidnapping. It was proof. They wanted it back. And they wanted Lisa back before she told anyone about Gene, the baby, and the room in the basement. So they sent the fake Evie, knowing it would lead us to the real Evie, who seemed like this helpless wreck of a woman. Someone who needed taking care of. God, they played us, Bee. They knew our every move before we did."

But there was one piece in Sam's scenario that still wasn't quite right: Lisa.

"Gabrielle," Phoebe said, turning to look at the girl in the backseat. "Was Lisa already there when they took you, or did she come later?"

"What?" Sam asked. "What are you talking about, Bee?"

The girl bit her lip, looked up at Phoebe, and nodded. "She was there. She was the true queen."

The car drifted from the passing lane into the right lane as Sam turned to look in the backseat. A horn blasted.

"Sam!" Phoebe cried. "Keep your eyes on the road. If you get us all killed, we'll never find the baby."

"I don't understand," Sam muttered, eyes focused on the dark highway, hands gripping the wheel as he straightened up the car. "Whose baby is it? Who is this girl? Where the hell is Lisa?"

"The baby's Lisa's, right?" Phoebe said.

Gabrielle nodded.

"Did you have a baby too?" Phoebe asked, remembering what Franny said about the milk leaking from the girl's breasts.

She nodded again. "My baby died. They gave me Lisa's."

"Where is Lisa?" Sam asked again.

Gabrielle began to cry. Phoebe understood. Lisa was under one of the white crosses in the orchard. Whether she died giving birth or they killed her because they had no use for her after, she was gone.

"And did your babies have the same father?" Phoebe asked.

Gabrielle nodded. "Teilo. The Dark Man. King of the Fairies. He'll come for you too," she said, staring right at Phoebe. "You'll see soon enough. You have something he wants."

Phoebe's stomach clenched.

"I don't get it," Sam said. "What the fuck is going on?"

"They took another girl," Phoebe explained. "I saw the name Gabrielle written on the wall in the locked room in the basement. Then when we were talking to Hazel, I realized this isn't Lisa. You were right all along, Sam."

"But why?" Sam asked. "Why take a second girl?"

"I'm not sure exactly," Phoebe said. "A companion maybe? But there's something else I'm not understanding. If your mother knew Hazel really believed in the fairies, which she must, because she wrote the diary, then how did she not suspect her when Lisa went missing? Why didn't she send the police after Hazel right away?"

Sam shrugged.

Phoebe pulled Phyllis's red diary from her back pocket and opened it:

End of Summer, 13 years old
Dear Diary,

Yesterday, Sister apologized for how awful she'd been. She said she was sorry she'd been so caught up in Teilo. Of course I should go off and marry David when I get a little older. She was happy for me. Really. We had a picnic on a blanket she'd laid out in the woods. She made cupcakes and brought a thermos of hot, sweet tea. After, I felt very sleepy.

"Close your eyes," she said. "Lay down awhile."

When I opened my eyes again, David was there.

I looked for Sister, but she was nowhere to be seen.

"We love each other very much, don't we?" David said, lifting my skirt. He unbuckled his belt.

"What are you doing?" I tried to ask, but what came out was a faint, buzzing June bug of a sound. I tried to sit up, but my body felt too heavy, as if I were made of bags of heavy sand.

Then he was on top of me. Inside me. I tried to roll away, but his arms pinned me to the blanket.

I closed my eyes.

When I opened them again, it wasn't David's face I saw.

Teilo's black eyes gazed back at me. And only then I realized that they were a lot like Grandfather's. And then he smiled and I felt that familiar constricting feeling in my throat.

"Silly girl," he said.

"Sam, how old was your mother when Lisa was born?" Phoebe asked.

"I don't know exactly. Twenty, I think. Why?"

Phoebe didn't answer but went back to reading.

Late Spring, 14 years old
Dear Diary,

Sister is the one who told David I was pregnant. She said that was the kind of girl I was—the kind who wasn't careful, who would go into the woods with just any boy who asked.

I tried to tell him the truth: that she led me into the woods. That it was his face I saw at first. It was a terrible trick the two of them had played on me.

"My grandfather's in on it too," I explained. "He's evil. He has powers. Sometimes . . . sometimes, I think he's not human."

David started to walk away. I grabbed his shoulder, made him turn toward me.

"I love you," I said. "All my life, I will love only you."

David shook his head, backed away from me slowly like I was brandishing a weapon. Somehow or other, I'd become a dangerous girl. A girl capable of anything in his eyes.

Sister was a great comfort to David. He kept coming around. She fed him tea and cake and stories. Stories

*about me and how I'd always been a little off in the
head. About how on the back side of our hill, there was
a town that used to be but wasn't anymore; about how
I, her poor crazy sister, believed there were fairies there.*

*When Sister told me that she was getting married,
that she was going to be Mrs. David Nazzaro, it
came as no surprise. But still, it was like she shoved a
corkscrew in my heart, then twisted and pulled. Pop. A
toast to you and yours. May you live happily ever after.*

*"It's just for show, though," Sister said. "I will
always be Teilo's bride. So will you. And you, you're
special. He chose you, Hazel. He chose you to give
him a son—half fairy, half human. The child you
carry will walk between the worlds."*

"Oh my God," Phoebe said, staring down at the diary.

"What?" Sam asked.

Gabrielle looked at Phoebe and giggled. "You can't change
what's happened. Or what's going to happen," she said. "One of
the guardians, she used to come sit with us. She'd tell us stories.
Stories about us. She said that everything happened for a reason.
We didn't always understand the reason, but Teilo did. Not the
fake Teilo, that's not who she meant, but the real one. We all
had our destinies, she used to say."

Destiny. Is that what this was all about? Phoebe touched her
belly.

"Bullshit," Sam said, peering back at Gabrielle in the rearview
mirror. "Who told you all this? Hazel? Evie's mother?"

"No," Gabrielle said. "The older one. Lisa's mother. She was
Teilo's queen once, too."

PART V

The Happy Family

If you believe, people will doubt you. Call you crazy. There will come a time when you must make a choice—when your true beliefs will be put to the test.

Us or them?

The world of magic or the mundane drudgery of going through life with blinders on.

You choose.

CHAPTER 50

Phoebe

They were coming up on Harmony when Phoebe got to the last few pages of the diary.

Spring, Age 15
Dear Diary,
The baby looks like his father. That's what Sister says. She and David are married now, and we all live together in our house, just as Teilo promised. Grandfather's gone, struck by lightning just after Sister and David got married. It's funny though, sometimes I wake up in the night and can still feel his cold, bony fingers wrapped around my wrist. Mother's gone to a home since the stroke messed up her brain. Folks in town say our family sure has had its run of bad luck. They bring casseroles and cakes but never set foot in the door. In fact, they seem to be holding their breath as they stand on the porch, nervously looking in, as if bad luck were a germ you could inhale.

Sometimes I see it like that too. This big old mushroom cloud hanging over our house. And if you followed it down to the source, you'd end up in Reliance. You'd find Teilo there, dancing in the shadows, laughing.

Sister and David coo over Gene. They play patty-cake and sing silly songs that make Gene giggle and blow bubbles.

I've tried, but I can't make myself love him.

No matter how many baths I give him, he smells like the woods. Like Reliance.

It's the Fairy in him, Sister says.

And the extra fingers, they're supposed to be a sign of magic, but to me, they're all wrong.

It breaks me into a million pieces to watch David with Gene. Sometimes I have to turn away because the tears are coming hard and fast.

Last week he caught me watching him, crying.

"What is it?" David asked. He'd just rocked Gene to sleep. Sister was out at the market. It's worse when she's away because then I can pretend it's just me and David and Gene here.

"Sometimes I wish things had turned out differently," I tell him. "I wish you and I—"

His eyes blazed and he looked away. "You made your choice."

I laughed. "What choice?"

And then I told him. I told him everything. Even the things Sister had forbidden me to say. I told him about Teilo and the woods, the book we found, and

*how we each promised our firstborn. I told him that
Teilo was watching us all the time, using us, playing us
like instruments.*

*He shook his head. "You're nuts," he told me. "You
don't make any sense."*

Maybe he was right. Maybe I am the crazy one.

*"I know that's what my sister tells you, but please,
David, please, if you ever cared for me at all, then
do me one favor. Try to imagine for one minute what
it would mean if I was right. I know you think that
my sister is good as gold, but what if she's not? What
if the only reason you're here is because they want
something of you?"*

"Who is they?" he asked.

*"Teilo. The fairies. They're using you, David. I'm
not sure what for—appearances, probably. Or maybe
it's just to amuse them because they know how it
tortures me."*

*"Phyllis and I are married. We don't keep secrets
from each other."*

*I laughed again. I couldn't help it. "This house is
nothing but a thick, tangled nest of secrets. You'll see
soon enough. "*

He said nothing.

"Do you love her?" I asked.

He winced a little.

*I smiled. "You know I'm right, don't you? I'm
guessing you know something's not right here. Maybe
you've felt him. Or even seen him watching from the
shadows."*

He looked panicked now, making me surer than ever that I was right.

"You have, haven't you?"

"I should go," he said, taking a step back.

"And I'm also guessing you don't love her. Not like you loved me. Remember, Dave? How you were going to take me away from all of this? We were going to California?"

He stepped forward then and took me in his arms. He was trembling. His lips found mine and I knew it was wrong, I knew there would be repercussions, but in the moment, I just didn't care.

Fall, 15 years old
Dear Diary,

I'm being sent away. Banished, Sister calls it. Me and little Gene and David's little unborn son or daughter are moving to an old farmhouse owned by some elderly distant aunt. She has an apple orchard. I'll pick apples, learn to run the cider press. When she passes on, the farm will be mine. It's all arranged.

I'm never to live in Harmony again.

I'm to stay away from David. No contact. Not until I prove I can control myself.

"And what if I refuse?" I asked.

"You can't," Sister said.

"I don't care what he does to me," I said. "Teilo can't hurt me any more than he already has."

Sister shook her head. "You stupid little whore. He'll go after David."

So I packed up little Gene's things, my clothes, a
few books, and I got in the car without even saying
good-bye.

Phoebe closed the diary. They were passing the Lord's Prayer rock.

"Evie's your sister," she said.

Sam nodded. "I know," Sam said, as if he was finally seeing something that had been in front of his face all along. "I mean, I didn't know it for a fact, but part of me always kind of felt it. I think Lisa knew, though. It was one of those things that I think everyone knew but no one dared say out loud. Everyone was too busy inventing their own twisted versions of the truth. It was easier to blame every mistake, every bad thing that happened, on the goddamn fairies."

Phoebe blew out a breath. "I don't think we know what we're up against," she said.

"Stories," Sam said. "Fables. Fairy tales."

"But if people believe in them so strongly, doesn't that give them power? More power maybe than even the truth?"

CHAPTER 51

Gene

MAY 29, FIFTEEN YEARS AGO

He's a ghost. Here, but not here. Walking between the worlds. Moving in shadows. A shadow man himself, more phantom than living, breathing being. He's been in the dark so long, he doesn't remember the light.

He's the Hoochie-Coochie Man. The Hurdy-Gurdy Man. The Bogeyman.

Boo.

Mister Slinky slinking around. Peeping Tom. He's Tom, Dick, and Harry. See Dick run. See Dick find Jane, smile at her. Think unmentionables.

He doesn't know movies, just the ones described to him by Evie. No TV where he lives, deep underground. No satellite or cable or movie of the week.

He knows books, though. The silly, predictable romances with their pink covers and ape-chested men. He knows *Frankenstein*, "Cinderella," and "Rumpelstiltskin" where the horrid little man spins straw into gold for the miller's daughter, who promises him her firstborn.

That is not my name, he taunts, trying to make her guess.

Hurdy-Gurdy. Hurdy-Gurdy.

"You are a prince among men," his mother used to say. As if that made up for things. As if that would be enough.

Enough.

For a long time, loving Lisa was enough. Just the feeling sitting inside his chest banging away like a gorilla in a cage. It was the strongest feeling he'd ever known. This need, this ache to meet her, to be near her. He'd heard stories of her his whole life. Stories from Evie, who crept down to the basement after each trip to the Nazzaros, full of stories of adventures. Things Lisa did. Stories Lisa told. Lisa. Lisa. Lisa. Lisa became the sun the world orbited around.

Round and round. All around the mulberry bush, the monkey chased the weasel. The monkey thought 'twas all in fun. Pop! goes the weasel.

They played a game, he and Evie. A game where she pretended to be Lisa. She acted like Lisa, spoke like Lisa, wrapped a towel around her head and said, "Don't I have the most beautiful hair you've ever seen?"

Yes, Gene nodded. Yes. Yes. Yes. He let himself touch it, his fingers lost in the soft terry cloth.

And when it would end, when Evie would get called back upstairs for chores or homework or dinner, she'd drop the towel and say, "Oh Gene, I wish you could meet her for real!"

He wished too. He ached with the wish.

Evie snuck snapshots to him. Lisa on the beach. Lisa biting into a candy apple at the fair, her lips crimson and sticky. He'd touch her lips in the picture, then taste his own dirty fingertip, teeth buzzing from the sweetness he imagined. Evie gave him a tape of Lisa telling stories. He listened to it over and over, until the tape got fuzzy and her voice filled his brain and stayed there, talking to him in his dreams, keeping him company when he was alone every day for hours.

The worst was when Evie was at school. His mother would bring him lunch sometimes, when she remembered. Cheap greasy peanut butter on stale bread. Watery soup. She didn't speak, didn't look at him, just dropped off the food and latched the door from the outside. She used to talk to him, used to read him stories, but as he got older, she just quit seeing him. It was like he was turning invisible. Like his skin and flesh, even the organs inside him, got so pale they were translucent. *Translucent.* That was a word Evie taught him. "Like mica," she told him. "And window glass. Plastic bags you put apples and broccoli in at the store. They're all translucent."

"You're the smartest person on earth," he told Evie and she smiled wide, her teeth like a shark's.

She snuck down after school, bringing treats: half an apple, new pencils, books from the school library. She was the one who'd taught him to read and write. To do math. He'd learned right along with her after school each day; together they'd struggled over vocabulary lists, science reports, fractions. She brought him newspapers. Books of fairy tales. Books on magic and natural history. Boy Scout manuals.

"There's nothing you can't learn from a book," she told him.

He taught himself to sew. He built elaborate mousetraps out of rubber bands, wire, and old coffee cans. Sometimes, at night, when their mother was out cold, Evie would unlock the door and they'd go outside together. They'd take long walks through the woods and old orchards.

He asked Evie a million questions. What was Lisa's middle name? Maude. Favorite color? Green. Favorite season? Fall. What did Lisa love best in the world, more than anything? Fairy tales.

A plan began to form. He would go to the woods behind her house. He would pretend to be someone else—someone brave and powerful and full of magic. And he would give her the most wonderful gift of her life—a magic book. He snuck into his mother's room one night when she was out cold and found the book hidden under her bed. *The Book of Fairies*. She'd shown it to him before, told him it was written by his father and that she and Phyllis had found it down in Reliance when they were girls.

You can only watch," Evie warned. "You mustn't ever let her see you. You mustn't speak to her or make contact in any way. If Mom and Phyllis find out you're there and that I helped you, we're both dead."

He nodded. Nod. Nod.

He knew the rules. He was supposed to stay in the basement. Live underground. No one could see him. He was that special. A walking secret. But when you spend your whole life being a secret, your biggest wish is that you had someone to tell it to.

Evie took their mother's keys the night before, let him out of his room, opened the trunk of the car, and hid him there among their bags. She gave him a knapsack with matches, their great-grandfather's binoculars, peanut butter, a loaf of bread, and an old plain-faced white Halloween mask to put on "just in case." He snuck in *The Book of Fairies* and two trinkets he'd found in his mother's bedside table drawer: an old penny and a medal that said SAINT CHRISTOPHER PROTECT US. He didn't have much to give, but Lisa would like these. He knew she would. Evie drew a map of the house, yard, and woods, showing where Reliance was, and put it in his shirt pocket.

"We'll be in Cape Cod for three days, so you're on your own then. When I get back, I'll bring you food as often as I can. God, I can't believe I let you talk me into this. Promise me you'll be good, Gene. Promise you'll stay hidden."

"Promise," he said. And she closed the lid of the trunk gently over him.

CHAPTER 52

Phoebe

Home.

This could be a scene from a Norman Rockwell painting: Phyllis in the rocking chair, giving her infant grandson a bottle. But Phoebe knew better. She knew that the grandson was also a grand-nephew and there, lurking in the doorway that led to the kitchen, was the man who lured Lisa away by pretending to be the King of the Fairies. A man Sam's height with the palest skin Phoebe had ever seen. Black hair and eyes and six fingers on each hand.

An icy dagger ripped through Phoebe as his eyes met hers across the room.

Hazel's hidden child. The supposed son of Teilo, King of the Fairies. *Half fairy, half human,* Hazel had said. *He walks between the worlds.*

Sam hadn't knocked—had burst 'in through the front door into the living room, Phoebe and Gabrielle right behind him.

"Mom?" Sam said. Phyllis looked up, smiled.

"Hello, Sam," she said. "We've been expecting you."

"What the hell is going on?" He was squinting in disbelief at his mother and the baby.

Phyllis kept rocking, cooed at the baby in her arms. A tiny thing, with dark hair and eyes, who wouldn't stop fussing. He pushed the bottle out of his mouth with his strong tongue, made an unhappy face. Phoebe had this idea that her maternal instinct should kick in, making her adore the tiny infant. But the truth was, she found him startlingly unappealing—grotesque even. He was so pale, his skin so thin that you could see a network of blue veins pulsing. And his cry sounded more animal than human— the squeal of a starving piglet, a creature who would never be satisfied.

Phyllis sang:

> *Say, say my playmate*
> *Come out and play with me*
> *And bring your dollies three*
> *Climb up my apple tree*
> *Holler down my rain barrel*
> *Slide down my cellar door*
> *And we'll be jolly friends, forever more!*

Phoebe shivered. The baby opened its mouth and screamed until it was purple-faced and breathless.

In front of Phyllis, on the well-polished coffee table covered in the runner Phyllis herself had crocheted, was *The Book of Fairies.* The cover was a deep green color and well worn. Phoebe longed to pick it up and at last see what secrets were shut inside.

She wondered if it was really the same book Hazel and Phyllis had found in the woods when they were girls.

Out of the corner of her eye, Phoebe caught a glimpse of a man-shaped form leaning against the mantel, shaking his head. *You know better*, he seemed to say.

She blinked and he was gone.

The room, which had once seemed so warm and inviting to Phoebe, suddenly felt small and airless. The jars of potpourri were sickly sweet, making her feel light-headed and ill. Her eyes went to the photos on the mantel: Sam, Lisa, Mom, and Dad smiling on a beach. The happy family. From another frame, Sam's great-grandfather, Dr. Eugene O'Toole, glared at them with glimmering dark eyes.

Phoebe realized how very wrong she'd been about this house, this family. It was far darker, more dangerous than the places she'd grown up in. In the dingy little apartments her mother rented, everything was out in the open. Their lives were dirty and squalid, but they didn't pretend to be anything else. Here, things seemed so normal, so perfect, but it was all a deception.

"I think," said Phyllis, looking at Gabrielle, "that little Maxwell would like to come see you. He isn't very interested in the bottle. And he's hungry. Would that be okay, dear?"

Gabrielle gave a deep nod, more like a bow, and stepped forward to take the squalling baby. Phyllis rose, giving them the rocking chair. Gabrielle lifted her shirt and the baby dove in and started to suck. Gabrielle rocked, hummed to the baby, a contented smile on her face. Little Maxwell's rigid body relaxed at last.

"A baby needs a mother," Phyllis said, shrugging and smiling. "And a mother needs a baby."

"But she's not his mother, right?" Sam asked, watching the nursing infant with dismay. "It's Lisa's baby and this isn't Lisa."

"She's the only mother Max has ever known. If Lisa was here, she'd care for the baby. But she's not. Now shall I put on some tea so we can visit awhile? I think we have a lot to talk about."

"What happened to Lisa, Mom?" Sam asked.

Phyllis flinched. "There were some . . . complications when she gave birth."

Now it was Phoebe who flinched. She hoped no one noticed.

"My God," Sam said. "She's been alive all these years, living in that little room in Hazel's basement? And you knew? You went and visited her?"

Phyllis nodded.

"She was your child!"

"Yes. But she made her own choices. You remember how she was, Sam. So fiercely determined to walk her own path."

"She was twelve, Mom," Sam said, his voice cracking.

Phyllis made a clucking sound, shook her head. *Too bad, too bad.*

"It was you in the woods, wasn't it?" Sam said, looking at Gene, studying his strange, pale cousin. Gene didn't respond, didn't even look in Sam's direction. His eyes looked glassy and vacant. Phoebe wondered if he'd even heard Sam.

"Gene," Phyllis said, "will you go make us a pot of tea, dear. And get some of those cookies from the tin in the cupboard." The pale man nodded, then slipped away into the kitchen. He walked slowly, with a limp.

"You knew where she was. What was happening. You were in on it all along," Sam said.

Phyllis leaned forward, speaking in a hushed voice. "There

are things you don't know. Things I tried to shield you from. For your own good, Sam. And for the good of the family."

Sam gave a stormy-sounding laugh. "The family? But I'm your family, Mom. Lisa was your family! Why would you protect Gene over us?"

Phyllis sighed, knitted her fingers together. She looked from Sam to Phoebe as she considered how best to continue. "Your aunt Hazel was pregnant at thirteen, the result of an incestuous relationship with our grandfather."

Interesting, Phoebe thought. *No mention of Teilo.*

"But I thought she got pregnant when she was sixteen," Sam said.

Phyllis nodded, her face tightening, the corners of her mouth turning down. "That was with Evie."

"And Dad was Evie's father, right?" Sam said.

"Good heavens, no! Did she tell you that? It was an orderly at the nursing home she worked at. She had a schoolgirl crush on David, and I think, in her fantasy world, he became Evie's father." Phyllis cleared her throat and continued. "I don't know how long the abuse with our grandfather went on. But she was pregnant at thirteen and there was no question whose child it was. The decision was made to tell the world that the baby had died in childbirth. But Hazel wanted to keep him. And Grandfather let her. But there were rules. The first rule was that he had to be hidden away. The second, he wasn't to be told who his father was. So Hazel raised the boy to believe that he was fathered by the King of the Fairies. She told him the same stories we'd heard growing up. About how there was a door to another world in Reliance. How our grandfather was a fairy changeling left behind. I think that Hazel came to believe they were the truth."

The six fingers weren't a sign of fairy blood but a sign of genetic mutation, of inbreeding.

"But I read Hazel's diary," Phoebe said. "*You* believed in Teilo. You told Hazel he was Gene's father."

Phyllis sighed. "Yes. I played along with the fantasy. It seemed easier for her to deal with than the truth. So I encouraged the delusion. Hazel was always . . . imaginative. She was like Lisa that way." Phyllis turned and looked at the photo of Lisa and Sam on the mantel, and smiled ruefully.

"My God," Sam said. "Gene never stood a chance."

"Think of it, Sam," Phyllis said, looking up at him, eyes wide. "An imaginative boy growing up all alone in that house, raised on a steady diet of fairy tales. The only friend he had was his sister, Evie, who was sworn to secrecy. She brought him gifts. Told him stories about the world, about his family, you and Lisa. He loved Lisa even before he saw her. Evie brought him photos, recordings of Lisa's stories. Then, when he was sixteen, he convinced Evie to help him stow away in the car so he could see her himself."

"He was coming for Lisa," Sam said. "And Evie knew it."

Phyllis nodded. "Apparently, he promised her he wouldn't make contact. He would just watch. But we all know how that turned out."

"Did you know?" Sam asked his mother. "Did you know he was out there?"

Phyllis shook her head. "Not until it was too late. Evie tried to stop him. She did her best."

"That's why she told Gerald and Becca," Phoebe said. "I bet she was hoping he'd pick Becca instead. And when that didn't work, she showed the book to people, trying to put the whole thing out in the open, bring in outsiders to put a stop to it. And that last night, she dressed up like Lisa so he'd take her instead of Lisa."

It was heartbreaking, really. Phoebe could see it all too well—poor Evie, alone with this secret. She'd let Gene out, brought him to Lisa. She must have felt responsible, as if her own invisible, lifelong friend had suddenly come to life, making dangerous plans, and she was the only one who could stop him. But she couldn't, could she?

"Where's Evie now?" Phoebe asked.

"I have no idea," Phyllis said, but Phoebe wondered if she was lying. What had Phyllis and Hazel done with her? Had Evie played out her part and now become useless—a liability, even? Phoebe remembered Gabrielle saying it was Evie who had let her go. Had she crossed a line? Was there a new grave behind Hazel's house?

"So Gene takes Lisa and the way you people chose to deal with it was to have not just one child hidden in the basement but two?" Sam snarled. "This is insane, Mom!"

Phyllis pursed her lips, took in a breath, and continued. "We suspected Lisa was pregnant, which turned out to be true. If people found out, they would have learned about Gene. So we decided to just hide her for a while. Until the baby was born. I admit it wasn't the best plan, but we were a little crazy and desperate. Dave had overdosed again and was in a coma. I was a mess. I don't know how else to explain it. But it seemed like an answer. We'd make it look like she'd run away. Then, after she'd had the baby, we'd bring her back."

Phoebe tried to understand how that might have ever seemed like a good plan.

"But you didn't bring her back," Sam said. "You kept her there. *For fifteen years*, Mom!"

Phoebe thought of Evie again. This lonely girl now had two secret friends in the basement. Even if she knew it was wrong, she must have enjoyed their company. Fed on the fact that she was their lifeline to the outside world. She was a misfit, no real outside friends. Having control over the secret world in her basement must have given her a huge sense of power.

It was sadly ironic that she'd chosen agoraphobia as her made-up illness when she'd helped keep Lisa and Gabrielle prisoner, literally unable to leave the house for all those years. And maybe she really was waiting, hoping for a chance to free them. But this thing she was up against, this family legacy all mixed up with fairy legends, was just too big for one girl to take on alone.

Phyllis pursed her lips. "Lisa lost the first baby. And she was such a wreck. We were waiting for her to get stronger. To want to come home. But I think, I think something broke inside her then. She seemed to forget all about her other life, her life with her family. In her mind, she'd crossed over to the fairy world. And she seemed happy. Hazel convinced me that it was better if we leave her there. She had Gene and Evie. And then Gabrielle came along. She was a runaway Gene met up in Burlington. He brought her home and she and Lisa became fast friends. Gene went on pretending to be the Fairy King. No one ever meant any harm. We were all just making the best of the situation. Taking something black and ugly and giving it sparkle and shine."

Sam shook his head, stepped back, away from his mother. "You turned Lisa's entire life into some twisted game of make-believe!"

She scowled. "Is that so bad, Sam? Tell me, which would you rather be—the Queen of the Fairies or some poor twelve-year-old girl knocked up by your half-retarded cousin?"

"Let's go," Sam said to Phoebe. "Let's get out of here and call the police."

Phyllis laughed. "And what are you going to tell them, Sammy?"

"That you kidnapped and killed your own daughter."

Phyllis shook her head. "No. My daughter's right here." Phyllis leaned down and stroked Gabrielle's unkempt hair. "She's come home after all these years with a baby. It's a miracle."

So the game of make-believe was going to continue. Phoebe understood—it hadn't been just for Lisa's benefit but for Phyllis's as well. It was a trick Phyllis had no doubt learned growing up in her own family: when things look grim, rewrite the story. Blur the line between reality and imagination.

Then Phoebe looked at poor, logical Sam, wondering how on earth he'd managed to be born into such a family. Sam gave her a desperate look. Then a shadow crossed his face and he looked away.

He's thinking of our baby.

It was a funny thing to think that she had resisted the idea of having a child because it would continue her own screwed-up family line, and now here was Sam with the same dilemma.

Maybe they truly were meant for each other after all.

Phoebe reached out her hand to his, and to her surprise, he didn't pull away. He grabbed it and held on tight.

"They can do DNA tests," Sam said. "Go see the room in Hazel's basement. They can dig up the bodies in the orchard—Lisa, Gabrielle's baby, the other babies Lisa had."

"Are you so sure, Sam?" Phyllis asked, her voice mocking. "Are you sure they'll find anything at all?"

Sam's hand went limp in her own.

Phoebe thought about everything that had happened at the cabin—how when they got back, it was cleaned up, all the evidence gone. How easily they'd turned Sam and Phoebe into the criminals.

Phoebe looked from Sam to Phyllis.

"We all just did the best we could," Phyllis said.

Sam let his hand slip from Phoebe's, shook his head, and staggered backward toward the door, like a man who'd been shot making one last-ditch effort at a getaway.

PART VI

Something That Goes On Forever

If you have read this book all the way
to the end, you know the truth. We
are here, walking among you. We are
stronger, faster, smarter. We walk with
silent footsteps. We can see into your
dreams.

And we lie.

Always remember that we lie.

CHAPTER 53

Phoebe

The panic phone was ringing.

Phoebe hated to call it that, but she smiled because that was the name Franny had given it. The panic phone. The secret cell phone they used only for communicating back and forth with Franny and Jim—their one remaining connection to their old lives.

"Hello," Phoebe said, almost out of breath from hurrying to the phone but chirpy, excited that Franny had called. Franny had been calling a lot lately to ask, "Any baby yet?" And tonight, Phoebe would tell her, "Soon, Auntie Franny, soon," because she'd been having little contractions all day. Practice contractions, her obstetrician said. Phoebe waited for Franny's oh-so-predictable first question, but it didn't come.

"Hello?" she said again. "Franny?"

"Phoebe? It's Evie."

Impossible.

Phoebe glanced at the door, praying Sam would walk in, tell her what to do, what to say. He was out picking up some last-minute things for the baby.

Should she hang up? Hang up, then smash the panic phone, using her regular cell phone to call Franny, to say it was panic time for real?

Phoebe took in a frightened breath, rubbed her enormous belly. She'd been hanging a mobile in the nursery, above the crib. Stars and moon that moved in a circular pattern and played "Twinkle Twinkle Little Star."

"How did you get this number?" Phoebe said. "Where are you? We didn't know if you were alive or dead."

Sam and Phoebe had gone to the police with everything they knew, but it had done little good. Hazel and Phyllis denied the story completely and expressed tremendous worry over Sam and Phoebe's mental health, even suggesting to the police that they suspected the young couple might be using drugs.

"Poor Sammy," Phyllis said. "He never got over the loss of his sister. It's damaged him so badly that now he's making up wild stories."

There was no sign of Evie. When the police went to the basement apartment near the university, they discovered it hadn't been rented in months. Becca had quit her job at Price Chopper and left town. And there was not one shred of evidence to prove the existence of Gabrielle, Gene, or the baby. The cinder-block room in Hazel's basement had been turned into a root cellar. The secret room was full of bookcases and a reading chair.

"A library," the cops explained. "Not exactly the bogeyman's secret hideout."

The police had found no graveyard behind Hazel's house, only a badly neglected patch of tomatoes.

"I told you so," Phyllis whispered to them once, as they

watched two cops poke halfheartedly at the dirt. She smiled so warmly, lookers-on would have thought she was soothing them with words of love.

"What now?" Phoebe asked Sam when they were alone.

"We leave. We get as far away from my fucked-up family as we can."

And so, with the help of Franny and Jim, Sam and Phoebe just slipped away. They sold their house and went to Colorado, where Jim had some friends with a farm outside of Boulder. There was an old carriage house they could stay in. Sam worked on the farm for room and board.

"You've got to stay under the radar for a while," Franny had insisted. "If you really don't want to be found, you've gotta work under the table, don't get your own apartment or put your name on anything. Ditch all your credit cards. Use only cash. If you have to get a library card or anything, use a different name."

A name like Mary Stevens, Phoebe thought, remembering the girl who had come to them with only chalk, a key, and a library card. Now she was just a few steps away from becoming that girl, a girl on the run with little more than the clothes on her back.

Phoebe could hear Evie breathing on the phone.

"I'm not dead," Evie said.

"So I gathered. Where are you?"

"Where are you?" Evie asked.

"What do you want?" Phoebe asked.

There was a pause. More breathing. Then, at last, Evie spoke. "I'm calling for Lisa. Because of Lisa. Because what happened . . . it was my fault. I couldn't save her. Couldn't save her baby. But maybe it's not too late for you."

"What do you mean?" Phoebe asked, irritated as hell, about two seconds away from hanging up on Evie.

"Your baby's in danger," she whispered.

"What?" Phoebe said.

"It's all a lie," Evie said. "You know that, right?"

"What is?" Phoebe said. The baby moved inside her, turning. She was a gymnast in training, this little one.

"There *is* a Dark Man, Phoebe. A real Teilo. Everything they're doing is for him. Phyllis, Hazel, Gene. They've all given themselves over to him. You can't stop them. My father tried and look what happened to him."

"Are you talking about David?"

"Yes."

"Phyllis said he wasn't your father. And besides, he killed himself."

"A hell of a coincidence, though, right? Before we went away to Cape Cod, he told me and my mom that he was tired of the secrets. He was going to put a stop to it—tell the world about Teilo and poor Gene in the basement. He wanted to take me and my mom away from all of it. He said he'd never stopped loving her."

"So what? Are you saying someone drugged him? To keep him quiet and stop him from leaving Phyllis?"

"I don't know," Evie said. "But something happened while we were gone. Teilo found a way to stop him. There was this drawing my father had done in his sketchbook—a man without a face. Teilo paid him a visit, all right." Evie caught her breath before continuing. "And then, that last night before his second overdose, he tried once more to put a stop to all the craziness. I told him I was worried they were going to take Lisa and he tried to call the police. The next morning, when we woke up, he was being taken away in an ambulance."

"But there is no Teilo, Evie! It was Gene all along," Phoebe said. "He was the one in the woods. He got Lisa pregnant. They were just trying to protect Gene. To keep all their dirty little family secrets hidden!"

"Listen to me. The secrets they're keeping are way bigger than that. Lisa wasn't pregnant that summer—not yet. They chose to take her, Phoebe. Gene didn't pull her out of that hole. My mother and Phyllis did."

"But Gene . . ."

"Gene may have started it, but once Lisa got her period, Phyllis knew she was ready. Ready to be Teilo's bride. So she used the work Gene had already done to abduct her own daughter."

"Evie, for God's sake. I don't know if you believe this shit or if you're still playing their game, or what. There are no fairies, no Teilo—it's a pack of fucked-up lies!"

"If you want to save your baby, you've got to believe me: Gene is not Teilo! He's Teilo's son. But Teilo is so much more. And you know that. Just . . . stop for a minute. Think. You've known him all along, haven't you?"

Phoebe shivered.

Somewhere in the back of her mind, a trapdoor under a bed opened and there was a clawlike scrabbling sound as something let itself out.

"I've heard them talking," Evie said. "They say Teilo chose you to give him Sam's firstborn."

"But that's impossible. How—"

"He wouldn't choose just anyone. You know that, right? You know who you are."

"Who I am?" Phoebe stammered.

"Haven't you sensed it your whole life? That you're different from other people. You don't fit in, no matter how hard you try. You know things you shouldn't. You see things other people don't."

"I don't understand what this—"

"You're his daughter. Teilo's flesh and blood. Half human, half fairy. You walk between the worlds."

Phoebe leaned against the crib, holding on to it.

"No," she said, shaking her head. *My father was just some guy my mom met in a bar. A drifter. He picked fruit and tobacco.* She thought the words but couldn't say them. The air felt suddenly thin. The walls were closing in, making Phoebe feel as if she were in a tunnel. And there, at the end, was her Dark Man, waiting for her.

"We all have our destinies, Phoebe. And you know, you understand, don't you, that the child you're carrying belongs to him?"

Phoebe disconnected the call and flung the phone across the room, just as a strong contraction rolled through her, bringing her to her knees.

Breathe, baby! Breathe! You're doing great. We're almost there." Sam stood beside her, flushed and expectant. Behind him, the doctor and nurse worked.

"Push now," they said.

Phoebe heard them through the thick haze of pain and medication, heard them, but wasn't entirely sure she had any control over her body. But she tried.

"Good," they said.

"Oh my God!" Sam said. "There's the head!"

"Push, honey," the nurse said.

Once the idea sunk in, Sam had fallen in love with the idea of being a father. Once he understood he'd promised his firstborn to his invisible cousin, not to some terrifying supernatural being, he seemed downright joyous about fatherhood. He threw himself into it with a fury, reading books on parenting, coming home with organic unbleached cotton diapers and onesies.

He painted the nursery with environmentally friendly non-toxic paint and stenciled Humpty-Dumpty borders.

Phoebe watched him up on the ladder, hand painting all those fragile, smiling little eggs in short pants sitting on a wall.

All the king's horses
And all the king's men
Couldn't put Humpty together again

But what if there really was a Teilo?

What if she really had been chosen—if the very reason she'd even been born is because Teilo planned it, seducing her mother, watching over Phoebe her whole life, waiting to bring her to Sam.

The idea gnawed at Phoebe. She told Sam about the phone call from Evie when they were on their way to the hospital.

"She said I was Teilo's daughter," she told him.

"She's a nut," he said, putting his hand on her belly. "You know that—she was victimized by my psychotic mother and aunt, and I pity her, I truly do. But in the end, she is just as crazy as they are.

All this foolish worrying isn't good for you or the baby, Phoebe. We're done with those people. Let's just focus on us. Us and our baby, who we're going to be holding in our arms very, very soon."

Doing great, Mom," the doctor said through his blue surgical mask. "One more big push and you can meet your baby."

Phoebe closed her eyes, concentrated on the entire lower half of her body, which she couldn't really feel but trusted was there. There was the faintest sensation of pressure, and the pain. There was always the pain. Even through the drugs, she felt like this baby was splitting her in half like an overripe seed. She pushed. She pushed with all the strength left in her, making a low, guttural, whalelike cry.

"Oh my God!" Sam said again, his voice shaking.

I've given birth to something inhuman, Phoebe thought. *A lamprey with row after row of teeth.*

The baby squalled. Phoebe opened her eyes.

"It's a girl," the doctor announced. "A beautiful baby girl."

Phoebe looked up to see a tiny form, covered in mucus and blood, all arms and legs, the tiniest tuft of wet, matted hair.

And there, behind her baby girl, the doctor, nurse, and Sam, a figure hovered in the doorway. Just a silhouette—a tall, dark shadow, watching.

"Who is that?" Phoebe asked.

"It's our baby," Sam said, coming to take her hand, kiss her. "Our daughter."

"No," Phoebe said, "in the doorway."

Sam turned. "There's no one there, babe."

"Do you want to cut the cord, Dad?" the doctor asked. And

Sam was gone again down to the other end of the bed. When he reappeared, he held their infant daughter in his arms, cleaned up, swaddled in a fuzzy flannel blanket. He leaned down and carefully placed the baby on her chest.

"I think she's hungry," Sam said, as the baby pecked and snuffled at her breast, mouth open, eyes squeezed shut. Sam helped guide her to the nipple. Phoebe stroked her damp hair, breathed her in while she sucked and gulped, latched on determinedly.

"Willa," Phoebe said. "She's definitely a Willa."

Phoebe closed her eyes. Smiled. Her daughter. She was here. Healthy. Perfect. Ten fingers and ten toes.

"I love you," Sam said. Then he kissed the baby's hair. "You too, little Willa," he said.

The doctor and nurse hovered, then drifted out. Another nurse came in.

"You rest now," she said.

Phoebe let her eyes close, holding the baby to her chest, Sam beside her.

I'm just going to take her for a minute," the nurse said, startling Phoebe from sleep. She'd been dreaming about her mother. Her ma had been sitting on the edge of the bed, cooing at Willa, her clothes inside out and dripping wet.

"We need to check her bilirubin levels," the nurse explained. "I'll be back in a minute." She smiled cheerfully down at Phoebe, her hair a perfect blond bob.

"Sam?" Phoebe said, handing the baby over. The nurse smelled faintly of cigarette smoke covered up with perfume. "Where's Sam?"

"I'm not sure, sweetie. Probably just went for a cup of a coffee or to get some fresh air."

Phoebe nodded.

"He'll be right back, I'm sure," she said, giving Phoebe's hand a comforting squeeze.

The young nurse took the baby, said, "Come on, little peanut. I'll have you back to your mamma in a jiffy."

Phoebe sat up, looked out the door after them into the fluorescent-lit hallway. She saw only shadows. Heard muffled voices. Somewhere, something beeped once, twice, three times. A doctor was paged. A cart rolled by, pushed by a man in green scrubs.

Phoebe rubbed her eyes, leaned over to the rolling table next to the bed, and got herself a drink of water.

"Mommy," she said to herself, smiling, still not really believing it. But she was a mother. And she was going to be a damn good one, too, in spite of how she'd been raised. She'd figured out that to be a good parent, all she needed to do was imagine what her own mother would do in any given situation, then do the exact opposite.

"You think it's that easy?" Her mother was there again, perched on the edge of the hospital bed. Phoebe blinked. Once. Twice.

Phoebe could read the labels and see the stitches of the seams of her mother's clothes. Water dripped off her ma, soaking through the thin hospital blanket and sheet, making Phoebe's feet damp. She stank of rot and cigarette smoke.

Her ma smiled at Phoebe, waxy blue lips pulling back mechanically. "You can't run from the Dark Man, lovie," she said. "Not once he gets inside you. Not when you've got something he wants."

Phoebe reached for the call bell on the bed rail but couldn't find it. She scrambled frantically, and just as she'd given up and was about to start screaming instead, the young nurse returned, carrying the baby, still swaddled. Phoebe glanced down at the foot of the bed. There was no one there. The covers were dry.

"Everything's fine," the nurse said. "She looks perfect."

Phoebe nodded, held out her arms, pulled little Willa to her and held her tight.

But something was wrong.

This was not her child.

The hair and eyes were darker, the skin more translucent. And the smell was all wrong—this child was dank and mushroomlike. The baby started to cry. It was a high-pitched, frantic cry, strangled sounding.

"This isn't her," Phoebe said.

"Excuse me?" said the nurse.

"This isn't my baby."

"Of course it's your baby." The perfect blond hair was slightly askew. A wig. My God. It was someone wearing a wig. And underneath the smile, the makeup, didn't she recognize this face?

"Becca?"

The nurse took a step back. "I'm sorry?"

"What have you done with my child?"

"I'll go and get the doctor," the nurse said, turning. As she walked, no—practically ran—from the room, the cuff of the left leg of her pants rose up just high enough that Phoebe could see she wasn't wearing socks. She had on silver running shoes with black laces. And there, on her ankle, was a tattoo. Teilo's mark.

Phoebe began to scream.

Wʜat is it, babe?" Sam asked, hurrying in, two nurses behind him.

"It's not Willa. The nurse took her. She switched her."

"No one took her," one of the nurses said. "She's been in here with you the whole time. Look at her bracelet—it says 'Baby female Nazzaro. And see the band we've got around her ankle? It's an electronic sensor—if anyone tried to leave the unit with her, an alarm would go off."

Sam stroked Phoebe's arm. "It's her, Bee. It's Willa. Maybe you were dreaming."

"I was not dreaming," Phoebe hissed at Sam. "Where were you?"

"I had to go down to Patient Registration. They needed a copy of our insurance card."

How had they known? They must have been watching, waiting.

"The girl who took her had blond hair, but it was a wig. And silver sneakers. A tattoo on her ankle. I think it was Becca, Sam."

"Pinkie?" he said, frowning, a shadow of disbelief crossing his face. "I don't think so, Bee."

The nurse shook her head. "We don't have anyone working here who looks like that," she said.

"She was here!"

"You have to be buzzed in to get on the floor," the nurse said. "No one like that was here. I was at the nurse's station. I would know."

The second nurse left the room, returning quickly with the doctor.

"Please," Phoebe said. "You have to listen. She's got to be in the hospital, still. You can stop her. Sam, please! Go look for her. She's got our baby!"

Sam shook his head. "She's right here, Bee. You've got her in your arms."

Phoebe looked at the squalling, pale-faced child, pushed her away. "This is not my baby!"

Sam took the baby in his arms, rocked her, which just made her squall louder.

The doctor left the room and returned with a needle. He shot something into Phoebe's IV line.

"Please," she said. "Just look at her. This is not the baby you delivered."

"You need to rest now," he told her.

She heard Sam say something in a worried voice about post-partum psychosis. A history of alcoholism and mental illness in the family. "Her mother committed suicide," he whispered.

"No," Phoebe moaned. "Listen—" She fought to keep her eyes open, but it was no use.

As she closed them, she saw it again, clearer this time.

There, hovering in the doorway to her room, was the Dark Man. A form made entirely of shadow, he seemed to gather light and swallow it like a black hole. It was something you could get lost inside. Something that went on forever. And there, where his face should be, she was sure she could see the flash of a smile.

ACKNOWLEDGMENTS

I'd like to thank:

My agent, Dan Lazar, for all he does.

My editor, Jeanette Perez, and the whole team at Harper, for helping to shape the book into what it is today, and for being so understanding and supportive when I had to put everything on hold during my mother's illness.

My father, Donald McMahon, who talks up my books to everyone, from the oil delivery guy to strangers in the checkout line at Stop & Shop.

Alicia Partridge, for her honest feedback and clever ideas.

Kenny Klein, for sharing his knowledge of fairies, and letting me read *Through the Faerie Glass* before it was published.

And as always, Drea and Zella, who go on believing in me, no matter what.

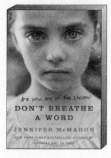
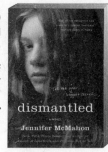

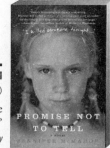